D0783732

CROW'S NEST

A Novel of the Possible

Gvg Miller

G.V. Miller

Beaver's Pond Press, Inc.
Edina, Minnesota

Unless ascribed to others, chapter quotations are by the author.

ISBN 1-59298-057-0

Library of Congress Catalog Number: 2004102102

Book design and typesetting: Mori Studio
Front cover design: Fuzzy Duck Design, *fuzzyduck.com*
Front cover illustration: David Olmstead, *davidolmstead.com*

Printed in the United States of America

First Printing: April 2004

07 06 05 04   6 5 4 3 2 1

Beaver's Pond Press, Inc.

7104 Ohms Lane, Suite 216
Edina, MN 55439
(952) 829-8818
www.BeaversPondPress.com

To order, visit *www.BookHouseFulfillment.com* or call 1-800-901-3480. Reseller and special sales discounts available.

Acknowledgements

Many of the thoughts that follow were affected by my association with Donna Taylor and our mutual buddy, the Teacher (*Book of the 8's*, Newleaf-dist.com).

On the other hand, the Teacher is probably choking on some positions put forth in Crow's Nest. But that's all right. Crow's Nest is, after all, a "Novel of the Possible," and my take on reality is just as valid or faulty as the next person's (or being's). Until the ultimate price of admission is paid, our beliefs, our faith, must sustain each of us—in our own way.

After rewriting Crow's Nest several times, I knew it still wasn't quite right, and I didn't know why. I then met Katherine Kleingartner in an appropriately coincidental fashion, but I instantly felt that she might be the one to provide the missing link. She brought out the best in my writing abilities—finding openings in that creative wall that I previously didn't even know could be penetrated. Once past the doorway, a whole new world opened itself to me, just waiting to be explored. My thanks to "Kat," and I hope we get to do it again.

My thanks also go to Jeff Phillips, director of engineering at KARE-11 television in Minneapolis. Jeff took the time to tour the studio with me and provide a beginning lesson on the procedures and technology behind the media that we viewers take for granted every day.

 # Author's Notes

1. Mustang owners everywhere will know that these icons of the American driving experience no longer have full-size spare tires, nor storage wells, as depicted in Chapter Three. The choices available were to either ignore this small problem or change the vehicle to something less desirable but technically correct. I like the Mustang, and it was the right car for the story. End of story...

2. Residents and visitors alike of Monument Valley will know that I have taken several liberties with the physical facts of the area. Certainly no disrespect was intended—only concern for the smooth transition of the story. You know, and I know, how special and powerful is the area you call home.

What do you believe in?

please visit www.crowsnest-thebook.com

To Mom and Dad, wherever you are in the continuum, another final goodbye with a thank you:

*Your gift of preparation
was buried deep within me,
but I finally found it...*

To Jeri, once again my partner this life:

*...And I found it
because of you.*

———————————

And to my very old friend in Philadelphia who has been in my thoughts almost daily for forty years. Apparently, we were not meant to share the same real estate this time around, yet our one year together has been more influential to me than I think either of us can comprehend.

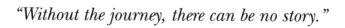

"Without the journey, there can be no story."

—Katherine Kleingartner, Editor Extraordinaire

Prologue

*Los Angeles, Saturday morning,
twenty minutes after midnight*

If any medics had been around, they would have
pronounced the man dead at 00:20 hrs. Without I.D.,
they would have processed him as a John Doe; Age:
approximately 70; Sex: male; Height: 6 foot; Weight:
maybe 140 pounds, probably less; Address: unknown,
but location and appearance suggested he was homeless; Cause of Death: Now, that's where things got a little complicated. It looked like natural causes because
there was no evidence of trauma, but death was
undoubtedly assisted by 55 years of smoking, 3,000
bottles of Ripple, many years of malnutrition, several
attacks of broken heart, numerous bouts of depression, and in the end, the man had just plain worn out.

John Doe's real name isn't important to the events
of the next five days, but his body is. At 12:16 A.M., as
he lay in the alley propped up against a Dumpster and
existing in a fog of semiconsciousness, a door opened,
either across the alley or at the far end of his mind—
he couldn't be sure which. At first it opened just a
crack with a very bright light shining through. It
opened a little further and a small girl's head poked
through the opening and inquired, "Daddy?" John
Doe, unable to rally his neurons, nonetheless knew

that the voice belonged to his little Sasha, gone now for many decades. "Daddy, it's time to come home. We miss you, Daddy. It's time." For the first time in years, John Doe felt something akin to joy as he felt himself rise up and move toward the doorway. Surprised at the effortlessness of the motion, he stopped and intuitively looked back to where he had been sitting: The lifeless shell of his miserable existence was still there. He turned back to an inviting little hand, knowing that his work this lifetime was now complete. Just then, the door opened wider, and the silhouette of a fully grown stranger over-shadowed little Sasha. The shape glided through the girl and the doorway and continued toward the departing spirit of John Doe. They met midpoint in the alley and passed through each other, seam-lessly, like the shadows of two people passing each other on a side-walk. John Doe walked into the light, allowed his tiny Sasha to grasp his hand, and then the door closed behind them. The stranger's sil-houette continued to the now-vacant body and entered—filling the mass of flesh just as water fills a sponge. The body stirred a little from the new and revitalized presence within, and then the man arose, left his dying place and walked to the end of the alley to begin the task assigned him

---

Washington, D.C., Sunday morning

Waking up and getting moving had never been difficult for Truman Lawrence. He allowed himself the luxury of coming fully awake while sitting on the toilet for five long minutes before taking a coolish shower just to get the juices flowing. His next stop was the exercise room, where he began his daily routine of stretching, tread-mill, and Nautilus workout. An hour later, sweating the poisons from the temple of his body, he sat at the prepared window table in his bed-room. He slowly partook of some V8 juice and began speed-reading the six newspapers set before him, topped by the *Minneapolis Star Tribune, St. Paul Pioneer Press,* and the *Duluth News Tribune.* Simon, his butler of fourteen years, arrived with a breakfast consisting of one poached egg, a bowl of mixed fruit, and half a bagel. After another fif-teen minutes, having completed breakfast and the newspapers,

Lawrence returned to the shower and completed his morning ritual by finally emerging downstairs in a dark Brooks Brother's suit, white shirt, conservative tie, and black Redwing loafers. He would have preferred the fit and quality of Allen Edmonds, but they came from Wisconsin, whereas the Redwings were true-blue Minnesotan, and three hundred workers might not appreciate their elected senator wearing the product of an out-of-state competitor.

As he stood at the foyer mirror, making last-minute adjustments to his vestments, Truman Lawrence caught his eyes in the reflection and briefly stared at his other personality. Despite outward appearances of normalcy, the man in front of the mirror was not a happy camper this fine morning. He now knew that a serious challenge to his plans was in the offing, and he would have to risk exposure of his true self and intents to meet this challenge. Worse, no matter how unlikely it seemed, he could actually lose the battle. He always knew that this moment would come—he had lived with its inevitability for over thirty years—but no matter how well prepared one is for a life-or-death challenge, there's a big difference between knowing it's coming versus having it arrive at your doorstep, ringing the bell. On the other hand, as was the case throughout all of history, meeting and defeating a challenge of this magnitude would have an immeasurable effect on his power and the ensuing completion of his goals. That was the upside, the side to be focused upon.

He accepted the Burberry trench coat offered by Simon as protection against the early fall chill, opened the front door and stepped toward the waiting limousine. With a Secret Service agent attending the opened door, Lawrence bent down, entered, and greeted the man sitting opposite, "Adam...."

Adam Dempsey, who had spent half his life with Lawrence, stared at his associate, savior, and—for the rest of the world's consumption—boss. The two men co-existed in a very entangled relationship that necessarily withstood the ravages of time, attacks, arguments, and emotions. Naturally, they knew each other well—as well as, and perhaps better than, a husband knows his wife. Consequently, Adam could instantly see that something was amiss with his associate, the honorable Senator from Minnesota and current independent candidate for vice president of the United States of America.

"What's the problem, Truman?"

As the limousine and Secret Service Suburban left the driveway for the airport, Truman remained focused on the beautiful autumn colors passing by, then he answered the question, "He's here, Adam—the one we've been waiting for. He arrived last night—or perhaps Saturday, somewhere out West." The Senator paused for a moment as the foliage of a particularly intense sugar maple distracted him. In just a few seconds, his mind walked a gambit of visions and emotions. Autumn had always been his favorite time of year, yet it had a love-hate dichotomy to it: the beauty of the leaves belied the coming of death as those very same leaves would soon fall in droves—not unlike soldiers on the battlefield. The coming cold, damp, and bleak air—austere on the one hand, promised rest and renewal for the future on the other hand. The question was, would he be part of that future? Would he prevail? In the naïve colloquialisms of humans, who would still be standing at the end.....good, or evil? With a sigh, he left the sugar maple behind and continued his advisory to Adam. "He'll be heading this way by now, so I've got my eyes out looking for him." Lawrence allowed the gravity of the announcement to sink in for a moment before turning to his man and completing the thought:

"It's begun."

Day One

"When opportunity knocks, we can do one of three things: ignore it, embrace it...or run like hell."

chapter one

Beware of Hitchhikers

Monument Valley, Arizona/Utah

A thousand feet above the desert floor, a rare Peregrine falcon cut lazy circles in the thinning air, tweaking one wing tip then the other, constantly making minute adjustments to its flight profile. To the casual observer on terra firma, it might appear that the predator was enjoying himself—out for a late morning stroll, so to speak; but for the falcon, the business at hand was deadly serious. Parents may have taught the bird *how* to acquire its meals, but the *need* to do so was controlled by ancient predatory instincts—and an empty stomach.

The raptor's eyes caught the movement of the red Mustang far below—not the red, actually, or the make and model—just the movement. Eons of programming demanded that the bird consider the moving object for his lunch, but almost instantly the same programming determined the object to be unsuitable for the expenditure of precious energies.

His reconnaissance continued, and a minute later his patience was rewarded with another movement, far ahead and almost beyond his visual envelope, but not quite. This object passed all intuitive tests: size, type of motion, location, distance, and speed. One by one the parameters were all accepted, and without another thought, the bird of prey, making sure the sun would be behind him, rolled hard left, swept his wings back against the organic fuselage, and became as streamlined a killing machine as anything in the Air Force. Quickly attaining terminal velocity and confirming the well-known human corollary that the shortest distance between two points is a straight line, the falcon approached his target with amazing speed—nearly as fast as an Indy race car. His meal-to-be was a solitary crow about three hundred feet above the valley floor, and with a "side-swipe" of his talons, the blue-plate special was knocked senseless and fell to earth. The bird of prey, wings spread in full regalia, landed inches from the crow and quickly administered the coup de grâce, making sure that there would be no escaping destiny this day.

The crow was not the only victim of destiny on the high desert that fine morning. Having been in just the right place at just the right time and looking in exactly the right direction, the driver of the Mustang had been fortunate to have witnessed the event. He continued to glance over toward the projected impact area, hoping to see the predator lift off; but there was no movement visible, testimony that lunch was being eaten on the spot.

Cruise-control still engaged, the red sports coupe maintained the leisurely sixty-five mph set by its owner, a speed ensuring that he wouldn't be a menace to those coming up from behind while allowing acceptable time for enjoying the surrounding landscape. The driver's left hand found the window controls, lowered the front two, then his right hand turned off the CD player, leaving Otis to watch the ships roll in by himself: "Rest in peace, buddy."

Justin Maley, freelance journalist and struggling novelist took a long breath of the dry desert air whirling through the now-open car, thoroughly enjoying one of life's great pleasures—driving alone on a lightly used highway, bladder empty, weather perfect, gas tank full, and surrounded by inspiring scenery. Life just doesn't get any better. It's also one of those increasingly rare interludes when no one can get in your face, no ringing phone can stop cold the most important idea you've had in a month of Sundays, and most importantly, the mind can finally open up and let "it" all hang out.

For Maley, the "it" was imagination, something in very short supply of late. *The brain is dead, long live the brain.* It's kind of hard to write a bestseller, or even a worst seller, when imagination is only firing on seven cylinders. Oh, there was no shortage of impromptu ideas firing off in his mind, but they would burn brightly for a few hours, perhaps a day, and then just fade away. The frustration was beginning to take its toll: first on self-confidence, then on productivity, and finally becoming a self-propagating loop. Creatively speaking, Maley was just as dried up as the desert surrounding him which, in a round-about fashion, was how he got to be here—highway 163, just north of Kayenta, in the "never-ceases-to-amaze-me" state of Arizona, or Utah—around here, it was hard to tell the two apart.

In the best tradition of Okie philosophers, Maley's father had been fond of saying, "Do something, even if it's wrong." Good advice is seldom taken until it's needed; and heaven knew, as did Justin, that his need had become great, and that doing anything was better than remaining stuck in the rut he was in. So, in an attempt to exit the doldrums, the writer had had one of his better ideas in months: get out of town. Not just a weekend fling, mind you, but a genuine, cross-country, take-all-the-time-you-need kind of journey. And forget the Interstates. Like the thread that weaves the tapestry called America, it's the back roads that would provide the kind of inspiration the writer hungered for. Justin silently thanked his deceased parents for the hundreth time for leaving him the resources for extended trips like this.

After a week of crisscrossing eastern California, southern Nevada and northern Arizona, Maley was approaching an area that had been on his list of "must sees" for years: Monument Valley. He was already kind of in it, but the best was just ahead, and as the '02 Mustang approached the end of a long plateau, Maley could begin to see over the horizon the caps of the monoliths that gave the area its name. He was sightseeing so well, in fact, he almost missed the turn-off for a scenic overlook.

Braking hard, he made the turn, and was struck by the extent of the place. Evidently, this viewpoint had been built in the days of budget surpluses, for not only did it consist of an unusually large parking area and a kids' playground, it came complete with respectable restroom facilities (rather than something with a crescent moon affixed to the door). The approach road must have cost a fortune, as it was at least a half-mile long, all the better to isolate the "serious" viewer from the stress-contaminated drivers back on the highway. The moment Justin parked the Mustang and shut off the engine, the supposed intent of the builders became clear: it was almost totally quiet, with a passing car on the highway barely audible. In fact, the only sound at all was that of the high plains wind whipping unobstructed through his car windows. And if all this were designed as accompaniment to the big show, the view, then the effort was a complete success. Once it sunk in what he was seeing, what lay before him for miles and miles, Justin was momentarily staggered. It was one of those vistas that no artist could possibly duplicate, although many had probably tried. A photographer would stand a better chance, but unless his lens could match the peripheral vision of the human eye, his attempt, too, would fall well short of the real McCoy.

Grateful to be in no hurry, under no deadline of any sort, Maley looked around for a bench on which to park for a while, and finding several, chose one way out on a small promontory further isolated from everything else by a good hundred feet. He collected his binoculars, a granola bar, and a bottle of water from the car, and then noticed for the first time—miracle of miracles—he had the place entirely to himself. *You're kidding. Hello, Operator.....? Yea...I'd like to reserve the best vista point in Arizona all for myself for a couple of hours. No problem? Thanks.* As he headed for "his" bench, the only downside to an otherwise perfect moment in time was the unexpected appearance of several crows, detected not visually, but by the sound known 'round the world—one of the few things that God had blown (well, okay, crows *and* mosquitoes).

Before sitting down, Justin unconsciously checked the bench for any gifts from previous visitors: things like spilt coke, chewing gum, bird crap—the sort of thing that can ruin an otherwise great day. Finding no unpleasant surprises, his brain *did* register plenty of carved greetings of another kind: "Jon + Kelly", "QG+KA" encircled by a heart, "Travis and Kate—Forever," and one carving with a date, "Dick Loves Doris, '43." *Hmm, sixty-one years ago.* A smile came to his face as his imagination felt a spark, "Hello Dick, how're things goin'? You and Doris still alive, still together? Got lots of kids?" Greeting over, the engineer part of the writer (a very small part) marveled that the bench was still there after so long a time, mute testimony to the dry desert air and the durability of the thing: one of those institutional kinds with the concrete ends and full two-inch board planking.

Justin turned back to his purpose for being there. He sat on Dick and Doris—returning them to their peaceful oblivion—and felt a huge sigh emanating from his feet, rising through his body, and finally exiting his nostrils, taking with it all the psychic poisons that had been messing with his head for so long. *It's a good picture, Justin; just hope it's real.*

Every soul of every body on the planet needs a respite now and then, whether the soul in question knows it or not. Being unaware is no excuse and does nothing to lessen the need. In fact, if anything, lack of awareness is probably symptomatic of *greater* need. But it's hard to get into the proper frame of mind when one works all day, prepares meals, washes clothes, tends to family, removes the snow or mows the lawn, and then falls into bed, going quickly to sleep (hopefully) during the weather segment of the dependably depressing news broadcast. Despite all the responsibilities and hardships in life, nourishment for the soul is just as vital as nourishment for the stomach, with the lack of the former often going unnoticed until one is already in some pretty deep shit. Quite a few folks intuitively know about this need and are quick to pause their daily routine, if given half a chance, for any special moment that might come along—typically something like a spectacular sunset, a moonscape, or an inspiring chunk of landscape. Vacations *do* count, but using the analogy of the stomach again, how would that organ feel if it were gorged for two weeks, only to be deprived of sustenance for the remaining fifty weeks of the year? And the cosmic soul patrol makes no differentiation between bodies in this regard. The need is as great for the ditch digger as it is for the mathematician—or for a spiritually starved journalist. Just as dried up as his creativity, Justin's soul was in dire need of attention. There had been no sunsets, landscapes, or moonscapes in the writer's reality for many a month. He had been living in the shadow of an extended eclipse, but all that was about to change.

So Maley began to fill-up the fuel tank of his soul. It wasn't hard. Not here. Actually, it's never "hard" because in this regard, the soul is *easy.* Give the soul a few minutes now and then of quiet, conscious feel-good, and you can almost sense the gauge needle heading toward the top. The difficult part is giving it the quiet, the consciousness, and the feel-good—all qualities that seem increasingly in short supply. Justin Maley had created the time, his location provided the quiet and feel-good, so he now went to work on the consciousness—unconsciously, of course. For him, this was the kind of place to visit to untangle a mind tied up in knots. For someone else, it might be sailing on a vast expanse of ocean, or climbing a mountain, or gliding high above the Earth. Whatever the venue, all other priorities were briefly rescinded. Even without being able to name it, or understand it, Justin could feel it all. Without really knowing what he was doing, his heart opened wide, allowing the healing victuals to massage his aching spirit.

All around him and as far as his eyes could see, the high desert plateau, technically a valley, sprouted mammoth spires reaching far into the sky. There weren't all that many of them, which was just as well, as density would only serve to take away from the effect of the few. The colors appeared to be the common desert stone reds to browns and would be even more striking in early morning or late afternoon, with the rising and setting of the sun. Just as with life, however, the prominent colors overshadowed all the myriad tones that contributed to the whole palette: the rusts, the smudges, the fresh, the dying, the excited—every color imaginable, and they were all here for the discerning eye to behold if the time were taken to delve beyond the surface. Everywhere, little sage bushes dotted the desert surface as if a pointillist artist were attempting to carpet 3,000 square miles. It was all beautiful and breathtaking, but Justin's eyes always returned to the spires, the monuments. A part of him knew that wind and water erosion were the true artists here, but another part, the creative part, would have none of that. This was God's playground—or could it be His battlefield? It had that feel to it and Justin momentarily envisioned giant beings representing good and evil choosing this very spot, on planet Earth, in the Alpha quadrant of the Milky Way galaxy to face-off and determine who would rule the Universe. And perhaps the losers had been frozen forever into stone monuments; or, and the writer smiled, maybe God had frozen both sides for their foolishness. The vision faded, but not the underlying realization: for the second time in his life, he was experiencing a power place.

Five years earlier, Maley had taken a trip down the mighty Colorado through Cataract Canyon, just a few hundred miles north of his present location. The primary goal of the adventure had been to experience the highly touted rapids, some reaching level six in size and intensity. But his nephew Quinn, captain of the boat, had prepared Justin to expect a lot more on the trip than just rapids, which are actually few and far between. Within thirty minutes of the big J-rig departing Moab, the writer knew his nephew had not exaggerated. Less than a mile from their departure point, a giant rock formation, easily the size of the Mt. Rushmore, emerged from the river's edge. Consisting of strata upon strata that created a geological calendar spanning millions of years, the massif would have been staggering even if its layers had been parallel to the surface. But it wasn't. The formation punched out of the earth at a thirty-degree inclination, providing silent testimony to the cataclysmic upheavals that had formed the region. The forces that could cause such an emergence were truly mind-blowing. The gorge quickly became narrower and much, much higher. Pretty soon, all the passengers on board were craning their necks to find the sky. Later, when the writer thought about this transition from "civilization" to—the unknown—the image had come to mind of entering Mother Nature's esophagus, eaten alive as it were, to emerge four days later a subtly different human being. The trip had had a profound effect on Justin, one that would be with him the remainder of his life. And the feeling that would not, could not, leave his mind was the awesome power of the area. It never stopped, not until after they left the pool the journalist later called "Amazing Grace" dome at the far north end of Lake Powell; and what an appropriate ending the dome had been. Captain Quinn had slowed the J-boat and turned starboard into a small inlet carved by nature's chisel into the sheer rock walls. With the outboard shut down and the boat secured, the intent was clear: bask in the sun or bask in the crystal clear water, or do both. Justin had rolled over the pontoon's side into the chilly Colorado, feeling water molecules touch his torso that had begun as snowflakes four months earlier and a thousand miles northward. Following a sliver of deep water, he saw a small opening in solid rock just twenty yards ahead. It was dark beyond the opening—and ominous, yet Maley knew that something special *must* be waiting just beyond. He entered.

A natural rock dome was his reward for the risk taken. Perhaps twenty feet across and fifteen feet high, the dome was far from dark. A hole in the ceiling penetrated entirely through the rock to the surface above and through this hole, a shaft of intense sunlight speared the cavern and penetrated the deep water which he was treading. The incredible beauty, the secretness of the place, left Justin feeling enormously small in the grand scheme of the planet, of the Universe.

Fellow travelers swam in, then swam out—except for one: a middle aged woman stayed longer, and after a while, she and Justin were the lone occupants of the dome—Justin off to a side, she in the center. The woman silently swam to the shaft of sunlight. The beam fell directly on her head; the dome was utterly quiet. To the writer, the woman became an ethereal vision of oneness with the place, but then she took both of them to a whole other level: she began singing "Amazing Grace" in the most angelic voice imaginable. Her voice was oh so soft, but the dome brought her heart and every nuance to every cell of Justin's soul. He had never felt anything remotely that intense before in his life and, later on, he wondered if he ever would again.

A horn from the boat broke the spell, but not before the woman and Justin looked each other in the eye—and smiled. A million words, a million emotions were exchanged in that moment, then they both returned to their lives.

The J-rig left the inlet, entered Lake Powell, and an hour later they all returned to the reality of trucks, buses, Cessnas, appointments, and deadlines.

Now, five years later, Maley was feeling some deja-vu. Here he was again, same kind of power, same kind of feeling, and Justin briefly wondered if he might be about to embark on a similar journey as the one down the Colorado. At the moment, he was absolutely convinced that there was more to this place than just "wind and water erosion." God was alive and well for Justin at that moment, and this was His cathedral.

As he recalled the river experience and considered the current one, he realized that no other place on the planet had ever aroused such emotions in himself—this "power place" kind of feeling. It was no small comparison, for the writer had traveled extensively on assignments, visiting the strange, the beautiful, and the awesome on several continents. Even here in the States, no other place seemed to exude this level of power; not malevolent, but not benevolent either—just raw, neutral power.

"Perfection" entered his thoughts. Whatever the origination of Monument Valley, it was perfect: the carpet of green-tinged scrub, the expanse of flatness (or close to it) providing stark contrast to the majestic spires, the colors—nothing out of place, nothing here that didn't belong. Like most ecologically anesthetized inhabitants of the planet, it never occurred to Justin, not even for an instant, that the highway that brought him to his current state of bliss belonged here about as much as a black stripe painted across a Van Gogh landscape. Such was man's dependence on, and acceptance of, *progress.*

As Maley sat bathing in nature's offerings, his mind dared to examine more closely the voids in his existence that had been plaguing him for so long. There was a hole in his life—a flatness all his own—of missing companionship, missing inspiration, missing reason for being, missing understanding of what life was all about, and a missing vision of what he wanted in his future. It didn't help any that Justin was a "runner." He was slow to dive into new things and by the time he figured out what he wanted to do, it was frequently too late— with life, opportunities, and significant others waving goodbye as they lost patience with the man's lack of commitment.

Somewhere behind him, the cacophony of the crows was on the increase, reminding anyone within earshot that, although it may be the eagle and hawk that get the glory, it's the crows that get the lion's share of human attention, even if it be in disgust. As he did his best to ignore them, a reflected flash of light caught Justin's attention, somewhere on a spire to the left and very distant. Maley recalled the opening scene from the movie "Vertical Limit," probably filmed on one of these very spires, and so assumed the light had come from some piece of equipment carried by a present-day climber. He kept his eyes on the rock formation while bringing his binoculars between himself and his target. But the distance was simply too great, even for the powerful Zeiss 20x60 lenses, a long-ago gift from his dad with an attached enigmatic message, "Stay focused." Holding onto the double-barreled spy glass, Maley began a slow scan of the landscape around him, from the far left moving to the right, looking for anything of interest invisible to his naked eye. The amazing optics offered great detail of the nearer rock formations with uncountable crevices scarring their faces and providing the textures and shadow lines that gave the monoliths their familiar character. He scanned the high desert floor as well, half-expecting to see John Wayne and Slim Pickens riding for their lives on horseback with John Ford in hot pursuit—not with a Winchester, but with his trusty movie camera.

But the scene was devoid of *human* life, and his scan continued. As his arc approached front and center, highway 163 entered the aperture, and with it, a dark blue SUV heading north. Just before the highway and SUV left Justin's scan, the SUV's brake lights came on and the nose of the vehicle took a noticeable drop downward—apparently slowing quickly. It was an odd enough move way out here that it required a brief explanation for the writer's curiosity, so he stayed with the truck, first with the binoculars, then lowering them for the overall panoramic view, but instantly raising them again as the distance precluded any detail at all of whatever was happening so far away. And then, through the lenses, he saw the reason for the SUV's maneuver as it came to a full stop next to a human figure sitting alongside the roadway and leaning against a signpost. Again, Justin lowered the glasses, for people always prefer their unaided vision to the supplemented kind, but it was a lost cause. Without the binoculars, neither the SUV with its stop, nor the human next to it would ever have entered his awareness. So, the glasses came back up and what Maley saw next only served to ratchet up his interest level a full measure: a light-colored hand, at least it looked like a hand, came forth from the huddled mass, and in what appeared as a perfunctory gesture, waved the SUV to "be on its way." The truck, just as testily, did exactly that, and the hand returned to its hiding place. *What the hell?...*

For anyone, for everyone, experiencing a life-altering event is a rarity, and rarer still is the knowledge beforehand that it's about to occur. Maley wasn't one of those fortunates because, even as good as the Zeiss 20x60s were, they weren't powerful enough to see into the future. Justin Maley, freelance journalist and struggling novelist, was unaware that his life had just taken a permanent detour.

––––––––––––––

Remaining focused *(Yeah, Dad, I'm focused)* on the huddled mass of flesh, Justin tried to elicit any detail that might shed some light on— *it*, for at this point, any determination of gender was an impossibility. The clothes, beige in color, appeared to be standard fare, and it looked as though the figure were wearing an oversized floppy hat, prohibiting even a miniscule profile view of the head. Maley panned around the person, looking for any telltale clue to his/her provenance, but there was nothing, with the most significant non-clue being the absence of a car. Logic would have been better served with the presence of a disabled vehicle, but reality wasn't interested in logic today. That made the visitor a hitchhiker, or maybe just hiker; but what a weird place for a genuine, normal hiker to rest: Besides the intrusive and intense noise of passing cars and trucks, it was a downright dangerous place to hang one's hat. One moment of distraction to the driver of a 70,000-pound rig, and Mystery Man (the writer in him *had* to put some gender tag on the body) might well be added to the daily quota of road kill. So, why wouldn't Mystery Man accept a ride?

Justin willed the already-superior optics to do just a little better, like maybe X-ray vision, but in frustration, and with sore arms and eye sockets, he laid the binoculars back in his lap. There was just no way his curiosity would be assuaged from his present location, if at all. As hard as it was to take his eyes off the target zone, for without the glasses that's all it was, he turned to admire the rest of the vista before him and on toward his right. But when another car began the long downward grade, he instantly brought the binoculars back up and focused on Mystery Man. Again, the wave-off....

This time, Justin noticed that the knees were drawn up with the arms and head resting on them, and during the wave-off the head did not lift at all, which meant that the hiker wasn't even bothering to look at the cars or their drivers. Then he noticed something else—an addition to the already bizarre stage at the base of the hill: At the top of a telephone pole across the roadway from Mr. Weird, looking all comfy and content, was perched a bird of prey—and it looked vaguely familiar. Fate was shining on the human form, for at least the bird wasn't a vulture. Down came the glasses as Justin shook his head a little, emphasizing his confusion to no one but himself.

In the next ten minutes, eight more cars went by below, six of which stopped to render assistance to Mystery Man. It was becoming totally unreal, as the bony looking hand appeared and waved away each of them in succession. Maley went back to the scenery, stage right, but after a couple more repeats of the game, he finally admitted to himself that the scenic reverie had become a charade; so with soul tank more or less filled, he collected his stuff, bid farewell to Dick and Doris, and headed back to the Mustang, intent on getting some resolution to the enigma before him.

He wisely chose not to play chicken with an oncoming Peterbilt pulling a full load of lumber. As he pulled out behind the truck, he was relieved to see the truck swerve over into the opposing lane at the sight of Mystery Man ahead. Justin wondered what it must feel like to the guy when opposing traffic made the swing-over impossible: it had to be scary, with tornadic winds, and grossly dusty. The object of his increasing fascination was barely a quarter mile ahead now and Maley considered, surprisingly for the first time, just what exactly he intended to do to get the answers to his questions which—surprise again—were not yet well-defined either. *Better hurry-up, dummy!*

And then a sinking feeling began to emerge within him: what if the whole thing turns out to be anticlimactic? Given his history thus far, it was likely that Mystery Man would just wave Justin on like all the others. *What're ya goin' to do then, Justin 'ol buddy—jump out of the car, do a little dance, maybe find that obnoxious hand and pump it a few times? Anything to see the face—at least find out if it's a man or a woman.* But the time to "fish or cut bait" had arrived. Justin checked the rearview mirror to make sure he wasn't about to get run over by another truck, but the road was clear and so he began slowing down.

Suddenly, his expectations and fears from unpreparedness were replaced by surprise and anxiety, for Mystery Man was obviously beginning to stand up—or trying to. Like an elder or someone with a debilitating injury, the hiker was rolling to both knees and then pushing off the pavement with his hands.

Words of warning from the past can, and do, come screaming back into present consciousness at the strangest times, or perhaps it's *opportune* times. The last thing Justin expected to hear rolling around in his brain was his dead mother's voice and her admonishing words: "Never pick up hitchhikers, Justin;" and like they did twenty years in the past, her words were about to fall on deaf ears once more. In the last ten to twenty feet before the Mustang came abreast of the man—he was clearly, finally, a *man*—Maley could see the stranger's jaw working furiously, apparently angry, obviously talking either to the raptor or himself, but between the closed windows and engine noise, Maley could hear none of what was being said. With a life all its own, his index finger found the window controls and with mounting trepidation, Justin brought Mystery Man, mid-sentence, into his life:

"…sus H. Christ….What the hell took ya so long? I've been sittin' on that asphalt for three Goddamn hours and now my rheumatiz is goin' to be killin' me for a week." Without a hint of needing something as useless as *permission*, Mystery Man grabbed the door handle, but the Mustang's brain had locked both doors on take-off almost as if the machine knew what was coming and wanted no part of it, prompting the stranger to interrupt his diatribe with a derisive demonstration of sarcasm, "Do you mind...?"

As Justin sat there with his eyes and mouth opening larger and larger, two realizations came to him nanoseconds apart. First, the guy bore an uncanny resemblance to the actor Max von Sydow, including the most intense blue eyes he had ever seen. The other realization, a little late in coming, was that he'd just made a big mistake; actually, two mistakes, maybe: the first was stopping at all, the second being the opening of the window. He was on a cusp. He was beginning to feel it, and he knew he could still salvage mediocrity by simply stomping on the gas and leaving the weird ol' coot to choke on his dust. Only with the help of hindsight would Maley know if his choice, made in the next few seconds, would actually turn out to be a mistake or not. Therein lies the problem with choices. You frequently don't know until later, sometimes years later, if you screwed the pooch or if you done good, way back when. So, in the here and now, you have to listen for that voice in your head, the voice of your internal adviser who's supposed to help you stay out of trouble but sometimes gets his own wires crossed. It's about thought, logic, emotions, and ultimately, faith.

But since Justin's supply of all those elements was severely depleted, he automatically relied on past patterns: He ran. Fearing what he might be about to get into, that the old fart might be the Boogey Man, Justin chose to run like hell rather than embrace the unknown—and he stomped on the gas, indeed leaving the man covered in his gravel and dust.

A quick look in the rearview mirror showed Mystery Man's face following Justin as he drove off into oblivion—once again. However, now that he was "safe," his foot eased up on the gas pedal because it was time for the usual (hated), self-deprecating chastisement and loathing for his choices made (or *not* made—another form of choice). *What're you doin', numb nuts? You wanted different? Well that was different, all right. What's your problem? So what if he's the Boogey Man. You got something to lose in your precious, worthless life? All you ever do is run, you chicken shit. At the first sign of trouble or, or—involvement, you take off like a rocket. When ya goin' to find some grit, you worthless fuck? Well, it's*

19

too late now. He's gone, and just as well. He probably had fleas and who knows what else on him. Save your change-of-life stuff for something more predictable, safer. No! Turn this thing around now and go back. This is it, Justin. This is the big one. You don't do this now, you'll never do it, and you'll hate yourself forever. Fuck it. I'm hungry. Medicine Hat's just ahead. I'll get something to eat and think about it some more. Maybe the ol' fart will show up. Maybe we can....

Just then the organic missile came out of nowhere, flew over the car at what must have been at least a hundred mph, and headed straight down the roadway. A half mile ahead, the bird open his wing-brakes, lifted up slightly, and then settled down for a soft landing right in the middle of Justin's lane. He wasn't picking at carrion or anything; he just sat there looking back toward the oncoming car carrying a very confused and shaken-up journalist. Justin focused on the bird—the same raptor that had been by Mystery Man, and he somehow knew that the falcon was there for him, as impossible as that seemed. He slowed the Mustang, verifying that the road was still clear behind him. A car came from up ahead and sped by, but the bird did not move. Justin stopped the car about twenty feet away from—the messenger?—and thought about what was happening. Without warning, and with a great single flap of his wings, the falcon jumped into the air and landed on the Mustang's hood. Maley jumped in his seat because this up close and personal, the raptor took on a whole new level of intimidation. Looking head-on into the eyes of a known killer that uses its razor-sharp beak and talons to rip out the eyes and guts of it victims is a sobering experience. Maley was grateful for the quarter inch of glass between them, but he also knew the bird wasn't there to harm him—not directly, anyway. Somehow, the message was crystal clear: "Turn around right now or you're dead meat." Justin considered his options and the ramifications of each.

Moments like these are exceedingly rare in a human's life. The Universe seems to slow down to a crawl over a span of seconds. Sounds fade—all things fade, as opportunity invites you to consider changing your life forever. The possibilities course through your veins, hot and urgent. You know you're on the edge. Something crucially important lies far below in the abyss. Safety lies behind you. In a most definite manner, your life has already permanently changed, for a decision now to ignore opportunity's invitation is a choice that will haunt you until the day you die. It is a choice every bit as risky as the choice to step forward into fear and the unknown.

The raptor waited for an answer. Justin came back to the here and now and made his choice: He turned the wheels hard to make a u-turn. The bird took off, and Maley took the few minutes' return drive to consider what had happened and what it all meant. The "what" was simple enough, even though quite unbelievable, but the answer to what it all meant was a long ways from being clear. He sheepishly wondered if Mystery Man would badger him for his cowardice, but he'd just have to get over that. In the meantime, the strangeness of the entire event was cranking up his curiosity big time, and it felt really good. He could see the man ahead now, and as he passed him, he made a another u-turn, came abreast of Mystery Man, and mentally pushed the replay button.

"Well, Mr. Writer, did ya get it all figured out?" the man asked as he opened the now unlocked passenger door. Mystery Man climbed in, got all comfy, then realized they weren't moving; so he stopped his activities and stared at Justin with eyes every bit as intimidating as those of the falcon and with the same message: "*Go or die,*" as simple as that. Mystery Man's voice, on the other hand, conveyed no outward threat: "You're gonna catch some mighty big flies with that mouth there, Sonny-boy. What all were you doin' up there on the hill anyway?" It would seem that the sidebar with the falcon and the self-analysis had never happened.

Like a child caught with his hand in the cookie jar, Justin found himself stammering over some kind of inane excuse for his naughty activities, "I… I was…"

"Yea, I know what you *was*—you was gawkin'! And at my expense. While I was down here on my keister, achin' to the bone, you was gathern' wool. You was watchin' me, too. I could feel it—you know why?—cuz you got lousy boundaries, Sonny-boy. We're gonna hafta work on that or you're gonna end up driving me crazy. Now put it in gear, put your foot on the pedal, and let's get out of here."

But nothing happened—nothing in Justin's body could move because his brain had seemingly ceased to function, something like a short circuit. He was frozen just as surely as if a hypnotist had put him into a trance. Mystery Man knew the look, knew the driver would eventually come out of it, but "eventually" wasn't good enough right now. So he reached over, careful not to touch the patient, snapped his fingers directly in front of Justin's eyes, and fairly yelled, "Knock, knock, Puddin' Head, it's time to rock and roll, so get this hot rod movin'... Hit it!... NOW!"

It was enough to break the spell of shock. Maley closed his gaping hole, swallowed to replenish his dried-up mouth and—did as he was told, not taking his eyes off the stranger until it was time for the mirror and the pull-out. Thankfully, Mystery Man went suddenly quiet, apparently content for the moment to relax in a soft seat. After several minutes, and as Maley began to get hold of himself, a new sound emanated from his passenger: the telltale sound of slumber. He cocked his head for a better look-see, and sure enough, the stranger had begun gently snoring between regular and deep breaths. It was as though Mystery Man were some kind of wind-up toy won at the carnival, and after expending all the spring energy, the toy stopped dead in its tracks, waiting for someone to wind it up again. *God, why can't I go to sleep that easily?*

With the reliable cruise control re-set (probably the only point of stability on his crazy new path) Justin settled into his seat for the duration, however long that might be, and finally removed his white-knuckled hands from atop the steering wheel, placing them at about eight and four with elbows on the resting bolsters. Only after making sure that all was well with the roadway and the car did he allow his mind to attempt comprehension of what he had just experienced. *My God, what have I gotten myself into; and how the hell did he know I'm a writer?* But journalists ultimately deal with facts, so as the shock and concern began to wane a bit, he initiated the sorting-out process that had always served him so well. This time, however, it didn't work. His tried-and-true analytical formula relied on the presumption of logic and the possible. Remove both characteristics from reality and what was left was confusion and chaos, followed closely by the always lurking fear and self-doubt. Justin did okay right up to the moment he opened the car window, then it all fell apart. *He was expecting me, dammit. How can that be? I mean, a whole bunch of cars went through and he waved them all on without so much as a "fare thee well." Then I pull up, and he's all over me. And, holy shit, he KNEW I was up on the plateau checking him out. He knew!*

Like an old eight-track tape, it all went round and round on a con-
tinuous spool, *where it stops nobody knows*. But it did stop, abruptly, as a
new and final thought emerged from the soup: *he chose me*. And with
that realization, the inevitable: "*Why?*" Before Maley could begin to
even try and address the question, everything started to dissolve again
into the chaos that was hovering in wait just above, below, and to the
sides of his consciousness. For the first time in his life, he began to see
how an otherwise perfectly healthy specimen could actually and suddenly go nuts, simply by being unable to make sense of an unreal reality. It was uncomfortable. It was also frightening because he was no
longer the analytical but *neutral* observer. Justin, as a writer, was well-
versed in the effect of words, but in his most profound, most powerful articles, he knew that his words had never had the power, as measured by effect, as the few words spoken to him by the stranger. His
words had shaken the journalist to the core. He was in trouble, and
he was in danger of losing it, in the most literal sense of the word. And
there was no turning back the clock now, either. He had chosen. He
had committed. The only way to put an end to this short and crazy
mistake was to pull over, right now, and unceremoniously dump the
stranger back alongside the road for the next fool that might be
inclined to pick him up. But his internal advisor would have none of
that, and Justin somehow knew that his silent pleas for journalistic
and spiritual salvation were about to be answered—if he could just
keep it together.

*"In the world of politics, government, and power, **nothing** is as it seems. There are **always** other agendas invisible to all us worker bees. And the truly scary aspect of that reality is the fact that modern civilization could probably survive in no other way."*

chapter two

Beware of
Silver-Tongued Devils

New York City

A thousand feet above the Hudson River, a predator of a different sort was on its final approach for runway 16 at Westchester County Airport. Safely encapsulated within the G-V, the man wearing the dark Brooks Brothers suit sat comfortably in the thickly cushioned leather lounge chair, peering at the landscape below, which had included a very large hole in the ground in lower Manhattan. An almost imperceptible smile of satisfaction crossed the man's face. *We've come a long way, my friend.*

The flight from Washington had been short and unremarkable, but it allowed him some time to prepare for the TV interview scheduled for broadcast at 10:00 A.M. As was his custom, he declined any attempt to secure or limit interview questions prior to the event. In addition to looking good on his "political résumé," the practice enabled him to bash his opponents who *did* try to subscribe to the practice. Furthermore, it didn't matter. Unbeknownst to anyone other than Adam and his butler, Simon, the politician from Minnesota was able to pluck the imminent questions right out of the interviewer's mind before the question was asked. Such an ability would serve anyone in any occupation, but in the world of politics, it was frequently the difference between night and day, peace and war, or winning and losing.

Senator Truman Lawrence seemingly had the world in the palm of his hand, which was not far from the mark. Even successful business-men and politicians daydream from time to time, and a recurring vision of Senator Lawrence's was of a fatherly figure holding an exact, minia-ture replica of planet Earth within his palm. As always, between father and child, discipline and generosity—in equal measure, hopefully— were regularly provided. To his discredit, the father appeared to enjoy administering the former rather more often than the latter, with a little poke on one continent or another, or a gentle squeeze evenly distrib-uted upon the entire sphere. Discipline was a good thing. It reminded the children that the landlord could taketh away just as easily as giveth, and it tended to keep the more hot-headed rowdies on a short leash. And lest there be any doubt, there was a striking resemblance between the bearded father figure and the Senator from Minnesota.

The vice-presidential candidate was handsome by anyone's stan-dard—not in a male model or George Clooney sort of way; more like a younger Jimmy Stewart. But even if he were butt-ugly, his effect on peo-ple would likely have been the same: Charisma is a politician's best friend, and Lawrence had charisma in spades. He had a deep, silky voice that could have had a lucrative career on radio or in advertising. His luminescent green eyes disarmed many potential detractors who themselves became distracted and flustered by his eyes' mesmerizing quality. But most of all, the thoughts and words that came from what many grudgingly accepted as the quickest and sharpest mind in the political arena of the time, were what made him such a serious con-tender on the ticket. Senator Truman Lawrence always had an answer or solution to any question or problem, and his comments were put forth in the most erudite and lucid manner possible without the need for "uh's" or "ah's" or other delaying tactics so often required by those needing to clear their mental cobwebs before inserting foot into mouth. That many listeners vociferously disagreed with the words and thoughts being delivered with reassuring smoothness one moment, or brandished like a rapier the next, didn't matter one iota, for there were many who *did* like what they were hearing and who wanted more—lots more. As for the rest, their counterpoints provided the fuel for contro-versy and debate—something Lawrence truly looked forward to.

What was really bizarre about the whole thing was that Lawrence was just the *vice*-presidential candidate. The *presidential* candidate, James Reardon, was content to live on his laurels while letting his bull-dog running mate take all the heat. Reardon, a heavily decorated Vietnam POW, had been first a congressman, then a senator long enough to know the game forwards and backwards. It was he who had the political machinery greased and running as smoothly as a power plant turbine. His was the name that everyone and his or her dog knew and loved from Coast to Coast. He was the elder statesman (but not "too elder") who was respected by associates of all parties, both domestic and abroad. While Lawrence pissed off some people and made others smile, Reardon remained above the fracas, plying the straight and narrow course of respected presidential politics. His running mate implied politics *not-as-usual*, which provided the ticket with a very well-rounded constituency.

For the first time ever, this Independent Ticket was not a joke, not a spoiler, and not just the party of the disenchanted. This time, they really had a chance—largely due to the lackluster candidates offered by both the Democrats and the Republicans. Whereas the incumbents usually have a huge advantage, the president's once insurmountable approval ratings were now heading south of mediocre, leaving the Republicans wide open to a vicious trouncing by someone come November. The Independents didn't look for much in the way of Senate or House seats, simply because they didn't have the organization to take advantage of the current political climate—and that was the principle weakness of going Independent. But what they *did* have this time around were a couple of big guns—two, high profile, experienced, intelligent, unembarrassed (so far), and—most importantly—very ambitious political creatures that could see the blood oozing from the incumbents' party, while smelling the formaldehyde that filled the other.

The Independents' time had come.

For Truman Lawrence it was the inevitable conclusion to the series of events he had initiated thirty-five years earlier.

The graceful G-V landed and pulled to the general aviation terminal where a helicopter waited to fly Lawrence, Adam, and a Secret Service agent into Manhattan for the broadcast session.

Daniel Morgan had been a television news journalist for as long as James Reardon had been in Washington politics. In fact, he knew Reardon well, as well as anyone outside the close family circle. Morgan liked the presidential candidate, and would probably vote for him. The *probably* caveat came from the trepidation he felt whenever he saw, heard, or was around his friend's chosen running mate. Truman Lawrence simply did not pass muster with the newsman. It wasn't just that he had some radical ideas, very radical, actually, although developed with much thought and merit. In some ways, the guy was too good to be true, and perhaps that was where the problem lay: too good to be true usually was....

The biggest hang-up, though, was gut instinct. Daniel Morgan simply didn't like Truman Lawrence: didn't like him, and didn't trust him; and the combination made his job as neutral, objective journalist quite difficult. He found himself wanting to set up the candidate in order to expose lies or incompetence. Although, to a certain degree, this objective might be considered a part of his job description, Morgan was finding that his emotions were in jeopardy of turning his journalistic efforts into an obsession, and that was not okay. So, once again, he reeled in those emotions that most journalists must struggle with sooner or later in their careers when doing the "hard" assignments, and the anchor promised the angels of his chosen profession that he'd be a "good boy," at least for another day.

His secretary notified Morgan of the candidate's arrival in the building. The program was thirty minutes away and counting.

"Thank you for joining us, ladies and gentlemen. I'm Daniel Morgan, and our candidate profile today focuses on Truman Lawrence, independent vice-presidential running mate of James Reardon. This is the third, and final, interview with Senator Lawrence since we began this series nearly six months ago."

The red light on camera #2 went dark and was replaced by the light on camera #3, the middle camera designated for the wide shot of both men. Simultaneously, Daniel Morgan turned his head to face the man he didn't like, the man who could be a heartbeat away from replacing the man he *did* like. *Steady, Danny-boy, steady.*

"Senator Lawrence, thank you for being with us again today."

"Thank you for having me, Daniel. As always, it's a pleasure to be here."

"Senator, for the first time in memory, an Independent ticket has a real chance of taking the reins of the most powerful country on the planet. It's an amazing development—one I never imagined seeing—at least, not in my life time. How did this come to be, Senator Lawrence? How did the Independent Party move from its usual position as spoiler and actually become a serious contender?"

"Well, Daniel, there're two answers to your question. One involves the political parties in general, the other involves the incumbent president. Our Republic long ago evolved primarily into a two party system. There has always been much animosity between the Democrats and the Republicans, and consequently, it is the unspoken creed of each party to make life as miserable for the other as is possible. In the process, the welfare and benefit of the common citizen takes an unfortunately distant second place position in the politicians' agendas. The voters have always been aware of this, to some degree or another, but it has gotten so bad that citizens are finally ready to dump both parties.

"Do not misunderstand me when I say this, Daniel. Politicians are not necessarily narcissistic, power-hungry, or callous. In fact, most are not. Most take office with a serious desire of doing right by their constituents. However, we must all face reality: a politician's agenda isn't going to happen until he or she attains power and then holds onto that power by whatever nefarious means necessary. By definition, that means screwing the competition, making deals, and digging deep for campaign gifts. Both James Reardon and I are independently wealthy, and we have no old or new connections or needs involving big business or political parties in order to get elected. Our sole agenda is to do what's best for each American, and then to do what's best for the planet and every other citizen of our shrinking world.

"As for the incumbent," Lawrence continued, "I don't think there's any need for me to get into the President's disqualifications for running a country: You gentlemen and ladies of the media have pretty much done that already."

"Oh, and how's that, Senator?" Morgan asked casually.

Senator Lawrence, remaining focused on his host, responded matter-of-factly, as though the answer should have been obvious: "He's in over his head, of course. The man is qualified to run a corporation, even a state—and quite well, by all accounts—but not a country of 285 million persons, or one that has incredibly complex international relationships. That task requires more training, more preparation, and far more subtlety than the President has been blessed with. You know, Daniel," and now Lawrence turned back to camera #1—looking each and every viewer right in the eye, even though his words were technically directed at Morgan, "it's almost as if the occupant of the oval office has convinced himself that he won his presidency via a mandate from the people rather than by a single vote from the Supreme Court. Either he believes that a majority of Americans support his 'kick butt' policies, or he simply doesn't care that they don't."

The host of "News Makers" didn't miss a beat, despite the maze of different thoughts firing-off in his brain. Morgan said, "As far as a false mandate, I presume you're referring to the President's handling of the Iraqi situation?"

"In specific terms, yes. In general terms, the incumbent's charming, slightly reckless bravado plays fine in state politics, I'm sure. On the world stage, however, that kind of cavalier attitude will never produce the desired results in a civilization in which ego is a significant, almost required, characteristic of leadership. His 'lasso, wrestle, and hog-tie to the ground' form of diplomacy only angered world leaders beyond measure. I'm rather certain that their collective goal, while still in office in their own countries, will be to serve up crow to the President every chance they get, even if such a goal might not be in the best interests of their own citizens or the world at large. They want nothing more to do with him, and they are now patiently waiting for the next, *new*, president to mend the fences."

Morgan genuinely looked concerned with what he was hearing. "Surely, Senator, you're not suggesting that we kowtow to the demands of our European allies—allow their temper tantrums to dictate world policy?"

"And surely, Daniel, that's not what you heard me say. We live on an increasingly small planet—in terms of elbow room—and I'm quite certain that there's always going to be 'good-doers' and 'evil-doers' living here." The Senator had bowed the first two fingers of each hand to visually bracket "good" and "evil" with quotation marks to attribute the expression to some other mind. "That's the way it's always been, and I suppose that's the way the good Lord meant things to be. If we, and our closest allies, are going to keep evil at bay, then our house had better not be divided. That means we need to work together closely and amicably, and certainly not as though the United States of America is king of the hill. Expecting our European brethren to ask 'How high?' when our President says 'Jump,' is most definitely not a formula for success. In the meantime, those 'evil-doer villains' of the world roll on the floor in laughter, thoroughly enjoying the international soap opera. Daniel, it is absolutely crucial to work within the framework of a significant coalition before doing something as reckless as invading a sovereign nation, and I don't mean a paper-tiger coalition offering sound bites to the media. If the proper platform for such a move, the United Nations in this case, isn't up to the responsibility, then the organization should be altered through its governing bylaws or completely withdrawn from. It was insanity for Britain and the United States to invade Iraq on their own, with the predicted results as plain as day to most Middle East specialists and even our own CIA."

"I'll want to come back to this subject, Senator, but you just mentioned 'elbow room on the planet' which reminded me of a recent conversation I had with James Reardon in which he indicated that it would take years to clean up the results of the President's reversal of environmental laws. I assume you concur with that assessment?"

Senator Lawrence looked down at the table top and slowly shook his head. "Daniel," and he looked back up at his host with utmost sincerity, "we don't have near enough time on your program for me to take that subject where it rightfully needs to go. Yes, I agree with Jim's assessment. Sometimes it feels to me like we're about two shakes away from proving, perhaps not for the first time, that cockroaches and sharks are the superior life form on our planet—at least in terms of longevity. It would seem that human intelligence is not all that it's cracked up to be. It's bad enough to rape the planet of its resources, it's bad enough to pollute the atmosphere that sustains our lives, it's bad enough that we indiscriminately kill off species of animals either directly or through habitat destruction. What really," and Lawrence paused for a moment to find the exact right word for what he was feeling, "what really *shocks* me is the apparent unconsciousness with which these acts are done by everyone, everyday—with the prime example set, of course, by the current leader of our country. I think my biggest concern is that the President might actually be acting with *full* consciousness already, not with any interest for the environment, but rather for big business. Otherwise, how can anyone in his or her right mind initiate or support legislation that will ultimately wreak havoc on our planet, and sooner or later adversely affect every resident thereon? It is a discouraging sign of our times that the legacy of the most powerful leader on the planet may well be one of destruction rather than creation."

"Perhaps, Senator, but there are a lot of people out there whose livelihood depends on fewer environmental restrictions, not more. Are you saying to them, sir, right now, that their jobs need to be sacrificed?" Daniel Morgan was counting on the Senator's reputation for straight answers—no matter how tough the question—to sink his own ship. True to form, he didn't have to wait long.

Not bothering to look at Morgan, the Senator addressed his answer directly to lens center of camera #1: "No, Daniel, their livelihood will not be lost, but it *will* change. It has to. And to understand that need, we have to examine the entire economy of our country, along with our antiquated foreign policies and a leadership seriously lacking in vision."

Morgan chose to say nothing, inviting his guest to take the interview wherever it would end up.

"Daniel, virtually every problem Americans face today can be traced to the role of the United States as the world's policeman—as the world's problem solver. It is a role we have no business, no right, and no qualifications for assuming; and the sooner we all realize that and make doctrinal changes accordingly, the better off Americans will be—and possibly the rest of the world as well—but for sure our own people."

The anchor of "News Makers" used all his powers to keep a straight face, for he now knew that his program, right here, right now, would seal the fate of the Independent Party run on the White House. Interestingly, he was not yet quite sure what that "fate" was going to be. He wasn't yet sure if the man across from him was going to end up a "heel" or a "hero."

"Please elaborate, Senator Lawrence."

"Glad to…. Teddy Roosevelt coined the phrase, 'Walk softly, but carry a big stick.' That idea became the basis for our foreign policy, but for many years now, we've been neglecting the 'walk softly' part. That's when we became the obnoxious Americans. That's when the residents of other countries began saying to American tourists, 'We like you Americans, but not your politicians.' There's nothing wrong with having a big stick—in fact, it's a necessity in a world that allows evil to exist. It's just that it's time for America to mind its own business.

"Here's another well-worn cliché, Daniel, which applies directly to what I'm saying: 'Let he who is without sin cast the first stone.' We, the United States of America, are so unqualified to judge anyone else, much less 'fix' their problems, that it is just beyond belief that we could be so arrogant as to think otherwise. We can't fix our own problems, Daniel. We can't feed all our own starving children; we can't house all our own homeless families; we can't provide proper healthcare for all our citizens; we deny certain people their civil rights. Our children—the future of our country—are taught in understaffed, underfunded schools and taught by discouraged, underpaid teachers. In many ways, women are still second-class citizens in America. We execute people for crimes committed; forgotten citizens are routinely beat up—tortured by any other definition—while incarcerated. In terms of violent crime (reported or not), we are arguably the most violent country on the planet. You tell me, Daniel—other than carrying the biggest stick, how is it that we're qualified to police the world?"

"You mentioned something about all of our problems stemming from this realization?"

The camera caught Lawrence sipping some water before nodding his head and continuing.

"Isn't it obvious? The projection of power to support our role as planetary policeman requires billions upon billions of dollars. At the same time, the role endears us to no one. It does, in fact, make us a large and hated target in the eyes of many. The benefits of carrying the biggest stick have been few, while the suffering back home, as a result, has been high. Senator Reardon and I believe it's time for a major shift in doctrine. May I go on?"

The question was addressed, not only to Morgan, but to the program producer as well. Everyone in the studio already knew that the day's program was unlike any previous broadcast, with its potentially historical significance not lost upon anyone.

Morgan's eyes twitched sideways for a microsecond, an obvious indication that his IFB was carrying instructions from the control booth to his ear. Instructions received: "By all means, Senator."

"Some of the billions saved should go directly to programs correcting the problems I just mentioned. But…"

But Morgan wouldn't let him go on, not yet. "You can't just terminate a huge chunk of defense spending, Senator. Our economy couldn't deal with it. The stock market would tank!"

Lawrence had both hands in the air, shaking his head. "You're right, Daniel. I said 'some of the billions,' and the exact amount would have to be determined by careful analysis. But there's another chapter in this proposal: Utilizing existing defense contractors as much as possible—for stability's sake—it is our contention that it's absolutely necessary to further develop space and energy technologies."

Seeing that he wasn't going to be interrupted, Lawrence quickly went on.

"Our space programs have always paid off big time once newly developed technologies trickle-down to the private sector. Government pays for the development, the people reap the benefits—that's the way it's supposed to work. But the fly in the ointment is our reliance on oil, especially foreign oil, and most particularly Persian Gulf oil. Until that basic premise is changed, a change of doctrine cannot be fully implemented. Therefore, it is imperative that enormous increases in funding for alternative fuels be initiated at once. Specifically, Daniel, Senator Reardon and I will propose a ten-fold increase in research and development spending for fusion-generated energy. It is the one means of power production that can provide for all our energy needs in the future without scarring the landscape, and without polluting our environment. Through conservation and technology development, we must wean ourselves from oil dependence. In the end, Daniel, no one is going to lose his or her job—the jobs are just going to be different."

"If fusion power production is possible and so important, why hasn't it been the focus of previous administrations?" the host asked. "No one wants to be dependent on foreign oil—we've experienced the ramifications of that one before."

"Simple reasons for complex issues," Lawrence replied. "The technology has proven brutally difficult to crack, yet no scientist denies that fusion power, or something like it, will one day be common. In the here and now, though, none of the oil producers or oil companies is too anxious to see the demand for their products lessened by the development of new energy ideas. It's hard to blame them for that position when they have stock holders demanding high investment returns.

"Okay, Senator, it's time for us to take a break." Both men focused on camera #3 as Morgan previewed what was to come: "When we come back, I'd like to know more about the effects of your proposed doctrine change on our Middle East policies."

———————————————

Two hundred thirty miles to the south, back in the political seat of power of the U.S. of A. if not the Universe, Mike Metcalf lounged on the sofa in his office at the *Washington Post* watching Senator Lawrence on "News Makers," and the latest bullshit issuing forth from the wall-mounted TV set. Mike, being the star investigative reporter for the paper, rated this twelve-by-twelve cubicle with walls, just one step up, although a big one, from those open-air, stress-inducing cells in the center of the building floor. At least in here, he could fart without having to share the experience with three, count 'em, three fellow inmates. At thirty-six, Mike was fairly young to be in this exalted and enviable position, but he'd earned every stinking foot from the press room to his private office, as evidenced by the two Pulitzers conspicuously displayed on the credenza behind his small desk. They were highly visible to all visitors, including those editors who periodically tried to remind him of who was who, and what was what. The desk was on the small side because he'd become comfortable with the size during his years in the press pool, and because he had always wanted an office with a sofa. If one or the other piece of furniture had to go down in size, it would always be the desk. The sofa was an eight footer, leather, and very, very soft. It had to be, because the maestro spent many a night there while in the middle of pieces that were about to break and wreak havoc on someone, some company, or some governmental agency. Mike might be satisfied with a nine-year-old rust-bucket Volvo, but he had the finest, most expensive sofa to be found anywhere in the *Washington Post* building.

As Mike relaxed with his right arm tucked behind his head waiting for the commercials to end, he stared at the envelope in his other hand. It was amazing that the thing had gotten to him at all since there was no return address. That must have woken up the security people; but someone was sharp enough to recognize the potential importance of the content, and so the envelope had been dutifully delivered once biological sterilization was complete. The edge of the envelope bounced up and down on his abdomen as if it had a life of its own, and perhaps it did—or would. Right now, it was a cocked gun, looking for its target. And as the commercials ended, that target returned to the TV screen.

─────────────

Camera #3: "We're back with Senator Truman Lawrence, Independent vice-presidential candidate. Senator, if James Reardon is elected president, and you vice-president, you've indicated that you would reduce the role of the United States as—in your words—planetary policeman. How would that affect our commitments in Iraq, Israel, and the Middle East in general?"

Finally...

"Daniel, as part of our proposed new doctrine, it would become our policy to immediately and totally withdraw from Iraq, and to disengage from all interference in matters pertaining to the struggle between Palestinians and Israelis. We would reevaluate our foreign aid and loan guarantees to both groups, with an eye toward taking care of our own citizens first and foremost. If they want to work things out, fine. If they want to destroy one another, fine. But they'll do it without dragging us into World War III. We would leave it to them to either live in peace or live in misery, until death do them part."

There...put that in your pipe and smoke it!

The shock to the anchor was instant and almost palpable, as evidenced by a slightly hanging mouth and the spurted beginnings of some unintelligible word. But nothing was coming forth from the television journalist's vocal chords, resulting in the cardinal sin of live TV: dead air.

The show's producer saw the need to gently coax Morgan back into the here and now: through the host's earpiece, he prompted the anchor to simply ask Lawrence for a repeat of the staggering proposal. Poor Daniel Morgan, the aging patriarch of the airwaves was so flabbergasted by what had just been said that his brain seemed momentarily stroked out. Grateful to his producer, the anchor followed the suggestion and finally muttered: "Uh, would you repeat that Senator?" which the Senator dutifully did, straight face and all.

Two hundred thirty miles to the south, the envelope in a certain *Washington Post* reporter's hand froze mid-drop while he uttered a very quiet, "Oh my God."

In the oval office, the President could hardly control his glee as he picked up the phone and initiated a barbeque party for that afternoon.

In households across America, spoons loaded with cereal stopped midway to open mouths as even the politically un-astute realized they had just heard something politically unacceptable and maybe even important.

And across the ocean, at the eastern end of the Mediterranean, the espoused leaders of the Israeli and Palestinian people, for one brief moment in time, shared one thing in common: they both abruptly stopped what they were doing and waited for the other shoe to drop.

Back in New York, Lawrence tactfully waited for Morgan to compose himself, which didn't take too long, just longer that his producer liked. "Senator Lawrence, forgive me my shock, but you make that statement as if announcing that two plus two equals four. Obviously— obviously, such an action would have a horrendous effect on the area, as well as the rest of the world; but just as clear to me is the fact that you have either just lost your mind, as well as the election, or you and James Reardon have given this a lot of thought and are willing to risk everything on that one position. Which are we to believe?"

Lawrence laughed a deep and friendly laugh. "Well put, Daniel, and I assure you that I have neither lost my mind nor forfeited the election. You are correct, though: Jim and I have had many late night discussions about this issue, often heated and always passionate, for we both fervently believe that until the Israeli crisis, more than any other hot spot—including Iraq, Iran, and North Korea—is resolved, the world in general will be living on the edge. The two majority populations of Israel, with their 6 million people, have the capability of initiating a series of events that could ultimately lead to the effective ruination of our world—through a combination of military activities, terrorist activities, and economic meltdown. And their leadership knows it. It's time to isolate them and allow them to sink or swim on their own, without pulling down 5 billion others in the process. We've all been held hostage to our fears or to our 'do-good' concerns, for long enough."

"How?" Morgan was still in shock, but his brain was coming back online. "How in the world could this happen without the mass slaughter of entire peoples, probably the Palestinians, but maybe the Jews as well? The Arab states would go crazy. We would stand to lose the majority of our oil imports. The Arabs also hold enormous liquidity in our financial institutions, all of which would be subject to instant withdrawal. Our European allies, what's left of them, would turn on us like the jackals we would be for doing something this irresponsible. How can you possibly sit there with straight face and tell us that this is a viable policy?"

"You know, Daniel, in point of fact, I cannot provide you or anyone else a guarantee that our proposal will work—other than this: Both Senator Reardon and I absolutely believe it will, and we both believe that in ten or twenty years, when the historians document this day, they will discover that, as the leaders around the world listened to your broadcast, they were either shaking in their boots or they were applauding—either case being the result of their own belief that our proposal was necessary. Furthermore, we are collectively approaching a point of having no choice. It is the position of this Independent presidential ticket that we have reached the point wherein radical action must be taken in the absence of results by all other efforts thus far."

"Historically, you can watch American policies toward the Middle East go up and down like a yo-yo, depending on the make-up of

Congress and on who happens to be in the White House at the moment. Sometimes we're proactive, sometimes we tend to take a back seat. But the moment the bombs start to explode and the blood starts to flow, you can bet that the pressure is going to be on for the good ol' U.S. of A. to do something, and do it now. A new doctrine needs to be defined, initiated, and adhered to.

"And, unlike the spineless Democratic and Republican parties that are controlled by special interest groups, we are willing to put up or shut up. We are willing to stick our necks out. We are willing to do this because that's what Americans have always done. The sign says, 'Freedom is not free.' It never has been, never will be, Daniel. So, who's going to risk their political careers? —the Democrats, the Republicans? No—I don't think so."

"Hold on, Senator—you're talking about risking more than careers and reputations here. You're talking about risking world chaos, perhaps even world annihilation, with your 'bold move,' and I for one want no part of it." Clearly, Lawrence had finally gotten to Morgan, as the television journalist could no longer remain in the neutral zone, regardless of the warnings coming through his earpiece.

"Easy, Daniel, you're beginning to sound like an opposing presidential candidate."

Per the firm instructions of his producer, Morgan announced, "Ladies and gentlemen, we're going to take another break, and when we return, Senator Lawrence is going to reassure us all that his blueprint for world peace doesn't end up as a blueprint for world disaster. We'll be right back...."

With the red camera light turned off, and the mics confirmed to be dead, Morgan turned to Truman Lawrence and demanded to know, in unequivocal terms, that his friend James Reardon was the author of this platform and that Lawrence wasn't making some impromptu grandstand play. While both men received make-up touch-ups before the next segment, Lawrence reassured the anchor that Reardon was fully behind the strategy, and had actually written most of it. This bit of news left Morgan stunned with head shaking. Then the producer actually came by and pulled Morgan aside for verification that his premier anchor had recovered all his senses and was ready for prime time.

The three minutes were over in what felt like ten seconds. The floor director counted down the seconds with his silent fingers, and then camera #3 showed both men as they were queued for return to live broadcast.

"Ladies and gentlemen, just in case some of you tuned in late for this morning's edition of "News Makers," our guest this morning is Independent vice-presidential candidate, Senator Truman Lawrence, who has just announced a major change to the Independent ticket's platform. Senator Lawrence proposes that the United States back away from its traditional role as world's peacemaker and peacekeeper, and focus instead on domestic issues. In so doing, Senators Reardon and Lawrence, as Independent candidates for president and vice-president, respectively, are saying that Iraq should be abandoned immediately and that the Israelis and Palestinians would be on their own—to 'sink or swim'—I believe the Senator said, without any input or interference from America. Is that an accurate summation, Senator?"

"Yes, Daniel, that's close enough," Lawrence nodded.

"Senator, the possibilities—no, sir, the *probabilities*—become endless as the minutes go by here. You and Reardon would just unilaterally pull stakes and leave the Iraqis to fend for themselves?

"Yes."

Morgan stared at his guest as though the man were insane. "That's incredible, Senator. What would they do? Their leadership is in its infancy. Sadam's loyalists could possible resume power. The country would fall apart. There could be mass killings or starvation. The infrastructure would crumble. How can you possibly make such a suggestion?"

"Because the Iraqis don't want us there, Daniel."

"That's not a not good enough reason to abandon them," the anchor demanded. "They'd hate us forever, as well they should."

"Perhaps, but I think not. Daniel—you and all too many citizens of our great country have allowed the current administration to bamboozle you into believing we did the right and necessary thing in invading Iraq. They did it first through fear of weapons of mass destruction, then the benefits of eliminating Saddam Hussein, and finally using democracy as the supporting justification. As a final insult, they had the gall to use patriotism as both the carrot and the stick."

"Meaning what?" Morgan asked.

"Meaning that we had a patriotic duty to support our Commander in Chief, to support this war, and to support our troops; and that if we didn't support the war then we weren't supporting our troops, and therefore we weren't patriotic Americans. And that, Daniel, is an insult to my intelligence and my conscience, as it should be to everyone's." Looking directly into camera #1, the Senator completed his lecture: "I'm a patriot; I support our troops, and I support them by wanting them out of Iraq. The invasion of Iraq was a horrible mistake, and it's time to correct that error in judgment right now!"

Daniel Morgan was just beside himself with anger and criticisms, but if he wanted to still have a job next Sunday, he had to maintain his composure. Shaking his head, "Senator Lawrence, if we pull out of Iraq completely, I suspect the country will fall apart within weeks. Furthermo....."

"Define 'fall apart,' Daniel."

"It will revert to a dictatorship, the power will fail, the water and sewer systems will probably fail, there will be rampant bloodshed and executions, and the Bathists will probably return to power. That's what I mean by 'fall apart.'"

"I agree with you… one hundred percent."

All eyes in the studio refocused on the man of the hour, including those of the producer, director, and anchor. This time, the "dead air" was affective. Every viewer in the country (and Iraq), was so intently focused by now that the dead air served to increase the mounting tension. As Lawrence had an agenda, he chose to break the spell by explaining himself rather than risking the anchor or producer screwing it up:

"Look with a different eye at what's been going on in Iraq, Daniel. With our presence on the scene, every terrorist and terrorist-in-training is flocking into the country to ply their wares. As long as we are there, they will continue to do so, thereby disrupting all attempts at producing normalcy. But what *is* 'normalcy' in Iraq? Under Sadam Hussein, normalcy was daily corruption, daily killings, daily torture, and daily systems failure. When we leave, they will return to that which Iraqis seem to have been comfortable with for so many years. They will rely upon themselves—and they *are* a very creative people when it comes to survival—and they will rely on the government that develops from the strongest faction to get the infrastructure fully operational again."

"But what about democracy?" Morgan interjected.

"Forget democracy, Daniel. If the Iraqi people wanted democracy, they would have had democracy years ago." The anchor began to jump in again, but Lawrence stopped him. "Invariably, a people that wants democracy as their form of government has to fight for it—fight either some other country or their own despot leader. It's called revolution, Daniel, and if the Iraqi people were so hot to have democracy, they'd be willing to sacrifice everything, including their lives, to gain it. They have showed no inclination to do that yet. They are not ready. And besides, what makes you or anyone else think that they even want democracy? The region is so totally different from the West as to defy comparison. Everywhere you go in the Middle East, you find warlords, factions, tribes, religious sects, hatred, greed, and righteous indignation. Whether America remains in Iraq for years or leaves tomorrow, the results will be the same. The only difference will be the number of American soldiers who end up sacrificing their lives in total waste."

The Senator was now done and prepared to allow Daniel Morgan his best shot. The anchor jumped in: "So, you would have no problem telling the loved ones of all those soldiers killed thus far that their sons and daughters had died for nothing?"

Lawrence slowly shook his head, clearly indicating that his host simply did not understand the depths of the issue. "The longer our troops are in Iraq, the more body bags that will be sent home. Ultimately, James Reardon will be saving lives, Daniel. The man who sent our sons and daughters to a lost cause is the one responsible for all the lives lost for nothing, at monumental financial cost, and with major disruption to families at home who were just trying to get by."

"Excuse me, Senator, but this sounds like a formula for losing the war against terrorism," Morgan said, trying to sound convincing.

"Daniel, you have to let go of this 'win or lose the war thing' because there's no such thing anymore. We, the inhabitants of planet Earth, are a civilization in decline. The whole of civilization is losing and has been for years now, and it all stems from hatred between one person and another, one group and another, or one government and another. As far as decisive battles—forget it! Face-to-face battles on the plains of war are gone forever, Daniel. The advisors to the President should have made that clear to him. When overwhelming force threatens your homeland, you'll do whatever it takes to stop the invaders. You'll resort to terror and guerilla tactics—just like the North Vietnamese did in their fight with us, and just like American militias did in our fight for freedom from the British back in the eighteenth century."

Lawrence had raised his voice, creating an illusion of passion, but then, in a perfectly choreographed performance, he caught himself, backed off, and kindly reentered with the tour de force: "Daniel, when one is reasonably well-to-do, then life becomes a joy—an exciting, rewarding, wonderful experience, and something to look forward to in the days and months ahead. However, when you have little to nothing, life frequently becomes nothing more than a transitory experience; then the donation of your 150 pound hunk of flesh for a cause and a promise of a place in paradise becomes a goal to look forward to and ripe for manipulation by whichever charismatic figure happens to be in the neighborhood at the moment."

The Senator's philosophical ramblings were not saleable on national TV, so Morgan shifted focus back to something that was:

"And if we totally disengage from the Palestinian and Israeli conflict, won't the Israelis eradicate the Palestinians from the area, once and for all eliminating the threat the Palestinians have constantly posed to the Jewish people. What's going to prevent that from happening?" Morgan asked.

In his most charming, *"trust me, I know what I'm talking about"* voice, the good Senator laid it on thick as honey on a biscuit: "Fear, respect for life, responsibility, and a knowledge that truly civilized societies must eventually move past tribal feuds if they are to survive *and* prosper. For the very same reasons, the Palestinians will cease their terroristic activities toward the Israelis. And the two societies will work out their future together. The alternative will become unacceptable to the citizens of both cultures."

The look in Daniel Morgan's eyes said it all: at worst, he thought Lawrence had completely lost it; or at the very least, the Independent candidate for vice-president was the epitome of naiveté. The problem with TV was the short time span in which to respond to the overwhelming implications of Lawrence's proposal. It was just so monumental that Morgan was having difficulty choosing which hole in the dam to point out first. Ever the statesman, the Senator relieved the newsman of the burden.

"Daniel—picture for a moment an Israel, all cultures included, with a reasonable amount of prosperity and security—perhaps like Beirut in the '60s, with the borders and occupation issues removed from the equation. Under those conditions, do you think the residents of the area, the Palestinians and the Jews, would still prefer to kill and maim each other, or would they prefer to make money, celebrate family events, and play soccer? To choose the former is to outright declare these people as bloodthirsty tribes who live for violence, who live to fight, and I don't believe that."

"Is it possible that Israel would use such an opportunity to ruthlessly exterminate its Palestinian counterpart? Yes, it is possible. Israel has the muscle, and the will."

"And they'd do it," said Morgan emphatically.

"I think not, sir. Under a Reardon presidency, such an unjustified move by Israel would result in the cessation of *all* relations with Israel—for many, many years to come. From the United States' point of view, and I suspect from every other country as well, Israel would be dropped from the rolls of the human race, left to rot in isolation as the radical bad apple it had become.

"On the other side of the coin, the Palestinians would be warmly embraced, no doubt with large infusions of financial aid, mostly from the Gulf states that purportedly wish to help the situation, but from the West as well. The Palestinian people would quickly experience reasons to look at alternatives to blowing up their children. However, if their warlord leaders still choose blood over wine, then I'm sure they will receive that which they would deserve.

"If both sides come to their senses, and after a period of time of zero to minimal violence, after a spell of cooperation when a Jew and a Palestinian can walk side by side down an isolated road without killing each other or being killed, when they can share laughter together—then statehood and land swap issues can be successfully addressed; flexibility will be a possibility rather than an absurdity."

"You honestly believe that the Israeli and Palestinian leadership would agree to this plan?"

"You're missing the point, Daniel. Neither leader would have any choice in the matter. If the United States publicly and firmly pulls its players off the board, withdraws its financial aid for the betterment of our own citizens, the two sides will *have* to re-evaluate their respective positions. From their position of strength, the Israelis will probably have an easier time of it. The Palestinians, though, will have to spend some very serious time in front of the mirror."

"What do you mean by that, Senator?" Morgan wanted to know.

Lawrence shuffled the papers in front of him for a second, as well as focusing his attention on them—giving the viewers the impression that he was choosing his words carefully. Although the latter was true, the effort had been expended some time ago, back in Washington. Now, it was no more than a dramatic pause.

"Daniel," but again the Senator paused: last chance to reconsider before pissing off every Palestinian on the planet—which, of course, was exactly the intent. "As sad as it may be, the Palestinians are nothing more than the Arab's pawns in the chess game known as Middle East politics. All Muslim governments in the region are quite willing to use the Palestinians as their whuppin' stick against the Jews because recent history has already shown that 'official wars' against Israel have been abysmal failures for the Muslims. So, the prevailing philosophy is, 'if you can't beat them, at least punish them,' and who better to use for the task than the hapless Palestinians who at least have a 'cause' with which to justify their actions. Besides the Muslim leaders in the supporting countries, the beneficiaries of this policy are the Palestinian faction leaders who can be seen driving in their BMWs and SUVs while the rest of the Palestinian population must content themselves with twenty-year-old clunkers or even donkeys. And for some reason beyond all understanding to Westerners, the rank and file Palestinians have bought into this game—hook, line, and sinker. Before things change for the Palestinians, they'll have to look more closely at what they *really* want and what they want from their leadership—such as it is."

Lawrence wasn't done, and before Morgan could intercede, the Senator continued his line of thought, "Like two half-brothers who can't seem to get along, the adoptive parents must finally handcuff them together and throw them into the pond. They will sink or swim together. They will make it to the shore together or not at all. They will build sanctuary together, or they will die together. We must allow these countries to make their choices and live with the consequences, without any outside pressures.

"Look at a globe, Daniel. The area we're talking about is so small as to almost be invisible on the map, yet the actions that emanate from there are felt around the world—because we, the rest of the human race, allow ourselves to be manipulated by fear of the 'what if.' It's time to change the nature of the 'what if.' It's time to handcuff them together and throw them into the pond. It's time to move on."

"Senator Lawrence—what about the Jewish population in the United States. They will never allow this to happen."

"Perhaps, perhaps not. But consider this. As a result of our discussions and research on this matter, James and I discovered a looming commonality amongst everyone with whom we spoke. I repeat, Daniel—everyone. Despite the lip service support for both peoples of the area by their supposed benefactors, everyone is tired of this problem and everyone wants it to go away, except for those leaders and participants who directly benefit from continuing the game—those receiving power, money, and respect to kill and send young boys and girls to their deaths.

"And speaking of lip service, if that's what Americans want from their next president and vice-president, then Americans need to stick with either the Democrats or Republicans—it doesn't really matter which, as they're pretty much the same. As always, it's the Independent that truly stands for change. As radical as our ideas are for the Middle East, they're not the only radical changes we propose. Our revised platform policy statement will be released to the public in a few days, and that statement will get into substantial detail about our ideas, ideas that cover domestic policy as well as international issues. I urge all Americans to thoroughly review our detailed platform revisions. Then, Daniel, come November 11, we'll find out if it's time to move forward or remain stuck in this morass of stagnant policies that have been with us for so long."

The timing was perfect, leaving Morgan just the right interval to close out the show, thank his guest, and preview the following week's guests. Regardless of the tension the broadcast had generated, after the camera lights all went out, the studio went about its business as usual. But Daniel Morgan had one more thing to say to the Senator before leaving the studio.

"Senator Lawrence, I want to go on record and say to you that what you propose regarding the Middle East I think to be incredibly irresponsible and totally impossible to accomplish, and probably threatening to the world at large. And I can't believe that James

Reardon subscribes to this notion, which is something I intend to verify once I leave here today." With that, the newscaster turned on his heel and headed to the narrow confines of his office—and mind. Truman Lawrence turned to leave as well, but as he headed toward the studio door a technician approached him. "Senator Lawrence, sir...."

A Secret Service agent moved to stop the worker's approach, but Lawrence waved him back. The Senator stopped, acknowledged the man, and shook his hand.

"I liked what you said, Senator. I'm tired of that bullshit over there taking up all our time. We should be focusing on other things—more important things—like taking care of our own, ya know? You got my vote, Senator."

Lawrence genuinely smiled and thanked the technician before he, Adam, and his Secret Service agent headed through the doors to catch the helicopter back to Westchester. Forty minutes later, as the G-V passed through 10,000 ft., and in the privacy of the plush cabin, Lawrence finally asked Adam how the interview came across on the tube.

"Better than I ever expected, Truman—you silver-tongued devil, you." A few seconds of silence followed as both gentlemen savored the irony, and then, simultaneously, they both erupted in good-natured laughter.

"Your sincerity and confidence were the winning combination, Truman, and I suspect we grabbed a lot of silent majority votes today, while scaring the shit out of the intelligencia. It'll be fascinating to see how it plays out. By the way, anything new on our friend out West?"

"Yes, I took a quick look when I was alone before the broadcast. He *is* heading East. He's somewhere out in the desert, and it looks like he's driving with someone in a red car. I can't tell yet if it's a planned thing or just a casual encounter. Anyway, the eyes have got a bead on him now, and they'll keep watching. I'll check things again when we get home, then I'll turn it over to you and the troops. Both men smiled as the cabin attendant poured each of them a glass of champagne.

"Faith *is a wonderful characteristic unique to human beings, and one to which I cautiously subscribe. But we must always remember that* faith *is not the same thing as a signed affidavit from God.*"

chapter three

Max the Magician

Highway. 163, Arizona/Utah

A lot can happen in thirty minutes and thirty miles. For one thing, Justin's fear of an imminent visit to the Funny Farm was beginning to lessen. It's weird how the human body, and more precisely, the mind, is capable of dealing with fear, stress, the unknown, and danger. As long as injury and death, or worse—insanity—hold off for a bit, the mind begins to adjust, as part of the survival complex it would seem, while calmer thoughts take over. In Justin's case, the white noise hum of the engine and the tires on the roadway didn't hurt any. The assumption was that as long as his passenger remained asleep, and he was sawing some pretty big logs now, there would be no more bombs to deal with—a reprieve. Just like any other tourist, he actually risked a glance now and then at the scenery that had brought him here in the first place. So, common sense slowly returned, along with his analytical abilities. Always a superb organizer of words and thoughts, Maley attempted to catalog what had happened in the last couple of hours. And then one of those "blasts from the past" worked its way into his consciousness: as clear as day, he could see his dad's face and hear his words, "Be careful what you wish for, son—you may get it." The recollection brought a smile and a chuckle to his lips.

49

Well Justin, you dumb shit, you sure as hell found some inspiration. So, we have an old man, and he is borderline ancient, sitting alongside the highway, no broken car, no luggage—that's right! Mystery Man has nothing but the clothes on his back. He's obviously not a hiker, not even hitchhiker, as he refuses a multitude of rescue offers—until I showed up. Then, before I can even stop, he's getting up as though—no, not "as though"—he's getting up because he knows its me. He's expecting me. He also knows I've been at the vista point, and that I've been checking him out. And then, the inevitable return to the final argument: *He chose me.* The key issue in his analysis is the presumption that Mystery Man is a mind reader, but the resilient brain comes to terms with that by acknowledging that mind readers, though rare, do exist. This is not a first, and it's not as outrageous as little green men landing alongside the highway. *So Mystery Man is adept at reading minds—okay, I can deal with that.* And for the moment, that worked; it fit the pigeonhole labeled "reality," except for one little, teensy weensy thing: Justin the man, the human with emotions, didn't believe it. Maley, the journalist, was adept at delivering bullshit, and he was as good at doing it to himself as to others. But going deeper than the mindreader thing didn't fit within his current agenda—it got too close to a danger zone where the moth's wings get singed in the flame. At the moment, sanity demanded that the thought of Mystery Man being something more than just a mind-reader be saved for a later time, with more information at hand.

It was a fine idea, but ultimately it wouldn't help.

As his visitor snored away the minutes and miles, the writer took a time-out from his internalized thoughts to focus his attentions on the man sitting next to him—kind of a physical inventory. With quick glances while keeping the Mustang on track, Maley noticed he wore a ragged Carhartt jacket over a plaid flannel-looking shirt. The pants appeared to be Levis, but they were so faded it was hard to tell. On his feet were worn-out sneakers, Nikes by the appearance of the ubiquitous logo, with a few strips of duct tape patching the holes. Everything was old and heavily stained, and if he were on the streets of any big city the assumption would be that this was a homeless gent. The hat didn't fit the rest, though. It looked newer, of high quality and very unusual. It was round and floppy with an overly wide brim, and it lent a gnome-like appearance to the wearer. Actually, a better word than gnome would be "wizard." All it lacked was a tall pointy peak, and the man under it could have come right out of a Tolkien novel. All around the hat, a mane of moderately thick gray hair flowed over the man's shoulders and had obviously not been visited by scissors in quite awhile. And the face matched that persona: very old, wrinkled—almost craggy, with lots of red spider web lines. Surprisingly, there wasn't a lot of sagging skin. He was fairly tan, supporting the supposition of homelessness, and there was a crop of fuzzy hair growing out of his left ear. His arms were folded across his chest, exposing a right hand toward the driver. His hands, and fingers, were gnarly but not yet totally deformed from the rheumatism he had alluded to. There were no rings, and the fingernails were a little long and moderately dirty. Finally, he looked as though he hadn't shaved in at least several days.

With the physical parameters established, Justin peered more closely at the face, willing himself to see more than what was on the surface, to do his own bit of mind reading—turnabout is fair play, ya know?

Suddenly, the snoring stopped, the body stirred, and the mouth opened, but the eyes remained closed. "You don't wanna be doin' that Sonny-boy."

Oh shit. It was the cookie jar again. "Huh?"

"You heard me." Opening his eyes and turning toward the driver, Mystery Man went on, "I told you about your lousy boundaries, and here ya are messin' around again. The next time you go pokin' around where you don't belong, you're goin' to regret it. You got that Sonny-boy?"

Another bomb... Never a master of the quip, Maley wisely chose to leave the subject alone, particularly since he didn't have a leg to stand on. Instead, he chose a different route to let the stranger know there was a limit to the amount of shit he was going to take from some ol' geezer. So, in as irate a voice as he could muster, he retorted, "Listen up, old man, my name isn't 'Sonny-boy', you got that? My name is Justin Maley," and then he spelled it out for Mystery Man as if the elder were mentally challenged. It was weak but a little better than going catatonic again. "And while we're on the subject, what's your name?"

With the question, the passenger turned to stare out his window, and for a moment Justin forgot all evidence to the contrary and flashed: *Oh my God, he doesn't know his name. I've picked up some Alzheimer guy who must have gotten past the door buzzer alarm thing, escaping Nurse Ratched and looking for some sucker to aid him in his run for freedom.* But his brief flight of fantasy was shattered, once again, as the visitor turned back to him—is that a twinkle in his eye?—and delivered his next bomb:

"Just call me Max."

GodDAMNit—how does he do that? There had just been the one fleeting thought in Maley's mind that Mystery Man looked like the actor Max von Sydow, but it'd apparently been enough for the passenger to make a connection, and now he tossed the grenade back to Justin. Maley's head darted between the road and Mystery Man—okay, "Max," looking for some sign, something in blinking neon would do just fine thank you, informing the inquisitor of who, or what, was sitting next to him. But it wasn't to be, and now the passenger's eyelids began sagging, and pretty soon he was gone again.

And so was Maley. Max's slumber provided Justin ample opportunity to consider his situation, and allow his imagination to expand like it hadn't done in months. Without firm answers to the enigma sitting next to him, he was free to create his own, and he did so with gusto, heedless of the certainty that sooner or later reality, and Max, would most likely shoot down his own scenarios in flames.

The Mustang was coming up fast on Mexican Hat, and Justin the human, the one on the edge of fear and trepidation, fleetingly considered finding the local bus stop, dragging his charge over to the bench, laying a couple of twenties on him, and returning to the safe and secure world he'd known earlier that morning. It was a short-lived thought, though, as Maley the journalist would never forgive himself for abandoning a potentially amazing story. It was more than simple journalistic curiosity. The guy—Max—was clearly way out on the edge somewhere, and the folks that hang out that far are usually either bonkers or have something important to say or do, or both. Maley wanted to be there when the verdict came in. Furthermore, mind readers don't grow on trees, and being in the presence of such an anomaly was not something any journalist in his right mind would voluntarily terminate. But, it was all academic anyway because by the time he finished processing the thought, the dusty little town of Mexican Hat was just a fading image in his rearview mirror.

Maley carefully reached behind Max's seat to retrieve some lunch food and a fresh bottle of water out of the little cooler stashed there. Juggling food and steering wheel and fully focused on neither, he was unaware that Max had awoken with a start. "What was that?"

"Say what?" asked Maley.

Max continued his thought, less sure, "Is there something wrong?"

Now Maley looked over at him, shaking his head, "There's nothing wrong. I was just getting something to eat. Why?" But just to be sure, he did a quick scan in all directions, wondering if something dark and evil was about to descend. Max did his own brief scan but then settled down, without going back to sleep. To the nonpsychic driver of the Mustang, the passenger looked skeptical and a little nervous—kind of fidgety. All the gauges read nominal, the car felt fine, so Justin was about to put the incident out of his mind when a foreign sound barely entered his senses. It was the kind of sound that, being new and different, and therefore not belonging, can be cause for concern or not depending on if it gets worse, stays the same, or goes away; after all, cars do pick up new noises as they age. But this one was very slowly becoming worse—louder. Also, it felt like there might be a slight vibration coming on line. An alarm began going off in Justin's head, so he set down the food, removed the water bottle from his crotch, laid off the gas peddle, and took firmer command of his ship with hands at ten and two. Both the noise and vibration were becoming worse now as Justin developed the depressing feeling that always comes with an experience like this, especially when it happens away from home and a thousand miles from the nearest help—with anything more than "visually up the street" feeling like a thousand miles. The climax came with a tremendous bang and the immediate dropping of the right rear of the car, then the feel and sound of metal on asphalt, presumably the wheel without tire. Both occupants of the car knew then what had happened, and one of them was visibly relieved since it was easily fixable with the spare tire—not like a broken engine or something. Max the Mind Reader blew it this time, as he failed to detect the sinking feeling coming from the man across the console. Justin got the Mustang to the shoulder, stopped the car, shut off the ignition and then just sat there, slowly lowering his head to rest between his hands at the top of the steering wheel.

Max still didn't comprehend the actions and emotions of his host, probably because the reason for it was so ridiculous as to defy normal analysis. But no matter what was going on, the obvious solution wasn't being implemented and Max began to feel some impatience, so he asked, "Well?"

"Well what?" Maley didn't move or look up, as he muttered the absurd question from his hiding place.

With mounting confusion and frustration, Max started to get a little testy. "You gonna fix the flat, or ya gonna make 'the ol' geezer' do it for ya?"

"Can't...." and as Justin said it, he rotated his head, still resting on the steering wheel, and turned to stare out his window—not really looking at anything, just mentally preparing himself for the inevitable pounding from his passenger.

"Wha' d'ya mean 'can't'? Haven't ya ever changed a flat before?"

Barely above a whisper and cringing as he said it, Justin replied to his soon-to-be tormentor. "I can't because the spare's flat."

Still looking out the side window, the writer scrunched his face and stiffened his body in anticipation of the verbal body blows that had to be coming because, this time, beating *himself* up just wasn't going to be good enough. But what he got was silence. It was so surprising that before long he turned from the window to make sure Max hadn't fallen asleep again. Wrong...

It was Max's turn to be gathering flies, staring at Maley, shaking his head slowly in bewilderment, but there was also some humor, both in his face and his response. "You gotta be shit'n me. You left Santa Monica without a spare?" As the enormity of the screw-up took hold, he started getting more and more worked up. "What kinda moron leaves home on a 3,000-mile road trip without a spare tire? Are ya crazy, or just so spaced out ya don't know your ass from a hole in the ground? Oh, God, my buddies ain't gonna believe this shit. Ya know, when I chose you, I was expectin' some smarts, but now you got me worried some, Sonny-boy."

The truth hurts, of course, but Justin was an adult, a red-blooded *male* adult, so he did what every man does in these kinds of situations—he got defensive: He screamed at Max as though the passenger were to blame for the whole mess, "Hey, I don't need your shit! You got that? It's by my generosity you're not still sitting back there about to freeze your balls off. Okay? This is MY car you're sitting in, my gas your using, and by the looks of you, I'll bet you got nothin' to chip in with. So take your fucking opinions and shove 'em! Got it?"

"Listen up, Sonny-boy," Max yelled back. He may be an 'ol geezer, but he'd never taken crap from a 'kid' and he wasn't about to start now. "At the moment, your car ain't nothing but a 3,000-pound door stop, we ain't goin' nowhere, and we might both end up freezin' our balls off because," (and an accusatory finger came out from the Carhartt jacket, pointing right between Justin's eyes), "you dropped the ball! And in case ya didn't know it before, you now need me as much as I need you."

Testosterone released and stymied by their mutual outburst, they sat there staring at one another, eyeball to eyeball, still playing—playing "who blinks first"—and almost simultaneously a grin emerged on both faces, at first tentative, then becoming a genuine laugh—at themselves, at each other.

"You're kind of a crotchety old fart, aren't you?" Justin finally observed.

With a snort, and also a changing look of mild sadness, Max shrugged, "I don't know about the first part, but yeah, the second's true enough."

"By the way, Max, I didn't tell you I came from Santa Monica, did I?

"I reckon not. Lucky guess I suppose. Now go change the tire, and let's get out of here."

Yeah, sure, lucky guess.... Maley had begun to pick up his cell phone as Max's last words registered. He stopped keying nine-one-one after the nine, wondering if he'd heard the man correctly. "Max, what part of 'spare's flat' didn't you understand?" and he continued with the one, one, thanking God for cell phones in one breath, then cursing them all in the next for not having a range of at least a hundred miles.

Considering his next move, he didn't even look at the man next to him as Max responded, "Just humor me, okay?"

It's remarkable how fast the human brain can process information when the requirement to do so is activated. Faster than a Pentium chip, Maley began looking at the possible ramifications of the very strange request from Mystery Man—despite having an official name now, Max was definitely still a mystery. Maley's life entered slow-motion mode, watching his hand replace the useless cell phone in its cradle. His eyes remained on the device, not seeing, just processing. The difference between the Pentium and the human computer is one of emotions. The Pentium would lock-up and roast if it were subjected to what Maley were *feeling* right then.

Hold it....hold it. Time out. What does he mean: "Humor me?" What could he possibly mean with those two words? Historically, "Humor me" means something like: "trust me, everything's going to be okay, don't ask any questions, have faith." Is he implying what I think he's implying? No way! Mind reading's one thing, but this is a whole new level. This is "beam me up, Scotty" shit. Things like this are....well, impossible. Right? Oh, man....

Justin sighed a big one as he came back to functional reality. Some part of him did not want to know the answer to this dilemma, but the blown-out tire could not be ignored. One way or another, the issue had to be dealt with. Either he had to hail down some help—or he had to open the trunk. Not a big deal, really—not usually. It was just that, this time, the one option was normal while the other belonged in the "Twilight Zone." *All this torment because of two little words.* Still not looking directly at the man sitting just inches away, Justin began, then stopped, the absolutely necessary inquiry, "Max...?" He couldn't complete the words, but neither could he stop the thought. And it wouldn't matter what Max said anyway because, in matters this great, words are cheap—while the proof is in the pudding, or with the case at hand, in the trunk of the Mustang. So, he reached over and opened the glove compartment and pressed the little yellow release button that could, right then, be opening himself up to all kinds of new and frightening "things." Justin felt, more than heard, the releasing of the trunk lid latch, so he opened the door and stepped onto the shoulder, eyeballing the just slightly cracked lid as he determinedly walking around to the back. He gave himself a "rah-rah" cheer, both for comfort and to stall for just a second longer, but the moment had arrived to find out what cards the future was holding. *Okay numb nuts, it's time to shit or get off the pot....*

Whenever there's a chance of some nasty hiding in the dark, one has two options: First, go slow and stealthily (safe mode); or secondly, get it over with as fast as you can, damn the torpedoes—full speed ahead. Justin knew the trunk was full of "stuff" in addition to luggage, all of it covering the useless spare tucked away in its storage compartment; therefore, nothing was going to jump out and grab him by the throat—figuratively speaking, of course. Still, all his bravado, all his nonchalance was tempered by the growing belief that what lay under the lid could change everything for him for the rest of his life, not that that hadn't happened already anyway. The decision to intentionally proceed, in full awareness, with a potentially life-altering event is no small matter.

Come on Justin, it's just a stinkin' flat tire.

No it's not. It's fixed, and HE did it!

He raised the trunk lid, not slowly, not frantically, but deliberately, and nothing jumped out. *Safe to proceed...*

Like hell it is...

Justin became frustrated with the mind trip he was laying on himself. He was self-perpetuating a self-created ridiculous level of stress and fear. With a change of plan, he dived into the mess, throwing books, magazines, luggage either aside or out on the shoulder of the road, and within seconds, the cover to the spare compartment was exposed and cleared of all obstructions—except those of the mind. Without any more bullshit, he removed the cover, exposing the tire and wheel below, but right then, right at the crux, the writer-who-seeks-inspiration, froze. *Touch it, Justin... all you have to do is touch it and you'll know, you'll feel it, and you'll know if the guy up front is just some 'ol crazy carnie trickster somehow messin' with your head—or, if he's—other.*

And for every action, there's an equal reaction. *You sure you wanna go there, 'ol buddy? You sure you wouldn't rather just go back to Santa Monica and get back to sending those nice, safe, lucrative articles to the* New Yorker *and* Smithsonian?

Fuck it! He pounded the spare with the heel of his right fist—and it was filled with air and hard as a rock.

————————————

Epiphany: a sudden moment of understanding; a flash of insight; the emergence of a truth with life-changing consequence. For some, an epiphany will come from a near-death experience. For many women, it will occur with the emergence of a new life from their bellies, watching as the first breath of air is consumed. For a scientist, it may be the result of a discovery that changes all previous precepts on the nature of the Universe. For Justin, it was a born-again flat tire, and it was a moment that would be with him forever.

For many seconds, Maley stood there staring into the hole that was the Mustang's trunk, staring at the spare, void of thought, void of understanding. Eventually, the practical side of the man took control, that part that says "you need to eat now, or sleep now, or pee now, or wash now." Without fear or curiosity, or emotion, the numb younger man pulled the wheel out and began the process of changing out the dead tire which had completely failed and was a mass of ragged pieces. Without fully considering the significance, the thought came to his mind of how lucky they had been that the blow-out had occurred on a rear wheel rather than up front, and that there had been enough warning to slow down before the failure, and that they had been on a straight stretch of road rather than a curve with a thousand-foot drop-off. Somewhere around tightening the third lug nut, a crow began "cawing" over his right shoulder. The new sound drew him back in a little, so he offered the bird some of his attention. The black bird was sitting on a power line about fourty feet away and seemed to be staring right at Justin. "Yeah, yeah, what do you want? You here to give me a message, or to mock me?" *Most likely the latter...*

As fate would have it, the crow's mission was neither...

With the shredded tire replaced, Justin repacked the trunk, slowly returning to the land of thinkers and feelers in the process. Once he got back in the driver's seat, he knew the shit was going to hit the fan between him and Max, and he had to get his thoughts together beforehand. The looming question in his mind, besides the true identity and purpose of Max, was the original condition of the spare tire. Had he blown it? Did he have a major brain fart? Was it not flat to begin with? And, therefore, had Max actually done nothing special? So, Maley went back to the construction site in Redondo Beach, three weeks before, and began the replay. He'd pulled into the site, ignoring the "Do Not Enter" sign because journalists are special human beings that don't have to follow the rules. And for his arrogance, he'd unknowingly driven over the corner of some angle steel stored on the ground close to the superintendent's shack. The steel ripped open the sidewall of the tire, therefore guaranteeing its unfixability—not like some nail puncture. No, the tire was definitely toast, and it ended up in the spare tire cavity to be replaced the next chance he got. And there it was—the biggie. Was there any chance that he'd replaced the tire without remembering doing so? The replay went into slow motion, covering each day in minute detail, minute enough to finally shake his head and confirm to himself that it just hadn't happened.

Max the Warlock was on the hook and it was time to confront him.

Maley returned to the driver's seat, but stayed away from the controls, focusing instead on the man who held all the cards, who had all the answers. "Talk to me, Max," Justin began. "Tell me who you are or what you are, where you're from, what's going on, where we're going, and how you did the tire thing. I want to know it all, and I need to know it now."

"I can't tell you. Not yet. It's too soon." End of speech.

But Maley was not to be put off. Max had now done the impossible and all of a sudden it *was* analogous to, and just as awesome as, little green men landing nearby in the desert. Max had just laughed at all the *known* laws of physics. Either he was some kind of charlatan or he had some really good connections, and either way, it was time for the truth.

"No, Max. You can't do the stuff you've been doing and expect to just go on without an explanation. There's a big difference between mind reading and doing what you just did with the tire. We're in the majors now, and we're not going anywhere until I hear what you've got to say. We'll stay here all night if need be."

"No we won't," Max said, now turning to look Maley in the eye. "We can't. There's danger out here, for me, and therefore for you." His voice dropped a little lower, and Maley thought there might even be a hint of fear in the blue eyes. "If I'm stopped before I complete what I need to do, the consequences will be unimaginable. A moving target is harder to find than a stationary one, so we have to go—now. It may already be too late, and the light is beginning to fade. Please…"

Always the sucker for a plaintive "please," Maley backed off a little, looking for a more circumspect approach to achieving the desired results. "I don't understand, Max, why can't…. Wait a minute. What's the matter with you? You don't sound the same as the grouchy 'ol fart of a few minutes ago. You okay?"

This caught Max off-guard, and before he could think of a better, misleading answer, he responded, "I don't know, maybe I'm just schizo, or somthin'."

"What?" Justin said with real concern. "You're kidding! You mean, on top of everything else I now get to deal with a split personality?"

"Yeah, that's more or less what it is. Which one do you like better?" Max added with a chuckle.

Distracted by another caw from the crow outside, Justin shook his head, "This just gets better and better." After a pause to consider this latest bit of info, he went on with his challenge: "But I still don't see why you…"

"Because you're not on the bus yet, Justin," Max cut off the driver's thought. "In the words of one of your favorites, 'You're either on the bus, or off the bus.' In your case, you've got a foot on the first step while your other foot is still firmly on the ground—and ready to bolt." Mystery Man let Maley stew on the picture for a second, then continued. "There's no blame, Justin. Our journey began just a few hours ago, and in that time, all your cherished illusions have been turned upside down. You're intrigued, and your curiosity has kept you in the game—so far. But deep down, understandably, you're scared shitless; and that, by they way, won't get any better, I promise you. I'm on a mission; I need help, and yes, I chose you. But until I know you're on the bus, irrevocably committed, I'm not going to spill my guts, and you're just going to have to deal with it," and smiling now, Max added, "or drag my worthless carcass to some bus stop bench in the next town."

That last was good for a laugh from Maley, "Max, you witch…. How in the world am I supposed to make this 'grand commitment' without knowing what I'm getting myself into?"

"Faith, Sonny-boy, faith—and intuition. Those are your basic tools, so use 'em. Am I one of the good guys or one of the bad guys?"

Maley seriously considered the question, but for the moment, there was no more to be said by either man, so Justin fired up the 4.6 liter V-8, dropped it in gear, and headed for Bluff, their probable destination for the night, unless stops weren't allowed in the old man's journey. Setting the cruise control, checking gauges and mirrors, Justin again let his mind drift. *The Electric Kool-Aid Acid Test* had been one of his favorite books long ago, a fact that Max had obviously gleaned, and an image of Kesey, Wolfe, the Merry Pranksters, and the Day-Glo bus scrolled across the windscreen before him. *God, they would have loved this—even without the acid.* Max's words hit home like a hammer. He *was* scared. This was the unknown, and although none had visited them as yet, danger was implied. Homo Sapiens have a natural aversion to knowingly walking into danger, and here he was being invited to do just that. But, somehow, the potential for physical danger was less a concern than the ongoing weirdness of his passenger. *He* was the scariest part of this whole thing, *he* the mind reader, *he* who fixes flat tires by—what?—simply thinking about it? God, the CIA would have a field day with Max, tucked away, of course, in a reinforced concrete cube in the middle of nowhere, thrilled and worried at the same time.

And what do you suppose his "mission" is, Justin?

The eight-track of his mind was doing its loop thing again, with no more resolution than when it had started. An hour later, with the setting sun, they cruised into Bluff. Speaking for himself, the driver announced the need for dinner and a good night's sleep. Max, who had been sleeping again had awoken right on cue, and for the first time so far, didn't argue with his 'helper' and agreed to getting a first-floor room at some "obscure" motel.

Justin cruised through the desert metropolis looking for a gas station and a place to eat with, preferably, an attached motel. He found the station, tanked up, and got directions to a motel at the far end of town, which had a country-western restaurant and club across the parking lot. After Justin got them a room, Max requested that he park across the parking lot from the motel, close to the restaurant, explaining seriously, "If they recognize your car by now, I don't want it too close to us."

Okay...

So they dumped their stuff in the room and headed back outside for some food, never noticing the red orbs on either side of the head of the crow roosting on the power line overhead. They didn't see its head swivel, as it watched them enter the club. They didn't notice the red orbs going dark once again, before the bird flew off into the darkness.

———————————

Lawrence opened his eyes and slowly came back into his body from the trance. He got up and returned to the library where Adam had been waiting for his boss, with an atlas and a snifter of B & B on the coffee table in front of him. Lawrence sat opposite Adam, turned the atlas book around and opened it to Arizona, studying it for a few seconds before locating the map for Utah. As if the map were a Ouija board and his finger the pointer, he moved down the state, across canyons and rivers, and came to a stop right on the town of Bluff. "He's in a country bar, I think at the north end of town."

While Adam got up and went over to the phone at the desk, Lawrence frowned at the decidedly thin nature of the intelligence provided him. After all, what can one expect from a bird brain? But the image had been clear; it was up to the reader to analyze and use the information, thin or not.

Adam returned to the davenport and reported, "The boys are in Blanding, less than an hour's drive to the north. They know the club where he's at, and they're on their way."

"They understand how it has to be done? Complete destruction, nothing left, and all that?" Lawrence inquired, more like verified.

"Don't worry, Truman—the troops know what's going on, and what's at stake. They'll take care of it. By morning, we'll have clear sailing all the way."

Senator Lawrence stood to go upstairs and to bed. After all, it was nearing 10:30 in Washington. "You remind me of me on TV this morning, Adam—with your reassurances. I trust your results will be better than the ones I promised the voters."

Adam didn't respond—it wasn't the appropriate moment to respond to the implied threat. Nevertheless, after Lawrence left the room, Adam called Blanding again just to make sure there was nothing left unsaid. Then he settled in for what might turn out to be a long night.

———

Upon returning to their room, both men took turns in the shower, Max going first. When Justin was finished, he found Max glued to the tube, watching an "All in the Family" marathon, and he was enjoying the "new" program immensely. So Justin joined him, and for the next hour all tension in their respective lives seemed to evaporate. Their laughter started building as they watched Archie pretending to load a single bullet into an imaginary revolver, then putting it to his head in a version of Russian roulette; all the while Edith is in *her* chair rambling on about something, oblivious to his antics, off in her own world portrayed so perfectly. The laughter in the motel room crescendoed as Archie "successfully" completed his task and feigned death—complete with lolling tongue. Edith, of course, never broke her stride continuing to do her thing next to her "dead" husband. It was a good release, a safe release for both men as they replenished their bodies. With the morning, business as usual would return soon enough.

They watched the evening news, including the bombshell proposal by the independent vice-presidential candidate, Senator Truman Lawrence.

"Now there's one scary dude," observed Justin.

"Hmm—you have no idea…," said Max as he slid off the bed for a last pit stop.

Whether from fatigue or the crush of all the other thoughts playing pinball in his head, Justin missed the clue. But one thing he'd learned that day was a personalized definition of "paranoia," and it was starting to incubate in him in a healthy way. So, out of character, he made the window his last stop before turning in. Opening the curtains a crack, he looked for—what?—Boogey Men? *Hell, I don't even know what I'm looking for.* But all was quiet and normal, whatever that might mean, so he closed the curtain and went to bed. It was 10:47 P.M., and the weirdest day of his life was over—but he also knew his journey had just begun.

Justin turned out the light…

Day Two

*"In matters pertaining to the 'other side,' things like—
life after death, souls, God, immaculate conceptions,
sons and daughters of God, salvation—I'm absolutely
certain that **I know** absolutely nothing for certain…*

…But the possibilities are endless…"

chapter four

On the Bus

Bluff, Utah

...Justin turned on the light and groggily looked at the Sony clock radio which said it was 12:38 A.M. The screams in his dream had been painfully, frighteningly real, but he could not remember where the screams had come from. Then, as he had turned on the light, he understood with startling clarity: The screams had not been in his dream; they were real and they were coming from outside the motel room door. Justin got into his body fast, jumped out of bed, and separated the blackout curtains. Everything became clear in an instant as flames could be seen coming from the roof of the country-western bar across the parking lot.

Instinctually, Maley went to Max's bed and shook him repeatedly until he awoke. With the reflection of the growing flames dancing across the ceiling, Max quickly understood that an emergency was in progress. Old body or not, he almost leaped from the bed to join Justin at the window.

Justin determined that the screams were on the decline, but he wasn't seeing any of the patrons that should have been running from the building, and very few people were outside the bar in the parking lot. "It's not even one o'clock yet, so where're all the customers; why aren't they running from the building?"

The question hung in the air for maybe three seconds before Max pulled it in and ran with it: "Justin—look at the doors—they're chained closed!"

Maley's eyes found the double front doors and immediately noticed the rapid shaking as someone inside repeatedly tried to slam them open to no avail. Suddenly, Justin sensed the panic, the fear, the realization of those inside that their last moment of life was about to be extinguished. Smoke poured from every crack and orifice of the building now, while the roof flames grew higher and higher. A siren's soft wail quickly became louder as the volunteer fire department approached the fully involved structure.

Max was saying something to Justin, but his words were overpowered by Maley's shock and emotions: The staggering death one hundred feet away of so many people merged with the writer's mind and heart so completely that Max had to spin Justin around, shake him, and yell right into his face to get through to him. "Wake up, Sonnyboy—we've got to get out of here."

"What're you talkin' about Max? We've got to help them. We've got to go open the doors. We can't leave!" and Justin moved toward the motel room door. Between the awesomeness of the fire, the screams for help, and the implied menace of the chained doors, Justin was so wound up he was shaking.

Max grabbed Justin's arm and with a strength belying his wilted frame, forced his companion's back to the window. "Justin, for Christ's sake, wake up! It's already too late. Look!" They both stared in fascination as, at just that instant, the entire roof caved-in in an enormous roar and billowing of flames into the cloudless night. The flames must have been visible for a hundred miles.

"Justin...," but Justin was gone again, gone into the unreality of the reality, into the mesmerizing flames. He came back with the strike of Max's hand across his face. "You young fool—who do you think that fire was for? Huh? Someone just murdered who knows how many people, with full intent and knowledge of what they were doing, and not giving a rip. And I'm here to tell ya the target of that fire was me. Me, Justin—you got that? I can also tell you, with complete certainty, that the killers will know within a few hours that I was not inside the place and therefore am not dead yet. When they discover that little fact, they'll not hesitate to come over here and do the exact same thing to this entire motel. We have to get out of here, Justin, and I mean now, while there's still lots of confusion around. You followin' me, or do I need to find another partner?"

Several seconds without staring at the fire, without merging with the dying victims across the parking lot, allowed Maley to get it together, to hear Max and to focus on what had been said. Max had spoken earlier of potential danger, and here it was. It was time for Justin Maley to choose his fork in the road, the path that would no longer be possible to retrace and make go away. One path to sanity, safety, and security; the other path to danger, chaos, and the unknown. Then he smiled—he actually smiled, for it was, after everything that had, and had not, happened in his life, an easy choice.

He looked at Max, looked at the room, then said, "Make sure there's nothing of ours left. I'll get the car across the lot, swing it around to the room. Only when you see me, right outside with the door open do you come out and we take off. Okay?"

Max nodded, "Got it. Be casual, Justin. And keep an eye out. I guarantee you the killers are out there, checking their work—looking."

Maley opened the door, relieved to find the parking lot now loading up with probably every resident of the motel and maybe the town. Unfortunately, only the firefighters and emergency people were actually walking around the parking lot; so, as he made his way across the lot to the Mustang, Maley must have stood out to anyone looking for the odd out-of-place movement. He got to the car, had it unlocked before reaching the door handle, got in, and started the big V-8. The roar was reassuring, and he was very pleased with himself for filling the tank the night before, and not with that 87 crap either. The engine was drinking 92 octane and was ready to romp and stomp. He looked for signs of trouble, and finding none, pulled out of his spot and headed for their room, having to thread his way through throngs of people— all of whom were focused on the conflagration and not on him. *Good.* He stopped in front of the room, took one more look around, then opened the passenger door and beckoned for Max to get in. Max did so, and Justin slowly, casually, stealthily pulled away, doing a U-turn in the lot to head back toward the highway.

Relief was just beginning to touch Justin's reality, right up to that moment the Mustang apexed the curve of the U-turn. But just then, lights came on from the direction of the far end of the parking lot where only the bigger vehicles parked. What caught his attention was the shear number and brightness of the lights—it looked like a dozen of them—and they were all pointed his way. Justin tried to identify the vehicle supporting such a rack of candlepower, and risking semipermanent retinal damage in the process, he recognized a Dodge pickup, the new kind with the big, oval, gaping (eat-Mustangs-for-lunch type) grill, in imitation of its larger eighteen-wheel brothers. It was also higher off the ground than usual. In fact, it looked huge. It looked like it could roll right over Justin's little car. And it was black—midnight black—bad-boy black, and Justin had no doubt as to its intentions.

As the Mustang came out of the U-turn, heading straight for the driveway apron at the highway, the mirror confirmed everything: even in the darkness at the back of the parking lot, Justin could see dust and dirt flying everywhere as the truck broke its leash and flew out of its holding pen—with but one evil thing on its mind. And the driver of the truck obviously couldn't care less if he ran over a few people in the parking lot in pursuit of his objective because he began filling the mirror of the Mustang before Maley could even whisper, *"Oh shit."* Maley could also see that the rig had one of those huge pipe things in front for pushing boulders, trees, cows—and Mustangs—off the road. All the thing lacked was a mount with twin fifties, but maybe one of those was in the back—probably was…

All this perceptive input happened in a heartbeat, for the truck was just a hair away from ramming the Mustang right at the entrance to the highway, when Justin screamed with fear and adrenaline, then turned the wheel hard to the left and floored it.

Yelling, "Hold on, Max, they're after us," Maley was gripping the steering wheel so tight a crowbar would be needed by the coroner to pry his cold, dead fingers loose. The truck missed the back of the Mustang by inches only, and couldn't brake quickly enough to keep out of the ditch on the far side of the highway. Nonetheless, the monster was not to be stopped, having an evil helper at its side; and it turned into the ditch, followed it for a few hundred feet, then worked back up the slope and emerged like a crazed beast through the night air and onto the asphalt. At maximum throttle, it fishtailed a bit before settling down and entering the chase in earnest. By now, the Mustang was approaching one hundred mph, Justin's heart rate was double that, and he was losing a quart of precious bodily fluids per minute, fortunately, all of it in sweat—so far.

"Jesus Christ, Max, he's gaining on us. I don't believe it—I'm doing one-ten and he's gaining in that tank of a truck." And then fear really sank in, as Justin realized he'd already subconsciously been counting on his hot rod Mustang to outrun a pickup truck any day of the week. If that wasn't going to happen, then they were in some awfully deep shit.

Their lives were on the line, there was no question about that, so Justin had no choice but to keep the Mustang floored, as the speedometer passed one hundred twenty mph. The noise was both frightening and exhilarating—frightening at the moment, exhilarating in retrospect for some later date, if they survived the night. But the truck was still, slowly, gaining on them, and Justin wondered how many ponies were left in his Mustang. The speedometer was now pegged. All the while, Max was taking turns looking forward, turning to look backwards, and just generally looking scared shitless. Justin had the instinct to check the gauges, all of which still read okay. Then, out of the blue, he had a thought, followed by a chuckle that no one could hear but him:

Yelling to be heard, "Hey Max—am I on the bus now? Huh? Am I Max? I think I'm on the bus now, Max. What do you think?" The attempt at bantering humor was cut short as Maley saw a sign in the high beams for a highway turn off ahead. Faster than any ol' Pentium, his mind realized that on this straight and beautiful highway, the truck, which had to be sporting a full-blown, thousand horsepower engine, was going to run right over them sooner, rather than later. Their only chance was going to be a highway with curves where the Mustang's lower center of gravity had to have an advantage over the truck's height. So, after an instant of analysis Maley slowed just enough to take the turn to the right onto highway 262, with the two right side tires hardly making contact with the pavement. He used up all the far shoulder with his turn, but the Mustang held on, and he punched it once again as he came back onto the straightaway.

Some gratification was quick in coming as this highway was obviously narrower, less used, less maintained, and less straight. In the mirror, he thought he saw the lights of the truck become stationary—

maybe as a result of sliding out at the turn. But whatever it was, after a few seconds, the lights flared again, like the rotating beam from a lighthouse as its aperture briefly hits you straight on.

Nonetheless, the Mustang had gained precious seconds, and Justin used the advantage to slow down, just a little, to get a better grip on the road and terrain situation. The last thing he wanted to do was to do the truck's job for them, through his own recklessness. *Hah! That's a joke. Let's not be reckless, Justin buddy—ya'll might have an accident or somethin'.* He almost laughed—almost, but gritted his teeth instead.

After a few short miles, Maley knew he'd made the right decision. The highway seemed to have straight runs for a short distance, then there would be a series of moderate to tight turns, before straightening out again. The net result was a perceived, slim growth in the lead ahead of their pursuers, but since he didn't know any of these highways at all, it was just as possible that there'd be no consistency ahead. If straightaways became the norm, he and Max would quickly return to the same situation they had been in back on the main highway. In the meantime, he had to work with what he knew, and a plan began to develop in his head based on what he'd seen of the truck's braking ability back at the motel. Justin estimated the truck to be maybe thirty to forty seconds behind, but that might be long enough. It would have to be...

Maley saw the outline of a windmill ahead in the moonlight, and the distraction almost ruined his whole night, for just before the windmill, the road took what turned out to be a ninety-degree hard turn to the south. Since the terrain on either side of the road was still flat, he kept going, looking for a better spot.

Six or seven miles ahead, Maley saw another yellow warning sign coming up and he began slowing down, just in case it was what he hoped for. From a distance, he could make out the "sharp turn" symbol on the sign, and even in the bright moonlight, he was unable to see any structures or hillside ahead at the end of the straight stretch. In an instant of thought, he committed to his plan, stomping hard on the brakes and pulling up to the warning sign, which now clearly advised a twenty mph speed for the curve to the left. Next to him, Max went ballistic, "What the hell ya doin'? They'll be on us in seconds!"

"Max, eventually these guys are goin' to nail us—they're just too fast. We've got to try and take them out, and this is the place. It's time to trust your partner, Max..." So, Max went quiet, and watched.

Without actually stopping, Justin put the right side of the Mustang's bumper against the four-by-four sign post and easily broke it off. As he gassed the engine, he figured he had twenty or thirty seconds left before the truck came within visual range of their target. He approached the end of the straightaway and performed the same service to the second, and final, warning sign with the huge arrow pointing toward the left.

Straight ahead beyond the curve in the road, Justin could see nothing—meaning it dropped down a bank, rather than staying flat or going uphill. He didn't know how far it dropped, but he was fairly sure that no vehicle would be returning to the road if it went down there. He put the transmission in reverse, laid rubber as he backed up fast, past the first sign, and then put it back into drive. He turned-off his headlights—leaving only the parking lights on, which also allowed the tail lights to remain on. Then he waited…

The Mustang probably enjoyed the break, but the rumble from its twin exhausts sounded as though it were also enjoying the flexing of its muscles. It sounded perfect, the gauges read nominal—just a little hot, and Justin issued a whispered thank you to his trusty steed. But the reverie came to an end as lights began bouncing off rock formations, then disappearing, then coming back. The truck was almost out of the curves and approaching the straightaway. With their windows down, listening for the beast, they began to hear its roar, growing louder and louder. Without warning it came out of the last curve onto the straightaway and headed right for the Mustang a scant quarter-mile ahead.

Justin gave it some gas, indicating movement, but he didn't floor it. Without the headlights, he was semi-blind, but he'd already seen what was ahead and was prepared. He also counted on getting some help from all the lights on the Dodge, without them being as much help for the driver of the truck. The truck was gaining fast now, coming on strong with the smell of blood coming from just ahead. It was a dicey game—luring the truck closer and closer at full speed, without blowing the timing and becoming roadkill in the end after all.

Maley was doing fifty now. "God, he must be doing over a hundred," Maley said to no one, to Max, to anyone. The lights had become unbelievably bright, and they helped Justin see the curve ahead, dimly, but enough. The truck was only a few hundred feet behind them as the curve and drop-off rapidly came up in front of them.

"Hold on, Max," Maley yelled as he simultaneously turned the wheel hard to the left, turned on the headlights, and then stomped on the brakes. Tires squealing, they spun, did a couple of three-sixties, and came to a stop on the shoulder, avoiding the drop-off by no more than ten feet.

But the truck was gone. They had heard the scream of its brakes, but it hadn't had a chance, as it went straight off the road, flying through the air, with lights projecting downward steeper and steeper. At about the same moment the Mustang came to rest, they heard a horrible crashing and grinding of metal echoing from some distance, followed by an explosion and a reflection of flames. It was over. And Justin yelled, "Yea!" and shook his fist in the air in triumph.

Maley shut down the Mustang, opened the door and ran back to the point the truck had become a two-ton glider. Perhaps one or two hundred feet below, he could easily see the burning, tangled mess of what had once been a gleaming truck. His heart began to slow down now. No longer needed, the adrenaline pumping voraciously through his veins slowed down as well, and returned to its storage tanks, awaiting the next event in his life when it would be required.

As his body returned to normalcy, so did his brain—and his conscience. Maley was not a killer, and there was at least one man down there who was dead as a result of his premeditated, planned actions. He could have dwelled on any number of things at that moment and as unfair as it was, he got stuck on that thought: *He was alive, and now he's dead. And I killed him.*

Behind him, just a few feet away, he heard Max's voice—soft, soothing, massaging the conflicted conscience: "No, Justin—tonight you saved my life, and yours, and perhaps 5 billion others. That's what you need to think about—not what's down there."

Maley turned and in the darkness looked at the shadow figure of Max. "Who are you, Max? What's going on?"

The old man slipped his arm through Justin's, maybe for physical support, but more likely to acknowledge a new level of friendship and connection, and he led them both back to the Mustang. "Well, for one thing, my name isn't really Max..."

Everything was different now that they were no longer running for their lives. Despite the fact that it was 2:25 in the morning, both men felt wide awake, at least for a little while longer, as the Mustang made its way east and south on highway. 262. They went through the sleeping town of Montezuma Creek, where almost every outdoor sign implied some connection with the oil and gas industry. They drove slowly, no longer in any hurry, enjoying the luxury of not having to focus too hard on the road and any hazards coming up from behind or toward them from the front and the future. They were both content to leave the map in the glove box as long as the road led them in a more or less easterly direction. They passed the town of Aneth—where another sign indicated U.S. Highway 160, twenty miles ahead. Justin remembered that highway from earlier map studies and knew that it would take them well east to the big interstate that ran north/south through the large cities of Colorado.

And they talked. Or rather, Max talked. Justin listened. At first, he struggled just to allow what he was hearing into his brain without cracking up and shutting down. Then he asked questions, all the while feeling incredulous, but at the same time *wanting* to believe what he was hearing. If he'd heard it from some stranger off the street, he would have laughed and ignored everything. But he couldn't do that any longer, and not with Max. He was on the bus now, and he had seen and heard things that were one hundred percent inexplicable by any rational means. So the writer took it all in, cataloged it, and saved it for that future day when, and if, a story was ready to be told.

They had started off with the simplest of all questions: "So what's your real name, Max?" The answer was anything but simple: "You talkin' about me, or this body?" Max replied with a chuckle. He continued when Justin didn't bite. In the dark of the car he couldn't see the glower on his partner's face, but he knew it was there. "Where I come from, nobody has names—they're not needed. As far as this body—I don't know what its name was. I picked it up in some alley in Los Angeles."

It was a hell of a way to start a conversation. Justin made another astral cell call: *Hello, Operator?....Yea, send the meat wagon, I got another one for ya...*

75

"Okay, Max, you've got my attention. So, forget the body. By 'me,' I assume you're talking about the mind, or soul, or being—something like that, right?"

"Right," came the reluctant answer. Max clearly wasn't looking forward to opening the floodgates of his background.

Maley braced himself: "You some kind of body snatcher, Max? Where do you come from anyway?"

There was a pause before Max explained, not so much from wanting to hide anything as much as just trying to find the right words. "I guess you would call it the *continuum,* or the *other side.*" Max turned his head toward the passenger window as he concluded the location explanation—a little quieter, too: "It's where you go when you die....."

After a second of stunned shock, Justin jumped all over that one: "You mean—heaven?" and he started to giggle a little as Max cringed. "Does that mean you're an angel, Max? You sure don't look like an angel, and you sure as hell don't talk like one."

"I knew you would say somethin' like that."

"Hey, Max—I'm a WASP, ya know? White, Anglo-Saxon Protestant, just in case you might be somethin' else. That means when people die, they go to heaven, or maybe hell—you know, depending on if they were naughty or nice. So, we talkin' about the same place or not?" Justin's disbelief and fascination were coming through loud and clear, around a core of humor. Max still had his attention, but he had to get to the crux of the thing or risk losing his compadre's interest and help. Still, this was dangerous ground, and the words just weren't flowing the way he had hoped. He tried a side-step before coming back to the main dance: "Most of you humans have finally come to the correct conclusion that the Universe is infinite. Is it such a stretch that the possibilities of *existence* within the Universe are also infinite?" He hoped for some agreement-type reaction from Maley but all he got was confused-looking silence.

Justin could feel the discomfort and hesitation coming from stage right, and with this being a semicrucial barrier to get past, he pulled the Mustang over somewhere just before Montezuma Creek, put it in park, and turned off the engine.

"Listen up, Max." It was Justin's turn to use soft, soothing tones with the uptight—what, visitor? He needed to make Max all comfy, get him to lower the walls that were keeping what he knew all safe and sound on *his* side of the Universe. "I'm already in disbelief. I'm already blown away. That started yesterday with the first words out of your mouth. Everything about our journey so far has been incredible. Nothing makes sense. Nothing is explainable by ordinary logic. Therefore, you do not have to tip toe around the truth, Max. I may react with trepidation, or laughter, or major skepticism, but that's okay. That's just gut reaction to hearing the impossible after thirty years of normal Earth-type programming. And lastly, someone is trying to kill us. As bizarre as this all sounds to me, I need to hear everything because I would prefer to keep on living. I don't even know who the players are, for Christ's sake. Okay, Max? So just take it one step at a time. Connect the dots from point 'A' to point 'B' to point 'Z'. Ready? Go..."

His efforts worked. Max settled down in his seat, the tension in his body oozing out the opened window and carried away with the wind. "I'm what you would call a soul. I'll refer to the 'other side' as the continuum or the other side, but never as heaven—or hell. The continuum is where souls live when they're not in a body on one planet or another. I needed to come into a fully adult body, which is almost never done. Obviously, we usually come into a new baby's body. When you have to come into an adult body, the correct procedure is to find one that's about to die, and come into it as that body's normal soul is itself leaving. We call it a 'walk-in.' The whole thing is quite complicated, as you might imagine."

"Indeed..." Justin was straining to hear every syllable, without cracking up in the process.

"But I managed although I wasn't prepared for the sorry state of the body I got stuck with. Anyway, I thumbed rides out of Los Angeles until I got to that desert back there. Then I parked it to wait for you. I'm on a mission—a very important mission. I needed help from a local, which turned out to be you, and I need to get to the East Coast as soon as possible, but surreptitiously and without endangering any more innocents along the way than can be helped."

Holy buckets! Justin's mind shifted into overdrive. "And just what is this mission of yours, Max?"

Maley could barely make out Max's eyes boring into his own—looking for help, for acceptance, and not rejection, once again reluctant to stick his neck out too far. But it finally came: "I need to stop Truman Lawrence from becoming president of the United States."

Justin's jaw flopped open at this final, but staggering, assault to his senses and his intelligence, but before probing Max for more detail, he corrected the old man's choice of words. "He's not running for president, Max. He's running for vice-president."

Max shook his head, "You've heard the expression about the vice-president being just a heartbeat away from the presidency?" Justin nodded his head, so Max went on, "In the case of Truman Lawrence, the transition would be as quick as a snap of his fingers, and almost as simple. I've been sent here to stop him before he has the opportunity to do just that."

"For anyone with a TV set, the language of politicians is depressingly transparent during election campaigns: Their advertisements are so full of hypocrisy, and deceitful half-truths and half-lies that they make it impossible for us to trust any of them with our future or our lives."

chapter five

Repercussions

Washington, D.C.

Lawrence awoke with a start at 5:35 A.M. He knew
the time because whenever he opened his eyes in bed,
they always fell, first-thing, on the large-numeral clock
on the dresser. Waking with a start was not normal for
the confident Senator and, historically, it meant that
something was wrong.

A voice in his head urged him to view the morning
news, so, again out of character, he reached for the
remote and brought CNN into his morning ritual. At
seven minutes past the half-hour, he had missed one or
more headline items, but he knew they would be
repeated at a quarter 'til. He got up, found the toilet,
turned on the smaller TV set on the bathroom counter,
and waited. At a quarter to the hour, he received con-
firmation that his instincts were right again:

"And now, repeating the morning's headlines, the
death toll now stands at forty-two from an overnight
fire at a restaurant-club in a remote part of southeastern Utah. Satellite crews are on the way to Bluff, Utah
where it is still dark, so we'll have video for you later
this morning. In the meantime, local law enforce-
ment officials are calling this a clear and obvious case
of murder as all doors of the building had been
chained or screwed shut, making escape impossible.

The perpetrators had thrown firebombs into the club before closing and chaining the last door. Witnesses said the building was fully involved in less than two minutes. The fire was so intense that the building collapsed in on itself just as local volunteer firefighters began to arrive. Witnesses also said that another person was killed in an apparent hit and run by a black pickup truck that sped away from the scene. Officials declined to say if there was a connection between the two incidents. State officials are on their way to the scene now, as well as agents of the FBI, at the request of the governor. We'll have more for you on this tragic story as information comes in."

A fly on the wall might have noticed a slight frown punctuating the calm countenance of the Senator, as he concluded his business. After his exercise routine, a note resting on his juice tray informed Lawrence that Adam Dempsey was in the library, as he had been all night. *Fine—let him wait.* Lawrence proceeded with his second shower, dressed, ate breakfast, and gleaned the highlights of the newspapers. It was no surprise that the Utah incident had shown up in none of the papers—too late for that. *Score one for television...*

At precisely 8:00 A.M., Senator Lawrence opened, passed through, then closed the heavy, double sliding oak doors of the library. He was greeted with, "Good morning, Truman, how are..."

Adam couldn't finish his greeting. It wasn't that he was interrupted by the boss, although, technically speaking, one could argue the fact. To issue words from the mouth requires air to be expelled from the lungs. If the bronchia are instantly closed off, that could presumably be considered an "interruption"—amongst other side affects.

Truman sauntered over to the coffee urn, poured a cup, adding one teaspoon of artificial sugar and a little low-fat Half & Half. He pointedly ignored the man sitting at the Chippendale table who was in the process of dying from lack of oxygen, grasping his throat with one hand, holding onto his chair with the other. His eyes had a distinct bulging quality, as fear and convulsions took over any semblance of normal body control. A bluish tinge encroached upon his facial pallor, as the lack of oxygen began the shut-down process. Somewhere deep in his consciousness, Adam knew of Lawrence's ability to do this "thing," but being at the receiving end was a far cry from an intellectual awareness. And as he began to feel consciousness slip away, he wondered if he'd wake up on the other side, or on the library floor.

He supposed it depended on how badly he'd screwed up in the eyes of his chief.

Truman walked to the full-height bay windows overlooking his personal rose garden, admired the view, sipped his coffee, and considered if it was time to replace the cretin behind him. The answer, regretfully, was no. It would be considered distinctly bad taste for a United States Senator to place an Employment Opportunities ad for "Devil's Helper." Oh, there would be no shortage of applicants—not with the recent spate of "top floor" resignations and lay-offs. It's just that busy Senators don't have time to cull through and separate the truly qualified from the simply gifted wanna-be's. So, with an effortless twist of some neurons, Truman allowed a few milliliters of air to enter Adam's lungs—not enough to ease his pain, paralysis, and fear, but enough to sustain his life.

Such a handy tool, really, being able to constrict a person's bronchia. When he, as a being, came into young Truman Lawrence's body thirty-three years ago, he knew that he had powers totally unknown to, and unused by, normal humans. Still, as with all beings, he had to work with his chosen body, rather than separately from it, and the body was untrained—inexperienced. With the urging of his guest being, young Truman had very big plans, and he for sure had no time for the movies or other juvenile distractions. Nonetheless, when he heard of a certain energy-torture thing performed by some evil guy in a science fiction movie, he gave it a look-see, as research, you understand. And when the evil Darth Vader did his number on the obnoxious admiral, or whatever he was, Truman was thrilled with the possibilities and couldn't wait to experiment on his own.

Even for a special lad of Truman's capabilities, it simply doesn't work to say, "Choke!" There's always been more to the craft than that, so Truman studiously pulled out the anatomy books and researched his target area. He quickly ascertained that messing with the thick and fibrous trachea would require more effort than efficiency demanded. But just as clear was the vulnerability of the major bronchia as, but just before, they became the lungs. They appeared pliable enough to accept a little squeeze—just there, so to speak—to effectively cease the transfer of air to the lungs. Oh, this was so exciting…

He started off with lower mammalian lifeforms, pointing his hand at the creatures just like a junior warlock might do. Almost instantly, he received gratification, and so he moved up the food chain. Cats and dogs became easy targets as they were everywhere, and with dogs, their lack of proper boundaries assured them of special attention—particularly those foolish animals given to greeting Truman by sniffing his crotch. Sometimes his victims would provide the ultimate sacrifice to the education of Truman Lawrence. Sometimes they would be released from his figurative grip with no permanent damage. And somewhere along the line, he discovered that there was no need whatever of using his hand and arm as a magic wand. It was all in his mind, entirely invisible to the outside world—except for the end result. Eventually, he reached the top of the mammalian food chain, and he sought out an appropriate human subject for his ministrations. As there were plenty of mean people in the world, even in Duluth, his search was short-lived. Jim Losey, a varsity wrestler in high school, was always a little too loud, a little too rough, and just a little too cool. He used his reputation, first, to intimidate his lowly fellow classmates. If, for some reason, that was insufficient, he would not hesitate to push, grab, twist, or otherwise inflict pain at inconspicuous times and in places immune to the watchful eyes of school staff. If a serious threat to his school supremacy emerged, he was also delighted to partake in pugilistic bouts well away from school grounds. But Losey was big and dangerous; everyone knew it, and no one wanted any part of him.

It was purely coincidental that Jim Losey ended up sitting directly below Truman Lawrence at a high school football game in October of 1976. It was also accidental that the girl seated behind Truman bumped his shoulder a little too hard, causing the full, and open, giant cup of Coke in Truman's hand to spill some of its contents on Losey's shoulder. The wrestler jumped up, began yelling at Truman who, confident of his superior place in life, eyeballed the bully without fear and refused to grovel or apologize. Bad move—for both young men.

Losey looked into the eyes of the upstart, and then he casually lifted his own Coke above Truman's head, and poured every ounce of it on the boy who regularly killed living things for afternoon entertainment.

Two days later, the local newspaper expressed shock and regret over the loss of the high school's star wrestler by unknown causes. The autopsy showed that Jim Losey had mysteriously suffocated, which immediately indicated foul play. No explanation was ever forthcoming, but Truman Lawrence's persuasive technique was well on the way to being perfected.

Senator Lawrence switched off the pleasant moment of reverie, turned back from the window, and eased into the chair opposite the pathetic creature that had been so near death. "You know, Adam," as he looked at his wrist watch, "When I found you in that reform school so many years ago, and I witnessed your activities with your captured rat, I knew that you were destined to be with me as I followed my calling in this life. Besides your sadistic nature, you were quite cunning with your little beasties, and I, perhaps incorrectly, interpreted that cunning as a form of intelligence. You see, I knew back then that I would have need of an army of troops scattered here and there all over the world. I knew that to get the right levels of loyalty and viciousness, I'd have to forgo superior intelligence in these troops. So, I came to rely on you, and your smarts, to keep them in line and to keep them from doing something as stupid as last night's disaster. You might as well have nuked the place, Adam—the news coverage couldn't be much worse.

Lawrence finally released his grip on Adam's throat, growing tired of the wheezing sounds and the frantic eyeball pleading. Adam took successive, enormous gulps of air—an autonomic response by his body to get some oxygen back into his blood.

"You got complacent, Adam. You forgot your place. You forgot the potential penalty when someone fails me. And you've gotten much too comfortable thinking of me as your friend or partner. You are neither of those, you foolish man. You serve me at my pleasure, and you would do well not to forget that." Lawrence gave Adam a minute to digest the reminder before changing tactics. "Now, may I warm up your coffee?" Like the perfect host, Truman poured steaming brew into Adam's cup, then got to business. "So, what know you of the results of last night's activities?"

Adam cleared his throat (it was a little dry), took a sip of coffee, and reported, "It will be awhile before we have a list of those killed, but I assume our man was among them."

"He wasn't," this, from the Master, shouldn't have shocked Adam, but nonetheless did. Lawrence saw his curiosity and responded. "Adam, if I could sense when the being arrived on the planet, do you not think I would be able to tell when it had departed? Neither man was in the club when your morons struck. Now, what do you know of the whereabouts of the truck and its occupants? I presume the hit-and-run truck was theirs, right?"

Adam braced himself for the possibility of more retribution. The night had been a total cluster fuck, and the extent wasn't fully out on the table yet. "I haven't been able to raise either man, and I don't know where the truck is."

Lawrence looked at the man as though he couldn't believe what he was hearing but said, "I see," and after a few seconds of thought, continued with, "and what are the chances that either man or the truck could be traced back to you or me?"

Fortunately for Adam, there were enough cutouts and false trails to make that possibility nil, and he said so to the Senator. But Lawrence's trust level was below even its usual level, so he issued a clear instruction to his assistant: "Find both men and that truck, and eliminate all three. You hear me, Adam? I want nothing left of that threesome for some forensics guru to run through a test tube and come up with a lead.

"Sir—can't you eliminate them yourself—from here? I mean...," Adam gulped.

"You mean by doing to them what I was just now doing to you, Adam?" The sparkle in the Senator's eye was meant to remind and to intimidate Adam, and it worked admirably. "No. That one requires that I be within close range of the recipient of my attention. Besides, it wouldn't get rid of the bodies, nor the truck, and that's a must. Now be off. I have work to do."

Adam left the library, and the house, very relieved to be away from the man he loved and feared more than anything else on Earth.

―――――――――

Unlike the subject of his research eight miles away, Mike Metcalf, similar to many other investigative reporters, did not even open his eyes until around 9:00 A.M. It would be a minor miracle if he didn't trip over some misplaced article of clothing on his way to the bathroom, the door to which any mother in the known world would have slapped a padlock on and posted as being a "biohazard." The only *good* thing about the bathroom was the shower. As he frequently did, Mike could return to a semicomatose (not to be confused with semi-conscious) condition under steaming needles of hot water and remain that way for, well—at least an hour, as once happened. Since the water heater was central to the building, there was actually no telling how long it could last.

Metcalf didn't know a thing about cooking, so his common morning fare was two over medium, crispy hash-browns, white toast, whole milk, and coffee—"the usual"—at Peggy's café just down the street. If he were rushed, he'd pick up a few Krispy Kremes instead, their store being conveniently located next to Peggy's. It was a generally accepted axiom at the paper that, if some pissed-off target of the writer's exposés didn't end up killing him, coronary artery disease surely would. But at thirty-six years of age, everyone is still indestructible until shown evidence to the contrary—with a third and fourth opinion required for good measure.

Notwithstanding the disparity in lifestyle and working habits, Mike Metcalf was just as dedicated to achieving his goals as Truman Lawrence was to achieving his.

By the time he got to the paper, the Utah story was old news, on TV anyway, and hadn't even made the papers yet. In any case, it was hard and current news, which meant that it would be here this week, and gone the next, and therefore, not Metcalf's kind of story. Metcalf liked the "deep" stuff—the story that went back for years, preferably, but for sure for several months. He liked the plot twists, the secrets, the conspiracies, the skeletons in the closet, and the hidden memos. Better yet, he liked the memos and other paperwork that the villains were absolutely positive had been burned or shredded months or years before, only to be resurrected by some past employee who had been shat upon by the gods in their ivory towers.

Sometimes he was assigned a story by the gods in his own building. Usually, however, he developed his own—through his own instincts, or through the suggestion of an anonymous phone call. His editor was content to give him his lead, since, when his stories did break they were typically "gold": They always raised circulation, and they never, ever resulted in a lawsuit. As long as Metcalf made money (and earned Pulitzers) for the paper, Metcalf could pretty much soak in his shower twenty-three hours out of each day for all his editor cared.

His investigation into Truman Lawrence had begun almost a year ago, right after Reardon and Lawrence had made their candidacy public. It had started as one of those flukes, something that should never have happened, but had, and it had been wholly innocent. A joke had floated around the pool floor at the paper that Lawrence was so clean that he didn't even have skid marks on his underwear. And then one of the older staffers actually bet Metcalf a twenty-dollar bill that even the great bloodhound would be unable to find anything on the Senator.

Metcalf was definitely a betting man, and being in a somewhat slow period while waiting for things to break, he accepted the wager—not for the money, but out of principle and for the action. Until that day, he knew next to nothing about Truman Lawrence because the Senator was current news, and there had simply never been cause to go digging. So, he started looking but came up empty. So, he dug a little deeper—and he still came up with nothing. It appeared the Senator was so straight as to not even have had a past-due library fine. That, of course, was when the red flags went up.

Somewhere during the digging process, Metcalf lost interest in the twenty-dollar bet and became absorbed by "the man"—his position on issues, his history, his speeches, not to mention his choice to run as an Independent. It had begun as glimpses of headlines, but by the time he'd supposedly exhausted all sources for something "dirty," he had become as *surface* knowledgeable about the Senator as anyone. And what he had learned had both fascinated and worried him.

It's not often that an Independent went anywhere in politics, much less to such lofty heights as senator and vice-presidential candidate. By definition, an Independent is telling the entrenched political machinery in the country to shove it, and like any other pair of cahooting monopolies, the two supreme political organizations in the United States did not particularly care to be told to "shove it." Such attitudes implied to the world that the parties in question might have flaws. So, the two parties had each, at different times, done their level best to derail the politician from the Northland, but in fifteen years, nothing had worked. Lawrence was still the Minnesota powerhouse, and he was still embarrassing the GOP and the Democrats every time he crossed their paths.

Although everyone agreed that Truman Lawrence was as good a politician as had come down the pike in many a year, no one wanted to believe that he was *that* good, and they always turned to his family, his wealth, and his personal tragedies as examples of mitigating circumstances. So Metcalf took a look as well. Apparently, Lawrence came from an old money-and-name family from Duluth, heavily involved in the mining and timber industry in both the nineteenth and the twentieth centuries. Metcalf found reference to an early accident, back in 1970, that virtually wiped out the entire family with the exception of Truman, and he made a note to dig further into the early years of the wonder boy.

But what really garnered the reporter's attention was the disclosure of Truman Lawrence's finances. As of one year ago, the man was worth an estimated $6 billion, and that put him well nigh of the very few, very elite, and very behind-the-scenes power players worldwide—people who had little use or need for political borders and limitations. So, why in the world would the guy *choose* to get into the "kiss your baby's bottom" field of professional compromise, favors, and skullduggery? The more he dwelled on the question, the more Metcalf realized how important the answer might be.

Lawrence had long ago put his entire fortune into a blind trust, run by others who provided him with a yearly stipend of some $100 million. From his trust income over the years, Lawrence had put together an election war chest of over $125 million, far exceeding that of either Republican or Democratic parties. And just prior to the announcement of Reardon and Lawrence as an Independent ticket making a run on the White House, the Senator had taken delivery of his brand new Gulfstream V-SP jet, with a reputed price tag of some $40 million. He had made it known that he'd use his own plane in the campaign, while the presidential candidate, James Reardon, would use a chartered 757 for his much larger team and batch of reporters. The entire campaign was being financed by the candidates personally: Not one cent of PAC money or private donations was being accepted. Whatever donations came in were returned, with thanks, to the sender; and if that were not possible, then they were endorsed over to local charities. Score one for Reardon/Lawrence, Metcalf thought. They were making it abundantly clear to everyone that their influence could not be bought by anyone, and that must be scaring the crap out of special-interest America. Just imagine: the leadership of the free world beholden to no one. That right there was enough to assure them of a place in the *Guinness Book of Records*, assuming they won the election.

Metcalf followed up on a reference to the death of Lawrence's wife and little girl. It was very big news at the time, of course, but disappeared from the first page, and finally the last page, after about four weeks. As we all must, Truman had to get on with his life and his responsibilities to his constituents. It seems that Truman, his wife of five years, and their four-year-old daughter had been enjoying a rare interlude in their hectic lives, and were driving as a family—without chauffeur—up highway 61 on the Minnesota arrowhead, toward Grand Marais. It was a glorious morning for a drive, and the folk in Grand Marais remembered the family as looking so happy and content together. But on the return leg, the weather had suddenly turned utterly foul, as all local seamen knew the weather on and around Lake Gitchegumee is want to do. Instead of pulling the Mercedes off the coastal road and finding shelter, Truman plunged onward, presumably assuring his family that things would improve. But things didn't.

Later in the afternoon, when the squall on the largest of the Great Lakes did moderate and the "Gophers" came back out of their holes, the skid marks and broken barrier were discovered, along with the mangled remains of the huge sedan, a hundred feet down from the roadway. Inexplicably, given the condition of the wreck, the Senator was found alive and well thirty feet away from the impact point. It had taken over an hour to extricate the dead bodies of his wife and daughter from the vehicle. Metcalf studied the photograph that accompanied the article and his eyebrows furrowed into a brief frown of incomprehension that anyone could have survived the crash—a crash that had left the car about half its original length.

It was a horribly sad and difficult time, in the Duluth region especially, and many weeks passed before the references and flowers ceased. Eventually, life did return to normal. The results of the next senatorial election were a no-brainer, and the tragedy was finding renewed airtime now that Lawrence was running for vice-president. *America loves its tragedies, and those needing the sympathy tend to get the votes,* the reporter mused.

Metcalf summarized to himself: so here we have a man bucking the system, rich as God, plenty of family tragedy, loved by virtually every Minnesotan, smart as a whip, and promising that things will be different when he and Reardon are in office.

Metcalf, chuckled to himself with astute irony, and wondered what it was about Minnesota that encouraged independent politicians to even exist, much less providing them with a half-decent chance of beating the odds to win. Who would ever have guessed that a feather-boa-dressed, obnoxious, ex-professional wrestler would ever make it to first-chair in state politics? It had to be either a statement on the mental condition of the voters of the state, or a statement on conditions of the politicians running the state, or perhaps a little of both. However, if the voters of Minnesota were anything like those in about forty-nine other states, they were so fed up with partisan bullshit politics and the imbeciles practicing the sport (at the voters' expense) that they probably would have voted for Beavis or Butt-head.

In the here and now, though, there's a big difference between a genteel, well-read, well-spoken, filthy-rich Senator from Duluth, and a cigar chomping, in-your-face state Governor from Brooklyn Park. One had worked his way up the political ladder slowly and surely, and acted like a serious politician should; while the other had entered the scene kicking and screaming and insulting every current politician in sight as being the cause of the state's sorry state of affairs. The thing is, the wrestler was probably right. The people certainly thought so, and in a very big civil rights demonstration of what they thought of the jack-asses sitting on their collective butts in St. Paul, the bad-boy former Navy Seal was sent to the Capitol to clean things up. Rah, rah, and Raw.

Metcalf closed his mental sidebar on Jesse Ventura and got back to the business at hand: Reardon and Lawrence were a different breed of independent politician. They had some radical ideas for sure, but their presentation was palatable, even responsible. World leaders and members of Congress, alike, could talk the same language as the two candidates, whether they agreed or not, while debating the platforms, policies, and position statements offered.

From his first run at office as a County Commissioner, Lawrence had identified himself as an Independent, "wanting no connection or entanglements with the existing political machinery and all its trappings," was how he had put it at the time. For most wanna-be politicos, that kind of attitude and position would quickly mark the beginning of the end of their years in office. Oh, you might get elected to the odd-job position with the city, county, or even the state, but for any serious office leading to the "real circles of power," you had to play the party game. Or, you had to be so rich that you could thumb your nose at the other party-players. And even then, sometimes wealth wasn't enough. For Lawrence, it had been. He'd apparently known very early what he wanted to do when he grew up, and every decision he'd made had been measured against his long-term goals. He had played the game his way, won over the voters, suffered through a tragic fate, spent millions of dollars, and had come out on top—with but just a rung or two left to go.

Metcalf wrapped up his surface research, considered all that he'd read, and then decided that he actually liked the guy. Which was all right for a naïve citizen from the boondocks of the north, but for a cynical, rabid, investigative reporter covering the armpit of deceit, greed, and power, it was the kiss of death. He couldn't see how yet, but Lawrence had to be bent. Since his instincts had never let him down, Truman Lawrence went from the fridge to the back burner, to be watched and looked at when other assignments allowed.

His initial poking around, although innocent in nature, had raised some curious eyebrows. Word had gotten around, especially in Minnesota, that that "snotty Easterner was out for our beloved Truman." It didn't get too bad for Metcalf, as his was just a soft background check and was performed via phone and computer versus eyeball to eyeball in Minnesota, but the radar picket line went up around the Gopher state.

A few months after those events, Metcalf had received an anonymous letter in the mail—anonymous meaning no name, signature, or return address. It was postmarked Duluth. In easy to read large printing, the letter said: "Truman Lawrence must never be allowed to become president. You must stop him." That was it. Metcalf had found it strange that the sender would confuse "president" for "vice-president." He wondered if the sender knew something, but the letter was hardly any kind of smoking gun, so it too went into the kettle on the back burner.

And then, yesterday, the day of Truman Lawrence's mind-boggling proposal, security had brought Metcalf a second letter. Anonymous again, and postmarked Duluth, the block printing inside appeared to be the same as the first letter. Metcalf pulled out his copy of the first missive once more, the original having been stowed in the vault downstairs. The thing was like catnip—constantly calling to him, tantalizing him. He read it for the tenth time. "Why haven't you stopped him? Truman Lawrence is *not* what he appears to be. Talk to the psychiatrists in Florida. They know."

Lying on his oh-so-comfy sofa, staring at the wormhole ceiling panels overhead, the writer performed the same analysis he'd done so many times before. Whoever wrote the note is familiar with his stories and knows that he has done nothing on Lawrence. Secondly, the reporter found it mildly intriguing that the author of the note used the phrase "*what* he appears to be" rather than "*who* he appears to be." Given that the English in both letters had been grammatically correct, except for the reference to "president," and well-constructed, the mistake or choice was significant. And that was the key: was it a mistake or was it a choice? If it were by choice, the enigma of Truman Lawrence could become intense in a hurry. And finally, the reference to the shrinks in Florida. He didn't have a clue what that was about, but it tickled his curiosity.

At any rate, the answer, if there were one, was not in Washington. Metcalf sat up, preparing to enter the zone. He started doing his mental calculations, scheduling, lists of people to call, and lists of things he'd need. Then he stepped to his phone and dialed a three-digit number. "Bonnie, it's Mike. I need an airline reservation to Minneapolis. What? Yea, as soon as possible; open return—I don't know how long I'll be gone. Right. Thanks."

Senator Truman Lawrence had just moved to the front burner.

"Begin preparing, right now, for that day when a Stranger may approach you on the street and ask:

'What do you believe in?'

Although you have every right to tell the Stranger to take a hike, you nonetheless have an obligation to yourself, and to humanity, to know where you stand on the question."

chapter six

Revelations I

Southern Colorado

Somewhere between Cortez and Durango, the black of the night began giving way to a faint light in the East. The drive since Montezuma Creek had been easy and uneventful, as long as the revelations from Max were excluded. Throw those into the tour package, and it became the most *eventful* drive in Maley's life.

When Max had revealed his purpose in being here, Justin had managed to avoid the clichés that scrambled to be released—things like: "Say that again," or "Oh, my God," or "Holy Shit." He had heard Max just fine, and by now he was almost past being shocked—almost. Instead, he had just stared at his passenger, waiting for any sign that he was being "had" or any sign that Nurse Ratched had been right all along. Maley expected neither, and he wasn't disappointed. So, he had started the engine and pulled away, passing through Montezuma Creek on into the remaining night, heading East where the wicked witch lived (okay, warlock), and ready to hear it all...

"Okay, Max, I'm listening. Besides being a little out there on the edge with his ideas, what's the problem with Truman Lawrence?" But before Max could answer, Maley jumped back into the ring: "Wait a minute—wait a minute," and then he went quiet as his organic processing gears turned faster and faster.

"Max—are you implying that Lawrence had something to do with those guys last night, that he sent them to kill us? Holy buckets…" As he added this ingredient to the simmering stew of the last twenty-four hours, the final dish was served with a flurry: "Is he like you, Max? I mean, is the being in the Truman Lawrence body from the other side, like you?" Now that his writer's brain had dropped its load, he waited for some answers from his passenger.

But there was a momentary delay before Max responded. The two men looked at each other through the darkness between them—not able to see the details of each other's faces, but feeling details of each other nonetheless. As Max prepared to answer his partner's questions, he brought in more of his being's personality (and knowledge), and less of the adapted persona of his cantankerous wino host. He softened; he relaxed. He smiled as he began. "Very good, my boy. 'Yes', 'yes', and 'kind of.' Yes, Lawrence had something to do with those guys last night; and yes, Lawrence sent them to kill us—me, actually. The last part is a little more complicated. You have to understand something first. Every sentient body in the cosmos is in partnership with a being. A body without a being is a dead body, or at best, a comatose body. The difference between Truman and me versus the other 5 billion people on Earth, is that our bodies and beings are in full awareness of that partnership. My body and my being are as one: No secrets, full knowledge of what lies on the other side, full powers available, and full cognizance of the nature of the Universe. It's the same with Lawrence. That's not the way it's supposed to be, Justin. That's against the rules. Truman broke the rules, and now I've broken the rules in an effort to salvage the situation—to salvage the planet, actually. A body may eventually become fully aware of its being and what lies beyond, but only after much study and work while here on the planet. How old and wise the being is when it joins any given body will also affect the level of consciousness attained by the body, and how quickly. Although the being in your body may have the same knowledge and capability as mine, there's a wall, a block, that prevents you from having full access to your being, and which prevents you from remembering the ways of the continuum. It has to be that way, Justin. The taking of a body by a being would serve no purpose otherwise.

"What purpose?" Justin was in cruise control, just as the car was, as he worked furiously to take it all in, to understand it, and to file it. He had managed to excise from his body the cynical part of himself and lock it away, and to allow only his open-minded part to listen to Max's words. And that part of him, the seeker-of-truth part, was completely convinced that he was hearing the secrets for which all humans hungered.

Max hesitated briefly before explaining. "Justin, there's something else you have to understand first: I'm on thin ice here, and there's a limit to how much I can tell you. It's kind of a need-to-know deal." Then Max laughed, as a picture came to his mind. "I could tell you everything, but then I'd have to kill you." He giggled some more, then went on, "Great line, wherever it came from. Anyway, it's true. If you abuse the knowledge you get from me, some sort of action will be taken..."

"Like what?" Justin was suddenly Mr. Pragmatic once again.

"Oh, I don't know—lobotomy, maybe death."

Now Maley knew he was being had. "Max, don't do that. It's not funny."

After his chuckle faded, Max advised him, "I'm only half kidding, Justin. This really is serious stuff. Serious enough that I was almost denied the assistance of a helper while on the planet."

"Who almost denied it, Max? You make it sound like there's a governing committee on the other side, which is really kind of depressing. And you still haven't answered my question: What purpose? What's a being's purpose in taking a body?"

Max sighed. This was going to be harder than he feared. Human curiosity was a wonderful thing—until it was you facing the interrogator's lamp. "It has to do with Karma, growth, and—and boredom."

"Boredom? You gotta be kiddin' me." As the picture sunk in, Justin completed his response: "Oh, I can't wait to hear this..."

Max sank as he got in deeper and deeper over his head, but he was the one who had opened the door, and ultimately it would be his mess to clean up. "Take a time out, will ya, Justin? I've gotta think this through before I make matters any worse than they already are. I need to organize my thoughts instead of knee-jerk reacting to your questions. Okay?"

And it *was* fine with Maley. He was in no hurry, and the break gave him time to more thoroughly process what he had heard, and to formulate clarification questions for a future go around. Also, Max looked super tired, which came as no surprise. And sure enough, a few minutes later, Max was gone—sawin' more logs.

"Where are we?" Max asked with one eye open and arms folded across his chest. He'd slept for well over an hour.

"We're almost to Durango. I need to get some gas and food. You with me?" Max was, and Maley found a small truck stop on the edge of town with plenty of regular-type cars as well. After tanking up and checking the oil, Justin asked an attendant about replacing the shredded tire from yesterday while he and Max had breakfast. That was no problem, so they settled down for their daily dose of carbs and fat.

The place had ceiling-hung television sets all over, presumably for the truck drivers who never got to watch the things, and coming across each and every monitor was the story out of Utah. The death toll was now at forty-five, including the man run-over in the parking lot by a black Dodge pickup truck, for which there was a massive search in progress: It was assumed that the man, or men, in the truck might be a suspect in the fire. No mention was made of either Justin or Max, or the Mustang. The governor of Utah asked for, and was receiving assistance from the feds, especially since there was still a possibility that the fire had been an act of terrorism aimed at the heartland of America. Finally, the President of the United States was shown in the White House press room, expressing his deepest condolences to the families of those killed in the "despicable act of cowardice," and promising that the evil-doers would be apprehended and punished. Little did he know...

As their breakfast was being prepared, Max kept an eye out for any *local* evil-doers who might have been instructed to keep an eye out for the two men. "How long will it take to get to Washington?"

The question surprised Justin, who had to look at the alternatives and mileage. "There's an assumption there, Max, that I'm taking you all the way, that I have no plans of my own, or if I did have my own plans, they just went down the toilet." He was kidding Max, who knew it, but played along anyway.

"You're on the bus now, remember?" Max said, with eyes on the prowl. His met those of the grizzled short-order cook behind the stainless steel service counter. Their eyes locked just long enough for Max's alarms to go off, and for the cook to suspect the pair at table number nineteen were the ones. If he could have been certain, he would have liberally dosed their breakfast order with rat poison, and then called his boss up in Denver. But he wasn't sure, not yet, and he'd been instructed to keep this job until further notice, and killing customers was not a good way to keep a job. He waited.

"Why don't you just catch a plane, Max?" the journalist asked. "You could be there in hours instead of days?"

Max shook his head, "Because if Lawrence knows I'm on it, I guarantee you the plane would crash, and I would be partly responsible for all the innocents' deaths. It would be the perfect situation for him, assuming he was within range of the aircraft. He would not hesitate to bring it down, no matter how many others were on board. And a fiery inferno would ensure my inability to continue with my mission—at least this time around."

Maley was truly shocked with this bit of news. "Jesus, Max, you're saying he can just snap his fingers, or something, and bring down a jetliner? Are you sure? How do you know that?"

"Because I can. And if I can, he can."

Justin looked at the man sitting across from him in a whole different light—maybe one of respect, maybe of fear—but definitely different. "If you can do that, you should be able to make that coffee boil, right?" Apparently, it was test time.

"I'm not interested in performing parlor tricks for your entertainment, young man. Either you can take me at my word, or you can take a hike," Max said with genuine irritation.

"All right, all right," and the subject was dropped as breakfast was delivered. However, the creature standing before them with a platter in each hand was most definitely not their waitress. The thing standing before them was clearly male, in the vilest sense of the word. He was tall and quite large, with a beer belly so huge and pronounced that it must have been tethered to his waist by a half-inch cable. Although he was dressed in white, food and grease stains covered more of his pants than did the original color, and for a sanitary shirt, he wore a plain T-shirt that was obviously saturated in evaporating sweat. His burly arms were covered in thick hair denying a clear view of the tattoos underneath, and the man totally reeked. He was easily the most slovenly human being Justin had ever seen, causing his appetite to go right out the window. It was a forgone conclusion that the management of the place would have had a seizure if they knew this walking health code violation was schmoozing with the patrons, probably dropping cockroaches all over the place. The cook stood there, not moving, just staring at Max—not Justin, not even once— just Max. It became obvious to Maley what was going on, and he began looking for a two-foot meat cleaver to emerge from the folds of flesh, ready to add Max's head to the platter in his hand.

But then the oddest thing happened: he smiled; a big, show-all-the-teeth (what there were of them) kind of smile. He set the plates down, gentle as you please, and returned to his grease pit. Two pairs of eyes followed him all the way back through the swinging doors.

"We've been made," Max said.

"Yea, Max, I figured that one out all by myself. What happened? I thought he was going to pull out one of his knives, or something," Justin added.

Max smiled his conspiratorial smile, "We had a little 'talk.' I promised to get rid of his hemorrhoids for him if he would pretend he'd never seen us. He agreed."

"And you believe him?"

"Not for a second. But he's worried I'll give his piles back to him, so he'll be a good boy until we leave." Max picked up his fork and added, "Let's eat."

Maley was still repulsed by the idea and hesitated although his stomach had been screaming for fuel earlier. "Maybe he poisoned the food, Max."

"He didn't—I looked. Until he and I did our thing, he wasn't really sure we were the ones. It's good Justin. Dig in. Ya gotta eat, and besides, no one else is keeling over..." and he pointed around the dining room.

Justin began refueling and got back to previous business. "So, do you want a speed run to D.C. or back roads, or what?" Max wasn't sure, and looked the part, so Justin continued: "If we stay on the interstates, we could be there in a couple of days. Back roads will double that. Can you drive, Max?" Max shook his head. "Well, I'm pretty good at long-distance driving—staying awake, and all—but there's a limit. I'll have to get some rest sometime. Still, two to five days should do it, depending on—surprises. What do you have in mind once we get there?"

Now Max perked up a bit, for this was something he'd thought about before ever boarding the Earth express. "I need to meet him somewhere very public, someplace with lots of people. The Librarians—the ones in the continuum—did a little research and discovered there's a football game in Washington on Thursday night, and the opposing team is from Minnesota. We all decided that there was a good chance Lawrence would go. Anyway, that's plan 'A.'"

Maley nodded his head. "That's reasonable, but not a guarantee. What's your back-up plan if he doesn't show?"

"Don't have one yet, but I'll figure something out if I have to."

"What will happen at the stadium, Max?—assuming he shows up."

"I'm not sure yet. I'm still working out the details." Max knew exactly what would happen, but how do you explain to a human the continuum equivalent of a down and dirty brawl? The longer he could keep that one to himself the better.

Maley scrutinized his travel mate, trying to understand more about him—through osmosis, if nothing else. Then a thought occurred. "Max, why didn't you arrive on the East Coast instead of out West? It would have saved all this hassle, danger, and a lot of time."

"A couple of reasons: First of all, I wanted to give myself as much of a fighting chance with Lawrence as possible. Arriving on his turf would not help my cause. I figured he'd be able to detect my energy, so the farther away I was, the safer I'd be early on. Also, I had to select a writer who would document the reasons behind the whole battle thing. I thought of using a reporter at the *Washington Post* but he was all head and no heart. A warrior requires both. So, I chose you and I had to be in the right place at the right time to pick you up, and that was out here in the West." Justin looked sidelong at Max at what he perceived to be a "left-handed" compliment.

Fifteen minutes later, Justin paid the bill, then went to the restroom as Max headed out to the car. All four urinals were in use, so he found an empty stall, and standing there, watered his horse. Almost done, his sphincter suddenly froze tight as a drum when steam began emanating from the toilet bowl. Then he saw what looked like hundreds of tiny little bubbles rising from the bottom to the top, and the steam got thicker and hotter, and oh did it smell bad. "What the hell...?" was all he could mutter as he got his fly up and backed away through the stall door. The little bubbles became big bubbles, constantly brewing at the surface, and steam was pouring out of the bowl, just as if the toilet were.....boiling. *Max, you son of a bitch!*

The hundred-foot walk from the restroom to the car was enough to calm Justin down and to even get him to smile a little. When he climbed in, Max was sitting there, gagging on trying to keep a straight face, but couldn't hold it any longer after Justin started bitching at him. "Parlor trick" complete.

They pulled over to the shop, loaded the new tire, and returned to the highway. Above the driveway, a clutch of screaming crows jumped around on the pylon sign, unable, as always, to sit still for long, but when the Mustang pulled onto the roadway, heading east, one of the crows left the others. It followed directly behind the red coupe, albeit not quite as fast.

Inside the restaurant, looking through the window, the cook watched them pull onto the highway and then he walked, with a more comfortable gait, back to his kitchen and picked up the phone.

"Justin, what do you believe will happen to you when you die?" It appeared that Max was ready to pick up where they'd left off earlier in the morning, and without reluctance.

"I've long believed my body would become fertilizer while my soul went to wherever souls go to—to the continuum, I suppose." Justin almost stopped there but then kept going. "The continuum: now there's a word I would never have used to describe—heaven?—before I met you. You're confirming my belief structure on the one hand, and messing with my head on the other. Fascinating..."

Max nodded and grinned a little. "And there's the danger, my friend; what we're all worried about back on the other side. Call it the Max factor, and it's already started, and it will only get worse, or rather, more significant. The remainder of your life is changing, as we speak, from the direction it would have gone as early as twenty-four hours ago. My presence is affecting your choices. My words are affecting your belief structure. Every single thing humans do in their lives involves choice: good choice, bad choice, right choice, wrong choice. Everything. Beginning twenty-four hours ago, less than that actually, your choices began to be influenced in a way they were not meant to be in normal circumstances. For you, and for those whom you affect, destiny is being rewritten, right now. Furthermore, I have put you in harm's way. You could have been killed last night. You still could be in the near future—because of me and my mission. If you die as a result of my mission, that means that maybe some great and important, or terrible thing you were destined to do in the future will not happen. By extreme extension, all of society, or the planet, could be affected. You understand our problem now?"

It didn't take a rocket scientist to run the logic on that one, and Maley nodded his head, keeping his eyes on the road and the unique high desert scenery. The conundrum could get real deep, real fast. "So why are you even talking to me about this stuff, Max? Why are you displaying your bag of tricks, when you know the effect it will have on me?"

"Would you be here otherwise? Would you have picked me up yesterday had I not appeared as an *enigma* to you—a puzzle to solve? Would I still be in your car, rather than on a bus bench, had I not piqued your interest with a few surprises, thereby providing fuel for your waning imagination? I have de facto asked you to risk your life for my mission. That deserves a bit more explanation than a few grunts and commands, and I won't lie. So, you're getting the facts—in limited dosage. But there's another side to these revelations, too."

A break in Max's dialogue caused Justin to glance at his passenger, prompting, "And what's that...?"

"There are those in the continuum that feel the Earth, or rather, its occupants, need some help in figuring things out. As a civilization, you're in a rut—morally, consciously, and spiritually—and you've been stuck for a long time. Humans are way too busy playing computer games, or working for their fancy cars, or just scrounging for the food to survive to take the time for serious contemplation of how important nonlife might be to life. They're way too comfortable with defining existence in the four dimensions they think of as reality. They don't have a clue as to the effect several billion beings on the other side might have on the Universe, much less on planet Earth.

"Furthermore, it's too easy for your society to become the unintentional but willing partner of group-mind forces, whether they be evil or otherwise; and then later, the *duped* victim of those forces. Either way, the Karma's the same, but when a major evil event is in the works on Earth, the collateral damage can be significant—extending well beyond your planet. And the continuum is tired of cleaning up your messes. If you, as a society, were half as adept at reading auras as you are at making computers, video games, and cars, you wouldn't need a kick in the butt. You'd be able to see that the aura around Truman Lawrence is singularly without light or color, and that it's downright frightening. At the very least, your alarms would go off, and you would never feel comfortable with that kind of person in a position of power. And that's one of the reasons I chose you as my helper."

"Say what?"

"You, as a journalist, are in a position to document the behind-the-scenes part of my visit. I'll take care of the more visible stuff—the 'get their attention' part, if you know what I mean. But after I do my wake-up call, your fellow humans are going to want more, and you're the one that's going to give it to them. You're going to end up famous, Justin Maley. For all we know, maybe you were destined for this from birth. Who knows?"

"Time out, Max. I don't understand. Just a little while back, you and your buddies were all hot and bothered about any of this info coming out, and now you're saying you're going to go public in some big way, and you want me to write all about it. In case you missed it, there's a contradiction in there."

"Yea, contradictions are a bitch, aren't they?" Max commiserated, then he turned to his new friend and added, "Deal with it—we had to. We struggled with this very issue for—well, what would be a long time for you—until a decision was made. And I assure you there was dissention in the ranks. A decision has been made. A brief exception to policy will be allowed. Once only, hopefully, but still, not without risk."

"Risk to what? What could happen?" Maley was desperate to know.

"The risk is to stability, Justin. You see, it's all about balance—everything. Mother Nature does a real good job at maintaining balance, throughout the Universe, and we're loathe to do anything that will upset the apple cart. But we looked at the risk element and decided that leaving Truman Lawrence to his own devices was more risky than intervening. So, here I am, contradictions and all. And…"

"Stop—hold it, Max. I've got to come to closure on at least some of this stuff or I won't know which way is up. I'm already starting to forget some things I wanted to come back to. You're saying you're here to stop Lawrence from becoming vice-president, which also means, by the way, that Reardon will most likely be stopped from becoming president, because Lawrence is evil and plans to unbalance things here on Earth. Does that about cover it, Max? If so, I think you need to fill-in a few dozen holes."

"God, leave it to a journalist to mess up a perfectly good story!" Max responded impatiently. "I hope you'll do better than that when you write my biography, Sonny-boy."

Justin snickered, "I will, Max, but you see what I'm worried about and why having just some of the facts may be more dangerous than none at all? For instance, I assume that Truman Lawrence isn't the first or only evil person to inhabit our fine planet." He glanced at Max, who was shaking his head vigorously. "So, what is it about him and his brand of evil that needs to be stopped? Why has he drawn so much of the continuum's attention?"

Now Max smiled, "Maybe you won't do so bad after all. That's a good way to ask the question, and here's the answer: It's not the evil that bothers us. Hell, like you said, there's evil all over this planet— always has been, always will be. In fact, that's one of the reasons that visits to Earth are in such high demand—part of the Karma thing."

"And boredom…I haven't forgotten about that one, Max."

"Yes, and boredom. Anyway, our concern is with what the body/being combination of Truman Lawrence is capable of, and *desirous* of. It's the combination that's unique and so frightening. Here you have a body that is handsome, off-the-scale intelligent, well-spoken, preceded by sympathetic tragedy, already in a position of power, seeking more power, and highly electable at that. Now, you team up that body with a being that's been around eons longer than the one that controlled Adolph Hitler or Pol Pot, make the whole package totally conscious and aware, with an agenda that seeks nothing less than utter global chaos, and perhaps you can begin to see why he's gotten our attention. It's actually not uncommon for civilizations to fade away and disappear from existence, but it happens progressively, logically, and slowly. Lawrence is an anomaly that does-n't belong. If humanity is going to self-destruct, it needs to do it on its own and without help from some egomaniacal interloper."

As the driver looked a little dazed, Max obviously needed to explain further: "Let me approach the end result from a different angle. The Earth, as a physical planet, and as a civilization, is amaz-ingly balanced. I'll tell you more about this balance thing in a minute, just trust me. For all its apparent shortcomings, your planet, like all the Universe actually, is nicely balanced. As I said, Truman Lawrence has the ability and the desire to change that. If he is successful in his efforts, and the continuum believes he may very well be, by the time he gets done with this place, your civilization will be so out-of-balance as to be unsalvageable, and whenever that happens, the civilization in question invariably dies. And you can quote me on that."

The message was successfully delivered, as evidenced by a reflec-tive silence, and then a, "Holy buckets…"

"It's cause for pause, isn't it?"

"Why, Max? Why would he seek to do such a thing? Does this have something to do with Karma? It's insane…"

Max prepared to guide Justin through the illogic: "We don't think Lawrence's actions have anything to do with Karma. If they did, the continuum couldn't interfere, and I wouldn't be here. You would be on your own. And it's only insane if you don't know the big picture. He's doing it because his bent is toward the malevolent side of things, because he's apparently able to do it, and because—well, because he thinks it's kind of like a final exam."

Maley almost lost it on the last revelation. "What!? What did you say? He's going to destroy the world as part of some fucking test?" They both pondered the picture for a few seconds before Maley went on. "You gotta be crazy. Is everyone over there like you two? No won-der everybody wants to come here—I don't believe this crap. You mean this is like some kind of graduation or something?"

Max cocked his head, "Yea, that's exactly what it is—kind of."

It was nearly noon, the Mustang was ready for more gas, and Justin was hungry for something besides the verbal diarrhea this was quickly turning into. They were approaching I-25 and he pulled into a gas and convenience store that could provide all their earthly needs. After inserting the nozzle into the tank, Justin agreed to keep an eye on things while Max stretched, used the head, and got some food-type stuff (using Justin's money, of course). When he returned, Justin did the same thing. Inside the store, a TV was relaying the latest from the Utah inferno: identification of the bodies could take weeks, and the suspect pickup truck, with two dead bodies, had been found near Montezuma Creek, Utah. An aerial view of the scene showed the smashed truck at the bottom of a small gorge, with forensic people all around it. A crane was moving into position to lift the pickup from its present position to the back of a flatbed truck, and a white sheet of some sort could be seen covering the cab area. Finally, the death toll remained at forty-five, firty-seven if the two men in the pickup were included. Again, no mention was made of Max or Justin, or the Mustang. Justin paid for the gas and food and headed back to his car, where Max, ever the Mystery Man, had forgone eating and was fast asleep again.

"Black may not always be black. Sometimes black might be white, as in the absence of light—or consciousness."

chapter seven

The Lion's Den

Minneapolis, Minnesota

The Northwest Airlines A320 landed within five minutes of its scheduled arrival, meaning that, for the record, the plane was on time. The man seated in 2B, although a well-known and feared reporter in Washington, was just a certain Mike Metcalf in the down-to-earth State of Gophers, loons, Timberwolves, Vikings, Twins, Wild, Lynx, mosquitoes, 10,000 lakes, Jesse Ventura, and Truman Lawrence. He'd slept for most of the flight, and now he grabbed the tote and his carry-on for a quick exit from the aircraft. Bonnie, his secretary in the "pool," had reserved him a mid-size car at Budget and a room at the airport Hilton. His plan was to get the car, get to the hotel, and settle in for the evening in preparation for an early start to Duluth in the morning. He had decided against flying directly to his destination simply to avoid recognition any sooner than necessary: Metcalf knew full well that he was entering hostile territory. He'd use the evening to complete his research of everything he had on the candidate for vice-president of the United States of America, and he would do it from the anonymity of a hotel room one hundred fifty miles south of "Lawrenceville."

Metcalf got into his room shortly after 3:00 P.M., got all comfy, checked the honor bar for goodies, and settled on a can of cashews and a bottle of some local brew called James Page. Clearing the nearly worthless dinette table of the extraneous marketing junk, he spread out his stuff on the bed, selected this file or that and settled at the table for his reading, nuts, and beer— the latter being excellent.

As with all newspapers, the *Post* had an extensive collection of "bios" that would provide a snapshot of numerous famous, rich, or important people throughout the world. The larger the paper, the more extensive the collection of bios, and with the insertion of computers into the business world, bio collection was now larger than ever and instantly accessible via the Internet. Mike had printed out the *Post's* current bio of Lawrence just prior to his departure from the building, and in conjunction with additional research materials the *Post* staff had put together on Lawrence, he had quite a pile to select from. He gleaned the salient points as he read through the documents. It wasn't the first time he'd read Lawrence's package, but now it was being done with more than just idle curiosity over a twenty-dollar bet; and this time, he had more data on Lawrence's childhood and family. Metcalf was looking for the missing element, the hole, or the piece that didn't belong. Whatever it turned out to be, the master of the exposé was on the prowl. If it were there, he'd find it.

As Metcalf began reading, there was no way he would be able to read between the lines of the family history, which is where he needed to be for the task at hand. He was limited to the hard, cold, and fascinating facts, but the story went much deeper than that:

Truman Jonathan Lawrence had been born January 20, 1961, at St. Luke's Hospital in Duluth, Minnesota. His father had been Jonathan Miles Lawrence, and his mother had been Cassandra Allison Winthrop (maiden name). He had a twin sister, Allison, but she had died in 1970 in the same explosion and fire that had killed the father and mother, which was the first tragedy to befall Minnesota's favorite son.

The family was wealthy—had been for three generations. When Samual Lawrence, Truman's great-great grandfather, had immigrated to America in 1871, his wife, Anna, was already pregnant with their first child. Samual had brought a modest sum of money with him and had settled in Duluth where other family and friends from Scotland resided. The new arrivals were welcomed with open arms, and the men of the clan immediately went to work bringing Samual into the inner business workings of the growing interior seaport. At the time, lumber was the big opportunity, as it was the prime known resource of the area, and there was huge demand for the product all over the East and South, following the Civil War. Samual's new friends were involved in lease holdings, small mills, transportation (both land and sea), and marketing. They were all working on the edge because they were all small operators trying to become large-scale barons, but there was something missing from their combined talents: vision. Samual didn't know beans about botany and trees, about home construction, about freight wagons and ships. But he had vision—big, and lots of it, and he understood that all business endeavors required capital, and capital was money (usually), and money was just another kind of commodity that was meant to be bought low and sold high. It wasn't long before he was leasing great plots of timber-laden lands for next to nothing up front, with the promise (written, of course) to pay the owner of those lands twice the going rate once the timber was harvested. The land owners were thrilled to make the extra money for minimal delay and without risk, for there was a stipulated timeline in which Samual, and friends, had to harvest the timber, after which the deal was off, and the landowner could release his property to whomever he wanted, while keeping the earnest monies. Any number of factors could have occurred and cost Samual everything. But luck shone on the man, and in five years, he and his partners were all quite well-to-do.

If business savvy can be carried in the genes, genetic engineers of the twenty-first century would be fascinated with the Lawrence family. When timber began to disappear faster than it could be regrown, Samual began looking at other possibilities, most notably the iron ore industry that was beginning to take a firm hold in the areas west and north of Duluth. But this time, rather than becoming directly involved in the product, Samual, at the urging of his young, but brilliant son Jonathan, remained hidden from view as a silent partner, providing investment capital for the Taconite pioneers—men such as

Peter Mitchell, Charlemagne Tower, and John McCaskill. And as those giants of mining became richer, so did the Lawrence family.

A few years later, young Jonathan, already holding the reigns of the family business with the blessing of his father, began investing in lake shipping assets, for the Taconite had to get to the industrial cities of the East, and lake shipping was the most efficient method for delivery. But in all transactions, the Lawrence family had become content to be the silent player, allowing the mining and shipping owners to receive all the attention. Those owners, of course, knew who lived in the big house at the edge of Lake Superior, but the general population of the area just knew the names and something about banking—and that the family was very generous and always kind.

The Lawrence clan was quiet wealth: never extravagant, never obnoxious. Their one visible indication of money was their magnificent home on the bluff north of town, but even that was almost sedentary compared to the pictures of the robber-baron castles back East. Also, the family enjoyed travelling, and as they left for another Grand Tour of the Continent, or some exotic location in Africa or Asia, the less-fortunate mortals of Duluth might look in wonder at the mountainous pile of leather luggage and steamer trunks awaiting loading at the station.

The family remained steadfast in its business strategy for years, quietly providing capitalization for established businesses, and later on, for the riskier startups—helping those pioneers with wild and great ideas to get started. Many of the latter failed, but when one hit, it almost always covered the losses of the others, and then some. Jonathan, Jr. was an inspired investor in these startup companies, especially the new horseless carriage industry and the oil industry. His son, Franklin, would carry on the tradition of sniffing out the winners by taking the family into the new business machine arena, risking venture capital in new companies like IBM, Honeywell, and Xerox—always spreading the risk.

By the time Truman was born in 1961, the family was worth nearly half a billion dollars—the family consisting of Truman's parents, his sister, his grandfather and grandmother, his uncle, two aunts, and assorted children of same. In 1961, half a billion dollars would buy a lot more than it would thirty years later. Without the Forbes 400 list, no one in Duluth or anywhere else was aware that the family was among the five wealthiest in the country.

But not too many years after Truman's birth, the long run of good luck for the Lawrence family ran out—or so it would seem.

It started with Truman's near death in 1969. The family was quartered for the winter at their digs in Florida. Truman and some friends were frolicking in the pool, and in the confusion, no one realized that the eight-year-old was missing from the "frolickers." It wasn't until one of the children stepped on Truman's sunken and lax body did the screams of panic begin. It took awhile for the rent-a-lifeguard to distinguish between the playful screams and the panic screams, and by the time he retrieved Truman's unconscious form from the pool, the boy was quite blue. To the lifeguard's credit, he did everything right: expelling the water from the lungs and administering the then current resuscitation techniques. And he wouldn't stop. By the time the rescue squad arrived, the lifeguard was totally spent and collapsed alongside the comatose body. The rescue people continued the effort, but it was clear to everyone that it was way too late: It had been at least thirty minutes since Truman Lawrence had been dragged from the bottom of the pool. Even if they succeeded in reviving him now, having gone that length of time without oxygen to his brain, he most likely would have been vegetative for the remainder of his life.

He was declared dead, covered by a blanket, and the rescue crew filled out paper work while family members wailed or stood around in complete shock. Earlier, someone had had the foresight to remove the other children from the scene.

But just then, the first miracle happened, something right out of either a horror flick or a comedy, depending on the frame of mind of the viewing audience: The body under the blanket sat straight up. Two women screamed—the real blood-curdling kind of scream, but it was a man who passed out, collapsing right there on the patio. The two rescue people were all over Truman in a second, doing this and doing that, with a noticeable shake in the hands of one of the two. After a few minutes, it appeared not to be a fluke, or some kind of end-of-life muscle spasm. Truman was back amongst the living, but the question was soon looming in everyone's mind: in what capacity?

Enter miracle number two: The next day, at the hospital, the shrinks began their testing of the boy bright and early in the morning. After an hour, although they wanted to continue testing their patient for a few days longer, it was obvious to everyone in attendance

113

that Truman was going to be fine, as good as new, and let's get back to life as usual. Praise the Lord.

Well, not quite.

The psychiatric staff at the hospital were in a quandary. Alone, without the family present, they would hover about the boy's bed, study the EEG results, shake their collective heads, and pass sidelong glances at one another. Something was wrong. Not wrong, perhaps, but not right, either. Their patient was putting out consistent EEG results that none had ever seen before, and they were, frankly, a bit disturbing; frightening, actually. The results belonged to something that couldn't exist, at least, not yet. Brainwaves as active as those they were seeing belonged to some advanced creature in a science fiction story, not in a Florida hospital. However, just as with a pilot sighting of a UFO, not one of the doctors was prepared to take the heat of the questions and explanations that would follow if any of them brought the matter to the attention of the child's parents—people on whose bad side one did not want to be. For all intents and purposes, the boy appeared to be fine, so they made their silent, huddled agreements to leave it at that.

Within a month of the incident, the immediate family knew beyond any doubt that Truman was different. It took awhile longer for the extended family to come to this conclusion, but come they did. This was not the Truman Lawrence they had known and loved, and that had known and loved them, just a few months ago. He was distant, colder, possibly more intelligent, and it felt to his sister as though there were a cunningness in his eyes that was new and disturbing.

And there was one other thing. Although the boy was only eight years old, he frequently spoke and acted as though he were much, much older. It became so disconcerting and uncomfortable for his mother, father, and sister that one of them began thinking it would have been better had there not been a resurrection.

Since the family traveled a great deal and money was no object, both Allison and Truman were educated by private tutors who, of course, traveled with them, along with their Nanny, Martha Evans, who had been looking after them both since right after their birth. As cushy and interesting as the tutoring position appeared to be, there had only been one, so far, who had remained on station for more than the contracted twelve months, and that was the current instructor, Ms. Jennifer Bryant. This was her second year, but it would be her last. The kids had liked her, the parents had liked her, and she had been very fond of Allison and Truman. Truman's resurrection, however, changed all that. Collectively, Martha, Jennifer, and Allison spent more time around Truman than anyone else, and it was they who noticed, more than others, that something was amiss with the lad, something both wondrous—and not so wondrous.

His personality change was not enjoyed by anyone, but Ms. Jennifer was downright intrigued by the change in his mental acumen. The boy's cognitive processes seemed to have leaped several years since the "event." This pertained particularly to his reasoning abilities, perception of cause-and-effect relationships, and memory functions. Jennifer asked for, and received, permission to have another IQ test administered, but the results were decidedly disappointing, measuring a full eighteen points less than his first test two years prior. However, there was an anomaly brought privately to Jennifer's attention by the test administrator. There seemed to be incongruities in the test answers that fit a pattern indicating many *intentionally* incorrect answers. Not knowing what to make of this development, Jennifer almost let the matter drop, but on a fluke asked the administrator if she could identify all those problems with suspect answers. The woman smiled, seeing that they were both on the same wavelength. "Yes," she replied, "and if he had answered those questions properly, the result would have been a score of 201, a result way above anything I've seen in my career." This was more along the lines of what Jennifer had expected to begin with, but the reason for Truman's deception, if indeed it was, confused her and, taken together with his personality changes, bothered her a great deal. It was a good thing for her future health that she ultimately decided to just forget the entire incident.

Ms. Bryant fulfilled her current contractual obligation with the two children then resigned her position, much to the regret of the parents and Allison. Truman showed no such sorrow. In fact, he showed no emotion at all. Upon leaving the mansion back in Duluth, Jennifer promised to write Allison.

The following winter, the winter of 1970, Truman, Allison, their parents, the Nanny, and the newest tutor returned to Palm Beach, leaving fifty-below windchills for others to endure. Like the Pillsburys and the MacMillans, the Lawrences absolutely loved living in Minnesota, as long as they, were able to spend a certain three months of each year in Rome or Palm Beach. But unlike all previous years, the family that walked through the front door of the modest mansion on Florida's Atlantic coast did not look like they were glad to be there. In fact, to the dismay of staff, friends, and associates, the Lawrence family looked downright glum.

The days went by in the shadow of this mood from which there seemed to be no salvation. At the end of January, the rest of the Lawrence clan arrived from their various parts of the country, and in one case, Italy (they had chosen to endure Rome for the aforementioned three winter months). It was time for the annual conclave to renew relationships, which had always been close, and to discuss family business matters. No one focused on the fact that it was also the one year anniversary of Truman's near drowning. As part of the forced festivities, forced because the balance of the family quickly felt the mood thing and succumbed to it, the clan provisioned the carefully and lovingly maintained 177 foot Camper & Nicholsons motor yacht for a week's cruise in the Caribbean. Actually, it was the crew of six that did the provisioning, while the family adults played cribbage, croquet, and Canasta. The children were required to study, albeit, at the edge of the swimming pool.

For some of the family, another miracle was about to happen. The night before the planned departure, poor Truman came down with something that brought on a fever, vomiting, diarrhea, and headache. Clearly, he would not be doing any traveling for a few days. Largely at the insistence of the ailing boy, good sport that he was, the clan decided to depart on schedule, leaving Truman and the Nanny behind to catch up with the yacht in the Bahamas in two days, or Jamaica in four. As it pulled away from the dock the next morning, the transformation in mood of those passengers aboard Destiny's Dream was an amazing thing to behold, almost as if a veil had been lifted.

That very night, there was a knock at the front door of the Florida mansion, and standing at attention when the housekeeper opened the door was a captain of the United States Coast Guard. He presented his ID, informed the housekeeper of some distressing news he had, and asked to come in and meet with any of the adult Lawrence's that might be around. His distressing news was trumped with the

116

announcement that there *were* no adult Lawrences about, since all were aboard the yacht having a jolly good time down in the Caribbean. In the meantime, Truman had made what can only be described as a miraculous (yes, there's another one) recovery that seemingly began within one hour of the motor yacht's departure. He arrived in the entry foyer to relieve the captain of his burden: With great sadness, the captain was obliged to inform all present that a mysterious explosion had completely destroyed the Destiny's Dream, and no survivors had been found. It was assumed that all aboard had died, although the search for survivors would continue through the night and into the next morning. An investigation would obviously be required, but it appeared to have been an engine room fuel tank accident, even though that was virtually impossible with diesel fuel.

Metcalf finished reading the numerous reports and articles of the boating accident, along with the required obits, testimonies, grand funeral, etc. *Twelve family members, plus six crew, wiped out in one night. You talk about a major disruption in one's life, speaking of Truman, not to mention the mad scrambling that must have occurred in boardrooms all over the country.*

The reporter laid aside the printed matter, got another beer, and stepped to the window to see what there was to see—literally, but mostly figuratively. *The kid was nine years old, alone mostly, and instantly one of the richest people in the country, if not the world. He'd violently lost his mom and dad and his twin sister, plus assorted uncles, aunts, and cousins. How in the world did he manage to come away from that in one piece, psychologically speaking, and then go on to become a pillar and model citizen of his community?*

But, again, the nuances in the life of Truman Lawrence were invisible to the eyes of reporters. Only certain eyes within the continuum knew it all, and with grudging respect, they watched a master at work. And they worried:

Young Truman smiled, as things were going perfectly. The all-knowing authorities had ultimately chosen to leave him in the mansion in Duluth, along with his grandfather, the nursing staff, the house staff, and Martha Evans, the Nanny. The whole kit and caboodle would be overseen by Rudy Jergens, the family's personal attorney for many years, and by the child services department for St. Louis County. Truman's grandmother had died two years earlier, removing her from the equation. Everyone expected his grandfather to quickly join her from a broken heart and it would appear that he had tried, but the stroke had paralyzed rather than killed him, and he had required twenty-four-hour care ever since. The family had decided to move him into the main mansion, where all activities regarding his care could be better monitored. Since he seemed oblivious to everyone and everything around him, he and his nursing staff had remained in Duluth when the rest of the family had migrated South for the winter. The only pebble in the shoe of Truman's plans had been the requirement that he now attend school, public or private, instead of remaining holed up in an adult bastion that offered insufficient contact with children his own age. But it was a minor glitch to which he could easily adjust.

At nine years of age, Truman was too young to pursue his plans in any active sort of way, so he actually did devote the next few years to academics, especially in the areas of history and political science. And he did it while going to public schools, where he had more opportunities of connecting with "the masses." At age eleven, the straight-A student began serving the community in earnest. Since he couldn't drive, he either walked or rode his bike (no limousine for young Truman!) to nursing homes, or to fund-raisers for the Scouts, his church, or the Seaman's Retirement Fund. By his fourteenth year, he carefully began his *overt* political career by championing causes of little risk of pissing off the voters—things like the funding for a statue in a park, honoring this person or that group, or providing a plot of cleared ground for a gardening group that wanted to further beautify the city for visitors.

For several years, Truman had surreptitiously provided funds for various projects around the city and elsewhere in the county. It hadn't taken much effort to convince Jergens of the worthiness of such endeavors and the amounts spoken of barely made a dent in the annual return from his portfolio of investments. Since it was crucial to Truman that no one know where the funds came from, a separate checking account was set up through a different law office located in St. Paul. The name on the checks was "Appreciative Benefactors, Inc." and came with a post office box address. After some time and dozens of charitable gifts, the rumor mill began in earnest, and, as per Truman's plans, it wasn't long before the good citizens of Duluth began suspecting the true source of the gifts, helped a bit by "a slip of the tongue" of an unnamed law clerk in St. Paul, speaking on condition of anonymity to a reporter from Duluth.

Truman had known for years that he could read minds and that he had the power to stop motors, turn off lights, and move smaller things by thought alone. It was around his sixteenth birthday that he began systematically cataloging (mentally only, of course) his bag of tricks and the limits of his power. That was the year that "Star Wars" came out, providing Truman a demonstration of what would quickly become one of his favorite tools of persuasion—or punishment, as Jim Losey discovered later in the year.

Also on his sixteenth birthday, he awarded himself a brand new shiny Trans Am convertible, which he graciously used to transport fellow high schoolers around town—both male and female. It should be noted that Truman dated, and was a perfect gentleman, but his heart really wasn't in it. He had no interest in dating, only in appearances: "Look at me, I'm normal." It was all part of the Grand Plan—the domination of the world.

Upon graduating from high school, second in his class (Suma cum laude would have drawn more attention than he desired—just as running for president would twenty-seven years later), Truman amazingly chose to remain right there at home for his college education, enrolling in the University of Minnesota, Duluth campus, and majoring in political science. The admiring citizens of Duluth had long ago taken the bright and generous young man as their own, and a few even began speaking of his entering politics in a few years. Ah, Truman loved it when a plan came together!

As part of his college education, Truman visited various law-related facilities around town and the county. Amongst these were places of incarceration, and one in particular was a lock-down type reform school for boys. On his carefully guided tour, during which he made copius notes for his future exam papers, he noticed a boy coming their way who reeked of deception, and who appeared to be secretly hiding something in his shirt. He passed the group and entered a restroom. The tour guide had seemed not to notice the episode and was preparing to move on. On a hunch, Truman asked if he could visit the restoom for a moment and quickly catch up with the group, which would still be just down the hall. With approval, the curious college student quietly entered the restroom and found the target of his search in the far toilet stall, softly speaking to someone. Truman had discovered in his bag of tricks a knack for becoming nearly invisible—not literally, but so "unthere" in energy transmission as to be completely unnoticeable without a direct visual contact. He went into the zone and moved closer to the speaking stall. Peeking around the stanchion, Truman saw the boy sitting sideways on the toilet, facing the rear corner, caressing and cooing toward a huge rat cradled in the crook of his arm. Surprisingly, the rat, very much alive, was not squirming or fidgeting in any way. It seemed to be accepting the ministrations as though they were coming from a loving mother. Lawrence was fascinated, and he opened himself up to receiving the thoughts and emotions from within the mind in front of him. What he experienced was unlike anything he'd felt from anyone else in his life to date. He went deeper...deeper. He *became* the boy: A slovenly woman entered his bedroom, a bottle of wine in one hand, a condom in the other. Then a man dragged him outside by his hair, removed his belt, and began whipping him over every surface of his youthful body. Another boy of about the same age punched him in the stomach, took some money from his pocket, pushed him backwards into a mud puddle, then laughed.

For Truman, it was obvious that the vignettes were all horrific examples of abuse and meanness in the boy's life. He merged again: Then a picture came to view of the school bully being hit over the head with something in the locker room shower area. Nobody else appeared to be around, so the boy before him uncoiled the nearby garden hose used for washing the shower walls and floor, rammed the nozzle up the bully's rectum as far as it would go, turned the water on full, and then left the shower room. Another picture became hot and bright, so hot that Truman nearly cut the connection between the two of them. The boy's house was on fire, and the audio image of screams attested to the presence of both Mom and Dad inside.

Apparently the authorities suspected the boy in these events but, without proof, could do no more than put him in this place as a troubled orphan. Just then, though, Lawrence knew he'd found a missing link in his formula for success. To accomplish his long-term goals, he would need a small army of troops around the world, and that army would need a general—a cunning, vicious, loyal, and intelligent leader capable of fulfilling Truman's demands. That the boy before him was the correct choice was confirmed when something made him look over his left shoulder and finally notice Truman observing him so closely. In that instant, the rat bit the boy—not with a nip, but a deep, prolonged, hold-on-for-dear-life gnashing of teeth. The boy, without any sound at all, mouthed a scream of agony, looking Truman directly in the eye while doing so. Truman returned the stare, not blinking, not moving. Then the boy looked at the rat and began pulling body parts off, one at a time. The animal screamed and screamed and screamed, until its head was removed from its torso. The boy dropped the remains into the toilet, and flushed.

"Hello, Adam. My name is Truman."

"How do you know my name?"

"I know everything, Adam—everything. When you leave this place, I will take care of you. When the time comes, you will become my right hand, and together we will change the world." Truman approached Adam and touched his cheek—both with the affection the boy so desperately needed, and with the mental image of who his benefactor was. Adam gasped, then, with a whimper, placed a bloodied hand over Truman's, and whispered, "Yes, Master." Truman turned, and left.

While in graduate school, Truman turned twenty-one and immediately announced his candidacy for the County Commissioner's seat that was to be vacated by the ailing Bill Ingersoll. The soon-to-be candidate filled out the proper paperwork and announced himself as an Independent for the simple reason that, in his humble opinion, the DFL and Republican parties were just two sides of the same coin, and he, Truman Lawrence, was out to do great and wonderful things, and different things, for St. Louis County. No one had any illusions that he would go any further than the borders of his home county.

Even before the County Commissioner election, the mysterious Appreciative Benefactor checks began showing up in other parts of the state, far and wide. At first, recipients just counted their blessings, and dollars, and let it go at that. But tipped-off reporters began following the trail, and the story broke when it was ascertained that millions of dollars were falling from heaven upon those organizations in need. But the stroke of genius was when the checks began finding their way into the bank accounts of those poor citizens upon whom the Fickle Finger of Fate had laid a turd. The idea came to Truman one night while watching the local news, and the latest hard luck case was presented for human interest and sympathy. A family of four, living in a poorer section of town, had lost everything in a house fire. The story went on for a couple of minutes, and Truman's mind began drifting; but his yawn froze midway when the storyteller announced that donations were being collected by the Norwest Bank of Duluth. The light bulb went on, and the next day, an Appreciative Benefactor's check for $1,000 was mailed to Norwest Bank Duluth. The legal office in St. Paul was instructed to quietly hire someone to track all such personal disasters within the state, and subsequently, send a similar check to each one.

Now the media really went nuts. This was just too close to a Santa Claus mystery to be passed up. Furthermore, it was a never-ending story since life served up a personal disaster for someone in the state almost daily. There was no way to trace the gifts back to Lawrence because the only connection was through the law office in St. Paul, and as good as they were with tiny little hints, when it came to the big confession, they went mum, completely, and with no exceptions. In the meantime, everyone in the state of Minnesota knew who the true benefactor was, or, at least, thought they knew.

Truman Lawrence was a shoe-in for the Commissioner's seat. For the following five years, he performed his responsibilities well, doing his bit to make St. Louis County a healthy, thriving place to live and work, offering up new economic, ecological, and legal ideas that would make the state stand up and take notice. In the meantime, Lawrence wrote a book on the nature of politics, as he understood the subject (and he understood the subject quite well), and what needed to change for the upcoming millenium to get off to a good start. The book didn't sell well, which was no surprise to anyone, but it further increased his notoriety and credibility, especially amongst those who ate, drank, and slept politics. Both mainstream parties wooed the upcoming Star of the North, but to no avail. Lawrence had no use for them and would never allow himself to be put under the thumb of their ruling committees—either on the state or national level.

His ultimate plan was progressing nicely, and in 1987, he officially made the announcement that everyone had finally come to expect: He would run for United States Congress, in the eighth Congressional district, with the election coming up in 1988. He opened up his election headquarters office in Duluth, and besides the normal political staff and advisors he hired, he brought in one Adam Dempsey, a stranger to the political landscape, as well as just plain strange. But to the amazement of the pros, the guy learned quickly and actually became astute in the "greatest game on Earth." But mostly, he kept to himself, meeting with Truman at odd hours, and performing duties that no one else knew of. When an administrator questioned Truman about the foreign travel expenses for Adam, the administrator was reassigned to another office, and Adam's expenses were redirected to the St. Paul legal firm.

Again, to no one's surprise, Truman Lawrence won the election handily, moved to Washington, and generally did well for his constituency. Lawrence was biding his time, not making any mistakes, doing the correct schmoozing both in Washington and back home, and developing a reputation as a solid player who honored his word, but who would not bow to anyone. He also developed a reputation as a brilliant strategist, a great speaker, and a man of unlimited ambition. Depending on one's point of view and agenda, there was both relief and regret that the man with so much potential had chosen to remain an Independent.

As soon as his age would permit, Congressman Lawrence filed the paperwork with the FEC that would also effectively announce his run for the Senate seat becoming available with the '94 election. This move, too, came as no particular surprise to anyone, but most thought that, as an Independent, his political career had already topped out. Wrong.

The long and short of it was that Truman pretty much bought the senatorial election—with money, smarts, and emotional tragedy (his wife and daughter's deaths). His unconfirmed, but suspected, financial generosity back home set the stage; and his early, extensive, and very creative TV marketing campaign ultimately paid off big time. But even with all that, the voters would not have succumbed to his charms if he hadn't had something good to say. And he did; all of it centered around cleaning up Washington, getting rid of the fat cats, changing campaign laws, getting rid of pork, and on, and on, and on. It was all old news but said in a new and different way, by a man most people had come to trust and respect; and said by a handsome, well-spoken, charismatic gentlemen who would never, ever lead his people astray. His victory margin was significant, indicating a mandate to go to Washington and kick ass. But Truman Lawrence had his sights on bigger game than Washington, D.C.

By the time Metcalf had finished all the *official and limited* background stuff, he was still ready to vote for the man himself—almost. He looked at his watch and agreed with his stomach that it was time to stop feeding his head and go downstairs to find some real food. He left his room, walking slowly toward the elevator while thinking about tomorrow—wondering where he might find Jennifer Bryant and Martha Evans.

"No matter how powerful each of us is, no matter how cool, how smart, how self-confident, how humble, how rich, how pious, or how pretty or handsome we might be, we are all subject to the First Law of Continuum Dynamics:

Karma Rules!

There are no exceptions......"

chapter eight

Roadkill—Mindkill

Southeastern Colorado

Justin was beginning to worry that he'd made a mistake taking the "road less traveled." There was absolutely nothing out here, including potential witnesses to thwart any crime that might be about to unfold. It was the antithesis to the advisory: "safety in public places," as if that concern had been a big deal to their pursuers to begin with. However, there was nothing to do but keep going, crank it up a bit more and hope that the occasional fellow traveler wasn't a radar-toting Smokey.

The journalist in Justin had about a thousand questions to pop on the geezer next time he awoke, knowing full well that he'd remember about three of them, and maybe get one or two answered before sleep claimed the traveler once again. For the past two hours, he'd been left to his own thought processes and imagination to sort out Max's last words. The highpoints had been the importance of "balance," Lawrence's preference for evil, Lawrence's ability to do what he envisions, and—here's the really sick part, Lawrence has a final exam coming up for humanity. It was all a mind blower. Maley had been tempted to awaken Max on several occasions when he just couldn't deal with the unanswered quandaries any longer, but he was beginning to realize how important sleep was to the old man—both on a daily defensive basis, and ultimately in preparation to do battle with the object of his visit to Earth. *God, listen to me. I sound like I've bought this story hook, line, and sinker.* And he had, of course, which elicited a smile. As implausible, hell, make that impossible, as it all seemed when taken as a whole, the individual elements could support no other conclusion—not any longer.

Max announced his return to the living with, "I gotta pee."

"Right. Nice to see you, too." Justin couldn't resist the dig. He pulled over on the shoulder, because there was obviously no place else to perform the act. Having seen about ten cars and trucks in the last hour, Justin now fully expected a couple hundred to come cruising by real slow like, with mothers and kids pointed their way and laughing. But he was spared the embarrassment, as they did their thing and then stretched for a few minutes.

"What time is it Sonny-boy? And where are we?"

"The time is 2:45, and we're on Hwy 160, east of Trinidad, still in Colorado, but not too far from Kansas. Back a ways, when you were asleep, I opted to get off the interstate and take the back roads—at least for a while. Also, we would've had to go way north or south to pick up an interstate going east. But I'm not sure it was the right choice. It doesn't feel good to me out here. It reminds me of a movie I saw once—but I guess you've never seen a movie, have ya?"

Max shook his head in humor, "Justin—I've had more bodies than you can shake a stick at, and between 'em all, I've seen just about everything, I suppose. Yea, it reminds me of 'North by Northwest,' too, but without the cornfields, and I don't like it much either. These old bones tell me they're goin' to make another try on us pretty soon. Let's get movin'. It'd be nice to find some more maneuvering room."

Back in the car, cruise control set, Max offered, "Go ahead and ask your questions, Justin, or do you want me to just pick up where I left off?"

The statement reminded Justin of just how far into the "Twilight Zone" he was, and his automatic grin confirmed that he was enjoying the trip—well, part of it, anyway. "You're right, Max, I've got a ton of questions, but if you can revisit in greater detail the same stuff you were talking about before your beauty nap, that would probably help me with the whole. Can you do that?"

Max didn't respond at first. Instead, he looked around, obviously getting back on track, and looking for the path of least resistance that would allow some enlightenment to find its way into Justin's heart and mind.

"I think the key to everything will be for you to understand the nature and importance of the 'balance' I mentioned," Max began. "I suspect you already know the significance of balance, or equilibrium, on a day-to-day level; but, like everyone else here, you don't extend that significance to its logical limit. You're familiar with the make-up of the atom, with its nucleus, protons, electrons, neutrons, etc.? As you know, the atom is usually in a state of equilibrium—a natural state of balance that keeps it comfortably bound together. Granted, some atoms are slightly less balanced than others, and a few have a difficult time keeping it together at all. And when nature or humans mess around with some atoms, all hell can break loose. In this regard, the Earth, civilization, and the Universe are just like the atom. Balance is a state of contentment, and it governs everything from the lowliest atom to the entire cosmos. Any problem so far?"

"No," Justin replied. "That makes sense, and I can see where it would apply to all things natural. I assume it's people that tend to screw things up, right?"

"Yes and no. First of all, the word 'people' is a distinctly human word that you shouldn't get hung up on. My definition of 'people' is any sentient race, and there are thousands out there. Secondly, there's very little chance, virtually none in fact, that any civilization is going to mess up the balance of their own planet, much less the entire Universe."

"Whoa—I don't buy that. Look what we're doing to our own planet. We're screwing it up pretty good, I'd say. We're killing off species, polluting everything in site, overpopulating the surface— well, you know what I'm talking about. We'll end up wiping ourselves out if we don't get our act together."

"You're exactly right," Max smiled, ready to pounce. "Listen to your words, Justin. 'We'll wipe ourselves out,' is what you said, and it's true. Planet Earth, however, will do just fine, thank you, 'pass the lava please.'"

The logic began to sink in but not completely. Justin asked, "But still, we're hurting the planet—aren't we? How can that not effect the balance?"

"No, Justin, you're not hurting the planet—you're only hurting yourselves. Planets take care of themselves. If they begin to go out of balance, they do something to correct that situation, and if the planet's corrective action isn't real healthy for the resident population—well, that's just too bad. It never happens overnight, mind you, but planets are in no hurry. Only 'people' are in a hurry. Planetary balance to you means pure water, clean atmosphere, snow-capped mountains, great big whales, lush and extensive forests, and happy children without cavities or nasty boils all over their faces. I've got a news flash for you Sonny-boy. Planet Earth couldn't care less about that stuff. That's because planet Earth isn't sentient, doesn't have emotions, and would be as perfectly happy spewing sulfuric acid as it is spewing out oxygen and water."

Maley didn't look happy about this turn of events as he sat there glooming and dooming.

"Sorry to ruin your day there, Gooch," Max said, but he wasn't really.

"Then why the hell should we care so much about treating it right?" It appeared that Justin was so agitated that his brain had stopped functioning.

But Max was prepared to be patient at the moment, "Because to do otherwise has several ramifications, not the least of which is the extinction of the human race. And that's a possibility that the continuum will not idly stand by and watch happen without intervening—unless it's a mass group-Karma thing, then once again, we have no choice but to stay out of the way."

"Max, tell me you're not saying that trying to take care of the planet isn't important. I just can't believe that. It's got to be...."

"Okay, one more time, real slow like: I'm saying to you that humans do not need to take care of the planet. The planet does not need your help. The planet is doing just fine with, or without any intervention from homo saps. Got it?"

"Bullshit!—what about the whales and the trees? Are you telling me we might as well go cut down all the old-growth redwood groves? If that's what you're saying, you're full of it, Max."

Max swung his head away in mock nausea and with consummate derision replied, "Oh, God, another tree hugger...."

"Shove it, Max. Those trees are alive, and they have beings, too. All trees are alive, not to mention the fact that they give us oxygen. They're living things that need to be protected." Justin was really getting pissed off. As is often the case, the problem stemmed from misunderstanding and miscommunication, more than substance. Wars had begun over less.

"You done? Trees, even the mighty redwoods, are definitely living things. No argument. Okay? But Justin, there is one very big difference between a living thing and a *sentient* living thing. Trees, no matter how grand, are not sentient lifeforms. I remember from past lives reading books that refer to great trees having beings attached to them. Pure poppy-cock! Only sentient bodies receive souls. And on the other side in the continuum, there's a soul for every sentient life form in the Universe. Can you imagine how many beings there'd have to be if every grand tree, rock, waterway, ocean, and cave in the Universe had one?

"Damn it, Justin, don't look at me like that. You think trees are special? You think the magnificent redwoods are special? What about the little maple sapling? Not as special? How come? Where do you draw the difference between a tree with a being and one without? Hmm— something about that doesn't pass the smell test. But humans consider the redwoods almost as a race of living giants, and the reason they have come to feel so special, besides their awesome grandeur, is because they've been blessed with enormous group mind consciousness."

A momentary silence befell the Mustang, both men allowing the words to sink in. Justin was also getting tired—physically, from sleep deprivation, and mentally from having to focus on the hazards of driving a two-lane highway. It also didn't help that the lowering sun was beginning to cause some serious glare in his mirrors. He'd be glad to find a place to hole up for the night if that were possible. But with Max's last words, something had just clicked—not well-defined yet, but coming. "Go on. What's this group consciousness thing?"

Max didn't jump in right away. "This could get complicated, Justin, and I don't want to stray from the 'balance' issue yet. Let me do this my way, okay?" Maley nodded.

"Let's finish with the physical planet. I was saying that the planet doesn't care what you do or don't do to it, and that's because it will adjust to maintain its balance no matter what. For your information, by the way, there are many civilizations in the Universe that would consider the Earth to be an exceedingly ugly and uninviting place. That's right. Not all sentient beings are carbon-based, Justin. The Ro-Teks bathe in a liquid that would dissolve your flesh to the bone in about a minute."

"Anyway, when you express concern for your planet's welfare, you need to separate the physical planet from the civilization that inhabits it. Did you hear that? The planet will do fine, no matter what you do to it. Eventually, it may not look the same, but it doesn't care about that, because to care, you must be sentient. However, you, as a civilization, will *not* do fine if you keep mucking things up. In that regard, you are very capable of destroying the somewhat fragile environment that supports your life. That's what you need to stay focused on, and your efforts in that regard will necessarily effect the human-defined *quality* of the physical planet. Unlike the hearty cockroach, the human race has specific needs for survival, and strict attention must be placed on maintaining the balance that works for you. Otherwise, you will all too easily join the ranks of the extinct. When balance is the criteria by which survival is measured, the phrase 'cause and effect' takes on a greater level of significance. You, as a people, need to get this into your thick heads—all of you, all 5 billion of you—and overcrowding is one of your biggest problems, of course.

"Imagine the balance (meaning survival) of civilizations as represented by a teeter-totter in a kids' playground. As long as the length of each side, as well as the load on each side, are equal, the teeter-totter is in balance and all is well. Now, it doesn't matter if the length of each side is one inch or if it's ten feet. Right?"

Maley smiled, "Right."

Max smiled, too, because he could see, now, that Justin knew where he was going with this, which meant that it was starting to sink in. "Most civilizations in the Universe live on a teeter-totter with very, very short sides. Cause and effect for them requires almost instant action, or they risk extinction. That also means that they are very conscious, by necessity. So, balance for them is held within a narrow range. There are, however, a few planets supporting civilizations that live on a teeter-totter with sides, metaphorically speaking, ten feet long. The human race is one of them. As a consequence, cause and effect moves much slower here. It can be quite awhile before anyone, or the group consciousness, knows that there's a imbalance problem looming that needs to be corrected. This delay in discovery and correction leaves you guys wide open for all kinds of mischief, usually in the form of a person with an agenda who achieves a high level of power, and who is totally devoid of consciousness as to long-term ramifications of the agenda. Then, of course, there's the wanna-be despots, fueled by hatred, whose goal is power, chaos, and murder. But there's a good side to all of this, too. For us folk on the other side, when we're ready to tackle some Karmic issues, our preferred choice of destination is good old planet Earth. With that long teeter-totter effect, the possibilities for working through Karma issues are almost endless.

"The preternatural loss of your civilization at the hands of Truman Lawrence would be a severe blow to the continuum—not an end-all, but a great loss nonetheless. And this is.....LOOK OUT!" Max shouted, and his eyes went huge as he frantically pointed straight ahead.

Justin had just glanced at the man doing the talking—the man sharing the secrets of the Universe, but his eyes had left the road and bad things seem to wait for that one moment in time when you take your eyes off the ball, off the road, off consciousness, and then your ass gets nailed but good. The eighteen-wheel semi that Justin had been non-chalantly tracking in its approach toward them had suddenly begun to swerve into Justin's lane and the Mustang's path. A head-on impact was one or two seconds away, and at a combined speed of one hundred forty mph, the Mustang would end up about the size of a toaster. Justin had a split second to respond. Pulling onto the right shoulder was not an option as the rig continued to swerve over the right line as well, anticipating Justin's thinking. One option only: pull into the opposing lane and hope no one was coming on behind the truck. NOW! He did it, but he was jumping from the pan into the fire because the first truck's twin had been hiding in his rear quarter, and the moment Maley pulled over, he was looking head-on at a bulldog emblem well above the height of the Mustang. The first truck went by them with inches to spare but with so much wind turbulence it felt like they would get sucked under his trailing wheels anyway. Still only one option. NOW! And he went onto the opposing shoulder and off the road, again missing the second rig by virtually nothing. The second jerk of the wheel was too much for the Mustang, and on the loose gravel alongside the road, it spun out, doing a couple of three-sixties before coming to a stop in a tangle of enormous sage brush. The loss of friction on the loose gravel had probably kept the car from rolling and, most likely, killing them both. As the car was now pointing toward the West, Maley could still make out the tail-end of both trucks as they continued on their way. Two other vehicles had stopped on the shoulder having witnessed the entire event, and the occupants of both came running to the red coupe.

"You guys all right? Anybody hurt?" was the universal question coming from three or four mouths. *Depends on how you rate scared to death, sir.*

But Maley knew what they meant, and it was time for a body inventory. Max was wide-awake, just stunned. They looked at each other, eyes meeting in silent acknowledgement that they should both be dead, but had instead dodged the Grim Reaper once again. They both began moving their bodies, gently at first, then with greater motion, just to make sure something unrealized hadn't gotten banged up. They got out of the car, walked around a bit, and declared themselves ready for action. The Mustang had gone through an old and rotten sign post that dented the door panel on Max's side. But other than that and a few scratches, it looked ready to carry on, assuming it wasn't stuck in the hard-packed sandy soil. Ironically, the V-8 had never stalled or otherwise shutdown: still purring like a kitten, in fact. Maley got back behind the wheel, put it back in gear, and slowly headed for the highway. The soil had enough binders in it to hold together and allow transport, so the eager helpers walked behind the Mustang back to their own cars.

With all heart rates returning to normal, everyone took stock of the situation: Everyone had seen what had happened, all agreed that it had looked intentional—at least by the rig that pulled into Justin's lane, and no one had gotten any identifying information regarding the trucks. Without the latter, the story was dead. They all knew it but continued to scratch their collective heads in thought before realizing they were all wasting time. And so, it was time to get on with their lives. Max and Justin thanked them all, but they remained at the scene, while the others went on their way.

"Max, we've lucked-out three times now, four if you include the blow-out, and the odds are piling up against us. We need a plan that will even the odds, or eventually they'll get us. Got any ideas?"

"Yea, the first thing we have to do is find a different car. This jalopy of yours stands out like a sore thumb, and I'm sure that's how they're tracking us. Don't get me wrong—they have other tools, too, but as long as we're in this thing, they don't need to try too hard."

"You expect me to dump my Mustang?" Justin asked, starting to feel argumentative. Max didn't reply. He didn't have to. He just gave the writer his "you Moron" look, and Justin caved with a sigh: "Yea, yea…all right…"

"We also need to get back to civilization, where we'll have more options. Taking the side roads obviously isn't the answer. Where are we now?" Max asked.

Maley pulled out the map book, put it on the hood and opened up Kansas. "We're right about here, almost to this junction. We'll either have to turn left for Garden City, or right to pick up another highway for Dodge City. We're really in the boonies, Max. Sorry."

"You've heard the expression: 'Any landing you can walk away from was a *good* landing'?" the old man offered. As Justin smiled and nodded his head, Max went on. "We're still here, aren't we, Sonny-boy? You're doin' fine. How much more driving have ya got in you?"

Maley looked at the map and pointed, "I can get us to here, here, or here," referring to Wichita, McPhersson, or Salina, "but then I've got to have some sleep—some uninterrupted sleep, hopefully."

"Okay, this is what we're going to do…" Max showed Maley how they would survive unscathed until at least the next morning, then they got back in the car and continued toward Wichita.

"How are they trackin' us Max? When I got off I-25 onto 160, I looked real close and there was nobody else that turned-off behind me. I was alone for a long time. So how did they know we were on 160?"

"It's the crows. That's why I enlisted the help of that raptor back in Arizona—that, and to make sure you didn't run too far before coming to your senses." The last was said with a little mirth and closing eyes. It was time for Max's replenishment, and the driver wanted to join him real bad. Instead, he looked out the windshield: one eye on the road, the other looking for crows.

As they had agreed to do, Maley, dead tired by now, pulled off highway 54 at the turn-off for the Wichita airport. Even after three hours, Max was still asleep, but it was time for him to come back in. "Yo, Max," Justin said as he gave him a couple of good shakes. "It's time to play spy, Max, wake up."

The Bringer of Strange Things stirred, opened one blue eye, and asked for a location, which Maley provided, as he pulled into long-term parking and easily found an innocuous space amongst a thousand other cars. When he shut down the engine, he actually patted his baby, thanking it for getting them this far in one piece, and promising to come back for it in a week or so.

"You won't need that long, Sonny-boy. You'll be back by Friday, or not at all," Max corrected him.

Maley noted, not *we*, but *you*—will be back on Friday. They made sure they had everything, which pretty much meant that Maley had his one rolling duffel bag, then they walked toward the terminal. They saw the baggage claim sign, went to that part of the building and found a waiting cab that would take them into downtown, to a "good" hotel. In the quiet of the back seat, Justin asked, "Max, what's going to happen Thursday night? Why did you say that 'I'd be back by Friday'? Where'll you be?"

Looking out the windows as a tourist would is always a good way to avoid answering a tough question, but it was only good for a few moments of stalling before the ploy became obvious. "Max..."

"I heard ya, and I don't feel like talkin' about it right now." Meaning: shut up.

They rode in silence the rest of the way, checking out Wichita at night from some freeway. Maley kept checking out the driver, looking to see if the driver was checking them out. Just then his memory produced the lyrics from a Buffalo Springfield song, generating a nervous laugh: "Paranoia strikes deep, and into your life it will creep." Maley shook his head in wonder as he considered where he was in the universal scheme of things at the moment compared to forty-eight hours ago. He'd gone from being a creatively dried-up journalist to being so full he didn't know where to start. The reality of his present situation also raised his heart rate as he truly wondered if he would be alive or dead at the end of the journey. Given the dedication of the competition, by all rights, he and Max should already be worm food.

His reverie ended as the cab pulled up in front of the Hyatt Regency. Maley paid the driver, led Max into the lobby, but halted and turned to face his friend, with the intention of watching the cabby through the window. The driver was on his radio in what looked like normal dispatch communications, and then he casually drove off.

They allowed thirty seconds or so to pass, then they went back outdoors and waited. Less than ten minutes later, another cab pulled up to drop off a fare, and Max and Justin commandeered the empty cab for their own use. The cabby began to complain, but a hundred-dollar bill calmed him down instantly, especially when he realized they were just going a few blocks away to another hotel.

Playing spy games would work for only so long, and depended on the level of competence of their pursuers. Justin had to assume that Lawrence and company knew who he was by now and that any credit card transactions would be traced quickly. Maley had discovered years ago in his travels to dusty hell-holes in foreign lands that cash was always accepted, whereas plastic was frequently good only for defeating locked doors. The habit of carrying a wad of American greenbacks had never left him, for which he was immensely grateful at the moment.

So, paying cash up front, Maley got a room with two beds, and once they got there, a call to room service took care of dinner. As far as Maley knew, there was no need to go out until morning. He then got on the phone, deciding to use the room phone rather than his cell phone, and called Greyhound for the morning bus schedule to Washington, D.C. With that done, he staggered to the shower, while Max waited for the food to arrive, and found another cable channel featuring Archie Bunker.

Their dinner came without incident, meaning no assassin bellboy, and Max began eating at once while his was still semi-warm. Justin joined him a minute later and immediately wanted answers to questions—answers that could only be provided when Max was awake, which didn't seem to be too often or for very long. "You've left me with a lot of loose ends out there Max."

"Like what?" Max knew just fine, but it was important for him to hear Justin's questions because hearing the question often told you how much the asker knew—or, in this case, understood.

"Come on, Max, you know. How about the 'group consciousness' thing, or the reason Lawrence is doing this, and what it is he intends to do—as in details, and the final exam bullshit. Oh, and by the way, I keep getting sidetracked and forgetting to ask you: is the continuum heaven or not?"

The laughter exploded from Max's mouth, along with a chunk of chewed-up steak and something that looked like bits of baked potato. As disgusting as the sight was, his reaction had been so spontaneous and unexpected that Justin got caught up in the humor of it as well, and they both belly laughed for several seconds. But it had to come to an end, which meant Max had to clean up his mess. "Okay, Sonny-boy, which of those topics would you like to dive into before you fall asleep, or should we just jump right in and get religious? I been wondering when you were gonna get around to that one—surprised it took ya so long."

The old geezer was right about the sleep thing, Justin knew. Despite his ravenous curiosity, in five minutes, or less, he would probably keel over and be off to dreamland. "Here we go again, Max— more distractions, more delays. But you're gonna be in trouble tomorrow, my friend, because I won't have to drive anymore which means I can devote all my attention to picking your brains. And I'll warn you right now: I'm going to want to know all about heaven and hell, God, Satan, Islam, Buddhism, Jesus, etc., etc."

Maley, as he prepared for the sack, couldn't see the wistful look that overcame Max, not until he came out of the bathroom and luxuriated under the cool and crisp sheets of the bed. "Where'd you go, Max? You look like you just saw a ghost—a good ghost."

The Strange-One smiled in acknowledgement, "Get all comfy, young man, and I'll tell you a bedtime story," and that's exactly what they both did.

"I met Jesus one time—the being that is, not the body, just before he took the body that became so famous. This was in the continuum, of course, and I came across him saying his goodbyes to other beings that he'd congregated with throughout the eons. You see, he was *passing beyond,* never to be seen, felt, or heard from again. We were all blipping around, as we're prone to do when we visit one another over there, and our energies fixed on each other for a moment. He was very, very ancient already, as you might expect of one who was about to pass beyond. We merged momentarily, and I was bathed in the recollection of his experiences; and the wisdom that came from him was so beautiful—and simple. And then he was gone. But you know what?"

"Uh, uh," the man under the sheets managed to get out, wanting to hear it all, while struggling mightily to fight off the call of the great white biscuit.

"Something happened, whether by accident or grand design we never discovered, and instead of leaving us forever, he was put into a body one more time—a human body, on planet Earth, in the tiny little berg of Bethlehem. And guess what. He came into that baby body knowing everything: Instead of all memories and powers being shutdown for the duration while 'in-country,' he remembered the continuum, he remembered purpose, his accumulated wisdom was intact, and he had all his powers. He could have been a real tiger, Justin, and—well, I guess he was, just in a different way.

A groggy writer queried, "Why didn't the other side just put a block on his memory and powers?"

"It doesn't work that way, my boy." Laughing and waving his hand around, Max fancifully gestured to the ether: "Rule number twenty-three, section D, sub-paragraph iv. specifically prohibits any messing around of a being/body combo by the continuum once the being is in place—except for very special situations like this one with me and Lawrence. We were stuck, and so was the Jesus being/body. He was the only one that could change things—and boy did he ever. He could have left earlier, meaning allowing the body to be killed earlier, but that wasn't his style. He chose to play the hand he was dealt, but at the same time, it's kind of hard to play dumb when you know the secrets of the Universe. But anyway, I find it kind of amusing that a whole new religion was built around an accident. Don't you think that's kind of weird?"

Too late, for Justin hadn't made it to the end. With his head cocked to one side, soft snoring sounds were coming from Justin's open mouth.

Max sighed. "Oh well, probably better he didn't hear it all anyway." Max didn't head for his bed. Instead, he pulled the padded club chair over by the door to the room, and sat down, not with his back to the door, but facing it head-on. "Alright—you boys want a piece of me, or my friend, come and get it." A more formidable bodyguard the world had never seen.

Day Three

"Back in the days when knowledge was a rare and mysterious thing, teachers, shamans, and philosophers were among the most revered (and feared) personages of the land. Today, now that teachers and philosophers have done their job (and everyone is so smart), they are rewarded by being one rung up from the bottom of the professional appreciation ladder.

"The very bottom of the ladder is reserved for the highly trained social worker whose job is to prevent our angrier forgotten citizens from returning us all to those former days of glory for the teachers, philosophers, and shamans."

chapter nine

Regroup

Washington, D.C.

Astonishingly or not, depending on one's viewpoint and level of cynicism, the "Utah Massacre," was no longer the top story above the fold. With a few simple keystrokes and a fresher supply of blood, its coveted position had been taken over by the latest account of killings in Israel, the administration's futile efforts to make Iraq a "free" country, and the public's reaction to the radical Reardon/Lawrence proposal.

Lawrence completed his review of the morning papers with a smile, as the Middle East debacle was simmering well all on its own, with minimal input from him. He was also a little relieved to find a headline above and more important than the Utah mess. With any luck, that story would be off the front page completely by the end of the week.

On a sour note, Truman knew his nemesis was alive and well, even before confronting Adam, simply because he could feel the being's energy with the antennae of his body—or rather, more like an itch inside a cast on a broken leg—an itch that won't go away and can't be reached. He silently cursed the need to enlist mindless mercenaries that would not question what they were doing, who they were doing it for, or what the end goal might be. The Senator descended the stairs, entered the library, and found Adam on his cell phone. At the sight of his boss, the functionary hurried the call along, knowing that the man would want an update immediately.

"The Mustang's been found at the Wichita airport," Adam announced as he closed the phone's cover. "I've got our people doing computer searches of the airlines to find out where they went, which airline they used, and what time they left. They'll call me back in a few minutes." He closely watched Lawrence, trying to ascertain mood and possible reaction, even though, deep down, he knew it was a futile effort. As he had seen often enough, and recently experienced in a most personal way, the man from hell could readily kill while reading from "The Prophet," and do so without missing a beat or creasing his serene face.

"Truman, this whole thing would be over quickly if you would just get involved yourself. Are you still unwilling to do that?" Adam asked, hoping beyond hope that Lawrence would change his mind. After yesterday morning's lesson, Adam was intensely aware that his future depended on his performance in eliminating his boss's mortal enemy, a supposition that missed the realization that the boat he was in was also shared by Truman Lawrence, and that a catastrophic leak would sink both of them—with no survivors expected.

"And how would you have me explain the trip, not to mention the ensuing events, to the reporters that would tag along or find me wherever I might end up?" Lawrence responded icily to the question. "The only place I can logically travel to on a moment's notice, without raising undue curiosity, is Minnesota; and even then there'll be one or two journalists dogging my every move. That problem is the primary reason I chose to run as vice-president rather than president. Reardon can have all the fame, all the glory, and all the staff as far as I'm concerned." After a brief pause, the Senator went on, "Furthermore, Adam, just in case you're operating under the wrong assumption, if and when our visitor and I ever come together to do battle, it is not a forgone conclusion that I shall be the victor. You'd do well to remember that the next time you do a motivation check. It would be much better for both of us for your bungling band of butchers to take him out long before he becomes a direct and personal threat to yours truly."

Adam's cell phone began beeping before Truman completed the thought, but Adam got the reality message loud and clear, as he answered the phone, "Yea, what've you got?" There was a good 60 seconds of silence as he listened to the minion on the other end, then, "Okay, check the bus stations, train stations, car rental places. If that doesn't turn up anything, assume he might have bought another car, so you'll have to check DMV, or whatever they call it in Kansas. See if you can find anyone at the hotel that remembers them, or talked to them. Maybe someone heard something about where they were going." Another pause, then, "Right, you got it. All right, good work—later."

"Okay," Adam began while organizing his thoughts; "There's no record of them catching a plane to anywhere. It would help if we knew the name of the old guy, but the younger one is Justin Maley, a writer from Los Angeles. Since they met up in Arizona, there's no telling if there's a connection between the two, but that's probably beside the point. Anyway, there's nothing on Maley in the airline computers, so either they didn't get on a plane, or this Maley has fake ID and fake credit cards, and/or paid cash. Even if he did pay cash, he'd have to have a fake ID to get a ticket, or his name would have shown up in the computer. All of that's unlikely, and besides, we show a Justin Maley at the Radisson Broadview Hotel in downtown Wichita last night.

"My guess is they parked at the airport to throw us off—smart move, too—and then they took a cab or a shuttle to the hotel, checked in all normal like, and stayed holed up in their room 'til this morning. They checked out early, but we've got no trail after that. I presume you heard me tell the boys what to do next, right?"

Lawrence nodded, once again at the window, breathing in the quiet beauty of which he tried to surround himself. Planet Earth was such a perfect place—in all ways.

Adam had learned long ago that the boss wasn't one for idle chit-chat; that silence was preferred unless there was something important to say. He also knew, from the look and lack of energy, that the man was in deep-think mode—trying to feel the nuances of his prey. So, he wisely let him be, waiting for the eventual word or words of wisdom.

Truman remained lost in his thoughts and in the garden view for several minutes. His eyes noticed the bright red of a male cardinal at the feeder, and his ears heard the distinctive song of an oriole somewhere hidden. There was much life in the garden, always ready to replace the death and decay—much like the planet that he had chosen for the completion of his work. Several crows noisily approached the garden, landing on a nearby tree branch. As always, their noise and presence disrupted the peace and calm of everything around them, and Lawrence momentarily considered zapping them where they sat for so intruding upon his reverie. But he stopped, for one does not arbitrarily execute the spies that bring the news, even if there's no shortage of them. The spell, however, had been broken. Keeping his eyes on the ominous creatures in the tree, he addressed Adam: "Focus on the bus stations, Adam. They will not have taken a train. Like a plane, a train is a traveling coffin with no easy escape. Nor will they have rented a car—too easy to trace, because, like you said, they will not have false ID or credit cards."

Lawrence finally turned away from the window and faced his right-handman. "They're on a bus, Adam, coming this way. Find them—and kill them."

*"The unspeakable cruelty that some humans
are capable of is exceeded only by the infinite compassion
frequently demonstrated by most."*

chapter ten

Explosive News

Duluth, Minnesota

Metcalf inherently felt uncomfortable in any city that, if not surrounded by water, didn't have at least a significant lake or river adjacent to it—probably something to do with wanting to be able to make a quick getaway. Claustrophobia is not limited to being locked in a bedroom closet, as any claustrophobe will tell you. It wasn't a huge thing for the reporter, but he was nonetheless very relieved to come down the long grade on I-35 with a sweeping view of both Duluth and the magnificent Lake Superior that stretched far to the east, and out-of-sight. A hundred miles back, after getting an early start out of the Twin Cities, he'd passed a town with the incongruous name of Wyoming while he'd been on the horn with Bonnie back in Washington. Besides checking in, he needed several things from her that he would call back on when he arrived in the port city.

Now that he was here and had the info from Bonnie, he could get down to work. Michael Metcalf didn't get to his exalted position by being dimwitted. His smarts and his experience told him that if the "Wicked Witch of the East" (himself) came breezing into town looking for info on the town's favorite son, he (himself) would get exactly zip. In the first place, it's

149

a rare reporter that's looking to do a "good-guy" piece on a major political player. In the second place, once the good citizens of Duluth determined the true identity of the Wicked Witch, doors all around town would slam shut like so many standing pieces in a domino set that were triggered to tumble. And that was the upside. The downside might easily include an armed escort to the city limits, or a night in jail, "which do you prefer Mr. Metcalf?" Small town yokels tended to get a mite protective of their daughters—and their home-grown Senators. Although Duluth isn't exactly small, it isn't Chicago either. But that was the upside again, because in Chicago, if you went after a favorite son, you might easily end up in a gutter in a not so friendly part of the city. It's a crazy business, exposing the deepest and darkest secrets of a corporation—or a powerful citizen.

Metcalf's game plan was simple, and he thought he'd know within a few hours if some kind of story existed to follow up on or if he would be catching an evening plane back home or perhaps to Florida. He was fairly sure now that there was no paper-trail kind of smoking gun waiting to be found. There had just been too much coverage and interest in the Senator's life for that kind of thing to go unnoticed. If there were something there, it would be in the head, or heads, of someone in the know. Most people in Lawrence's life from the '60s and '70s were long gone—some from natural causes, but most from an explosion aboard a very expensive, very sophisticated yacht, perfectly maintained and operated by a crew of six. The two people that Metcalf wanted to find most were Martha Evans, the nanny, and Jennifer Bryant, the tutor for Allison and Truman. If anyone had the goods on the good Senator, it would be either Martha Evans or Jennifer Bryant. Their whereabouts was what Bonnie had worked on that morning.

Bonnie had learned that Martha Evans, most recently of Grand Marais, had died of natural causes six years previously. Just like that, Metcalf's potential source inventory had shrunk by fifty percent, which made his job half as difficult and perhaps impossible at the same time.

Jennifer Bryant had been a challenge, but Bonnie was the master of such searches and had discovered that Ms. Bryant was now Mrs. Harlan Brown, having married in 1972. Although she had originally come from Denver, she had apparently chosen to stay in

Duluth following her tenure with the Lawrence children. Her husband, Harlan, was a very successful chiropractor with several clinics in the arrowhead region of Minnesota. They lived in the hills above Duluth, and that was Metcalf's destination at the moment.

But the address Bonnie had given him could not be matched to any house on the twisty lane, and the reporter soon found that he had become lost in the foreign environment. Eventually, the road he was on made its way back downhill to a larger street with an old service station on the corner—the kind of dilapidated place that every city wanted to get rid of. The only person there to help Metcalf with directions was currently under a vehicle on one of those roller platforms. He grudgingly came out from under a truck and got pissed off real fast when he realized that his efforts wouldn't even result in a dollar's worth of gas. If the big city reporter had developed a little more paranoia, like a certain journalist out West, he might have noticed a significant change in attitude when the gas station owner saw the name and address being referred to. The man stared at Metcalf as the reporter walked away with the necessary information. The man also wrote down the license number of the car the stranger was driving, then he went inside and made a call.

Metcalf had no idea if she, her husband, or anyone would be home. Furthermore, he was very aware that a surprise knock on the door could easily cause consternation, followed by dismissal. But rather than risk the same over the phone, he always preferred the off chance that a face-to-face encounter stood a better chance of an invitation for coffee, or some other midwestern courtesy. At the very least, it afforded him the chance to see some facial or body reaction to his purpose for being there.

The reporter finally found the hidden home. He parked on the street and walked up the long driveway to the entry stoop. No one, nor their car, was visible, but that meant nothing. A few seconds after ringing the doorbell, a woman opened the door wide—obviously with no experience living on the East Coast where the peephole would have been used first, then the identification query, followed, maybe, by a slightly opened door with two or three chains in place and a Louisville Slugger in the umbrella stand.

She was in her fifties by his guess, very attractive, and probably would have been on every guy's "want to date" list back in high school and college. Her hair was cut short, her green eyes were alive and sparkling, and the lack of Northland sun seemed to have been kind to her skin. Jennifer Bryant Brown was the picture of good health and contentment. The reporter wondered if he was about to spoil the latter.

"Yes?" kind of tentative, maybe expecting him to be a salesman or a representative of a proactive church, but still polite and not hostile.

"Good morning. My name is Michael Metcalf of the *Washington Post,* and I wonder if you might be Jennifer Brown, formerly Jennifer Bryant?"

The woman looked at him in the strangest way. There was resolve there, and curiosity, but also a reluctance to go any further with whatever he wanted. But she didn't close the door. Could she have been expecting him? Impossible....

"I am. What do you want, Mr. Metcalf?" she asked.

"Mrs. Brown, I'm doing a deep background story on Truman Lawrence, and I understand that you tutored him and his sister back in the late '60s. Is that correct?" *Please, please, answer the question,* for he knew that once "they" answered the first, innocuous question, the rest came more easily.

Mrs. Brown did not hesitate, being very sure of herself and comfortable: "I am that person. And you're the reporter that broke the story on corruption in the GAO, are you not, Mr. Metcalf?"

She knows me, or my work, that is. Is that good or bad? "Yes, Ma'am, that's me." It was a moment for straightforward honesty—no pushing, no sales job. She was obviously astute and was determining for herself if this discussion would go any further or die on the spot. He'd been here before. It was time to remain quiet.

After a full five seconds of staring him down, of considering every nuance of his face with her eyes, she took the lead: "If you're doing a story on Truman Lawrence, it's because you wish to terminate his political aspirations. True?"

It was also time, apparently, to be brutally direct. "That's correct, Mrs. Brown," he answered, never flinching as their eye contact continued. More silence, more deliberation—then a noticeable sigh....

"You do good work, Mr. Metcalf, and we share a common desire. Would you care for some coffee or tea?"

Yes! "Coffee would be great, thank you, with some sugar and cream." She turned and led him through the house into the kitchen and family room area. The house was quiet, and he assumed they were alone. A strange-looking cat was lying on a throw blanket in a lounge chair. It raised its head in mild interest over the unfamiliar energy, but quickly returned to the business of sleep. Knowing that small talk was essential for easing tensions, Metcalf asked about the cat.

"Her name is Suki, she's a wedge-head blue-point Siamese, and if you're really interested in cats, that's great, but I doubt that. Small talk is not necessary Mr. Metcalf. I'm a willing interviewee, so ask your questions.

Mrs. Brown's bluntness was as disconcerting to the reporter as it was refreshing. "No problem. You may be the only person alive who knew the Senator before 1970, when his whole family died, and to put it simply, I'm curious to know what you remember of those times." Ever cautious, afraid to flush the covey, the reporter kept the inquiry very general, for the moment. He pulled out a small tape recorder, held it up to Mrs. Brown, and asked, "Okay?" She nodded.

Again, she looked at him in a strange way, trying to probe his mind with her eyes, frowning a little. "You surprise me. I would have expected you to be a crusty curmudgeon that went right for the throat, take no prisoners and all that stuff. Instead, you're being all sensitive and considerate. Is that for my benefit? You afraid I'll change my mind and demand that you leave?"

"It's happened before..."

Jennifer nodded her head in understanding. "Well, let me ease your mind. In my opinion, Truman Lawrence is one of the most dangerous men in the world. The young boy I began teaching in 1967 was definitely not the same young boy I left in 1969. If such things were not impossible, I'd swear that some kind of alien took over his body when he recovered from his drowning—an evil, malevolent alien, with a smile on its face. If this Reardon gets elected president, I have no doubt at all as to who will actually be running the country, and probably the world, eventually. It wouldn't even surprise me to learn one morning in the future that President Reardon had mysteriously died in his sleep with Vice-president Lawrence coming to the rescue on his white steed and in his shining armor." She placed his coffee cup on the table, along with a condiment service, two cookies, and a linen napkin. She repeated the move for herself. Metcalf, who had seen and heard just about everything in his life, stared at the woman, all agog, and muttered to himself, *Holy shit!*

She sat opposite him, smiling, and teased, "Cat got your tongue, Mr. Metcalf?"

Metcalf resisted the urge to jump up, come around the table and hug Mrs. Brown until she squealed. She may have just provided him the lead paragraph of a story, but there would be no printed story until there was substantive evidence to corroborate her assertions, and the likelihood of that happening was nil. To his knowledge, the presence of aliens on the planet had never been proven, and he had no illusions about being the one to change that fact. Nonetheless, her position, the confidence and assertiveness of it, and the matter-of-fact, no-hysterics delivery of it, was a real eye opener. And—AND—it supported the weirdness of the word usage in the note he'd received back in Washington: that part where 'what' was used instead of the proper 'who.' Fascinating. It begged the question, of course, if Jennifer Brown was the author of the two letters.

"Mrs. Brown," he began after regaining his composure, "did you write two letters to me at the *Post*. They had no return address, but they both came from Duluth. Were they yours?"

"No. What was in them?" she asked.

There was no point in withholding their contents, so he brought out his copies, smoothed their creases, and laid them upon the table. As he did so, he watched her reaction very carefully, looking for the slightest twinge of reaction, but there was none.

After reading the contents, she observed, "So, at least one other person in this world doesn't think he's the Second Son. Are these the originals or copies?"

"Copies. Why?"

"Because the originals, if on nicer stationery, could possibly be traced to a particular store here in Duluth. If you're intent on finding the author, that kind of thing could help," she offered.

Metcalf nodded in agreement, "An expert on the subject told me the paper is carried by every office supply company in the country. Tracing a buyer would be impossible. But you keep right on thinking because without something solid, there's not going to be any story. A lot of Americans like this guy—see him as kind of like your previous governor but not as rough around the edges. And everyone's tired of the Middle East problems seemingly affecting all our lives every single day. He may be full of crap in some respects, but he knows how to talk to the voters. Right now, today, and with the pathetic condition of the two major parties, it wouldn't surprise me to see Reardon and Lawrence get elected. It's scary. Now, if you will, tell me more about Truman the kid. Everything I have access to is limited to cold, hard facts—nothing between the lines."

So Jennifer Bryant Brown began with the day thirty-six years earlier when she responded to an advertisement in a Montessori newsletter for a live-in, full-time tutor for a twin brother and sister in Duluth. She had responded on a whim, being between jobs in Denver, and was surprised to be invited to Duluth for an interview—all expenses paid, mind you. She met both the father and mother, but the majority of the extensive interview had been with the mother and her sister. She hadn't expected to meet the children unless the interview was going well, and that was exactly the case. Her presence was requested the next day and on that occasion, the children were there. She had enjoyed them immediately, noticing an amazing bond between the two, presumably because they were twins. The long and short of it was that she had taken the position, with a very interesting and lucrative contract. The contract period was for one year. Her salary of $20,000 per year was enormous at the time, but there was a catch: She would receive half her salary each month, with the other half going into an escrow account. If she left before the end of her contract, she would forfeit that portion in escrow. On the other hand, if she completed her contract, she was promised a $5,000 bonus, in addition to the escrowed funds. As all her basic living expenses were covered by the family household, the financial arrangement was exceedingly generous, so she took the position.

Within a few months, she understood why no tutor had lasted more than a year. The kids were wonderful, as was the money. Even the parents were solicitous and kind. The problem was the chaos caused by constant traveling. It was very difficult to get settled into a routine, and just as that might be about to happen, they'd pull up stakes and head off to some other exotic locale. Part of the process was fascinating, as well as being a valuable learning experience for the kids. But it became stressful for the tutors, as evidenced by their annual departures.

Jennifer, however, was able to cope with it well enough to extend her contract for a second year, which delighted kids and parents alike since all considered the woman the greatest teacher ever. It was in the winter of that second year that everything came unraveled—right after Truman's drowning and recovery.

"Care for more coffee, Mr. Metcalf?" she asked.

"Yes, please. Were you poolside when the accident occurred?" he wanted to know.

"Yes. In fact, it was I who raised the alarm. I couldn't find Truman in the group of splashing kids. Then one of the kids stepped on Truman—he was lying motionless at the bottom of the pool, directly under the others. The lifeguard was in and out of the water in under ten seconds and went right to work on the boy."

The host filled both their coffee cups and offered some more cookies. The reporter watched her movements—precise and efficient. This was not a person given to excesses or exaggerations.

Jennifer continued the story—that part that had never found its way into newspapers or the 11:00 P.M. news—10:00 P.M. in Duluth. She described the arrival of the emergency team, the despair of all those present, the heroic efforts of the lifeguard and fire department rescue squad to revive her student—all to no avail. Finally, she ended the account with the defeated look of the medics, the covering of the body with a blanket, and the placing of Truman on a gurney that raised up for ease of rolling along the path to the front of the house.

"I went to the gurney, to touch his arm or head—I don't know; I just wanted to say goodbye, and I stood there crying and reflecting on who he'd been, and who he might have become. That's when it happened—when he sat straight up with a jerk. He had come alive after being dead for thirty minutes. The blanket fell off his face, and he turned his head and looked me right in the eyes; then he smiled and he said, "Truman's back." I don't know what kept me from fainting, but I didn't, and I stared right back at him, in shock I'm sure. I didn't put it together until later, but that was the first moment, the first clue for me that this was a Truman Lawrence different from the one that I'd known for a year and a half. The smile he'd shown me wasn't the loving, caring Truman smile, but a distant, secretive smile—

and completely insincere. It confused me, and frightened me, besides the fact that he had just risen from the dead."

The teacher went on to describe the hospital stay, the testing by the psychiatrists and therapists, and the return to everyday normal life. Except, she said, there was nothing "normal" about it. "By the way, whoever wrote those two letters to you must have been at the Florida hospital at the time—perhaps a staff member, since he, or she, knew about the psychiatrists.

"To anyone who didn't know Truman," she continued, "nothing had changed. He was his old charming self. To those of us with daily contact, however, his name might as well have been Tom, Dick, or Harry. The Truman personality was gone, Mr. Metcalf. Try to imagine the effect if you can. It was very unnerving. As bizarre as it was for me, it was downright horrifying for Allison. Here was her eight-year-old brother with whom she had always had such a strong bond, and all of a sudden, there's no longer a bond at all—nothing, zero. She took it very badly, and it began to affect her whole life. She ceased being the lover of life. Her insatiable curiosity took a ho-hum turn, as did her openness and affection. If you ask me, I suspect she was heading for big trouble with depression and other related problems."

"But the boat accident took care of that," the reporter interjected.

"Yes. Did your research turn up anything on Truman's mental acumen following the drowning?" As Metcalf gave a quick shake of his head, Jennifer Brown related to him the apparent change in his academic abilities, her request to have him tested again, the results of his IQ test, and her subsequent discussions with the administrator regarding certain anomalies. "The administrator of the test told me that if his IQ were the 201 she suspected it to be, he would probably be the most intelligent person she'd ever encountered, perhaps of all time. Hers was no self-serving claim, Mr. Metcalf. It confirmed what I had already come to suspect. If Truman had faked the test results, there was little purpose in my challenging him as to the reason. Obviously, he was trying, in his own failing way, to dumb-down to the old Truman's level, which was above normal to begin with. He could pull-off that strategy with a test here and there, but on a day-to-day level, there was no hiding his superior intellect."

"For instance?" the reporter prodded.

Jennifer thought for a few seconds, then offered, "Whenever a question-and-answer-type game show came on the television that required some serious knowledge, Truman always knew the answers—no matter how obscure the question—always, and that was much different than before the drowning. There's something else, also—quite disturbing, now that I recall it: Sometimes during conversations, whether on TV or at social functions at the house, I would hear him speak the words of the talker *before* the talker began speaking. It was very weird."

"Did you ever ask him about this ability?" the intrigued reporter asked.

"No."

"Why?"

"Because I was afraid....." The pause gave them both time to massage their own thoughts.

Finally, "Where are you going with this, Mrs. Brown?" as fascinating as this all was, it was time to cut to the chase.

The teacher snickered and looked past her guest, over his right shoulder, beyond today—to the past.

"Mr. Metcalf, no one would have been surprised had the doctors come to us and predicted that Truman would be different from then on. After thirty minutes of dubious, mechanical induction of oxygen to his brain, we all expected the worst. We all know that a traumatic episode like that, if not fatal, is almost certainly the precursor for years of psychotherapy. We all expected it; we were all prepared for it. None of us was prepared for the stranger that returned to the house two days later. We gave it time, as time heals all wounds—right? Wrong—it just got worse. On all levels but one, the resurrected Truman Lawrence was a superior human being. The missing element was right here," and the teacher touched her chest. "Truman Lawrence no longer had a heart. He was emotionless; he was cold, and that shit-eating grin he'd developed couldn't conceal the fact."

"There's only one logical deduction that can be made from such a development, Mr. Metcalf, but unfortunately, that deduction is impossible. Therefore, we're left with a paradox, a mystery, and this one never did show signs of just disappearing into oblivion."

"And just what is your impossible deduction?" he asked

"Why, that his body was taken over by some alien presence, of course. He's possessed." Jennifer Brown smiled, and went on, "Try printing that—see how far you get with that little exposé."

The two looked at each other in silence for a good minute. The ticking of a grandfather clock could be heard in the background, causing Metcalf to check his watch and consequently breaking the spell. "I suspect there's absolutely nothing to substantiate any of what you've said?"

She shook her head.

"So, you fulfilled your contract, then you left?"

"Yes. It was very painful, especially for Allison—and for me. If I could have, I would have taken Allison with me. You know, the parents didn't even try to change my mind. They knew, Mr. Metcalf. They knew that something wasn't quite right, that their home and family were a health hazard to be avoided, and in hindsight, there was some danger there for all who remained. They wished me well and gave me a very sizeable departing gift. Truman, by the way, wasn't the least interested in saying goodbye. He was somewhere else, tearing off butterflies' wings, I suspect. And, in retrospect, that was probably the greatest proof of all that Truman was no longer Truman. The boy I knew would have been an emotional wreck at my departure—clinging, crying, wanting to go with me." She shook her head again. "There was none of that. Allison and I wrote to each other for a while, but three or four months later, my letters went unanswered, and I stopped writing. In another couple of months, the family was back in Florida, and then the boat blew up. The rest you know."

There was silence again, a final silence, as the reporter rose and made his way toward the door. He released a huge sigh, and thanked Mrs. Brown for her hospitality and openness.

"What will you do now, Mr. Metcalf?"

"I'll be catching the next plane for Washington and continue with my other projects."

"You're not going to follow up on Lawrence, go to Florida, try to expose him in some way?"

"With what, Mrs. Brown? This is one of those dead-end stories that we frequently run into. You have experience with the man as a boy, and you have an opinion—an interesting one to be sure, but there's obviously no story, no evidence, no witnesses—other than yourself, and I've wasted enough time on this one already." He stood, put his recorder away, thanked her again, and turned for the front door. She almost jumped from the table to follow him, clearly not wanting the reporter to leave, but apparently unable to stop him.

"Mr. Metcalf…"

He was at the door, opened it, and turned to face her. "Mrs. Brown, it is obvious that you have very strong feelings about this man, and for all I know, you could be right on. Hell, I'm sure that something about him is wrong. But you have given me nothing to sink my teeth into, and I will not write a story that will damage another person's character without unimpeachable evidence to support what I'm saying. Now, unless you have the proverbial smoking gun stashed away in an attic foot locker or something, we both need to let this go. Do you have such an item, Mrs. Brown?"

Jennifer stood there in the entry, stared into the reporter's eyes, but said nothing.

"I thought not. Goodbye, Mrs. Brown, and thank you again." The reporter went down the steps of the stoop and had taken one stride along the walkway when her words stopped him cold.

"Allison's alive, Mr. Metcalf. She survived the explosion."

Frank Mulligan had casually taken the call on the fourth ring, not being familiar with the phone number on the caller ID. The voice at the other end, however, was instantly familiar as that of the Swede, a lowlife if there ever were one, and therefore a great asset to have in one's pocket.

Mulligan was a licensed private detective, complete with office and secretary, but he had only one regular client, and that one client seldom needed his services. It was as good a sweetheart deal as there ever was, as an office and a secretary didn't eat up much of his $20,000 per month retainer, and the balance was all his. One could do a lot worse. On the other hand, when his phone rang with a Washington, D.C. area code, he'd better be ready and available for anything—and he was. Adam Dempsey had hired Mulligan right after Truman Lawrence moved to Washington as a junior congressman. His purview was inordinately simple and general: protect the good name of one Truman Lawrence, and don't get caught doing it. Dempsey had chosen well when he enlisted the aid of Mulligan. The man was smart, a little brazen, and absolutely knew how to take care of himself. There were rumors regarding the latter...

Mulligan had been given few specific instructions, but one of them regarded a Ms. Jennifer (Bryant) Brown, former tutor of a young Truman Lawrence, and Martha Evans, the kid's nanny. If either name came up in any way other than Teacher of the Year, or some such thing, Washington wanted to know about it—yesterday. The special instructions had been made clear to Mulligan, and he had made his own local minions aware of the instructions as well. So, when the Swede called about a man seeking directions to Ms. Bryant's house, the first thing the detective did was to get one of his gophers into the office, hand him a digital camera, and send him to observe the subject's house. If the Ford with Minnesota plate ZRT312 were still there, the gopher was to wait, watch, remain unseen, and get a picture of the visitor if possible. With that done, he called the number in Washington—a number he had memorized long ago. The answering party was not the Dempsey guy but some broad that took the information and the license plate number. She assured Mulligan that someone would get back to him within the hour.

The return call didn't take an hour, not even five minutes. This time Adam Dempsey was on the phone, got the story straight from the horse's mouth, and then told Mulligan he absolutely had to get a picture. Adam then put Mulligan on hold to take another call and when he came back on the line, Mulligan thought he was talking to some entirely different person, as determined by stress level and pitch of voice. The man in Washington was nervous, and his revelation told Mulligan why: the license plate was for a Budget rental car that had been rented last night in Minneapolis to one Michael Metcalf, whom everyone in Washington knew, Adam informed Mulligan, was an investigative reporter for the *Washington Post*. The shit was about to hit the fan.

In every investigative reporter's professional life, there's a distinct, staccato moment in time before which there is no story, and after which, there is. Something or someone falls into place, like the last piece of a jigsaw puzzle, and the whole collage suddenly pulsates with a life of its own. From that moment, it becomes a story looking for a place to happen, and there's no stopping it.

In truth, Metcalf didn't know if that moment had just occurred, but it sure felt like it, and those slap-across-the-face feelings are rare. He was turned away from Jennifer Brown when she dropped her bomb, so she was unable to see the look in his eyes and on his face. It was the look of personal victory, as if he had just discovered some incalculable piece of information that was going to change the world. That, of course, remained to be seen. He turned back to face a very-serious-looking woman who was at once frightened and relieved to be free of a heavy burden.

"I think we should go back inside," Metcalf said, pulling his trusty recorder back out of his pocket.

She led the way, but this time she headed for a desk in the living room. From a cleverly hidden secret nook in the desk, Jennifer pulled out a piece of paper upon which were a name, address, phone number, and an email address. She made a copy and handed that to the reporter. "Don't lose this, and don't, under any circumstances, allow anyone else to get their hands on it."

"Talk to me, Jennifer. May I call you Jennifer?" She actually looked at him before responding, realizing that this would earmark a subtle change in their relationship. She nodded. "How did she survive? Where is she now?" forgetting he had that answer resting in his hand. "Has she been hiding? Why?" He knew he had to stop with the questions if she were to begin answering any of them, but excitement is an emotion difficult to control.

"She lives in a small cottage in the woods about forty miles from here—very isolated. Although she has moments of lucidity, she's mostly gone bye-bye—not crazy, just not normal. She can't drive, but she's mostly able to care for herself. She cooks and stays clean. Unless she gets worse, her doctor thinks she can live independently indefinitely. She's the one that wrote those two letters to you. I take her for drives—she loves to ride through the forests and along the shoreline—and on two occasions, she asked for a mailbox. I questioned the wisdom of such a move, but she insisted the letters go out, and she also assured me there was no way they could be traced back to her.

"I'm not her keeper, Mr. Metcalf. Harlan and I help her as we can, but she's free to do as she pleases. Harlan and I are the only two people in the world who know who she really is—until now, that is. When she's lucid, she remembers everything, and she knows the evil her brother is—or believes he is. She's obviously aware of his political ambitions and, more than anyone, she knows how important it is to stop him."

"How did she survive the explosion?"

"According to Allison, everyone on the yacht was asleep except for one or two of the crew. Allison had been asleep also, but she woke up from a dream—or, at least, she thought it was a dream. In the dream, her brother was in the engine room doing something with tools. It had to be a dream since Truman was still in Florida, sick with the flu. But when she woke up, she had the nagging feeling it wasn't a dream, more like a vision. So, she got up, put her robe and slippers on, and went aft to determine the veracity of her vision. Upon entry into the engine room, she indeed saw her brother fiddling with something, but it wasn't quite her brother. What she saw was an outline with a hazy image of Truman within the outline. Please remember, Mr. Metcalf...."

"Please, call me Michael."

"Remember, Michael, that this is all coming from an incredibly traumatized little girl who later suffered amnesia. I'm just relating to you what she told me. Anyway, she watched the ghostly image for a moment and then challenged the figure to explain what he was doing. She said the image didn't respond, as though it couldn't hear her—as if it were unaware she was even there. It was then that she smelled fumes, and noticed a cluster of dangling wires above her brother's image and to his left. A sign above the wires said 'Alarm,' with smaller printing below that she couldn't make out. She suddenly understood what the phantasm was up to, so she turned to run for help. She made it to the bridge and began screaming for the crewman there to follow her to the engine room, where her brother was doing something bad. That kind of talk, from a nine-year-old that was obviously having a bad dream, fell on deaf ears. The crewman tried to convince her that she had just had a nightmare and that she should go back to bed. But it all came to an end when a thunderous explosion emanated from the bowels of the yacht. Both Allison and the crewman looked down the passageway, seeking some sign of explanation and level of damage. The roar continued and then a wall of flame came racing around a passage corner and directly toward them. The last thing Allison remembers from the yacht was the crewman picking her up, kicking open a door and literally throwing her into the ocean, followed by one of those orange life rings. She was okay, and when she looked back at the boat, the above-deck structure was completely engulfed in flames, including the crewman who had just saved her. Allison grabbed the life ring and began drifting away from the wreck."

They had been sitting in the living room, but Jennifer realized that she had been neglecting her guest. "Are you hungry, Michael? I am. Let's go back to the kitchen and I'll fix us something." She led the way and began bringing out the ingredients for making sandwiches. The woman was on a roll now, finally unburdening herself of a secret weight she had carried for so many years.

"Allison wasn't sure how long she drifted, nor even the direction she was going. She does know that she floated for at least one complete cycle of day and night. For a while, she saw planes in the distance, probably searching for survivors, but she was just too small a target to be seen. Also, there was some weather coming, and the swells had started affecting view lines. She thinks she either fell asleep or became delirious because she lost track of time and doesn't remember how she ended up in the hut of a man she would come to call Robby—after Robinson Crusoe."

Jennifer put placemats on the table, brought the plates over with sandwiches and chips, and offered the reporter any of a variety of drink. When she sat down, she took a bite of her lunch and continued with Allison's recollections, full mouth and all. "She thinks she spent six months on that island with Robby. He was quite elderly, she said, and had apparently been living there for many years, eating off the land, repairing his hut with whatever flotsam he could salvage from the beach, or from plant and tree life. There was good water nearby—in short, everything that was needed for survival was there. This Robby character was kind to her, no funny business at all, and he taught her 'his hermit ways' as she referred to them. It was a slow learning process, as Robby didn't speak a word of English, and

Allison's French was only two years old in training. Much of what she learned was of the watch-and-see variety. As far as Robby knew, they were the only inhabitants of the island, and there was no way to communicate with the outside world. This was all apparently fine with Allison because, at the time, she didn't know she was Allison. She says she didn't remember a thing of her past."

"But that changed as the weeks went by. An image here, an event there, and sparks of memory began returning. She began remembering Duluth, me, Martha, her parents—and her brother. She started thinking a lot about her brother, beginning with the drowning incident and how everything had changed after that."

"This probably won't constitute corroboration for your story, Mr. Met—Michael, but Allison and I are in full agreement, despite the impossibility, that Truman's body was taken over by someone or something." She smiled at the reporter, and said, "How are you going to wrap up that package?" Metcalf slowly shook his head back and forth—there was nothing to say or do.

"Anyway, as her memory returned, she developed a mental list of needs and goals. She felt no burning need to get off the island; the island had probably been the safest place in the world for her over the previous few months. But she knew that sooner, rather than later, she would need to get back to civilization. The trick was to do so without alerting her brother to her presence, for she had no doubt that he would not be pleased to learn of her survival. Another 'accident' could then happen at any time. Obviously, no one would believe her story, so any kind of accusation was out of the question. The world probably thought she was dead, and it might be better if things remained that way.

"I remind you, Michael, that all this was coming from a nine-year-old. Necessity is the mother of invention, yes?

"Everything came to a head one day when Robby slept in way past Allison's wake-up time. This had never happened before and Allison knew right away that he was either very ill or dead. It was the latter. According to Allison, she didn't panic. She buried Robby, knowing that she now knew enough to survive but also knowing it was time to get off the island. Through limited vocabulary, pictures in the sand, and sign language, Robby had made it known to her that leaving the island shouldn't be difficult. A light raft would be easy to build, and the trade winds and currents would take her far enough out that someone on a boat, ship, or plane would eventually spot her. The big thing to remember was to take covering shelter for the sun, plenty of water, some food, and avoid the hurricane season. She hadn't been sure when hurricane season was, but the rest was easy. She built herself a small raft, secured a pole in the middle for her canopy, collected all the necessities, and shoved off—pushing off the sand as far as she could, then paddling. It wasn't long before she was adrift, once more, and heading away from the island."

"Did she ever figure out which island she was on?" the reporter asked.

"No—only that it was somewhere in the Bahamas Archipelago. It wasn't long before she was picked up by a couple in a sail boat enjoying their vacation. Her youthful appearance belied a sharp mind and a body that was in excellent condition—for being dead six months. Wanting to remain that way, Allison feigned amnesia this time around, and the couple bought the act completely, as they changed course for the nearest port city."

Jennifer began to giggle, obviously over some memory that came to the surface. "What is it?" Metcalf asked.

"Oh, I was just remembering Allison's recollection of her body's reaction to her first few days of normal food. The poor thing lived in the head for hours. One time, she knew she wouldn't make it, so she dropped her drawers right there on deck, held onto the railing, and squatted over the side."

"The nearest port of size was Grand Turk in the Turks and Caicos Islands. Given her age, the couple didn't anticipate any problem from her as they escorted their charge to the local government office. As they passed through a crowded market area, she took off running, found a place to hide, and later kept an eye on the couple's sloop so she'd know if and when they left. They were the only people that knew her face, and she didn't want to risk running into them on shore. They left several hours later, so she could then proceed with her plan: she found a phone, someone to help her, and she called me long distance, person-to-person, collect."

"She had your number? How?" Metcalf asked.

"She knew it by heart. We talked frequently when she was in Duluth. But even when the family was traveling, I'd get calls from her."

"That must have been a freaky phone call for you...."

"You have no idea. If it hadn't been so cryptic, I probably would have fainted. The operator said the call was from a Molly. The only Molly I knew was Allison's old doll. I accepted the call, and I knew instantly that it was her. She didn't want to talk too much on the phone, but she made it clear she needed my help. We made arrangements, I went to my bank and got a bunch of cash and traveler's checks, and I flew to Grand Turk as quickly as I could. I found the open market she had described, along with a certain café. I made the café my home until she sauntered in as confident as you please. I couldn't believe it. My little Allison was alive after all the grieving I'd done. God, we hugged and hugged, and then she told me everything, over heaping plates of food and Cokes."

"I was very proud of her, Michael. She had survived an ordeal that would have killed most others. And she seemed to be in pretty good shape emotionally. Little did I know...."

"So, how did she end up here?"

"It was actually easier than I expected it to be. I knew the absence of a passport would be a problem for her any place other than U.S. territory, so I found a funky air freight outfit that agreed, for a substantial price, to fly us to a remote little airfield on St. Thomas. That was the scary part, but once that was behind us, the rest was easy. However, it was while we were on St. Thomas that I saw Allison's first episode of some sort of psychological disorder. She seemed to forget who she was, who I was, where she was—in short, experiencing amnesia for real. She went into a semicatatonic state, although she didn't appear to be a danger to herself—you know, like swallowing her tongue or something similar. I was scared to death. I didn't know the island, and no one was around—which was probably a good thing. Otherwise, I'm sure I would have rushed to some hospital in a panic, and the truth would have all come out. Instead, I just found shelter and held her, hoping that she would be all right. Eventually, she seemed to fall asleep, as did I. When I woke up, she was lying in my arms looking at me, and she smiled and said, 'I love you.' I cried, she cried, and then we talked about what had happened. She remembered nothing about the spell she'd just experienced, but she also remembered nothing of the duration of the spell. She understood this could be a serious problem in our plans for returning to Minnesota, but what choice did we have?"

"We flew out of St. Thomas without problem, landed in Miami, then flew to Milwaukee. I didn't want to risk flying into the Twin Cities: there was just too good a chance that someone would recognize Allison, the 'Darling of Duluth,' you know. I rented a car at the airport and drove the rest of the way. As my connection with the family was completely over, I never had occasion to see any of them in person, and I assumed that my apartment would be a safe place for her. So, I had Allison move in with me, temporarily, until we could figure out a long-term strategy. The thing was, she could absolutely not go outside for risk of being recognized. She became a voluntary prisoner in my home. She didn't have another episode for about a week after our return, but then it was worse, and longer, than the first one."

"That living arrangement went on for over a year until I met the love of my life, and I no longer wanted to keep him away from my apartment. At first, I claimed Shannon—we'd taken to calling her a different name—as my niece from a troubled home in Miami. But as Harlan and I approached marriage, it was time to bring him into our secret. At first, of course, he was totally confused and didn't understand why we didn't go to the police and make it all public and all that sort of thing. But as we got further and further into the details: the history of the family and the abrupt change in Truman, and even our quirky suspicions, Harlan backed away from logic and decided to take a wait-and-see approach. After all, what was the harm, other than having a strange girl living with us?"

"We got married, and Shannon continued to live with us. When I discovered that I couldn't bear children, the devastation I felt was somewhat tempered by having Shannon as part of our family. By mutual consent amongst the three of us, she quietly became our surrogate child, and we all loved each other very much. We moved into this home where it was unlikely that any prying eyes would notice Shannon. I continued to home teach her, and that went well. Her episodes would come at unpredictable times, with unpredictable duration, but the characteristics were always the same. About ten years later, her episodes began getting consistently worse. Still, she steadfastly refused any sort of medical intervention. The greatest fear in her life was that Truman would discover her existence and come to kill us all. I, for one, believed her. And as Truman's career in politics began to evolve, Harlan began wondering if there might be substance to our suspicions after all."

"Somewhere around Shannon's twentieth birthday, she asked us if she could move into the cabin. The cabin was Harlan's parents' getaway and became ours when they died. We spent a lot of time there as a family, and she really loved the place, the forest, and all the critters; she thought it would make a perfect home for her. It was still secluded, without any connection whatever to her real identity. Other than the possible worsening of her episodes, she would be completely safe there, and so, we all agreed. She's been there ever since. She's a forty-three-year-old hermit, Michael, and she seems to have adjusted quite well. She writes prolifically but has made no attempt to publish her work—mostly poems and short stories, which I think are excellent. With the advent of the Internet, she has developed many chatroom-type relationships across the world. It's fascinating and wonderful, until she has another spell. I once didn't hear from her for two days, so I went up to check on her. She was gone, who knows where. I remained at the cabin waiting, and about twelve hours later she walked in, very dirty, but physically okay. She couldn't account for three days—the longest episode to date. She's okay with it. She's okay with the possibility that she could die as a result of some problem while in the middle of an episode. She's very clear about that."

"Will she see me, do you think?" Metcalf asked.

"I think so. When she mailed those two letters, she was quite aware that she was throwing a string out into the world, and that you might follow it back to its source—even as unlikely as that seemed to be. For that to happen, we both knew that the trail would go through me. She authorized me to use my own judgment in making her existence known to whomever. You passed the test, Michael. Now it's up to you."

"Let's go see her."

"Right now?"

"Yes, right now," Metcalf said, anxious to see where this could lead.

Jennifer went to the phone and made a call. After a long time, she said, "It's me, Honey, give me a call as soon as you can. Love you. Bye." She hung up the phone and thought for a second, then, "Where are you staying, Michael?"

"I don't know. I didn't know if I'd be staying overnight. Should I?"

"I don't want to just show up with you in tow, and there's no telling if she's just away for a minute or a day. We never know...." The phone rang, and if it had had a caller ID screen, Jennifer would have seen that the call wasn't from Shannon, but from some unfamiliar area code. She answered it and almost instantly a frown appeared between her eyes, and her whole countenance radiated worry. "Hold on...." and she handed the phone to Metcalf. "It's for you."

Michael took the phone at once, assuming it to be Bonnie, as she was the only person in the world who knew he might be here at this moment. "Metcalf ...."

"Mr. Metcalf, I have a call for you from Senator Truman Lawrence. Would you please hold for just a moment?"

Oh fuck!

"Mr. Metcalf? Are you there, sir?"

"Yes, I'm here. Put him on."

"Thank you, sir."

The reporter looked up at Jennifer who was desperate to know what was going on. He started to whisper the name to her, but was cut off by the television-familiar voice coming through the handset.

"Mr. Metcalf, I'm glad I was able to locate you."

"Hello, Senator Lawrence, what can I do for you?" Jennifer cupped a hand over her mouth in fear of letting out a yelp, and sat down across from Michael. She was obviously very frightened.

"Well, actually, Mr. Metcalf, I think it's what I can do for you. I understand you're doing some deep background on me, I presume in preparation for an article. In all honesty, Mr. Metcalf, this concerns me because the whole world knows that your articles are usually, shall we say, unflattering. In fairness to me and James Reardon and our campaign, I hope you will provide me the opportunity to fill in any blanks you might have come across, and also to comment on any blemishes you may discover. I'll be in Duluth in the morning and would be delighted to meet with you at, oh, say eleven at Leif Erikson Park. What say you to that, Mr. Metcalf?"

Metcalf was frantically and silently trying to weave his way through the bullshit, but there just wasn't time. Besides, it was a perfectly legitimate request as well as a generous offer, bullshit or not. And a "park" sounded public and safe enough. "Eleven will be fine, Senator. Where shall I meet you?"

"At the rose garden, Mr. Metcalf. I do love roses so much. I'll see you tomorrow then. Oh, and please give my regards to Ms. Jennifer—it's been much too long since I paid her a visit. Good day."

They both hung up, and Jennifer was all over Metcalf to know how the Senator knew where to find him. He shook his head and called Bonnie, who assured him that no one even remotely related to the Senator had been in touch with her. So, either he was using some kind of mumbo-jumbo magic or Metcalf was being watched.

"He must have someone here watching me, Jennifer. I'm so sorry not to have been more careful. I will, of course, stay away from you and from Alliso—Shannon—until I know what's going on." He reached into his pocket and removed the slip of paper Jennifer had given him earlier. "Here, you keep this—better that I don't have it right now." He held out his hand on the tabletop, and Jennifer took the piece of paper, then placed her hand over his.

"Michael—do you know what you're doing? This could be dangerous. Hell, I know it's dangerous. You pose a serious threat to him, and if Truman Lawrence is anything like what I suspect, you'll be walking into the lion's den. I'm worried for you, Michael." Jennifer was clearly holding back tears.

The reporter was touched. It had been many years since anyone had opened their heart to him in any fashion at all.

"I assume Leif Erikson Park is a public place?"

"It is. If you must do this, just make sure you don't go off alone with him anywhere."

"It'll be okay, Jennifer. Besides, this is what I do. If I'd called his office and requested an interview, they would have laughed at me. Now I'm getting a one-on-one. It doesn't get any better."

Metcalf left shortly thereafter, and took Jennifer's advice on a hotel selection, choosing the Canal Park Inn down at the waterfront. He took a drive before dinner, finding the park and the rose garden easily enough per the directions given him. It looked to be fine, and he began formulating his thoughts and questions for the interview the next morning.

*"**Faith** is a crucial element in the make-up of human beings. It matters not what foundation the faith rests upon, as long as it exists: It has to do with the belief in a Grand Mystery to be solved.*

*"As with all things in the Universe, **balance** exists for the faithful: The atheist's belief in the great Nothing is just as valid as, and complementary to, the religious person's belief in the great Something.*

*"A body without **faith** is a body without hope and is a hollow shell of what was once unlimited potential."*

chapter eleven

Revelations II

Kansas City, Missouri

The food at the bus station restaurant was the worst they had had on the whole trip, not that the journey was all that long yet. By the end of the meal, both men were purposefully making their way to the restroom where they would share a brotherhood dump together, à la Justin's fraternity days back in Norman, Oklahoma. Apparently, when in Kansas City, a visitor unfamiliar with the gastronomic landscape is advised to stick with steak and potatoes, or perhaps it was just bus station cafés in general. But their suffering was short-lived and certainly more digestible than a Mack Truck in the face or barbecued ribs (their own) in some cowboy clubhouse.

In reflection, the morning, beginning in Wichita, had been completely uneventful, the preferred state of affairs. Max had awakened Justin at 5:30 A.M., and received a graphic litany of bad words for his effort. But somewhere in the waking-up process, Justin noticed that Max's bed was undisturbed, and that there was a chair, with a blanket, in front of the door. His diatribe ceased when the significance of the two circumstances became apparent. "My bodyguard," he muttered and headed to the shower.

After Justin had paid their hotel bill, they had a light breakfast and then walked to the Wichita bus station on South Broadway where they bought tickets for Philadelphia, knowing full well that they would take a detour somewhere en route. They both did an initial check for suspicious characters but quickly gave up the hunt as the place was *full* of suspicious characters. They decided, instead, to wait for someone to devote special interest toward them, but in reality, they presumed to have a few hours grace period before they would need to fine-tune their paranoia antennae. By the time Adam's crew was discovering the Mustang at the Wichita airport, Max and Justin were heading out of town on a scenic cruiser, heading first for Kansas City.

The bus was surprisingly comfortable and reasonably quiet, and there was a pleasant sense of security being surrounded by people and riding high above the roadway. If they could remain anonymous, this could actually work out okay. So, they got all settled in, then Justin fulfilled his promise to his partner: "So, you're implying that Christianity was, and is, an accident?"

The old man chuckled, "I thought you were asleep when I made a reality adjustment to that part of your history."

"Max, now that you've opened Pandora's box, what's the connection between the continuum and religion?"

"Why—nothing; absolutely nothing. Religion is a man-made product, Justin, and those of us on the other side who enjoy observing the foibles of humankind on planet Earth find the whole invention utterly fascinating—particularly the day-to-day machinations."

"I suppose you're talking about the hypocrisy angle?" the younger man asked.

"Of course. It's everyday. It's virtually everywhere. And it never stops. It's almost overwhelming in its ludicrosity. Therefore, all us fans in the continuum gallery can't get enough of it. Nor, it seems, can humans. Oh, and here's the really bizarre part. When one of us takes a body on the planet, the required memory block goes up, we forget all about those observations, and we dive right back in with everyone else—join the crowd. Have I told you I was a pope in a previous life? Yea, well get this: I called myself Pope Innocent! Boy, it does get weird. Never a dull moment when you're in a body, Justin—never."

"But we wouldn't change a thing, don't ya know?" Max continued, and his words surprised Justin, who looked at the old man in confusion. Max, seeing the look, went on, "First of all, we can't change anything—not in soul form. Only when we're in bodies can we change anything, not that there's any certainty we will, mind you. But even if we could change things as souls, I don't think we would. Earth works, Justin, and if somethin' works, ya don't fix it."

"Max, how can you say that? How can you say 'the Earth works'? To refer to ourselves as a civilization seems more and more to be a contradiction in terms. All across the planet, people hurt and kill one another each and every day. Cruelty, in almost infinite variety, happens constantly."

"Yea, I know, and a lot of it frequently happens in God's name, right? Or with God's guidance, or His blessing, with God on whoever's side, and on and on. Isn't it wonderful?" Max picked up the day's newspaper. "Here's a case in point," he said, pointing to the latest headline from Israel. "This struggle, which has been going on for a lot longer than you can remember, by the way, involves two races, each with its own religion. Both peoples believe in God. Both peoples have God on their side. Both religions espouse generally wonderful and logical laws that would really and truly serve the people well if the followers would only observe the laws. The faithful dead of one religion will go either to Olam Ha-Ba, while the other deceased will go to a heavenly place filled with forty virgins."

Max could not contain himself, but nonetheless tried to control a wheezing giggle. "Sorry, Justin, but after awhile, it all just gets to be too much."

Justin sat there shaking his head, looking out the window. "You see what I mean, Max? Religions are crazy—and dangerous."

"Oh, they're not particularly dangerous yet, planetarily speaking; but still, you don't know the half of their craziness. Consider: Either there's a bunch of different Gods up there, down there, wherever," and he almost lost it again, "or these religions all share the same God. Which could it be? And here's the real mind-blower for me. These Israelis and Palestinians? Well, they're all related. They're all genetically connected. They all come from the same family—according to their religions. Each of their scriptures says that they came from Abraham's seed. Brothers and sisters are killing each other everyday, despite the admonitions of their 'good books,' despite the protestations of their God; but regardless, they still have God on their side."

That was it; Max the philosopher was gone again, laughing heartily, and this time it would be awhile before he recovered.

Justin the human being, the one who had to live on this planet day by day, was not amused. It was his backyard that was getting trashed, and he found no humor in the situation. Screw the Karma thing, and screw the balance thing, too. He just wanted the hate and killing and greed to stop, go away forever, and for the Earth to be one big happy place. Although there was no shortage of troublemakers around the world, the Middle East, birthplace of modern humanity, birthplace of the "Son of God," birthplace of compassion, seemed to also be the focal point of hatred and war on the planet. Maley knew a little of each religion—enough to know that, in a just Universe, God would be frowning on both sides. Ergo, either the residents of Palestine were complete morons, or the foundation of their respective religions was flawed, or both.

Justin wanted to lighten his mood, so he took another tack with the geezer: "So, Max, were you a nice pope?"

"Hell no. I killed, raped, pillaged, and plundered with the best of 'em—either directly or through my Holy Blessings. I did nothing to curtail the activities of Christianity's armies in their exuberance to clear out the countryside of nonbelievers—all in the Lord's name, of course. I'm still paying off the Karma from that trip. But, boy, did I ever get some gorgeous sculptures created. Some paintings, too, but especially sculptures. The artists in those days were something else, Sonny-boy. Those were good times. But the temptations were mighty. That was the downside, and that, of course, was what I wanted to work on when I chose to take a body. Best laid plans of mice and men..." and then the ex-pope got serious again. "You know, Justin, evil comes dressed in many styles."

"What do you mean?" It was obvious that Max had hit upon something of meaning to himself, probably some memory, and it looked like something he needed to share.

"Pretend that Jesus really was the son of God, and not an accident. Between you and me, Justin, even though he wasn't who everyone said he was, his heart was good, as were his words—religion or not. Anyway, when he sat at a table for his evening meal, do you see him with the jewel-encrusted golden cup and plate of a King?"

"No—simple and plain."

"Right. I'll never understand how his later followers could misconstrue his teachings and deportment so grossly. When I was pope, there wasn't a single simple mug or plate in the place. Not one! Everything in there was gold, brass, silver, rubies—something 'precious.' That whole place is a shrine representing some theology that is the absolute antithesis to what the man Jesus preached that day in the temple square as he faced off against the money changers. So, how in the world can the Vatican claim to represent the beliefs and teachings of Jesus under such conditions? The religion they represent encompasses the world and includes millions upon millions who are extremely poor and undernourished, yet those in the Vatican drink the blood of Christ from golden goblets every evening before snuggling into their comfy beds—right after whispering bedtime prayers for the lost souls of the Earth. It really is ironic, my friend—and bizarre."

Max's reverie ended abruptly. He came back in, looked at Justin with a refreshed twinkle in his eye, and closed the book on his Vatican days with a final rumination: "I wish the Jesus being hadn't left the continuum. It would be great fun to watch him come back into a body today and react to these managers of his legacy. You talk about a rip-roaring ass-kicking in the temple. Oh, folks..."

Now Justin joined Mystery Man in the light-hearted giggles. "That would be a sight, all right. But, Max—even as screwed up as religions have become, you feel no desire or need to change them?"

"Of course not—can't anyway, remember?—not without a body. I take it you're not getting the importance of Karma yet, and the importance of a high-conflict environment for working on Karma."

"High conflict?"

"Yea—war/peace; cruelty/kindness; hoarding/sharing; forgiveness/revenge; etc.—contradictions, like with the various religions. Things like that. That kind of environment gives the weak body plenty of opportunities to mess up—to choose poorly—to do things unconsciously. The teeter-totter sinks on the collect-bad-Karma side. But, by the same token, your planet offers the same opportunities to behave honorably—to choose well—to act consciously. Around here, Justin, we beings can fix an awful lot of screw-ups in just one lifetime—if, and when, the being/body partnership gets its act together.

"As a pope, I had a great opportunity to repair some Karma. Unfortunately, as a weakstick body, I succumbed to all the temptations, and succeeded in piling up a huge Karmic debt. C'est la vie. Still, you'd think that common sense would tend to keep people out of trouble. For instance, this Middle East thing: if a father is going to teach his kid to 'hate thy neighbor,' he also needs to teach his kid that what goes around, comes around. I mean—what's the problem? Don't they understand that little concept? That's kind of basic, ya know. So, early on, parents jump right in there and help their young children to build their own Karmic debt load to work on. Thanks a lot, Mom and Dad."

Justin thought about that for a second, then, "God—Max, how in the world does the planet stay balanced that way? The way you describe it, we should have gone down the toilet long ago."

"Don't worry about it, Justin. Just like the newspapers and the evening news, most of what you hear about is the bad stuff. There are just as many folks on your planet that make good, conscious choices as there are those who don't. Like I've said before, you're doing okay—your balance is in the green for go. That is, until a being/body comes along like Truman Lawrence. Then we've all got a problem."

"You haven't told me yet why he wants global chaos. And what, exactly does that mean, anyway? What's he going to do?"

"If left unchallenged, he will turn Earth into a wasteland," Max answered, "both physically and spiritually. He will help every human being find his or her own individual dark side and assist them all in bringing it to the forefront of their lives, exaggerating it, and using it to invade the space of others. Soon, the dark side will prevail in people-to-people interactions. This will become evident in increased killings, bigotry, hatred, rapes, levels of cruelty, narcissism—well, you know the drill. War, pestilence, starvation, and pollution will harvest humans in record numbers. He will make every effort to subdue the level of consciousness within the group mind, and he can do it, too. Once the group mind consciousness level goes, you, as a civilization are in very deep trouble. And understand this, Justin: The ultimate death of the human civilization is not his goal—that would be okay with him, but it's not what he wants—not at first, anyway. Misery needs an audience. Evil, too, needs an audience. Did you hear that, Justin? He does not necessarily want civilization to perish: just to be miserable. Truman Lawrence will want to be acknowledged as the absolute leader and bringer of both. He will want to bask in that acknowledgment. Only then will his work be complete. Only then will he be able to leave the continuum forever—at least, that's what he believes."

"To go where?"

"That's way beyond what you need to know, Justin, so forget it. Don't go there," Max adamantly replied.

Shit! "Okay, yesterday we were talking like this was a final exam or something. Is that still right?"

"In very loose terms, yes."

"Alright, so he completes his dammed test, he graduates, and then he gets to leave the continuum and go somewhere, someplace you won't tell…. Wait a minute! He'll 'pass beyond' the continuum? Is that what you mean?"

Max looked at Maley, trying to see what he'd just put together, but it was jumbled and coming too fast. His companion took the silence as a positive response and went on:

"Max, those are the same words you used to describe the Jesus being's departure. Are you telling me Truman Lawrence would end up in the same place?"

Without the need to keep his eyes on the road, Maley was able to devote full, uninterrupted attention to the old man sitting next to him, whom he was about to throttle. This couldn't be right because it was totally ridiculous. Nonetheless, Max was showing a slight grin, a "welcome to the big leagues, kid" kind of grin, accompanied by, "Congratulations, you got it. I suppose that sounds kind of crazy, huh?"

The very-frustrated Justin derisively snorted, threw up his hands in mock surrender, and said, "Oh, hell no. Fuck! What's the problem? Jesus and the Devil, walking side-by-side through the pearly gates. I suppose they're going to see their creator, God. Oh, yea, I see now—they'll take a seat on each side of Him, right? You know—the right hand of God, and, oops, the left hand of God as well. I got it now, Max. Geeze, whatever took me so long?"

"You understand perfectly, don't you?"

"Screw you, Max! I understand nothing because nothing of that line of bull makes any sense." Maley wanted to get up, leave the bus and the crazy coot sitting next to him, but that was not an option at the moment. Instead, he remained seated and stewed in frustration.

"No, I suppose not—not unless you're conscious of both sides of the teeter-totter. For bodies, for humans, the words are simple, but the actual living concept of balance is a different matter all together. When I say to you: 'Justin, balance includes the dark and the light,' you say to me 'Great—no problem.' However, when I tell you that Truman Lawrence is on one end of the teeter-totter, and Jesus is on the other, that they both came from the same place, and that they're both returning to the same place—well you have a little harder time with that one, don't you, Sonny-boy. You get kind of whippy on me."

"It's not that simple, Max."

"Au contraire, Justin. The great truths in life are always simple. It's humans that make them complicated—open to interpretation—no doubt by the popes, rabbis, and mullahs."

A pensive Justin kept the dialogue alive: "You're saying that Truman Lawrence is necessary? No—wait a minute, that's not right. Lawrence is an anomaly that you've come to reign in. What you're saying, though, is that good and evil exist at the same time, are both necessary, come from the same source, and will someday return to the same source. Is that it?"

Max blessed the writer with a generous smile. "Yes, that's it. Simple, eh?"

Maley went limp, way deep inside himself, all the while staring at the man who was in the process of changing his whole life, a man to whom he was feeling closer and closer, saying things that Justin wanted to believe—he thought. But Justin was just not ready to accept the Truth according to Max the Mysterious. He had to get past his own interpretations first; his own meddling in reality. He had to get out of the box and think differently.

Justin started up again, "The logical conclusion of this balance thing is that evil things, or bad things happen just as regularly as good things. Furthermore, they're necessary. Oh, shit, Max. That means that doing bad things is okay—like, like killing someone is okay?" Maley began vehemently shaking his head. "No way, Max, no way. I don't buy it."

"I wouldn't either, put that way. Nonetheless, you're on the right track. You just need to let me fill in some crucial blanks. Killing someone, murder, is a good example to use because it is so extreme." Max stopped abruptly, thinking of something else, then started up again. "One brief side trip, Justin, before I go on, and it's about extremes: The Universe does not tolerate extremes for long. Like a magnificent meteor shower that burns brightly for several nights or an epidemic that brings unspeakable despair, things extreme eventually fizzle just before a return to normalcy. And do not confuse 'normalcy' with mediocrity, my friend. All successful civilizations are just a notch or two either side of equilibrium. Perfect balance, although possible, is boring and leads to stagnation. Exceed the four-notch spread, however, and the civilization in question almost always perishes, regardless of which side of the teeter-totter it happens to be on.

"Now, murder is an extreme, and I'm talking Karmically, not just physically. Bodies don't matter. It's the being that matters. When a body is killed incorrectly, which is about ninety-nine percent of the time, the being is ripped from the body, from its Karmic work, and sent reeling back to the continuum. You with me? It's a very traumatic, devastating experience, and there's an enormous Karmic debt incurred by the one, or ones, doing the killing."

Max went on: "Murder is almost always an unconscious act, otherwise it would seldom happen. Forget wars—that's a different issue. And forget Truman Lawrence's kind of killing because he knows exactly what he's doing—it's completely conscious."

"So what?" Justin finally came to life. "What's the big deal about killing someone consciously or not? They're still dead—damage done. You're telling me that Lawrence can mess up the whole world without having to pay for it Karmically?" He shook his head some more, then, "Keep going, Max—you haven't reached me yet. Oh, and what was that bull about bodies not counting? If someone kills me, I'm not going to be too fucking happy about it, Max. You know what I mean?"

"Yes, it will be traumatic for you as a body, Justin, but just for a brief moment; then your body becomes an organic sack of sushi. Everything that really mattered goes back to the other side, where it came from, whereas your body lasted somewhere between zero and ninety years or so. Your family, if you had any, would suffer much more than you—which, by the way, is part of the Karmic price to be paid by the killer.

"When a body is murdered, the killer does not give any thought to the ramifications of his actions beyond his own personal emotions and the earthly risks involved—like being caught and executed. Oh, now there's an interesting scenario: execution, all legal like, slowly planned, appealed, etc., etc. That one can get real weird, especially if the powers that be execute the wrong person. Oh, man—stay away from that one, Justin; it gets so messy. Anyway, the killer doesn't have a clue about the continuum and Karma, and more importantly, the future. The killer, in most instances, has just altered the future of civilization. Did you hear that? The future of humankind has just been altered—maybe just a skosh, but maybe a whole bunch, too. You know the story: the victim was destined to someday be a partner in a union that would give birth to a prophet that would be able to stop the mess in the Middle East, thereby saving hundreds or thousands of lives. And now it's not going to happen because some scumbag had to go and kill one of the planned parents of the prophet. And that happens all the time, of course—dozens of times each day, but mostly right here in this 'land of freedom' of yours—the handgun capital of the planet. You wouldn't believe the adjustments that have had to be made over the centuries as a result of someone important to the future being arbitrarily bumped off in the present.

"Then we have the Truman Lawrences of the Universe, the troublemakers, the ones that throw a wrench in the works. But, I suppose they're also the ones that keep us on our toes."

Max's eyelids had been drooping for a while, and he finally informed Maley that he had to nod off for an hour or so. It was becoming a pattern to set a watch by, and Justin had no problem with having to wait to find out what made Truman Lawrence tick. At least he'd gotten a warning this time.

The nap turned from one hour into almost two, with Max conveniently coming back to "life" upon their entrance into Kansas City. A few minutes later, the bus driver announced that they would be coming into the terminal in ten minutes, that they'd be there for one hour, then continuing the trip on the same bus, bus number twenty-two. He stressed the importance of being back at the bus on time, as it would definitely leave at 1:16 P.M. sharp. To the future chagrin of Max and Justin (and probably others), he informed the passengers of the "decent" restaurant within the terminal.

"The greatness of civilizations must be measured not only by their magnificent achievements and their finest minds, but also by the condition of their most forgotten citizens."

chapter twelve

Bleeding Hearts

Washington, D.C.

Since the announcement on Sunday of the Independent ticket's proposals regarding the Middle East, the media had been clamoring for time with the candidates—time to clarify, time to challenge, time to belittle the ideas, time to do—whatever. It was an inevitable request and one that Truman Lawrence relished, more so than did his more sedate running mate. But Reardon was the top-half of the ticket, so his presence was required.

Following a private lunch together, during which Reardon's food received a liberal pinch of Lawrence's psychic magic dust—one simply couldn't leave a press conference this important up to mere mortals—they entered the Ballroom of the Willard Hotel, under noticeably increased Secret Service protection. The press conference began at 2:00 P.M. with an opening statement by presidential candidate James Reardon. It was an excellent lead-in address, as one might expect since it had been "fine-tuned" by Senator Lawrence, and it set a positive and feverish tone for the question-and-answer session to follow.

But before the candidates could field any questions, Reardon, who had begun complaining of stomach pains shortly after lunch, heaved his chunky beef and vegetable soup all over the podium table. For the most part, those close by saw the gags first and were able to retreat from harm's way before the first cluster bombs emerged from their launcher. Cameras, of course, were clicking away with ferocious intensity over the newsworthy event as, in gross embarrassment, Reardon left the area in search of a restroom with his security people in tow. As is always the case, the staffers were left with the unenviable task of cleaning up another presidential mess (well—almost presidential). Ever the quick-thinking, considerate gentleman, Truman Lawrence pulled the focus away from the brownish-green pile to the right of the podium as he moved to the left end of the table and picked up a wireless microphone. Thumping it a couple of times to verify its status, and to get the attention of the reporters and TV news people, Truman apologized for the disturbance, indicating that his running-mate had been complaining about stomach pains earlier, and that he was certain the event wasn't life-threatening (ha-ha). "In the meantime," he said, "neither of us would want to keep you waiting, and I'm sure Senator Reardon would want me to proceed with the press conference. Therefore, if you're ready, I'll take the first question."

That did the trick, and the pack all took their seats, with maybe thirty hands rising in unison, along with a few shouts. The Senator knew most by face and name, and he knew whom to select to point his comments in the preferred direction. "Yes, Tom."

Tom Stevens of the *New York Times* stood and began: "Senator, as I'm sure you know, virtually every expert on the Middle East, along with leaders the world over, have condemned your and Senator Reardon's proposal for the region as being, and I quote Stanley Morris here: 'an asinine proposal from an odd couple that clearly doesn't understand the dynamics of the region,' end quote. Any comment, sir?"

The Senator smiled and in his most charming, unassuming voice, replied, "Well, Tom, if you're a Stanley Morris fan, I reckon we might as well go home and close shop." There weren't many fans in the room of the ultra-rightwing Morris, so the comment was good for a general round of laughs. "First of all, Tom, there are at last count three world leaders and two Middle East specialists that have come forward in support of the idea—in general. Gratefully, Senator Reardon and myself no longer appear to be on the raft by ourselves," good for another laugh.

"But, Senator, what chance would you have of getting any legislation passed to support such an abandonment of Iraq, Israel, and our policies there?"—a follow-up from the *New York Times* reporter.

The question appeared to perturb Truman Lawrence, who gathered his thoughts and took his time in answering. Actually, the question didn't bother him at all, but it was show time, and in politics, showmanship is nine-tenths of everything, with substance making up the remaining tenth. Only the truly gullible believe that the leaders of a nation get elected for their intelligence, moral fiber, and leadership. They get elected because of an awesome political machine, charisma (for better or worse), money—and largely due to the ineptness of their competition.

A very serious-appearing Senator Lawrence responded: "Let's get something straight right now, ladies and gentlemen. James and I are very aware that this proposal could cost us any chance we may have had of winning the election. We didn't just dream up this plan as some sort of desperate sound bite. We've been working on this issue for quite some time, trying to figure out how to break the Jewish-Palestinian stalemate, and do so in a positive direction. The disaster we now face in Iraq only served to intensify the need for withdrawal from Middle East affairs. As you'll be reading from our detailed proposal in the press kits, we've done our homework and talked to many experts who believe the time is right for a change of policy, if carried out in the correct manner. Some of those experts are members of our own House and Senate, and I wouldn't be too quick to assume that we have no support. If the august members of those institutions can be convinced to vote their hearts and minds rather than their promises to political affiliations and PACs, you will find that many of our leaders are fed up with business as usual over there." A Secret Service agent approached Lawrence, handed him a note, and then withdrew.

After reading the note, the Senator advised the room that Reardon had bowed to the requests of his staff and gone to the hospital for a quick checkup, and that he expected to be back on the scene first thing in the morning. Lawrence pointed to a TV newswoman. "Lisa…"

"Senator, you just said, quoting, I hope, '…many experts who believe the time is right for a change of policy," and at this point the newswoman paused, raised her head and spoke directly to Lawrence as she emphasized, "if carried out in the correct manner.' End quote. What did you mean by that, sir?"

"What I mean is this, Lisa. Walking away from the Israel debacle in particular, and the Middle East in general, is a bold and potentially very dangerous move. When we do this, we must first of all have a clear consensus within our own country. We will be delivering a firm and historic message to everyone with this move, the effects of which will be lost on all parties if the support back home is marginal, with constant bickering between supporters and nonsupporters. Secondly, when the decision is made to proceed with the move, there can be no vacillation, no 'wishy-washy' stance on the matter within the Congressional membership. We must be forceful, consistent, and without any mixed messages—unlike what we have experienced for so many years now. Last, all key members of the administration itself must be in complete agreement with the plan, or they shouldn't be part of the team. We've all seen problems in that regard in the last four years, and we've been witness to the credibility stigma which ensued."

"Yes, Charlie," and Lawrence welcomed Charlie Yates to the capital. Charlie, senior reporter with the *Duluth News Tribune*, had followed Lawrence all through the politician's career.

"Sir—how can this possibly work? Logic says that the moment we wash our hands of the area, all hell's going to break loose, that the blood bath will be total, and that the whole world will side-off and get drawn into an inevitable war. Senator, the people back home with whom I've spoken are scared. They want to know we won't all die as a result of this kind of policy shift. The folks back home are all for you, Senator, but you're taking us to the edge with this one. What can you say to your constituents, sir?"

Oh, thank you Charlie, thank you. The room went silent with the import of the question and what might be a make-or-break response to the naively sincere newcomer from the Senator's hometown. Lawrence knew it as well, and milked the moment for everything it was worth while refreshing his throat with some water. For a moment, for that's all it took, he worked on the group mind within the room, mockingup an acceptance of what he was about to say, with subsequent positive accounts going back to their respective news organs. He looked at Charlie, then down to the lectern, and then lifted his head to take in the whole room—really thinking hard, preparing to open his heart to the good and innocent citizens of America.

"Charlie—there are no guarantees in life, besides death and taxes, of course," no laughing this time, just a twinkle in his eye verifying that we all know it's true. Slowly, deliberately, and oh so sincerely: "The way things stand today, we have no assurances whatever that the Middle East crisis isn't going to take a turn toward some unanticipated direction next week or next month and bring the whole house of cards tumbling down upon us all. What I do know, or at least believe, is this: it is the height of either arrogance or naiveté to think that the United States of America, or any other 'do-good' country can go into a foreign area of multiple, warring tribes, place our diplomats or soldiers between the factions, and expect a permanent cessation of hostilities, much less the end of underlying animosities. Besides being a nearly impossible endeavor, we have a poor record of getting it right. Inevitably, however bad the situation was before our arrival, it eventually becomes worse *with* our presence, and worse still after we depart in hopeless frustration, often bloodied.

"That doesn't make us a bad people, or a bad country, or inept. It only demonstrates how different are the various cultures on planet Earth. With good intentions, the American government has, for a long time now, made a point of trying to control hostilities in a land that has been experiencing hostilities ten times longer than the United States has even existed. As regards the Holy Land especially, has it not occurred to anyone that, like two people living in an abusive relationship, the Israelis and the Palestinians might be co-dependent—co-dependent on each other, on violence, on their mutual victimhood? If the Jews didn't have the Palestinians to focus on, and the Palestinians the Jews, might not each direct their frustrations and hatreds inward toward their own kind? You think that's ridiculous? Look at Lebanon, people. And I remind us all that there's no small amount of tension in Jewish Israel among members of the various faces of faith: the Haredim, the seriously observant Zionists, and the secular Jews.

"The Palestinians, of course, have lived as antagonistic tribes under various warlords for centuries, so destroying themselves would be nothing new."

Lawrence stopped for another sip of water but quickly went on before the media took it as a sign to begin asking more questions.

"No, ladies and gentlemen, until the people of the region—on both sides of the conflict—the herders, the students, the farmers, the shop keepers, the lenders, the mechanics, the builders—until the citizens tire of the incessant bloodshed and associated poverty, and come to terms with the fact that the other side isn't going to go away, that the land will have to be shared—until that day comes, there will be death and bombs and burials—impenetrable wall, or no. Either the people will choose leaders with the vision to make peaceful coexistence happen, or there will be extinctions—just as with any life form whose habitat has been decimated.

"The point is this: Neither the United States of America, nor our allies, have any business interfering in the day-to-day or year-to-year activities of two peoples who seem intent on destroying each other, and who will gladly bring the rest of the world along for the ride—if the rest of the world allows them to do so.

"In the meantime, because of present policy—more or less the same policy for the last fifty years—our presence in the region, either physically or diplomatically, provides false hand-holding assurances to everyone that nothing really, really bad is going to happen, hopefully—just the usual day-in and day-out skirmishes in which mothers, children, fathers and, rarely, a combatant are killed.

"The Arab world especially, but just about everyone seems to believe that the United States has veto power over any move the Israelis might be considering. I assure you that, even if the recent messages from 1600 Pennsylvania Avenue had been early, decisive, and consistent, the Israelis' terrorist cleanup of the last three years would have proceeded regardless. All efforts at reason dissipate when a nation-state believes its very existence is being threatened, and it no longer matters what the diplomatic repercussions might be. You deal with that when the gun to your head has been removed. But that's beside the point."

The Senator paused for another drink of water and to ascertain how the spiel was playing. As all occupants of the room seemed to be more or less mesmerized, he accepted that as a sign to continue without any change of tactic. Still, he reinforced the group mind once more before continuing—opportunities like this could not be wasted.

"One of the criticisms of our proposal is that, without our stabilizing presence, the two peoples will go on a rampage of killing, with the Palestinians within Israel quickly being wiped out. I don't buy that assessment, and here's why: First of all, Israel would be slitting its own throat *economically*. The irony of their mutual economic interdependence is laughable, given their willingness to spill each other's blood. In terms of brute strength, however, the Israelis have seldom looked for a fight, but when fight they must, it's usually they who are still standing when it's all over. Add to that the absolute given that they will never, ever, under any circumstances allow their homeland or race to be expelled or exterminated (by outside forces), and you have the makings of a 'stop at nothing' army of fighters. The Palestinians know this. The Arab world knows this as well. The Palestinians know that the Israelis could take them out in record time, should they choose to do so, and if the only thing that would keep Israeli tanks in their lauders would be the cessation of all hostilities, I believe the Palestinians would offer up an olive branch very quickly. The alternative is fairly obvious."

From the back of the room: "But the other Arab countries would intervene and come to the Palestinians' aid. Then we'd have a huge war and maybe even the elimination of Israel."

The Senator shook his head. "It will never happen, Lou, for a couple of reasons. The Muslim countries already know, have known for many years, that Israel is there to stay—unless the Israelis allow themselves to self-destruct. They found out the hard way via a couple of bloody-nose wars, and that was before Israel was generally known to have nukes. Any Muslim state, or states, that seriously go after Israel now know that the price for their possible success will most definitely be their doom. They won't do it, and no amount of begging or tears or blood coming from the Palestinians is going to change that. All the Muslim saber rattling we see and hear is face-saving political chess, using the Palestinians as the pawns. It's a sad commentary on the human condition; it's unnecessary, and the time has come for the game to end."

"What about oil, Senator Lawrence. Aren't you forgetting the gas lines of the '70s? If pushed too far, OPEC could retaliate again. Is it worth it?"

"You tell me, Janet—is it worth it? Is the long-term conversion of weapons into plowshares worth the threat of an oil slow-down, of having to conserve on our oil consumption, which is something we should be doing anyway? I'll leave that question for you to answer, but consider this: The Gulf region is no longer the only landlord of major oil reserves. Even more important, we, as a people, as a global civilization, are so interconnected that such a move by OPEC cannot be taken any longer without risking instability within their own countries. I remind you that not one Persian Gulf OPEC member state has a democratically elected government. Not one. That should tell us all something. They depend on the flow of oil-generated cash to maintain political stability just as much as we depend on the flow of oil to maintain economic stability.

"Yes, Rachael." Rachael Townsend of the *San Francisco Chronicle* had just returned from Tel Aviv, where she had personally witnessed a gruesome restaurant bombing.

"Senator Lawrence, assuming you're correct in your analysis of the situation, do you think peace can be achieved in the area with the present leadership?"

"No, Rachael, I don't," Truman shook his head, "and here's why. Ariel Sharon loves fighting. He'd rather fight than talk any day of the week. It's unfortunate that he can no longer be at the head of a tank column because that's his forté in life. He and Patton would have loved each other, or killed each other, and probably both. Don't misunderstand me here: If fighting is absolutely the only game in town, then Sharon is definitely Israel's best bet for a leader. He's decisive, he's brutal, and he knows how to win a battle. But as a visionary with peace and tranquility as the goal, he was lost before he ever took his first step. Unfortunately, the current political scene in Israel is so fractured, so— chaotic, it's difficult to see how any one leader could emerge with enough of a mandate to turn the country toward any sort of relief. And, as for Yaser Arafat, it doesn't really matter if he stays or goes."

"What do you mean?"

"You don't think Arafat really runs things over there, do you?" the Senator chided. "Remember, this is still a tribal society we're talking about. Arafat is the colorful, well-known mouthpiece that speaks for at least twelve faction leaders, and as such, he hasn't solely steered the Palestinian ship in years, if ever. I worry, however, that, as irrelevant as

Arafat is as a leader, he would make an extremely effective martyr. The Palestinian leadership will know this, of course, and I wouldn't put it past one of their warlords to murder him and plant evidence implicating a crazed Jewish settler as the assassin.

"Even when Arafat has left the stage—by whatever means—whoever replaces him will be in exactly the same boat, in terms of having the faction leaders to deal with. In the end, it will come back to the people—it always comes back to the people—and how much strife, corruption, and greed they are willing to put up with. When the Palestinian people have had enough of their generals and corrupt politicians, they'll let the world know."

Lawrence pointed to Mike Jensen of *Newsweek*. "Mike—Oh, how's little Sarah doing, Mike?" referring to the toddler's recent car accident.

"She's going to be fine, Senator—thanks for asking. Sir, by pulling back from Middle East affairs, couldn't that be construed as acquiescing to Osama bin Laden's demands and his stated motives for attacking the United States? And do we really want to send him, and the world, that kind of message?"

The Senator politely waited for the reporter to finish his questions although he began nodding in understanding early on.

"Mike, Senator Reardon and I are more concerned with substance than appearances. If doing 'a thing' is the proper action to take, should we not do that thing because of concern over appearances? The current administration might choose that course, Mike, but I for one consider deceptive moves like that to be demeaning to the American people, as well as to our allies."

"However, Mike, I want to answer your question more directly: As far as we've been able to ascertain, bin Laden's big objective was to punish the United States as the 'Great Satan,' and for our presence in Saudi Arabia, his homeland. Well, whatever moves we make in the area will be of our own choosing and in concert with the appropriate governments of the area, and not because of Osama bin Laden. If there's a message to be sent, that's it."

"A follow-up, Senator?" Jenson quickly asked, to which Lawrence nodded.

"Sir, do you have anything to say about the way the President has handled the Osama bin Laden situation? Is there anything you and Senator Reardon would have done differently?"

"Initially, no; both James and I concur with the way the President responded to the 9-11 attack by invading Afghanistan, seeking to root out and destroy bin Laden and his supporters, the Taliban. However, it is extremely unfortunate that the President allowed himself to be distracted from that rightful pursuit, having left the job only partially done. The more than 100,000 soldiers and support personnel that he has sent to Iraq in wasted effort would have been much more useful scouring the countryside of Afghanistan. As we all know, the Taliban is making a comeback. Kabul does not the country make, and warlords and tribal mentality rule the land outside of the capital. Without a very strong UN presence throughout Afghanistan, it is reasonable to expect the 'bad old days' to return. As much as James and I would prefer to bring the troops home from Iraq, there's still a job for them to do in Afghanistan, and that's where they should have been all along. The genius mad-man who has become such a thorn in our side is still alive and apparently well. I am dismayed that the Commander-in-Chief of the most powerful military in the world allowed our current nemesis to escape the arms of the justice he so rightfully deserves."

"And the Reardon-Lawrence ticket could do it better?" this from Franklin Thomas of the *Los Angeles Times*.

Truman Lawrence looked first at Franklin, then briefly at the others in the room, then down at the lectern. Clearly, ostensibly, and totally for the benefit of the cameras, he was a man debating with himself on whether to pursue the subject, or not. On that decision, though, there had never been any doubt. The act over, Senator Lawrence continued:

"I suppose you all recall how seldom the President has mentioned the name Osama bin Laden in recent months?" Everyone was aware of the fact, and Lawrence went right on. "Although James and I concur with the man's decision, I'm confident that our reasons for doing so are very different. I suspect that bin Laden's avoidance of capture or death had become such a serious embarrassment for the President and his administration that, by mutual agreement, all the senior staff determined not to speak his name or talk about him unless they were answering a direct question. Senator Reardon and I, on the other hand, minimize speaking bin Laden's name because doing so tends to deflect attention from what's really going on in the world of terrorism."

An eruption of questions issued forth from every mouth of every reporter and every TV news journalist in the room. The man on the podium had just taken the Independent Party to another new level of controversy. Lawrence held up his hands in the familiar way of asking for patience and silence, and as he was remaining in place, the media calmed down to hear the next sound bite.

"Ladies and gentlemen," Lawrence began again, and in a commanding, almost presidential voice, "Those persons willing and capable of projecting great evil upon our planet come along only in a great while. And do not think for a second that evil requires a reason to exist. It does not. Evil just is...." As expected, the anticipated next vice-president of the United States had the rapt attention of everyone in the room. "The stated purpose of these evil villains is invariably a deception for their real goal: self-gratification and nothing more. They like power. They like wealth. They like inflicting pain and misery—on anyone, including their own kind. For that reason, even when the U.S. is completely gone from the Middle East, the terror will not cease. Some other excuse will be found, is all, and we'll still have to root-out the bad guys on their home turf. This pattern will continue until the world's forgotten citizens no longer have a need to find themselves a charismatic leader who will provide them a reason for being."

"In the meantime, Osama bin Laden has earned his place on the list of most infamous characters in history. But remember this, my fellow citizens, if not bin Laden, there would have been someone else because the world was (and is) ripe for the emergence of the species. And we are all responsible...

"If you have faith, beliefs, or religion, you are responsible. If you have eyes, ears, mouth, so that you can see, hear, and speak, then you are responsible. If you have a working mind, whether adept at consciousness or not, then you are responsible. In our magnificence as a civilization, we have created the means for instant communication of thought and ideas, and the ability to travel anywhere on the planet within forty-eight hours. In our magnificence as a civilization, we have done pitifully little to eliminate the pain and suffering of hundreds of millions of our planetary brethren; we have done *nothing* to close the gap between the 'haves' and the 'have-nots.' We, meaning generally, 'the West,' have a tendency, when visiting countries *not* of 'the West,' to attempt to impress upon the locals just how superior we are. We do this, not only with our words—although we certainly have no hesitation to voice our abundant opinions—but mostly with just our presence and our attitude."

Lawrence took a sip of water, and continued his thoughts: "Please, do not misunderstand me. Terrorists are criminals, and they must be punished for their crimes. I know of no compassionate God of any religion that espouses the killing of men, women, and children who can only be considered innocents. Islam is no exception. Certain Muslims may choose to *interpret* the Koran as a Divine authorization for wholesale slaughter, but I consider that notion to be pure bunk.

"However, I'm at least as interested in eliminating the underlying cause motivating terrorism's soldiers, as I am in eliminating those who choose to practice its manifestations. Otherwise, there's no reason not to expect future acts of brutality."

A solitary hand arose about half-way back in the room, catching the other journalists off guard. Lawrence looked at the hand, pointed, and nodded his head, "Yes?"

"Senator—your waxing philosophical is not going to go over well with those people who lost friends and family on 9-11; nor is it going to ease their pain. Any words for them?"

Not recognizing the voice or the attached head, Truman asked, "And you are?"

"Travis Whitcomb, *Christian Science Monitor.*"

"Mr. Whitcomb—you're right, and I apologize to those folks who lost loved ones on that horrible day. In fact, though, nothing anyone can say could possibly make them feel any better. Not then, not now, not ever. They are victims, perhaps even more so than those who died because they still feel their pain every single day. It would be nice if those feelings never had to be felt again by anyone else. We will never be able to stop every terrorist act—we're just too big, too porous, too friendly, too open—and thank God. The only way to stop organized terrorism is to end the need, the root cause, whatever it may be. And stop it we must, for there's a lot more at risk here than the agonizing and permanent separation of families."

"Like what?"

"Like the end of civilization."

If the floor hadn't been carpeted, a pin could have been heard hitting its surface, so quiet was the ensuing reaction. If nothing else, Senator Lawrence knew how to get an audience's attention.

The gentleman smiled at the reaction, slowly nodded his head, and beat the journalists to the punch. "As was probably one of his intents on that fateful day three years ago, bin Laden demonstrated the vulnerability of America, and by extension, every other country in the world. By doing so, he shook our confidence.

"I'm here to tell you, ladies and gentlemen of the media—and all who read or watch your reports: Neither biologicals or bombs can do us in, but if we stop spending money, we'll be in very big trouble. And when we lose our confidence, we slow down our spending. You can verify this with any economist: no matter how fabulous are the physical assets behind any economy, if confidence is removed from the equation, the economy will falter and possibly fail. If the American economy fails, it will quickly drag the rest of the world with it, and we'll all return to the Dark Ages so fast it will make even the terrorists' heads spin. That's probably the biggest danger of terrorism, but here's another—one that we should be jumping all over right now!

"Since shortly after 9-11, and solely as a result of the terrorist attack, our government has been jailing people based on ethnic background, type of name, immigration status, and religion. This action was understandable, at least at first, as our government scrambled to protect its citizens from future attack, while also trying to apprehend those responsible for 9-11. I remind you that some of these incarcerated individuals have been held for over two years, without possibility of bail. And here's the really scary part, between you and me: they are not allowed legal representation, and they could quite literally be in jail for the remainder of their lives, or until the war on terrorism is declared officially over. Some of these people are confirmed American citizens. People—that kind of treatment is enough to make a terrorist out of anyone."

Even though the momentary silence provided by Senator Lawrence invited a plethora of questions, none was forthcoming. Everyone in the room knew that he wasn't done. The importance of the subject was perhaps even more vital than confidence in the economy.

"In the name of terrorism, in the name of protection from terrorists, our rights as United States citizens are being diminished—there's no doubt about it. If the principles upon which our founding fathers created our great land are shredded by our present-day leaders, then Osama bin Laden, Al-Qaeda, and terrorism have already won."

There's one more thing I need to say about this subject before moving on, and I direct my comments to you, the media, personally: you folks have been remiss in your duties and obligations to the citizens of our country. It's your job to stay on top of things. It's your job to report on little things like the loss of liberties. It's your job to question authority. Speaking of which, there's another aspect of this... *security thing*... that bothers me no end: Has it not occurred to any of you, as it has to me, that whenever the President wants something, all he has to do is say 'possible terror attack,' and he pretty much gets a free ride on whatever it is he wants?" Senator Lawrence raised his right arm level with his face and, in unison with his head, slowly shook his index finger back and forth. "I say to you fellow citizens, be wary of those who would protect you at just a small price of your freedom.

"Travis—I suspect I gave you a lot more than you bargained for, and I apologize for getting carried away. I do believe, however, that I answered your question.

"And now," Lawrence looked at his watch, "it's time to wrap this up. As I said, the in-depth details of our proposal are contained in your press kits, so enjoy the reading, and I really do look forward to more conversations like this in the days ahead. Good day...."

The news media were desperate to keep the man in place, and virtually screamed questions at him. But that, too, was a game that went on somewhere in Washington everyday. The media would yell questions, the target would smile and ignore them as he or she left the microphone. When it was obvious that no encore would be forthcoming, the crews scrambled for the table with the press kits, anxious to read more. To the media members, as just plain people rather than professional news hounds, there was something intriguing about what they had just heard, and they were curious.

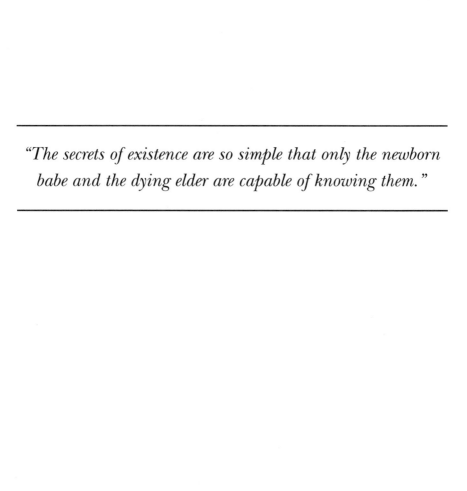

"The secrets of existence are so simple that only the newborn babe and the dying elder are capable of knowing them."

chapter thirteen

Revelations III

Kansas City, Missouri

True to his word, the bus driver backed out of the parking space at 1:16 P.M. Although there appeared to be about the same number of passengers as before, there were new faces for Max and Justin to examine: some people got off at KC, while new blood got on for the continuing trip East. Justin became confident that they hadn't been spotted so far, as he noticed no one suspicious in the new group.

Just as he was settling in for the long afternoon cruise, Max leaned over and whispered into his ear, "We've got company." Maley's jerk would have given away the secret if anyone had been watching, but he managed to casually look over the top of the seat in front of him, trying to spot something or someone he had missed. Max helped him, "Right side, about the eighth row, woman wearing a green baseball cap."

Maley saw her at once, as he had earlier, and was just as sure now, as he was then, that the good looking woman was no threat. "No way, Max. She's okay."

Mystery Man snorted and giggled some as he shook his head. "If you want to stay alive Sonny-boy, you'd better learn to look at more than the pretty faces. That girl's got no boundaries, just like you back when we first met. And she's got *his* energy all over her.

She's one of his troops, Justin. Mark my word. The only question is whether she'll try to take us out herself or wait for help. My guess is that she'll mosey back here to use the restroom, check us out to be sure, and then make a cell phone call. In the meantime, leave her be—don't be staring at her, no eye contact, but sure as hell keep your guard up."

A few minutes had gone by when the woman stood up, did some rearranging in the overhead rack, and then almost as a second thought, turned for the rear of the bus. As instructed, Justin kept his eyes forward, fighting the temptation to bore his eyes into hers. Max, on the other hand, did focus on her orbs, and he met hers head on for several, very telling seconds. She blinked first, but Max was now certain that they had been made.

The two men had specifically chosen the last row on the bus for their seats because they didn't want anyone sitting behind them. It wasn't pleasant being so close to the engine and the head, but that was the price of life. When the woman emerged from the poor excuse for a restroom, Justin half expected to see a bazooka precede the body, but it wasn't to be. She returned to her seat, sat down, then pulled a cell phone from her purse. The call lasted all of thirty seconds, and Max looked at Justin, Justin at Max, the eyes saying it all: They're coming.

"What do we do now?" asked Maley.

"Ask your next question, I suppose."

"Huh?" If Justin understood correctly, he couldn't believe what he had just heard.

"What do you propose to do, Justin? Get off the bus, walk for a spell, maybe all the way? I don't think so. I think we'll just hang right here and see what they have to offer. You see, my young friend, when they get this close, and for so long, my available options go way up. You ready for some more magic? In the meantime, we might as well enjoy the scenery, and you might as well continue your education. I believe we left off talking about the bad boy that's behind all this, right?" Justin nodded, but his expression indicated what he thought of the old man's plan.

"Let me tell ya about Truman Lawrence, or that part of him that's a being from the other side. As a being, he's old as the hills and a spoiled brat. And what do spoiled brats do? They break things, that's what they do. And why do they break things? Well, obviously to prove they can do it, to demonstrate that they can get away with it, and to reap attention—usually of the negative kind."

The proffered picture was painted with humor and served to lift Justin's sour glare, at least for a bit. "Max, you've indicated that the Truman being and the Jesus being are both very old, which I interpret as being mature and wise and all that stuff. How is it they can be so different from one another? I mean, the 'good-guy' or 'bad-guy' thing doesn't come out until they take a body, right?"

"Are you kidding?" The question surprised Max who thought he'd already explained the nature of beings in the continuum. Maybe not—"I think I told you that beings are pure energy, right? They have no mass, and they can't accomplish anything physical while in the continuum—they have to be in a body to do things here on Earth. Okay?" Maley nodded, and Max frowned, but then went on. "Have I ever implied to you that beings don't have any personality?"

Justin's attention jumped a level at this realization. "Are you serious?"

"Quite, and don't forget ego, either. We've got as much of that as you humans do."

A picture instantly developed in Justin's mind and he laughed, sharing the vision with his friend: "Oh, this is rich. I can see it now— a bunch of green energy dots, or whatever color you guys are, flying around the ether, bumping into each other, huffing and puffing, visiting, sharing stories—Is it like that, Max?"

"Kind of. We're all different, just like you humans are all different. In fact, we're the biggest factor in your personality differences here on Earth. So, it should come as no shock that Truman and Jesus are different, especially when you throw the ego in for good measure. Egos don't get any bigger than the one Truman Lawrence has, which had long been a problem for him on the other side. You see, even over there, maybe especially over there, it's hard to be humble when you're perfect!"

Maley rolled his eyes in the universal expression of "Give me a break," as his friend smiled at his own cleverness.

"When a being gets created, it has both good and evil potentials locked within. It is its own teeter-totter, and the being must find a balance within those few notches either side of equilibrium. Otherwise, like civilizations, a being will tend to self-destruct. As you already know, Truman's being is very old, very wise, very experienced and, by the way, very bored. He's been a troublemaker for a long time, which is the main reason he didn't pass beyond way back when—Oh, and did I mention that he's exceedingly powerful. I mean, it's a case of nobody in the continuum being able to spank the errant being, ya know what I mean? So he gets this notion that it's unfair he hasn't been allowed to pass beyond, so he figures he needs to pull off a grand finale of some sort. Now, bear in mind that the Truman being exists on that side of equilibrium that you would refer to as 'evil.' That's his bent in life and his desired means of manifesting. Some time back, he figured that if he could get rid of the 'good' side of his being, the minority part, then his dominant side would become massively stronger. The continuum made the mistake of ignoring him because such a thing, the complete splitting of a being, had never been done before—therefore, it must be impossible. Wrong."

Max asked Justin for one of the bottles of water and took a swig. They were about an hour out from KC and had about three more hours to St. Louis, with a scheduled pit stop in Columbia. Max got up to use the restroom, with the advisory to Justin that if his "girlfriend" made any sign of coming rearward, he was to scream bloody murder. That was fine with Justin, but nothing happened. Max returned relieved and picked up where he left off.

"Well, he did it—no one over there knows how—and he sure as hell picked up some juice in the process, but he had this little problem."

Maley saw it and jumped in, "A being can't do anything by itself. It has to have a body."

"Exactly—a being, without a body, can accomplish nothing in physical space/time. A body, without a being, knows nothing, but in actuality cannot even really exist. But great things happen when the two come together—and great things, Justin, apply equally to good or evil.

"So, here we've got this very powerful being, very full of himself, on the prowl for a body, but he needs the right kind of body and, *and* he's in a hurry. It's that last part that almost led to his undoing. To do what he wanted to do, he had to find a fetus being born to a family that already knew advantage in the extreme. You can see that what Truman Lawrence is doing now would not have been possible were he born to a lowly resident of some obscure town in the middle of Africa, for instance. No, it was Europe, America, or Japan for the Truman being, but the perfect fit was alluding him, which is to say: all the right bodies were already under contract to other beings in waiting. Somehow, he became aware that the Karmic cycle was about to end for a young boy whose circumstances might fit his needs. For you landlubbers, that means the being's work was finished this time around, and the kid's body would be dying soon. The Truman being saw an opportunity in the making and checked further. The body was the son of a very, very wealthy individual in the United States, was perfectly healthy, would no doubt one day be considered handsome, intelligent, and popular amongst all who knew him. He was eight Earth years old, which had the added benefit of shaving eight idle years off Truman's wait for the big time of adulthood, when he could really start doing 'things.'"

"Now, the taking over of an already living body by a being other than the contracted one had been done before a few times—special circumstances and needs and all that stuff, but it's a dicey procedure, and it has to be done just right. For one thing, it is sacrosanct that no being shall interfere with another being or body when the being/body are in union. It's like the Golden Rule, never to be violated. Secondly, if two beings are within the same body, even for an instant, the body always dies and usually cannot be salvaged, thereby defeating the whole purpose to begin with. It's like the ultimate burnout. On the other hand, if the new being waits too long after the first being departs, the body may not recover from its normal death. Like I said, it's dicey."

Donning his journalist cap, Justin was writing furiously in his journal, not wanting to miss a drop of this vintage, for it was the most fascinating lecture he had ever attended. Meanwhile, his "girlfriend" up front remained stationary, the bus droned onward, and the afternoon light levels began their slow fade.

"To make a long story short, the Truman being blew it. In his impetuousness and haste, he entered too early, doing temporary harm to the departing being, and nearly killing the boy permanently—permanently being a relative term. I mean, the boy would briefly die anyway even if the procedure were done correctly, but the body was gone for thirty minutes. It's testimony to the Truman being's power that he was able to bring the kid back at all, much less without permanent damage. But he did, and now you know the history of Senator Truman Lawrence, future King of the World."

"Did you come into this body that way, Max?"

"No—I did it right! I waited until this body's being left, as in completely out, and then I slid in. The guy was dead for only a few seconds, which is about all the time he could last. In all my observations of humans, I've never seen a body be in such bad shape and still be amongst the living."

"So why did you choose that particular body instead of an Arnold Schwarzenegger or something?"

"Who?"

"You know—a Charles Atlas—someone big, strong, and young..."

"Oh, you mean like Johnny Weissmuller..."

"Who?"

"Forget it. I chose this body because it seemed like the right thing to do at the time. I was careful to do it correctly, without engendering any more Karma than necessary. But also, I ran into my own time crunch and couldn't afford to be too choosy. Now I'm kinda regretting it. Arthritis is a pain." As the old man's unintended pun registered, he began cackling.

"So what was your time crunch?"

"We already knew that something had to be done about Lawrence. We'd been watching him for years, hoping against hope that something natural would happen to prevent him from accomplishing his goals. We kept thinking his being would burn up. Do you remember when I said the Universe doesn't tolerate extremes?" Justin nodded but kept on writing without lifting his head. "And remember that beings, as well as civilizations, exist in that two-notch zone either side of perfect balance?"

This time, Maley stopped his writing, thought for a moment, then looked at Max, "Yea, and after he split his being in two, he fell out of that zone, didn't he? He became one hundred percent evil."

The look on the nodding face of the master implied pride in his pupil. "That's right. So that's what we were all waiting for, but the son of a bitch fooled us again—he refused to croak. It became apparent we were going to have to do it the old fashion way: hard work and getting our hands dirty."

"You mean, someone was going to have to take a body and duke it out with Lawrence," Justin completed the thought.

"Uh huh—and guess who got the short straw? We'd been waiting for nature to take its course, and we almost waited too long. If he gets elected vice-president, it will be much more difficult to get to him without risking the lives of innocents, and that's bad news—we can't have any of that; at least, I don't want any. So, it had to be now. The problem, though, is I'm not sure I can whup his ass. I brought some major group mind-type power from the continuum, but your Senator Truman Lawrence has become one very bad dude."

"And what happens if you lose?"

"Then you might as well let your insurance policies lapse."

"Come on, Max. You guys must have a back-up plan...."

"I'm sure we do; I just don't know what it is yet."

"Christ, Max—you're talking about the fate of the Earth here, but the lackadaisical way you're dealing with it leaves something to be desired. Wait a minute—time out," and the writer went into think mode as something tickled his brain. Then, he grabbed it, "Why is the continuum getting involved in this? You've implied a 'hands-off' position from the other side, let nature do its thing, allow Karma to play out, and all that crap. Why not this time? In all the Universe, what's the big deal if planet Earth—check that, if human civilization—dies or survives?"

Max was slow to respond, as he always was when his perceptive companion got a little too close to the bigs. Still, he admired the curiosity and the investigative mind behind the probes. It was, after all, what they, "the Boys from the Continuum," had been counting on—the secret back-up plan. So, he answered the question: "Yea, well—there's the rub. You guys are kind of important to us. More than kind of, actually. Remember I said there were only a couple of civilizations that lived out on the far ends of the teeter-totter, rather than close-in to the fulcrum, and therefore there was more time to experience things and change things? Remember that?"

"Of course. You said we were one of just a few like that and that Earth was a good place for doing Karma work. I remember."

"So, maybe I didn't adequately emphasize the importance of that little fact..."

"Yes?"

"Yea. Well, there's an awful lot of beings in the continuum, Justin, and all of them have some sort of Karma to deal with. And since there's only three planets in the Universe with civilizations where Karma can effectively be worked on, that makes those three civilizations pretty damned popular, if you know what I mean. I'm talkin' about signing up ten years in advance for a reservation—that kind of thing. So, the idea that one of those three civilizations might go down the toilet due to some evil, egomaniacal madman didn't sit too well with the boys. Therefore, the rules of the Universe were suspended until this matter is cleared up."

It bothered Max a little that Maley was looking at him like he'd lost his mind, and then the kid began shaking his head back and forth, then he got the smile: the "you're joshin' me, right?" kind of smile. It started to piss Max off, but he quickly replayed his words in his own mind and realized that "bizarre" had just gotten a new definition.

"You know, Max, it's beginning to sound like you guys could use some help up there: split personalities, boredom, egos run amok. Don't you have any dead shrinks amongst you?"

Snot-nosed, smart-ass kid. "Did you notice your use of the phrase 'up there' rather than 'down there'? You might want to be careful about the connotations of your assumptions, Sonny-boy."

They turned away from each other in a temporary truce, both with their own thoughts, far and near. Both checked the woman up front. They'd gotten caught up in Max's ramblings and had lost track of time and location, but the issue became moot as they pulled off the interstate at the Columbia exit. It was 2:10 P.M. and by mutual, unstated agreement, the paranoia antennae went to full alert.

———————————————————

It wasn't Columbia. Apparently, Truman's troops wanted more time to get their act together, to provide the best possible surprise party. The two men had agreed not to separate at the bus station and to not get trapped in some place like the restroom—meaning the meager facilities aboard a moving vessel would have to do. They resupplied their bottled water and bought a few snack food items, then reboarded the bus to hell. The young woman followed them, and when the bus pulled back onto I-70, she made her obligatory cell phone call. In a strange sort of way, that action provided some comfort: It indicated to Max and Justin that the fun and games lay somewhere ahead—most likely St. Louis—and that they had time to relax and contemplate the marvels of their respective worlds, or go to sleep—whichever came first.

Maley cat napped in between working on his notes; Max either cat napped or slept like a log. Their extraterrestrial discussions were taking a hiatus until they determined if they would be alive to appreciate the significance. And so they rolled into St. Louis about two hours later, where a change of bus and a ninety-minute layover almost guaranteed a crime of opportunity. To fantasize another free pass would be the height of wishful thinking.

The party began right after dinner—a dinner of food hopefully supplied by a vendor different from the one in Kansas City. Justin paid the bill, as always, and as they had little choice this time, they paid a casual visit to the restroom. They wisely chose to stay together. Showing the first signs of cunning, Max instantly knew that one of the bad guys was in a stall—awaiting their anticipated visit. Sure enough, from seemingly out of nowhere, four more "toughs" followed Max and Justin into the restroom. All seven of them played dumb until the two innocents already there had a chance to finish their business and leave, looking over their shoulders with concern on the way out. And then the fur flew, but not for Maley.

Maley felt himself being pushed into the far corner of the restroom with an advisory from his pusher, Max, to stay there. Facing the pack, Max stood in front of Justin in a clear effort to protect his charge. The five men, all looking like rejects from a James Dean motorcycle flick, had already brandished their weapons—not knives, not chains, but top of the line Glocks and Colts, all automatics and presumably containing illegal, full-capacity clips. Like the Valentine's Day massacre, the five stood in a line and pointed their guns at Max, and by extension, the man behind him. But their orders were clear: the older man was the target, and don't come back unless he's toast—absolutely, positively, completely, and without question.

They didn't come back....

209

Their clips were indeed full, containing something like fifteen rounds each. Fifteen times five shooters, not counting various hidden pistols, and the potential mayhem became considerable. The five aimed their automatics and applied the necessary six-pound trigger pressure to begin the bloodbath. Sounding like machine gun fire, Max and Justin should have been dead in less than a couple of seconds. The decibel level was incredible in the enclosed space, and despite the silliness of his choice, Justin automatically put his hands over his ears to protect his precious eardrums. Something was wrong—or right, thankfully. He realized that he felt no pain, that he wasn't pouring precious bodily fluids from dozens of holes, so he ventured a look beyond his own personal death/survival reality. Faster than his eyes could follow, Max's arms and hands played ping-pong with the fired bullets. His limbs were a blur of motion, even at a thousandth of a second shutter speed. Radiating a strange electroluminescent blue, the bullets were all ricocheting off Max's hands, and variously redecorating the restroom walls, mirrors, tile flooring—and the bad boy shooters themselves. Instant Karma.

Truman's troops didn't get to empty their clips. As many of the ricocheting bullets found flesh, the attackers faltered, one by one, until they were all on the floor, guns smoking with heat: pints of blood following the obligatory eighth-inch-per-foot slope to the floor drain, per code.

Max stayed with them long enough to make sure they were no longer a threat, then he turned to Justin. The look in Mystery Man's face was the scariest thing he had ever seen, easily trumping what he had felt when the five men had cornered them with likely death. Max was—was grinning? No, it couldn't be a grin, but it was something insane or feral, something real gone, definitely not normal—and definitely not okay. It was a look that didn't belong in a civilized world. It belonged to a climaxing Klingon or something like that. It was evil and it was, in the end, a grin of satiation.

The mesmerized spell Justin felt was broken as several police officers kicked the door open, but remained at the steel frame to get a handle on what awaited them. It was a tense moment as they were scared to death after hearing the invisible firefight coming from the other side of the door. Consequently, their trigger fingers were not in a discerning frame of mind at the moment.

210

The cops yelled for Max and Justin to put their hands on their head, turn around, and face the wall. When it became obvious that the threat factor was over, the tension in the room slowly, very slowly began to return to one hundred twenty beats per minute. When it came time to explain what had happened, the logic of the scene, along with some more magic from the magician, did wonders for getting the two men back on the road. The evidence supported Max's story. Two men had been there, three more came in, the yelling started, then they all pulled their guns and started shooting. It was all over in a few seconds, and somehow, despite worse odds than winning the Powerball, the two innocents avoided something like fifty rounds in a small space. The story was helped along by the clean cut appearance of the survivors, at least compared to that of the perps. None of the cops seemed to notice that, although most of the restroom was trashed from flying bullets and ricochets, the area in the corner, coincidentally close to where the two survivors had been found standing, seemed to be free of damage.

At any rate, between the logic of the statements, the apparent innocence of the two survivors, no court case to prepare for, and with a little mind diddling from Max, the two men were allowed to return to the bus ramps, board their new bus and wait for departure. The "event" had emptied the terminal like horses exiting a barn on fire, and it took thirty minutes or so for things to return to any semblance of normalcy; for the men's restroom, the timeframe would be considerably longer. Thirty-five minutes late, the bus left the terminal, complete with Justin's "girlfriend," as Max had become fond of describing her. As they waited and watched, within five minutes of departure, she was on the phone. Justin was tempted to grab the phone from her, hit the redial button just for kicks, and see who answered—bet it wouldn't be Momma. But he declined the urge, preferring to avoid any possibility of mind-meld.

Even though it had been almost an hour since the shooting, Justin was still wrapped up tight—better, for sure, but an experience like that didn't leave one's stream of consciousness for some time. He noticed that he felt clammy, probably from sweating profusely, with no place for the sweat to go but into his clothes. He wasn't shaking anymore, for which he was grateful. He looked out the window of the bus, not really noticing the cityscape until his eyes fell on the huge arch, so elegantly joining the sky at dusk. A smile formed of his lips and mouth in appreciation for the wondrous things that humans are capable of when the get their heads out...

"Max—you there Max?" Maley asked, while visually holding the arch until he could see it no more.

"Yes, Justin. What is it you want to know: how I did it, or the meaning of the look in my eyes at the end?"

Justin smiled at the perception as he turned back to his partner, somehow knowing it was honest this time and not the result of a mind probe. "I knew you were capable of magic, although that was a pretty spectacular demonstration. No, it was who you became at the end that I'm wondering about. You were scary, Max; more than scary. You were almost—hideous.

"It was the warrior's look of victory. The Evil One sent his troops to kill us, or in point of fact, to kill me. They came, we did battle, and I emerged victorious. The Evil One will not sleep this night, for I am a heartbeat closer to his camp. He cannot risk coming at me directly, so he sends his troops. They have made four attempts and all have perished for their efforts. He is losing. It angers him, and it will affect his judgment. I grow stronger; he grows weaker. It is the way of the warrior—it always has been. Now, I must rest...."

The Greyhound Scenic Cruiser hummed into the darkening skies of the East, as Max began snoring almost immediately. Justin was tired too—actually more exhausted than tired, but he would not sleep for a while, not until it was dark in the coach. He didn't want the woman to see both of them asleep at the same time for fear that she might try something on her own and catch them both vulnerable. So he worked on his journal, and considered what the words meant. He thought about his location and mind space at this time four days ago, before meeting the Mad Hatter. It seemed like ages ago because it was, in fact, a world apart from the Earth he was walking this day. How is it possible for a life to change so much, so quickly? The answer was sitting next to him, and also in an office in Washington, D.C.—he had a three-way date with destiny, and the big event was getting closer by the minute.

Day Four

*"Consciousness is forever hovering around us, waiting to be plucked and consumed, with just a little bit of work on our part. As the fruit can be either sweet or bitter, humans are selective (whether they know it or not) about those regions of their existence they deem worthy of consciousness—or more to the point—those areas **not** worthy of the effort. As you can see, it's all very complicated, despite its underlying simplicity."*

chapter fourteen

Truckin'

Western Ohio, I-70

Justin awoke with a jolt. It is a distinctly human trait that upon waking and being somewhat disoriented, the first thing that must be ascertained is the time. If a watch or clock is not readily available, the human body automatically and immediately goes into stress level I, with subsequently higher stress levels attained until the time of day is properly logged. If the latter is not done quickly enough, the whole day can be shot for the body in question. Fortunately, he wore a trusty Timex with the Indiglo night light feature, and it read 12:37 A.M.

The next necessity is to determine location. That's easy if you're in a familiar bed, but if the bed is traveling at seventy mph, one needs a map or a sign. Justin had the former but not the latter, and without some point of reference, the map was almost useless. The problem was that the bus had left the interstate, had turned onto a two-lane highway, and Maley didn't have a clue which highway it was or where they were going—until recently, the story of his life.

Before he had a chance to start freaking out, however, the bus slowed and began a turn into an enormous Truck Stop that was as busy as Grand Central Station in spite of the hour, or perhaps because of it.

The bus pulled into the pump area but kept its engine running, as the driver explained to everyone the need for fuel, pit stop, stretch, smoke break, coffee, and food. He informed the passengers they'd be there about forty-five minutes.

By now, Max was coming out of his stupor, wanted to know their location, and got a little testy when Maley reported ignorance. But at least he got the time, except—freak out, now—are we still Central Time or are we now Eastern? Knowing the correct time zone shouldn't be a big deal when you're in the middle of nowhere, in the middle of the night, with destiny as your only appointment.

Both Max and Justin were amazed at the truck traffic as they left the bus, making sure that their female traveling companion remained in front of them. An unfamiliar smell attached itself to their receptors, and they both accurately assumed it to be the smell of diesel-powered rigs. The air was thick with the stuff. Some of the trucks looked rather plain, and therefore, smaller. But some rigs seemed enormous with what looked to be hundreds of tiny lights aglow in the night—marking their presence for all to see, and as a warning to move aside for the comet passing through the night. Justin's ears caught a sound he vaguely remembered hearing periodically over the years, always wondering what it could be but never in a position of asking: it came from a truck out on the highway, slowing down in preparation for turning into the Truck Stop. It was a sound like someone slapping their hands on a table top real fast—faster at first, and very loud—slowing in beat just as the rig slowed. Maybe he could finally find out what it was. He liked it here. It felt kind of fun, kind of exciting, an unknown alternative life of constant movement—separate from day-to-day familiarity. He determined to spend some time with truckers when his current assignment came to an end, assuming he was still alive and kicking.

While Maley checked out the truck stop, Max had gone on ahead, used the restroom, and had grabbed them a corner table in the restaurant with glass all around for greater visibility of the truck pads, driveway and highway beyond. Assuming there were no bad guys waiting inside for them, there was little chance any could approach without being seen. Nonetheless, Max stayed focused primarily on the inside traffic, while Justin did the same for the outside. Otherwise, the two men relaxed, enjoyed themselves, and had a surprisingly good meal for so early in the morning.

There were two smokies seated at the table across from them, along with two drivers. They were all talking about recent truck thefts that were greater in number and bolder than was the norm. They mentioned the two in Kansas the day before, causing Max and Justin to curl their eyebrows at each other, and they mentioned a new hijacking just a couple of hours earlier back in Indianapolis—one of those huge tow trucks used to tow the biggest of rigs. They were talking about how "tricked out" it was and that it must be worth a fortune.

After the peach cobbler, Justin paid his respects to the restroom, casually inspecting the stalls for any gunslingers; but his visit was inconsequential until he left. He saw the woman from the bus briefly staring right at him as though she had been staring at the door and couldn't turn away quickly enough when her brain registered the man coming through the opening to be her target. She was on the phone again, but that too ended as Justin headed back to the corner table, stopping first to pick up a newspaper. That thirty-second delay was probably all that saved their lives.

Max, true to his word, was keeping an eye on the patrons of the restaurant as Justin walked toward him with his head buried in the headlines. Even though he was looking downward, the intensity of the headlamps shining through the glass caught Justin's eyes—just on the periphery, but it was enough. He looked up to see a mammoth green and yellow tow truck coming straight at him and Max—straight for the building—and the smoke was pouring out its twin stacks: it wasn't even attempting to slow down. Max caught the look of shock on Maley's face and turned to ascertain the reason. Being seated, though, he was too slow to react to the danger in time—as he felt a hand reach under his armpit and practically jerk the arm out of his socket. Maley had dropped the newspaper, set his feet, reached for Max, pulled the old man clear, and began his run—all in about one second.

The best move would have been sideways, but their path was blocked by the window wall on one side, and a clutch of departing guests on the other. So they had no choice but to run for the checkout counter—straight away from the oncoming truck, making it a race of time over distance. The two men had taken the first step of their sprint when the twelve-inch-high chrome bumper of the rig made contact with the side of the building. One instant, there was just chaos, panic, and fear; the next instant, massive destruction was added to the mix. Approaching the building at fifty mph, the truck was barely affected by the first wall of wood and glass; and between the bumper, the two front tires, and the underside of the carriage, Max and Justin's table was flattened to about six inches in height. Although they weren't there, the two cops and two drivers were—and all they could do in the end was cover their faces with an arm to ward off death—or evil, either one offering a one-way ticket to the other side. Their bodies, along with the deuces, four-tops, and banquettes flew through the air like splashes of water from a swimming pool after some kid has done his cannonball.

Justin knew better, but Max had to turn and look. He wanted to look, to see death coming, to feel it, to defeat it if possible—but most importantly, to participate in the experience. It was the antithesis of boredom, and anything was better than that, and that was just as big a reason for visiting Earth as was dealing with Karma: Life was a kick.

And the kick was gaining on them even though it had begun to slow down. The momentum of the 50,000-pound rig at fifty mph would have easily carried it through the length of the building, but the debris that came down with its passage was beginning to jam up the drivers and axles. It had been all of about four seconds since the truck attacked the building, as Max and Justin passed the unattended check-out counter and made a hard left for the exit door. The not-so-straight, and not-so-shiny chrome bumper of the tow truck came to a stop about ten feet beyond the counter. Steam was pouring from the mortally wounded Peterbilt, and the stench of diesel fuel filled the air. The roof of the truck cab had been sheared off from passing through multiple roof bar joists, leaving the driver still buckled in his seat with hands properly positioned at ten and two, but minus one head.

Almost every sentient body in the vicinity was now running toward, not from, the scene of disaster, but Max and Justin were interested in none of that. They needed to get away from the attention, quietly, and preferably without being seen. "We've got to find another way out of here, Justin. Can you rent a car in a place like this?" Justin boarded the coach, grabbed his duffel, and the two walked slowly, casually toward the back of the complex—away from prying eyes. Both knew that the bus was no longer viable as safe transportation. "No car rentals, Max, not from a truck stop. Besides, everyone's a little busy right now. I could maybe steal a car, but that solution won't last for long. We'd have to dump it soon or risk getting caught." Their discussion was interrupted as they both saw the woman come through a backdoor of the building, obviously looking for them. Their eyes met—hers and Max's—and she began to turn away, no doubt with the intent of making one of her phone calls.

"I've had enough of this shit," Max the Mouth intoned, and he raised his arm, pointed a couple of crooked fingers directly at the woman, letting loose a blue bolt of energy that traveled across the parking lot and enveloped the spy. The cell phone flew from her hand as her body appeared to be experiencing a few thousand volts of electricity. When Max ceased firing, she collapsed on the pavement, very still, and like the Peterbilt, smoke or steam lifted away from her. "That takes care of that pair of eyes. Now, how do we get out of here?" Max asked.

Justin closed his gaping mouth, looked down at Max's lowered arm, and reminded himself to never, ever piss the guy off again. "Max—is she…"

"As a doornail."

Back to their immediate needs, Justin pulled his attention away from Max and the dead woman to consider their options. Then he smiled. The best hiding place is the most obvious one, he remembered from somewhere, and the lot was absolutely packed with transportation. It was everywhere, and all they had to do was find a willing driver. And you talk about discreet—Lawrence's people would never find them riding in a private truck.

Most of the drivers were up front with everyone else in the restaurant area looking for survivors. But there was at least one that Justin could see, and he was doing something to his rig. "I'll be right back, Max. Stay here."

Maley walked toward the lone trucker who had a miniature baseball bat in his hand and was hitting each of the truck tires in turn. The man had finished and was returning to the cab as Maley intercepted him, sensing for a second that the driver's hand stiffened around the bat for a moment. Max could see them talking, then saw the driver look over Justin's shoulder in his direction. The man nodded his head and Justin walked back to fetch Max. "What did ya tell him?" Max wanted to know.

"That you escaped from Menlo Park and Nurse Ratched and that I was taking you back to Washington to live with me, but the car had broken down and maybe the psycho police were looking for us. I promised him you'd be a good boy."

"Very funny. Now, what did ya really say?"

"Actually, that's pretty close, replied Justin. He bought the story, and besides, the two hundred dollars I gave him didn't hurt any either. Let's go."

They walked toward the truck, looking in all directions for the "psycho police," and Max asked Justin what kind of man the driver was. "I don't know, Max—I'm not the mind reader here. But he seems okay; like a 'good ol' boy,' whatever that is. He's friendly enough, and he doesn't come across like any of Truman's troops that we've encountered. Okay?"

Besides which, he didn't bother to add, their options were limited. The driver was already in the cab as the two men crossed in front of the truck. Since Justin had begun to take an interest in the lifestyle, he also began mentally cataloguing the details of his surroundings. The truck on the left side of theirs was completely different in appearance, having a straight-up nose and appearing much taller. The rig on the other side had a long nose like theirs, but it looked more modern, or space-agey— or maybe it was more streamlined for efficiency. The nose on their ride was square and boxy and huge, with an emblem above his head with the letters "KW." In fact, the truck they were getting into looked generally square and boxy all over, except for the chrome shade thing over the windshield, which made the rig look like it was wearing a baseball cap. There was chrome all over the place, lots of those little marker lights, and Justin noticed the exhaust pipes—one on each side—looked as big as his waist. He smiled. This was going to be cool.

As he waited for Max to climb up inside, he stood next to an exterior mounted metal box on the side of the truck. In a moment of little background noise, he could hear the idling thunder coming from the cylinders of the engine—coming through the box, as though it were a direct link to the fires within. The truck next to them gave off a brief "whoosh" sound, just like a steam locomotive Justin had seen just last year, but it wasn't steam—it was air. It finally occurred to him that these were big machines, not just big cars, not toys, and the truckers sat astride their machines and guided them Coast to Coast, doing their part to keep the land of the free, free. Max finally got in, having to climb over the passenger seat and into the sleeper area behind the cab. Justin threw in his duffel bag behind Max and then climbed into the seat, which decompressed a little as it seemed to conform to his body. He closed the door—and entered another world.

"I saw you boys in the restaurant. I'm amazed you got outta there."

"Yea, me, too," Justin offered. "How come you didn't hang around afterwards?"

The driver snickered a little. "I've seen enough disasters in my life. I don't need to see another; besides, there was plenty of help in there already. And if I don't get this load of strawberries to Philly on time, I ain't gonna get paid." He was writing in a journal or something, so Maley perused the "cockpit."

It was smaller than he expected, after having felt the enormity of the whole package from the outside. However, the sleeping area extended beyond the cab a ways, and looked like two large adults could stretch out in it. The dashboard looked like it belonged in a small airplane, it had so many gauges and switches. There were two different levers on the steering column, but the really fascinating thing was the three gear shift sticks coming up out of the floor. *Three? How many gears does this thing have?* Finally, there was a cell phone in a holder and a coiled-up microphone hung overhead.

"You keep a journal?" the writer asked.

"It's my log book. Every driver's gotta have one—or two, or three," he giggled, at some private joke. You gotta prove to ol' Smokey that you're gettin' enough shuteye along with your drivin' time. You boys ready?"

Justin said, "I am," and looked at his partner, who was smiling himself now, and nodding his head. "Max is, too. That's Max, and I'm Justin."

"I'm Tony, but just call me Buck—that's my handle," and he pointed to the CB microphone overhead. Justin watched with unfeigned interest as Buck prepared the rig for departure. Depressing the clutch, he shifted the closest stick toward the back, and the second stick toward the front with a slight amount of gear grinding noise with each move. The third stick he left alone. He turned on the headlights, then pushed downward on a large yellow button, looked in both side mirrors, and let the clutch come out slowly, along with a little throttle. They began to move: straight ahead at first, then with a slow turn to the right when Buck was sure they had the clearance. They got to the main driveway, curved to the left and headed toward the highway. All three heads looked out Buck's side at the mass of tangled destruction that used to be a bustling restaurant. Red and blue revolving lights were everywhere, and now a portable crane was pulling into the lot. Scores of people were carefully sifting through the wreckage, while Max and Justin stealthily slipped back onto the highway. It was 2:40 A.M. and it was Eastern time, as Maley had confirmed in the restaurant before the cute little Cookoo Clock stopped ticking.

Buck did another right onto the two-lane highway, number unknown, increased the throttle until a certain rpm was reached, then shifted gears, using the left stick and depressing the clutch twice. It was a slow process following some procedure and not anything like shifting gears in a sports car. The engine again reached some rpm limit, and Buck shifted gears again, only this time he used the middle stick, and the change of gears was much quicker, but so was the need to shift gears for a third time, using the middle box once more. The operation reversed itself as they approached the on-ramp for I-70, turned right, and slowly worked their way up to interstate speeds.

Buck had noticed Justin's fascination with the gearboxes and enjoyed the rare opportunity to display his prowess. He repeated what Justin had already seen while explaining, "She's got a five and a four and a two setup." Pointing to the stick closest to him, Buck identified the boxes. "This here is the five-speed main box, this one's the four-speed 'Brownie,' and this one's the high-low splitter. The Brownie divides each of the main box gears into four smaller gears. Ya multiply 'em and you end up with twenty forward gears—forty when you throw in that 'Sweet Georgia Overdrive.'"

Both Justin and Max had been watching his hand operate the gears, and they both wondered what would happen now that he'd used up all the Brownie gears. Buck pulled the Brownie out of fourth and left it in neutral, switched over to the main box and shifted it from second to third, then went back to the Brownie and put it back into first, ready to start all over again. It was a complex maneuver, but the next time it came around, Buck truly dazzled them both with a "speed shift." Putting his left arm through the steering wheel spokes to maintain directional control, he grabbed the main box with his left hand, the Brownie with his right, depressed the clutch, and slid both boxes into neutral. He let the clutch out for just the exact amount of time, depressed it again, and simultaneously "snapped" both transmissions into the next appropriate gear, without so much as a whimper from the gears. All three men smiled and did a big, "Whoa!" at the display of training if not surgical precision. If it hadn't been so dangerous, high-fives probably would have been going around the cab.

"I don't usually do a snap shift like that unless I'm on a really bad grade. It's too dangerous, cuz if you miss it, you just took about a year off your transmission's life."

"I had no idea driving a truck was so complex," Maley observed.

"It ain't, usually—not anymore. This rig's different—older. This here's a 1975 Kenworth with a Cummins 375TA—that's 375 horse-power with turbo charger and after-cooler. She was my pop's truck 'til his arthritis and hemorrhoids got so bad he had ta stop drivin'. Broke his heart, cuz he loved to drive truck. He loved the feel of the pull, the sound of the turbo screamin', the feel and sound of power when you're doin' a long grade and barely holding 1800 rpm, and the heat's start'n to come up through the firewall. Man, it just don't get any better. Needless to say, I'm a chip off the old block. Anyway, most rigs just have a single stick now, with an air-slave-operated auxiliary transmission. It took all the fun out of drivin', and my pop wouldn't have none of that shit. So, in '75, he scraped together all his money for a downstroke on ol' Mable here—even mortgaged the farm—and got it just the way he wanted it. We partnered for a long time, but when he had to retire, he gave ol' Mable to me. She's been almost completely rebuilt, and runs as good as ever," and then he patted Mable's tush—the dashboard—in grateful appreciation. "She may be a little old, but that don't mean she's slow—that's from a song. Speakin' of which, you boys ready for some tunes?"

They hadn't thought about it, but sure, why not. Buck lifted a box off the floor between the seats and handed it to Max, "Here, Old Timer. You all bein' the guests, you pick out somethin' what looks good."

Max opened the box and felt through the CDs, not needing any light, of which there was none handy anyway. He lifted out his selection, removed the CD from its case, and handed it to Buck to insert into the slot. As soon as the first notes left the speakers, ol' Buck got all excited, "Hey guys, that's my favorite CD in the whole world!"

Justin smiled at the driver. "Really?" then he turned toward Max the Magician, shaking his head, "Wow, that's amazing...." Even in the dark of the sleeper, Justin could see the Cheshire grin and blinking of his partner's eye.

Buck fast-forwarded to his favorite song on his most favorite CD, cranked up the volume and the two guests prepared themselves for who knew what? A fast and furious drumbeat proceeded the same from a guitar, and then the first words confirmed their location in the unknown Universe: *"I pulled out of Pittsburgh and was rollin' down the Eastern seaboard..."*

"Gentlemen, meet Mr. Taj Mahal and the best damn truckin' song ever made."

With the melody, words, beat, and volume coming from the thousand-dollar sound system, it was impossible to sit still during "Six Days on the Road." They shucked and jived and bounced—and in the interlude of feel-good safe passage, they laughed and laughed. If there had been a mean ol' crow back there watching the rig speed down the highway, he would have reported flames coming from her stacks and the truck bouncing from side to side all over the road, but never touching it—just as if it were in a Roger Rabbit movie.

And on toward the wicked East they went....

"Humans celebrate when bodies are born.
Beings celebrate when bodies die."

—Donna Taylor
Lester Park, Duluth, 2003

chapter fifteen

May I be Your Guide

Duluth, Minnesota

The G-V landed at Duluth International Airport at 10:00 A.M. Central. Truman Lawrence and one Secret Service agent departed the plane and joined other agents, the black Suburban, and Truman's local limousine, all parked on the general aviation tarmac a few feet away from the aircraft. Adam Dempsey was not among the entourage.

For his sins, Adam had remained behind in Washington, miraculously lucky to still be alive, much less in one piece, but he was still nursing a very bruised back. He was trying to ascertain the present location for the bane of his existence—their existence. The closer the visitor got to Washington, the more freaked out Truman became, and the more injuries Adam sustained. The recollection of Truman's latest fit that morning came screaming back into his head—probably with a little telepathic assistance from his boss while en route to Duluth. The reminder was not wasted.

Truman had already been up and in the library when Adam arrived—that was the first bad sign; that he was dressed in a robe was the second. Clearly, the Senator already knew about the mess in St. Louis and later at the truck stop. The smart play would have been to turn and run as fast as possible, get out of range, and then come back when his boss had calmed down some, not that there was any guarantee that he would. Instead, Adam took one step more into the room when Truman swung around wearing a hideous scowl, raised his arm—hand and fingers extended, and sent out some kind of tractor beam thing that lifted Adam off the floor and then slammed him against the tall library bookcases. He didn't fall to the floor either. Lawrence held him in place with shoes two feet off the hardwood floor, as he yelled at him—the third bad sign, for Senator Lawrence never raised his voice. He enjoyed punishing his opponents with a smile and a soft voice, with his face just inches away from theirs, if possible—eyeball to eyeball, so to speak. But not today. Today, the man from hell was livid and yelling.

"You worthless piece of shit. If I had a ready replacement for you, you'd be dead; and you can rest assured I'm looking. That army of yours may be fine at starting revolutions here and there, but when it comes to stopping one old man, they're as useless as you are." Truman conveniently neglected to mention that the "one old man" was a walking army unto himself. His yelling stopped, but his scowl continued, and it was obvious that he wanted to kill his right-hand man of twenty years and that he needed the release of his frustrations and anger as much as anything else. However, common sense finally tipped the scales in Adam's favor, for the moment, and Adam fell to the floor in a heap as Truman turned and walked out the door.

An hour later, Truman re-entered the library, completely refreshed and ready to party, wearing Dockers and a University of Minnesota (Duluth) windbreaker over a golf shirt from the same institution. He approached the desk where Adam was on the phone, poured himself some coffee and patiently waited (another rarity) for Adam to complete his business. Knowing that the Senator was on a short fuse, Dempsey wisely terminated the call in just a few seconds.

"I'm leaving for Duluth now. You'll stay here and continue the search. By the way, you did well to find out about Metcalf. I didn't see that one coming, and depending on what he knows, he could be just as disastrous as this other one. Relax, take a hot tub, get a massage, take some Valium even. But Adam—make no mistake. Twenty years together or not, if our visitor isn't dead by this time tomorrow, you will be." Lawrence set down the coffee down and stood, but before heading to the door, he gave his man a parting shot across the bow, "And it won't be quick and painless, Adam. I trust you understand me?" This time his voice was soft with his face no more that a foot from Adam's. The smile, however, was nowhere to be found. Truman turned and left for a date along the magnificent shore of Lake Superior.

———————

It was turning into a beautiful fall morning: sunny, still, and clear. The weatherman, for all he knew, said it would be fifty-eight degrees today, and remain cloudless. Varying shades of red, yellow, orange, and brown were already showing up in the trees as autumn began early this far north. The waters of Lake Superior were calm in the windless morning, but calmness eluded Michael Metcalf, and it both surprised and unnerved him. Investigative reporters lived for interviews such as the one coming up—assuming that Lawrence kept his word. They would be meeting in a very public spot, and Metcalf would insist on recording the interview, or he would threaten to walk and work with what he already had. When the game got this deep, bluffs were seldom used and therefore such threats were taken seriously. He was supposedly in the catbird seat as evidenced by Lawrence's call to him, so why didn't he feel better about this meeting?

The answer, of course, lay in the disconcerting unknown surrounding the Senator. Although he appeared to be as clean as he could be in the present and near past, there was that little problem back when he was eight or nine. It had spooked Jennifer, it had spooked Allison, and now it was spooking the meanest, badest investigative reporter around. He knew he could fake it, but he couldn't shake it. It was real enough that he had called Jennifer Brown prior to leaving the hotel. She answered the phone, which assuaged his first paranoid fear, and she, too, was concerned for his welfare. He requested that she and her husband do some driving today; go somewhere, maybe up to see Allison, Shannon now, or otherwise just make themselves scarce. It was probably the wrong thing to say because the other end grew ominously quiet until a question came back to him that he didn't want to deal with: She asked, "If you feel that way about Lawrence, why are you still going to meet with him?"

The excuse, "because it's my job" rolled out of storage all too easily and quickly, despite the fact that in the end no job is worth one's life, and that was, after all, what was being bandied about over the phone line.

He arrived at Lief Erickson park at 10:30 and checked it out again, finding things unchanged since the night before. For the third time, he checked his windbreaker pocket, feeling the recorder there, along with two back-up tapes, four double A batteries, which in turn backed up the four fresh batteries he'd placed in the recorder that morning. There was nothing more to do than walk off the tension and maybe get something to drink from the Jubilee market across the street as he waited for Duluth's favorite son.

The Suburban and the limousine arrived out on the street five minutes early. From behind a column of the small rotunda off to the side of the rose garden, Metcalf watched three Secret Service agents quickly exit the vehicles and scan their surroundings behind their intimidating dark lenses. Then one of them, probably the lead agent, opened the rear door of the limo, and out stepped His Highness in his perfect casual garb befitting the impromptu one-day trip home. Regardless of his other excuses, the reporter knew The Man was here for one reason, and one reason only: himself. Metcalf was a problem, and the problem needed to be defused or massaged in some way that the reporter was about to discover.

Metcalf moved away from the rotunda and Lawrence saw him at once, waved, smiled, and immediately set off to join him in the garden. One agent remained at the vehicles while the other two remained a discreet distance away from their charge but close enough to be all over a potential attacker instantly.

As he approached Michael, the Senator paused for a moment, stepped into the garden proper, and despite all the rules, broke off a deep red rose bloom. He brought the bloom to his nose, inhaled deeply, and smiled a "Nirvana" kind of smile. He then continued toward the reporter, talking as he approached:

"I can't seem to resist the 'Mr. Lincoln,' and even though I shouldn't pinch off the blooms, the society does make some exceptions for me. Hello Michael—is it all right to use your Christian name?" and he shook the reporter's hand in a firm but friendly manner, a presidential manner. Metcalf smiled back, nodded his head, which presumably meant that the Senator could call him anything he wanted as long as he delivered the goods. "This is what I miss most about having to live in Washington," Lawrence said as he waved his arm over the garden. "When I was mapping out my future life, this is where I did much of my thinking—here and along the shoreline, walking for hours, figuring it all out."

"It must have been a real bitch in the middle of January," Metcalf observed without a trace of humor.

Responding more to the attitude than the words, Senator Lawrence ceased his reverie, turned to the reporter, and nailed his eyes. "Quite. Shall we have a seat over there?" The smile was gone— as were the pleasantries.

Metcalf verified the nearby location of the two agents, along with the presence of about ten other people in the vicinity, and followed Lawrence to one of a pair of back-to-back concrete benches, separated by perhaps fifteen feet. With one of the agents protecting the other bench, the two men had generous private space in which to converse while being virtually surrounded by park visitors. He removed his recorder, held it up for the Senator to clearly see, and received a nod. He turned it on, made sure it was working and then identified the date, time, location, and personnel present. With all the formalities complete, he set the recorder on the bench and got ready for some hardball. However, before he could ask his first question, before he could take charge and control of the interview, Senator Lawrence threw the first pitch:

"I take it from your attitude, Michael, that I can't yet count on your vote?"

Now, there was an understatement.

"No Senator, you can't, but I'm not sure why, and I was kinda hoping this interview would help clarify things for me personally. It's a strange dichotomy: when I did the research on you, the man, and then listened to, or read, your speeches and position statements, I actually felt excited and ready to cheer—here was a man who didn't give a rat's ass about the political ramifications of what he said, a man who spoke his mind and wasn't beholden to any PAC or corporation, and a man who really had a grasp on the world situation; and if I were the average Joe out there in blue collar land, you'd be my man in a heartbeat. You were perfect, Senator..."

"And that's when your alarms went off, I suppose," the Senator finished the sentence.

"Yes, sir. I've been in Washington long enough to know that when something, or someone, seems perfect, there is invariably a stink to be found somewhere. Washington is the capital of "the lesser evil," Senator. The 'perfect' politician is a contradiction in terms, and so I made it my mission to prove myself correct: that you had your own skeleton somewhere."

"And....."

"And—I haven't found it yet, but I'm getting close. We'll see—maybe after today...."

"Then, by all means, let's get started. I'm rather certain that by the time this interview is over, there will be no secrets left for you to unravel. Ask your first question, Michael."

Something important just whooshed by the reporter's brain, but it was moving too fast, and without enough of a handle to grasp to make any sense of. It would become an unfortunate pattern the entire interview. The reporter didn't want to freak out his target too early in the interview and thus force him behind a defensive wall, so he began with a slow pitch—something comfortable: "Sir, on both 'Newsmakers' and at yesterday's press conference, you implied that, not only will America *not* win the war on terrorism, or the war in Iraq, but that civilization is going downhill. As you know, that has disturbed many voters, as evidenced by the latest polls. Is there anything you would like to add to your statements on the issue?"

Truman Lawrence casually nodded while intently watching a crow in a nearby tree top. Without looking once at Metcalf, he added to the enigma that was gaining more and more media coverage: "Not to belabor the obvious, Michael, but the world is not the same place that it was twenty or thirty years ago. Because of the Internet, any half-way astute person with a modicum of curiosity can quickly ascertain the depth and significance of the disparities and polarizations now consuming our civilization. The issues will not be so much between 'good and evil' as so many of your kind like to believe, but between their own consciousness and unconsciousness, between the need to give and the desire to take, between a focus on the present rather than making sure there will be a 'present' in the future.

"The third world understands, well, the real facts of survival dynamics. But for the first world, the genteel race—in America, Japan, and Europe—the idea of survival is to have a bigger SUV, a bigger TV, a bigger refrigerator, a bigger home, a personal generator, and a job that will make it all happen. At the moment, the 'haves' live secure in the belief that they will survive any storm that comes along, while the 'have nots' are too busy surviving each day to give a rip about some metaphoric storm coming next year or ten years down the line. It is enormously ludicrous to me how wealth can so blind those who think they have it. While living in sublime comfort, it seems to not occur that money cannot buy clean air to breathe, that even a thousand dollars cannot buy a loaf of bread if there is none, or that the gas that runs their personal generator will soon run out and that additional fuel supplies may not exist. But the storm will come, my friend. Mark my words.

"And do you know when America's decline began? It began when circumstances dictated that both parents had to work—away from the home—leaving the child to fend for him- or herself. It began with the infants being dropped off at day care, bonding with the teacher, coming home late with strangers, going to bed, and then repeating the cycle for months or years on end. In our achievement as a modern civilization, the twenty-first century babysitter is the TV, computer, and cell phone. Where's the heart and soul of those children when they become adults, Michael? I can assure you that it lies not with making planet Earth a better place for all who inhabit it."

Metcalf was simply floored by the sociological, philosophical outpourings from the potential vice-president of the United States. Once again, he felt those stirrings inside that said this was the only man to lead the United States of America in these turbulent times. Nonetheless, there were other, more pressing questions to be answered; and there was Jennifer Brown, and Shannon, and a blown-up yacht to get to the bottom of. One step at a time.

"Senator, do you really think your Middle East proposal has a chance of working?" The response he received was the last thing on Earth he expected.

Still admiring the rose garden, but with a smirk and a shake of his head, "You don't really believe that crock of excrement do you, Michael?" Lawrence asked, although it was more a statement than a question. "I mean, as the most cynical reporter I've ever come across, as well as being reasonably bright, I would have thought you'd see right through that one."

Even in his shock, Metcalf was able to resist the temptation to bang on the side of his head for a reality check because what he thought he'd just heard was simply not possible. Nonetheless, he hazarded a clandestine look at his recorder to make sure, please God, that it was moving 'round and 'round.

"My, my—if you're buying into that one, things are going better than I ever could have imagined." He paused for a second to savor the moment, to savor another piece of evidence that his plan was moving along nicely. "Okay, well, to answer your question, there's not a chance in hell that my proposal will work—not this year, not next year, and not a hundred years from now. The players are just too far gone for logic or common sense to take root. Some Palestinian group will continue to kill Israelis, the Israelis will tire of waiting for cooler heads to prevail and they'll end up killing most of the resident Palestinians, and forcing the rest into refugee camps—concentration camps by any other name—isn't the irony delicious?"

Lawrence took a moment to let his words sink in, looked into the reporter's eyes, and furled his eyebrows. "Are you getting clarified, my ambitious friend?" The subtle smile spoke volumes about his understanding of the journalist's motivations. Truman turned back to the lake-that's-almost-an-ocean and continued his mind-blowing revelation, Metcalf hanging on every word. "It's almost like there's something in the water over there—something that makes for strife, warfare, hatred, bitterness, poverty, hopelessness—and no one can figure it out, much less do anything about it. Furthermore, if you remove the tribal combatants from the area and place them in virtually any civilized, productive country of the world, they'll get right with the program and become all civil and peaceful-like themselves. But, then, if they return to their homeland, their progressive thoughts and ideas are purged from their bodies and souls while they are handed a primer on hatred, along with a gun or a detonator to wear as an 'honorable' cloak of freedom."

A brief silence preceded a change of subject, one that was about to take the reporter to new and uncharted waters. Jennifer Brown's warning of the true nature of Lawrence was about to scroll across his brain:

"Did you know, Michael, that the Earth is a major battlefield for good and evil—both figuratively and literally? Beings from all over the Universe come here to participate or watch the action because, as with any big venue, the action here gets pretty hot and heavy. And as with any battlefield, there's usually a focal point—the hub from which the action emanates. On Earth, that place is none other than the land historically known as Palestine. How's that grab you?"

It grabbed the reporter just fine because his warning alarms had begun to go off in earnest, but they stopped short when his mind convinced itself that the stimuli lay, not in danger, but in the realization that Senator Truman Lawrence might well be insane. For the second time this day, it was the wrong conclusion (well, not totally wrong), and he was about to pay dearly for his self-deception.

The Senator snickered, "I've never seen a speechless reporter before," and then he went on. "The beings are gathering right now, Michael—even as we speak. You see, there's a possibility that a huge battle will occur within the next few days—an 'end of humanity' kind of battle." The thrill emanating from Lawrence was palpable, "Cosmic battles don't get any bigger than this one—or, at least, not any more important…"

"Are you involved, Senator?" Metcalf asked, sure he was being facetious, but wanting to give the man more rope with which to hang himself. Another glance confirmed the recorder was continuing to collect the bits and pieces of a major scoop.

"Why, yes, Michael, I am—and very perceptive of you to ask. Not wanting to toot my own horn too loudly, I'll just say for now that I'll be on center stage—if it actually comes down to that."

Suspicions confirmed—he's certifiable.

"But getting back to Israel and the Middle East, you know—it's interesting—whenever an outside force pays the area a visit, to pacify and civilize the place, don't you know—the indigenous tribes miraculously begin working together in efficient, if not loving, harmony against their common intruder. But the moment that intruder leaves this hot bed of insurrection, the tribes invariably return to fighting each other. I suppose it just verifies that the prevailing way of life in the region is 'us or them,' always 'us or them.' Whenever someone, usually some well-meaning, advanced outside government, tries to rewrite the playbook with 'us *and* them' ideas, the end result is invariably disastrous. And it's certainly been no different with the current tenants."

But, how is it possible for an insane man to become so wealthy, so powerful, and to achieve such an important position?

The Bringer of Bad News continued: "No, I'm afraid in the final analysis, it's simply not possible for the Jews and Palestinians to live together in peaceful coexistence. One or the other will ultimately need to be..."

The reporter realized that he had begun vacillating back and forth between the excitement of exposing a lunatic and the feeling that, witnesses or not, he was in grave danger.

"...eliminated from the area. Even if by some miracle they began to move toward serious peace talks, I would personally put a stop to the process at once. I assure you, if the players deviate from my game plan, I'll be glad to sponsor a few suicide bombings of my own. There's always some family over there willing to sell their son or daughter for a few pieces of silver, Michael. No problem."

Insane or not, and "not" wasn't really a serious consideration because it implied that the Senator might be speaking the truth with authoritative knowledge—which was way beyond the realm of possibility (wasn't it?), Metcalf should have picked up his toys and run like hell. But the ace investigative reporter for the *Washington Post* was having the time of his life—hearing and recording words that $100 million couldn't buy but which were being given to him, instead, on a platter; words that tomorrow or the next day would terminate a presidential campaign and send two prominent American political fixtures into political exile. Oh—and don't forget Pulitzer number three for dessert.

But, first things first, because even as unbelievable as it all was, Metcalf recognized the need to stay focused on the interview, the man, the questions, and the follow-ups. He checked the recorder again, and resisted the smile that wanted to come. Many new questions were popping into his head as the Senator continued to bury himself, but he wanted to save the big ones for later. "You're also assuming, sir, that the House and Senate would authorize such a plan, a—what is it, Senator, a pull-out?"

A slight wind had come up, from the southwest rather than off the lake. Although it was a gentle breeze in the protected park, low level whitecaps were beginning to form on the lake's vast surface. An audible sigh came from the Senator—a sigh of satisfaction, of being glad to be alive. In a fatherly gesture, Metcalf supposed, even though they were close in age, Truman raised his right arm from his lap and laid his hand over Metcalf's left forearm. It was a gentle move, meant to endear rather than intrude—to share a special moment or emotion. Metcalf had never really enjoyed the sensation of human touch, which had been a bothersome issue in the failed attempt at two marriages. This time was no exception, except for the fact that the "toucher" was not a wife seeking intimacy but one of the most powerful men in the country who was spilling his guts into a seventy-dollar recorder. Metcalf ate his discomfort in favor of perpetuating the moment and tried his best to ignore the five-fingered touch of foreign flesh.

"Look out there, Michael," said the Senator as his other arm rose to encompass the magnificent scene before them. "Isn't it beautiful with the wind creating the white caps? It's almost like looking out over the ocean but without the salt air. I miss the salty air of the Coast, but this is still wonderful. Don't worry yourself over Congress, Michael; you'd be amazed at how many of them are sick to death of the Jewish influence in our affairs, not to mention the ridiculous sums we are spending on a lost cause in Iraq. And there's certainly no love lost for the Palestinians or Arabs. In fact, just about everyone would like the whole thing to go away, as long as there was some assurance that a pull-out, as you call it, wouldn't ultimately cause a worse scenario than that which we have already. As President, I'll assuage their fears long enough to get all the necessary legislation passed."

"You mean 'vice-president', don't you sir? You said, 'president,' I believe."

"Did I? Hmm, slip of the tongue, I suppose," and again, with his left arm, he flicked away the "slip" as if it were a troublesome mosquito, "but between you and me, Michael, we both know that all the decisions will be coming from my office and not from Reardon's. It should be obvious to you that this is my show and that Reardon is just along for some legitimacy and votes. I doubt he'll last the first two months in office before a stroke removes him from the stress, poor thing. I will, of course, have no such limitations." And with the last, he turned to Metcalf, looked right through the reporter's eyes, and smiled again. "Right after my usurpation of the Oval Office, I'll be setting the wheels in motion that will mark the beginning of the end for the human species. My plan for America's withdrawal from the Middle East will ignite the fuse. But just as everything is about to fall apart in the quagmire that everyone secretly fears so greatly, yours truly will cause a wonderful—as yet undefined—event to occur that will temporarily bring peace and common sense back to the forefront. I will be elected to a second term, and during that term things will once again become unglued so that the magical machinations of Truman Lawrence will be desperately hoped for again. Alas, however, just as my efforts begin to show results, someone will point out that my second term shall not be long enough for me to finish my good work, poor America, poor world. A repeal of the twenty-second Amendment will be suggested, hotly debated, but finally passed just in the nick of time to prevent the next catastrophe from destroying everything. In the short term, everything will look rosy and everyone will love me. In the long term, though, humanity's fate will have been sealed."

Metcalf was astounded, and without removing his eyes from those of the astounder, he had to make sure, for professionalism's sake, that the interviewee knew how deep was the shit in which he was now standing. "Senator Lawrence," his voice began and was actually shaking a bit with excitement—and with growing concern, "I want to verify to you that I'm recording everything you're saying. You are aware of that, aren't you, sir?"

"Why, yes, Michael, I'm aware of that," and then softly, conspiratorially, "And are you aware yet that your life is in the process of ending?" Metcalf's eyes immediately focused, no longer caught up in the excitement and the fantasy of Pulitzer number three. Something of substantially greater importance had just been brought to his attention and required the adjustment of a billion or so neurons. "It began a few minutes ago when I placed my hand over your forearm," said the Senator, never wavering from his eye contact with the recipient of his pleasure.

With sudden recollection, the reporter remembered his distaste for human touch and decided to terminate the contact without further delay. He jerked his arm away from the Senator's grip—at least that was the instruction he sent from his brain to the muscles of his arm, and at first he was more surprised than frightened to look down and see that no movement of any sort had occurred. But fear quickly pushed aside surprise, and in a reaction that anyone could relate to, all logical thoughts were suspended while the body went into automatic fight or flight mode. The mind instructed the body, in general, but the legs specifically, to get the hell out of the park, out of Duluth, and maybe out of the state as fast as possible; and once again the body considered with fascination the fact that nothing was happening at the issuance of otherwise off-the-shelf muscular commands. He tried again, looking at his legs, willing them to at least twitch. But there was nothing. He was apparently talking on a dead line.

It finally sank in to the reporter with three desperate words he thought: *I can't move.* And then he said them out loud after looking back into the face of Lawrence, "I can't move." Apparently, there was no problem with moving his neck and head or with speaking.

"Yes, Michael, I know," the sweetness of the delivery rolled like molasses. Truman's hand remained gently in place over Metcalf's forearm. "Let us just enjoy the day for a few minutes until your fear subsides a bit, then I'll explain to you what is happening. Would that be alright with you, Michael?"

Would that be all right, Michael? Is that what he said? My God, what the hell's going on here? I can't move—I'm paralyzed—and he's asking me if "that would be all right." Just on the other side of the fear and confusion were the previous words: "and are you aware that your life is in the process of ending?" and when the absurd words were put into conjunction with the very real paralysis, Metcalf finally understood why the Senator had been so free with his comments. Somehow, witnesses or not, Michael was meant to die at this place, on this date. And then the same fear and resignation that a death row inmate must feel on his way to the execution chamber took hold of the reporter's body. He was already strapped to the table and the injections, or whatever Lawrence was doing, had begun. He was already dying, according to his killer, and there was presumably nothing he could do about it. The fear of the unknown came in a wave then—not a short and tall wave like at the Wedge of Newport Beach, but a long, growing wave that could be seen a long ways out—maybe like a Tsunami wave—that would build and build and then pick him up and carry him to his death.

Metcalf could suddenly hear the rumblings of what sounded like a diesel train approaching, and for a second he thought it might be part of the death process. But then, as the noise became overwhelming, he saw the forceful expulsion of exhaust smoke emanating from just beyond the concrete wall separating them from the giant lake. Apparently there were active tracks below that he'd missed on his initial inspection; and it wasn't, after all, some spiritual passenger train collecting souls for a one-way trip to paradise.

Without realizing he was doing it, a vision of his mother and him entered his awareness. His father came around the corner of the garage with a brand new, floppy-eared Cavalier King Charles Spaniel folded up in his arms. It had been the happiest day in his life. He began remembering other days, other experiences—all long forgotten. Then Metcalf returned to the here and now long enough to understand what he was doing. As he had so often read about, he was feeling near-death panic and flashing back over his whole life in the seconds remaining to him. If enough time were left, his whole life could probably be recalled from the deepest, most remote corners of his brain. He knew it was happening. He knew in another flash that the end of his sordid life was moments away, and he became very frightened.

But then anger entered the equation because it was all so unfair. What had he done to deserve this? Answer: Nothing! What gave that asshole the right to terminate his life? Answer: Nothing! He was being cheated out of years of life—and he couldn't do anything about it but complain. Or could he? How was he doing this, this—paralysis thing? Other than not being able to move, he felt fine—just scared and confused. Maybe he could yet break away...

"That's it, Michael. Let your curiosity come forward. Oh, yes, but how could you have possibly known that I read minds quite well. And to answer that other question, there is no longer any escaping your destiny, my friend. The path is set. Certain damage has already occurred in your body that cannot be reversed. I could have ended your life immediately, of course, but I thought that you, as an investigative reporter, would enjoy the whole dog and pony show, if you know what I mean. Did I assume correctly? I'm in no particular hurry and, well frankly, you're not going anywhere either, so why not try and enjoy the whole experience for what it is?"

"What it is? What do you mean?" the inane question amazed Metcalf, but he couldn't stop it from coming out because, despite the fear, his curiosity did seem to still be alive and well.

"Why, the miracle of death, of course—in its own way just as amazing as the miracle of birth. You see, you as a body will be separating from you as a being. Your body will die and be buried or cremated, but your being will return to the continuum and live forever. You will rejoin old friends and family from previous lives, you'll share experiences, talk about Karma, and actually, it's all rather boring now that I recall it. But for you, it should be quite an eye-opener as you pass over to the other side. If you want, I'll be your guide and walk you through the whole process, like beginning with your feet. There, you should be feeling some tingles now, right?"

It wasn't the least bit tingly feeling for Metcalf, but more like a growing case of a limb falling asleep and it was getting worse and very uncomfortable, and the look on his face and a moan must have been enough for Truman to realize that there was pain involved.

"Oh, let me take care of that—there, is that better?" And it was. "If you're adept at this sort of thing, controlling pain is very simple. But you see now, life has just left your feet and is coming slowly up your legs, leaving behind a dead shell that will feed the Earth. I've always been an avid supporter of recycling. Did you know that?"

Certifiable...

Now that he could feel some tangible evidence that the man sitting next to him could indeed do things inside his body (apparently, causing paralysis alone didn't count), Metcalf's perspective on his life, or the diminishing of it, changed yet again—perhaps for the last time. He realized from his pathetic question earlier that he could still talk, and move his head. In a last ditch effort to change the outcome of his final interview, he tried to scream for help, but to scream first requires a large intake of air for the vocal chords and his effort to do so instantly resulted in a coughing spell that took a good minute to recover from.

"Oh—I'm so sorry, Michael, I should have warned you about that. I've restricted your bronchial capacity to prevent just such an attempt to call for rescue but at the same time to permit a sufficient volume of air to sustain your brain and heart. Your other vital organs, I must report, are already in pretty bad shape."

241

"Why?" he asked quietly, not wanting to risk another round of coughing. "Who are you? How are you doing this?"

"Ah, the investigative reporter returns, curiosity healthy and intact, at least for a few more minutes. You ask why? You know why, my friend. You threatened me: my reputation, my career, my plans. You may be able to do that to some people and get away with no more that just hard feelings; however, the price of doing evil unto me is substantially greater. I have no qualms about terminating bodies and sending beings back to the other side. As to 'Who am I?', well that's not all that complicated. I'm just a little ol' body that happens to be controlled by a rather powerful being—instead of a body working unconsciously with a being, as is the case with virtually every other person in the world. I took over this body when it drowned back in the late '60s, but you probably know all about that incident.

Metcalf's body was changing constantly now—he could feel it. Somewhere down in his calves he could actually feel fluids being sucked upwards and he had to look down to make sure his legs weren't disappearing because that's what it felt like. Somehow, he knew it wasn't fluids leaving his body, but life force. His body was dying, one inch at a time, from his feet upward, and he was watching and feeling it all the way. It was both unbearably frightening and unceasingly fascinating. And his body was filling with sadness. "What's happening to me?"

"Well, essentially, I'm disconnecting your nervous system. I have to do it carefully, you see, or I could end up killing you faster than either of us wants. I need to allow some things to continue to operate while terminating other functions. It's an excruciatingly exact process that requires years of training and focus. I find it much more challenging than chess. We'll end up at your heart, of course, but your brain will be the last to go. If I'm especially careful, and I will try to be—just for you, Michael—you'll still be just barely alive when your being cuts the cord and pulls out of your body. Trust me, Michael, it is an exquisite experience, much better than sex."

"Who are you—I mean, what...."

"You mean, what is my purpose, my goal, my raison d'etre—something like that?"

Metcalf could feel his energy dissipating. Nodding his head seemed to be easier than generating an affirmative spoken reply.

"Hmm, strange, now that I think about it. I've never been asked that specific question before; I've never had to put my agenda into words before. I suppose I could just say, 'because I'm able to and because it's fun,' but there really is more to my motive than that. My purpose, Michael, is chaos and misery. I intend to bring human civilization to utter, complete, total, desperate, frightening chaos. And then, when they are at their most helpless, despicable, savage selves, I will step up to the plate and offer salvation. Price of admission: their souls. Sound familiar? Oh, the Karma!," and little beads of sweat began to exit millions of pores on the Senator's face in his anticipatory zeal. "It's an old theme, of course, and we've been prepping Earth for centuries. It's nearly time, and it will be my honor to gather the flock and lead them to the cliff. The Palestinian-Jewish thing will be the catalyst—the straw that breaks the camel's back, so to speak."

"How?" Although his body was fading, there still appeared to be nothing amiss yet with the reporter's brain.

"Assuming I end up in the director's chair—which is a fairly safe assumption, as you should know—I'll get the legislation passed that will prevent the United States from interfering in any way with affairs in the region. Without our influence, the European influence, usually irresolute at best, will be negligible. At that point, the Palestinians and the Jews will be free to decimate one another, should they choose— and they will choose, don't you know. By the way, I'll also be pushing antiterrorism bills through Congress designed to further protect American citizens from future attacks, with only a slight depreciation of their guaranteed rights. Unfortunately, as those slippery terrorists continue to thwart our protective systems, amendments to the laws will be required with, I'm afraid, additional parallel adjustments to personal rights. Alas, civil protection can exact a heavy price." The Senator smiled and chuckled a little as he concluded the scenario, "I'm sure you get the picture."

"But how...." Metcalf could not turn off his curiosity even though he could almost watch the "line of death" work its way up his pelvis.

"You mean, what will happen in Israel to send the whole of humanity over the edge? Simple, of course: the players do all the work while I sit back and direct from behind the scenes. They'll continue to hate each other (as directed by their mutual leaders), fight each other, and kill each other. Left to their own devices, one day

Hesbullah or Hammas (despite Arafat's pathetic efforts to reign them in) will go too far, and Israel will finally unleash their dogs of war, without limitations. A thousand years of psychological persecution will be expunged in a matter of days. The result will be the near annihilation of Palestinians within Israel's borders. The surviving few will be given the opportunity to go into permanent exile or live out their remaining lives in concentration camps. They will have no power, no government, no self-esteem, no self-respect, and absolutely no hope. All they will have is an underlying, seething, never-ending, always-growing, festering anger. It will be beyond hate. They will be silently livid with the vision of eventual revenge. And I, through my associates, will provide the means for them to have their revenge. I will provide the remaining radicals with a nuke—a nuke from Allah—and not some miniature suitcase bomb, either. No sirree, we'll get them a ten megaton, city-buster warhead, and then we'll help them figure out a way to get it into downtown Tel Aviv. And as they prepare to push the button, they'll let the good citizens of the Jewish capital know that Allah has approved their plan, that Muslims the world over will be celebrating tonight, and adios civilization as you've known it. That will mark the beginning of the end, Michael. It will all go downhill from there: holy wars, economic wars, racial wars—it will truly be beautiful.

"We've worked a long time for this moment, my friend. At long last, all the ingredients are finally in place to complete the recipe. As always, throughout history, the hatred is there. What's different from the past, though, is the availability of modern weaponry, making potential death and destruction much greater. And, as everyone knows, it's information dissemination that really defines our modern era. Now the blood and guts can be seen in every home in real time ('Where do I send a donation, please?'). Finally, population density has made it inevitable, like never before, to have an incident—some kind of incident—almost everyday. So, with all the ingredients on the table, the chef—me, I'm proud to admit—needs only shake things up a bit, bake at 10,000°F for a few seconds, and voilà, one Chaos Soufflé coming right up. Now, Mr. Metcalf, are you completely and totally clear?"

But Metcalf seemed to be missing or not quite totally there. "Michael—Michael, you still there, Michael? Are you still with me? I apologize for getting a little carried away, but it's a subject near and dear to my heart, and I've been shaping it for so long…"

"I—I don't want to die." But Metcalf was beginning to fade, and his words came out as a whisper. His breathing had become very shallow and he could feel the line moving up his abdomen now. It was almost like standing in an empty pool then having the water slowly fill and envelop your body—only in Metcalf's case, it was the reverse. He knew the end was near. He was scared. Despite the presence of the creature next to him, he felt alone—and lonely. He began to whimper.

"Well, it's a little late for that, now, isn't it? I trust you are in no discomfort. If you are, just tell me and I'll take care of it. I really do not want you to suffer. Do you see any unusual lights yet, Michael? The door should be opening pretty soon."

"Please…"

"What's that, Michael? I can't hear you."

"Pleeeze…"

"Don't beg, Michael. It doesn't become one of your stature. Oh, dear, there's a tear in your eye. Should I wipe it away for you?" Without waiting for an answer, Truman pulled a monogrammed ultrasoft handkerchief from his jacket pocket and delicately dabbed at the corner of Michael's eye—first the left one, then the other. "There—that's better."

"What's that you're thinking? …Jennifer?…. Oh, Jennifer Bryant. You're wondering if I'll hurt her? Well, I don't know. Show me what she knows, Michael, and then I'll tell you. No, no, Michael—you can't keep it from me. Ah, so Jennifer knows I blew up the yacht. Well, now, I wonder how she discovered that little bit of information? You're worried about someone else—and so is Jennifer. Hmm, who could that be? Let it out, Michael, you'll feel better afterward. No? Well, let me poke around a little—just there—yes, there it is. Okay, you're worried about Shannon. Shannon who? Oh, darn, you're fading just a little too much now, Michael. Hmm, I can't think of any Shannon I know. Well, I guess I'll have to pay Jennifer a visit—perhaps during my next trip home, when I have more time.

"…k ou…"

"I'm sorry, Michael, I missed that one all together. Try again, and I'll get down here real close."

"...uck...yo..." but it just wouldn't come out right. Nonetheless, Dr. Death gleaned the general sentiment.

"Oh, yes, I got it. The man's dying words, but not quite as articulate as one could have hoped for. I believe it's time, Michael. What do you think? Hmm, well, I suppose no answer is still an answer. Okay, then, here we go, one more little squeeze—Good bye, Michael—enjoy your trip."

It was impossible to tell if Lawrence shot a last bolt of something into Metcalf's body, but he let go of the former reporter's forearm and then placed his hand over the recording device. He left the machine running, but with the same ease he used to reroute the electrical signals in Metcalf's nervous system, he turned his hand into a high gauss magnet and erased the tape completely. He left the recorder right there, and went into the mindset of the thespian he'd been all his life: He began shaking the body next to him, then he jumped up from the bench and began yelling for help.

The Secret Service agents were at the bench in less than two seconds, the call for medics went out within five seconds after that, but the star reporter from the *Washington Post* was way beyond any Earthly assistance.

From any dictionary…

Evil: morally bad, wicked, causing pain or suffering

_"It's easy to spot an evil act when the event, or its aftermath,
is broadcast on television as victims lay dead or dying.
Less obvious, and ultimately more damaging to our future,
are the millions of 'events' we perpetrate upon one another
each and every day, year after year, century after century:
the unkind act, the angry blast of energy, the ignoring of the
suffering of our fellow humans, the casual violent attack, or
the ill-chosen word. The 9-11s may **shake** civilization, but
it's the daily acts of evil (or kindness) that **shape** it."_

chapter sixteen

Rocky Stumbles

Philadelphia, Pennsylvania

Leaving the comfort and safety of Mable's womb was not the happiest moment of their journey. For something like ten hours they had had no concerns at all, safe in the confidence that Truman Lawrence didn't have a clue as to their ten-twenty. They had listened to great songs, slept or sat in comfort without having to keep one eye opened, had plenty of fairly decent snack-type food and drink, had low-key conversations with a great truck driver from Alabama, and generally had a few hours' reprieve from possible mutilation and/or death. Justin had finally gotten an answer to his long-standing quandary about the "popping" noises that trucks make when slowing down—learning about Jake brakes and the way they open the exhaust valve just before the power stroke of the engine: all resistance with no power stroke means the truck slows down. Easy....

But the good times were now over as the enormous Kenworth arrived at its destination.

Buck had backed the big rig into a narrow passage between two other trucks with the consummate skill that no longer surprised his passengers at all. Remaining in the truck while Buck made arrangements for the off-loading of his strawberries and did all the necessary paper work, Justin and Max firmed up their plans for the next twenty-four hours. They had gotten Buck a little involved in their strategy sessions because it was nearly impossible to talk about the subject without his hearing every word. So, sometime around mid-morning, Max came up with a story in which he had seen some things out in the desert of California that he wasn't supposed to see, and some very nasty aerospace heavies had been trying to convince him to keep his yap shut. But Max, being Max, told them to shove it, and that's when things got "a might interestin'"—as in 'kind of dangerous.' Anyway, he told Buck he'd enlisted the help of his friend Justin the Journalist, and they were both making a beeline for the office of a friendly Senator in Washington, where they would be safe and have a sympathetic ear.

With the legend laid down, Buck put his thinking cap on, pulled in years of East Coast driving experience, and put a plan before them. What they should do, he insisted, was find a semi-dive of a hotel in Wilmington to hole-up in for the night, then catch a train in the morning to one of the outlying stations outside Washington. By following his plan, they would avoid the really big stations of Philadelphia and Washington, where the enemy's eyes might be in search of them. By staying overnight in Wilmington, which was just across the river from Philly and south a skosh, they would avoid layovers and other opportunities for being spotted. Wilmington, you see, he conspiratorially told his new friends, is on the mainline, so no delays. He went on to promise them that he'd personally take them to a truck stop he knew on the outskirts of Wilmington, talk to his fellow truckers and determine a suitable flop house for them that wasn't too far from the train station. Max and Justin loved the plan. Besides being smart, it limited their exposure just in finding a place to hang out for the night.

So, at 5:00 P.M., the three of them were having a leisurely dinner in Wilmington. Buck, as good as his word, had brought them to "his" truck stop, talked to a couple of locals, and gotten directions to The Balmoral, most certainly not to be confused with its namesake in Edinburgh. After dinner, the three of them walked out to Buck's rig together, and they were all getting kind of back-slapping dopey for being kick-ass kind of guys, but they were friends now, with two of them going into harm's way again. Buck pulled the compression release, fired up the Cummins, went through his set procedures of checking oil, thumping tires, and checking lights, then climbed into the driver's seat and slipped the main and Brownie into gear, gears quietly meshing in nominal fashion, and everything was a go. He smiled at his co-conspirators, released the parking brake and began to move, but just then, Max jumped up onto the running board with a message for Buck: "Buck, you watch football?"

"Hell, don't everyone?" the trucker said, "unless I'm on the road, but even then I'll sometimes take a break and try to pick up the game on my TV back there. Why?"

"If ya can, watch the Redskins game tomorrow night. Okay?"

"Ya got a line, Max?" he asked, but Max had jumped back down to the tarmac. "Who's gonna win, Max?" Buck shouted.

Max thought about it for a second, then yelled back, "I am..." to which the trucker looked at Max in a strange sort of way.

They watched Buck disappear onto the interstate ramp then walked the two blocks, as instructed, to the proper bus stop for reaching their destination. As they stepped over an apparently seldom-used pair of railroad tracks, a glint of semi-shiny metal caught Maley's eye—he stopped, bent over and retrieved a squashed piece of copper—formerly a penny. He remembered putting pennies on railroad tracks as a kid; most of the time you could find them but sometimes not. He was about to toss the piece of scrap, but Max held out his hand, requesting a look-see. As they kept walking, the old man became intently focused on the useless piece of metal and finally brought it close to Justin's eyes, pointing at it's surface. "See these four spots and this squiggly line, Justin?"

"Yea...."

"This thing's kind of what beings look like, in the raw, in the continuum."

Maley tried to find evidence of mirth and mischief in Max's face, and asked, "You're messing with me right?"

But Max was dead serious and then got a pissed-off look—now he *was* messing with his cohort. "Can I keep this? It might be a Talisman," and Justin waved it away to its new owner. They used two city buses to get to their destination, paid the up-front money and went to the second floor room. It could have been worse but not by much; however, the anonymity suited each of them just fine. The guy at the front desk hadn't asked for IDs, and upon presentation of the registration book, seemed perfectly happy at having Sean Connery and Ben Affleck as his guests. At least it was fairly quiet, so far, and the twin beds appeared to be without a resident bug population. Still, one thought twice about sitting down on anything, especially in the bathroom, and Maley briefly wondered if there were any disinfectant supplies available in the neighborhood. Not likely.

They tried to space out via the TV, but the reception was so lousy as to cause just the opposite effect.

"Max, do you have any special knowledge that Lawrence is going to be at that game tomorrow night?"

The old man got up, turned off the TV and got some water. "No, other than common sense. They're playing the Minnesota Vikings, you know, so everyone thought the chances would be pretty good that he'd go. That was one of the big factors in my choosing this week to pay y'all a little visit."

"Why?"

"Justin, you understand I need to do battle with him, right? I have no assurances that I'm gonna win. In fact, there's a greater possibility that I'll lose. Now, if this big event happens out behind some barn in the boonies, no one will know about it and nothing will have changed. My trip and all the help I've received, from you and the continuum, will have been wasted—and this will be real bad news for the human race. Got it? On the other hand, given the way we'll be fighting, even if I do lose he'll lose, too, as long as we're in a very public place. There'll be nothing normal about a fight between the two of us, Justin—trust me, you won't believe your eyeballs, nor will anyone else. The only chance he'd have would be to get away fast before I take the first swing, so to speak. But I don't intend to let him walk away. No sirree. If we're both in that stadium at the same time, I'll lock the doors and throw away the key. Caesar and the Roman Sports Commission would be proud. My only concern is that he might decide to stay away from all public assemblies if he knows I'm in the neighborhood, and that possibility is very real. He's no fool."

Maley listened to it all, and could not conceive of what a battle between the two would be like. He'd just have to wait for that image, so he changed the subject. Tomorrow was coming fast, and there was no telling what Friday would be like. For all he knew, this might be his last evening with Max.

"What's so important about 'group consciousness'?" he asked.

The change in direction caught Max by surprise—as did the question itself, and he smiled in appreciation of the journalist's mind as he answered. "As a body/being partnership, you've lost contact with the omniscience that's present in the continuum. One of the great challenges of coming back into bodies time after time is to try and bring full consciousness to the body in question. The first step in that process is to realize that there's something there at all—that something like the continuum at least exists. That, of course, is a huge leap of faith when there's no evidence to support the conclusion at all. Faith is a most powerful thing, Justin. Throughout the millennia, that leap of faith, that belief, has cost many their lives—often at the stake or in some other hideous manner. You follow?" Maley nodded, and Max went on after a pull of water—old throats dry out faster than younger ones, and being in a body that had smoked for years didn't help.

"Let's say that five or six of these 'enlightened' believers manage to survive the heretic patrols, come together, and discover that they are of like minds. So they begin getting together, probably cautiously at first, then with enthusiasm as they become more connected. Understand, Justin, that they may not agree on all things—which is to be expected and even desired—but they do adamantly agree on a few common things, one of which is the existence of something like the continuum, which is probably what brought them together in the first place. Like all curious humans, they want to know more. Hell, they want to know everything, and they want to know it right now. So they talk together, they study together, they 'what if' together, and what they quickly end up with is a group consciousness that is better able to put together the secrets of the Universe than each member of the group could do alone. Group consciousness is a consortium of body/beings for the purpose of learning and gaining an understanding of the Universe in which they exist, which also includes the small stuff—like how all the various parts of their planet work in conjunction with each other to provide a balanced environment in which the body/being partnerships can thrive." Max curled his eyebrows, sending a message to Maley that the current thought was completed, inviting comment, and questioning his audience's comprehension. Max's eyebrows had a lot to say.

"Are religious groups part of this group consciousness thing?"

"Of course. They're probably the most obvious, but understand: two people constitute a group of sorts. Virtually everyone on the planet is part of some group consciousness except for maybe the hermits, some homeless folks. But even they, when they temporarily come into contact with another human being, will participate in a brief collective consciousness—whether they're aware of it or not."

"And group consciousness can be used for both good and evil, I'll bet."

Max the Mentor smiled at his helper-turned-partner, and nodded. "You are understanding," he said.

"I suppose, Max, but it's not as easy as fallin' off a log. And it's okay for both kinds of group consciousness to exist at the same time because it's all part of the balance, and if we get too far off center balance we'll croak as a civilization—even if we're all good and wonderful human beings and there's no longer any bad things happening on Earth. Ya see, Max, that's where I start to lose it. I hear you, and I'll take it to the bank because I've come to trust you. But it's really hard to grasp that it's not okay to get rid of all the killing, hating, evil, prejudices, bullies, wars, greed, and various scum—and finally have a healthy planet with a big smiley face on it, visible from the moon. Ya know what I mean?"

Max was chuckling, "Well said, my young friend—you do have a way with words. And you know what? I basically feel the same way. Keep remembering the fulcrum of balance, and that all things survive on one side or the other of that fulcrum, or dead center. You and I live on the side with a leaning toward, now get this Justin, toward 'what we think of as' the good things vs. the bad things in life. The key word there, or words, were 'what we think of,' and that does not imply an absolute. The man three rooms down from here may exist on the other side of the fulcrum point and firmly believe that war is the perfect method for population control, that survival of the fittest is the Golden Rule as he mugs a little old lady for her Social Security check.

He would think that you and I are worthless gobs of spit that are getting in the way of planetary selective breeding. And, he would not be alone. And just like you and I, he would be right. Ain't it a bitch!"

Both men smiled at the irony of it all. "Justin—perhaps it's never occurred to you that half the richness of your life is the result of the actions and beliefs of the other side of that teeter-totter. Webster has given you convenient definitions for all the words you use in communication, but there's a big difference between academics and first-hand experience. For instance, Webster's definition of 'orgasm' doesn't quite live up to the actual event. Right? Think of living at equilibrium, or the fulcrum, as having the definition of a word without having the experience. That's what it's like there, at dead center, and why I told you that civilizations that live in equilibrium are boring and stagnant. It would also be similar to live on one side or the other of the fulcrum without actually experiencing that which exists on the other end of the teeter-totter.

"How significant to you would be the word, 'sublime' if you did not also have firsthand experience with the word, 'grotesque'?" and there went the eyebrows again. "Extend the same dichotomy to dark versus light, hateful versus compassionate, and good versus evil. Webster can provide definitions for each, but true meaning can come only from experiencing both within a balanced civilization."

Maley was leaning back in his rickety chair, taking it all in, and finally beginning to grin a little with understanding. The conundrum was beginning to dissolve as Max's words began to strike some chords of logic within Justin's core. For him, it was starting to pass the smell test.

"So, way back when—Colorado, I think—when you were beating me up about the consciousness of the giant redwoods, you mentioned group consciousness in relation to the trees. How does that work?"

"Group mind, not group consciousness—that's what I said. I suppose it's just semantics, but there's a difference. With the one, you bring in knowledge and understanding; with the other you do things. The group mind is what changes things, big and small, from hometown ethics to worldwide pollution cleanup, or no cleanup—depending on group consciousness. It's a big circle, all interrelated, which should come as no surprise. Your redwood tree thing is an interesting study in how it works and in how the little parts go to make up the whole.

"Picture yourself driving down the highway and, all of a sudden, a mile or so in front of you, is this behemoth of a tree rising some 300 feet into the sky. I dare say, it would nearly take your breath away. You, and perhaps your family, stop, get out, and spend time with this giant and its brethren. You feel the six-inch-thick bark, soft and spongy. You are staggered by your smallness and its girth; its age and your youth; its height and your shortness. It is a hot and sunny summer day and you note a unique aroma in the air—unique unto the redwoods and no other. Then you hear a low-frequency noise emanating from every-where; but infrequently. You soon realize that the sound is of the enormous branches rubbing against one another in a love dance high above you that is also unique to these rare trees. All of this contributes to an awe felt by you, and this awe causes you to deem the grove of Redwoods as being something very special upon the Earth. As you climb back into your car, you give the trees one last admiring look before driving off for the nearest Burger King. How'm I doing?"

"You were right on track until the end. I prefer Wendy's," Justin said with a smile.

"Consciously or not," Max went on, "you have just sent a huge jolt of energy into and all through that tree and/or grove. Your gift brought the trees healing energy, caring energy, and even conscious energy as you came to realize, briefly at least, how perfect the environment can be. You have left a gift behind, and it has joined all the others before you in creating an aura of energy around the grove that feels very much like conscious life. You, Justin, have just contributed to and participated in a group mind activity; and as you travel up the coast, you'll do it some more—at say a spectacular rock formation, or a canyon of ferns, or further east in Monument Valley, or at a river slicing its way through solid rock. As you become a more conscious human being, your threshold of awe will come out of the clouds, back to the soil, and that's when the little maple sapling will become just as big and significant a miracle to you as its three-hundred-foot distant cousin."

Max got up, having to move his stiffening bones, got some more water and occasioned a glance out the window to the street below. The sun was going down and there was quite a crowd going into a pool hall-bar across the street. No one seemed to be paying any special attention to The Balmoral, except maybe the health department.

He came back to the table, as Justin came out of the bathroom, advising: "You have to hold the handle down or it won't flush."

Max began where he had left off: "That's a sample of what an individual's untrained mind is capable of—by untrained, I refer to no direct and conscious connection to the continuum. Now, imagine the possibilities when many minds work together in concert for a specific goal. The results can become amazing, and again, the results can lean toward the dark or light, depending on the group mind at work. This is where religions come into play but also your cults and even the political action groups like the National Rifle Association. Things happen when a large group of people focus their energy on one subject or thing. The best example of all is on the front page of the newspaper everyday, and I'm talkin' about the Jewish race. The political power they possess and wield in world governments is another kind of awesome and completely belies the fact that there are only some 14 million of them on the whole planet. But those 14 million have experienced firsthand the opposite of 'good,' and the race-saving covenant they made amongst themselves is so singularly focused as to virtually defy any threat to their further existence. Theirs is the consummate use of the group mind."

"Speaking of which," Justin jumped in, "how do you think that plays into the proposal that Lawrence has made regarding the Middle East?"

"Hands off—keep away and let's see what happens?" Max asked, and then let the possible strategy roll around in his head a bit. "Okay, first of all, it's unlikely that he'd ever get official approval for that kind of position; however, in desperate times, almost anything can happen. Is the United States desperate enough yet? Probably not. But Lawrence is a silver-tongued devil," and he hesitated a second to make sure his play on words wasn't lost upon his companion...

"Yea, Max, I got it."

...and then Max continued. "He's got to get elected first, and this whole thing has sure put him and the other guy—what's his name—Reardon, yea, it sure has put them in the limelight. Right or wrong, controversy is good for that. My guess, in the end, is that Lawrence really wants to do this leave-'em-alone thing because he sees it as a way to jumpstart his ultimate program—chaos or bust.

"You know, the Jews have never been a race that shies away from bloodshed, when it's really necessary. But after experiencing the extermination of a third of their race during World War II, they've become downright merciless when it comes to protecting the ol' homeland. So, let's say that Reardon and Lawrence get elected, then Reardon mysteriously dies in office—which is a forgone conclusion. Truman becomes president and eventually gets what he's after in the Middle East. The region is left to its own devices, no help or hindrance from the United States and possibly its allies. What will happen?"

"Who knows, Max, but I think it's pretty obvious that if the Palestinians don't cool it, they're gonna get stomped on."

"Right. Now, I wouldn't put it past Lawrence and his crowd to help the Palestinians lob a few bombs into Israel. In fact, not just a few, but a lot. Hell, Truman would probably gladly pay for the suicide bombers to do their thing for God and country—remembering, of course, that God is on their side and no one else's. There's only so far Israel is gonna get pushed before they send in the tanks, and if things get bad enough, the Palestinians within Israel could get pretty much wiped out. All the while, the Arab countries are having a shit fit and want to invade Israel more than ever. But they can't..."

"Why? I mean, there's a hell of a lot more of them than there are Jews, so why not just overrun Israel and be done with it?"

"First off, they've already tried that and lost. Second, the same thing will happen again because, as tough a fighter as any Arab is, as a collective army, they leave much to be desired. It's the tribe thing. Deep down, the Arab countries are warlord states where cohesive cooperation is a rarity. They don't share the same level of group consciousness and group mind that the Israelis do. And lastly, they all know that Israel has nukes, and if Israel feels certain that its end is at hand, no one doubts that they'll lob a bomb into strategic cities and areas of the invading countries—as a parting gift to the victor. And that would probably suit Lawrence just fine. Take out the Arab oil fields and the level of world chaos would have to go up a few notches, don't you think? Yes, I'm rather certain that that scenario would play right into ol' Truman's hands."

"Ya know, Max, it just occurred to me that this whole group consciousness and group mind thing is a lot more complicated than it has to be. Furthermore, the problem with Lawrence wouldn't be a

258

problem, except for the fact that the population as a whole is pretty much unconscious. Right?" The old man nodded his head in a way that invited Justin to complete his thought.

"Okay, so who says it's not okay for bodies to be conscious of the being that comes into them at birth, as well as the continuum and all the knowledge and power that would go with the consciousness? Everything would be a lot more efficient if we were all fully conscious from birth. We would all know, for instance, that Lawrence was a bad dude that shouldn't attain any position of power. Doesn't that make sense?"

Max smiled at his friend because the logic was unassailable, but his reply squashed the thought instantly: "Good idea, my friend, but it doesn't work. It's been done and the results were catastrophic."

"How so? Wait a sec. What do you mean, 'it's been done?' You mean it used to be that way—right here on Earth? What happened?"

Max was nodding his head and trying to get a word in edgewise. "It's a long story, Justin, and one that I don't intend to get bogged down in, but a few million years ago, another race of bipeds lived on Earth, and when they developed enough to become seriously sentient, we beings in the continuum decided to try our first, and last, grand experiment—along the lines of what you just suggested. This race was nearly twice your size and could hold a lot of energy. We began slowly, carefully, and after a period of several generations, all members of the species were fully conscious of both sides: the body side and the continuum side."

"For a while, great and wonderful things happened, as you might imagine. Rather than spreading out, they chose to build spectacular cities at just a few locations on the globe. But sometime during the seventh or eighth generation, problems began to occur—problems directly related to full consciousness-based abilities."

Justin was stunned, and it was obvious that he wanted to know everything, no matter how long it might take. "What kind of problems, Max?"

"Justin—I repeat: I'm not going to get into this, but I'll give you a clue that should lead to clarity: What do you think the result would be if the entire population of Earth were made up of Lawrences on one side of the teeter totter, and Max's on the other side?"

It was a good clue. He nodded in instant understanding, and snickered. "God, it must have been a psychic blood bath."

"Precisely. It didn't happen overnight, but eventually the population of the species began quickly heading toward zero. That's when the continuum realized they had no business being in the psychogenetics field, and we bailed out. We then patiently waited for Homosapiens to develop before beginning the procedures we currently use. For better or worse, this way works."

"Why hasn't anyone found the ruins of these cities, or some other evidence of this race?"

"Because in trying to correct our errors, we attempted to wipe all vestiges of our failure off the face of the planet. We nearly succeeded, but the supply of physical bodies became extinct before the task was complete. As I recall, there are still a couple of cities, smaller ones, remaining somewhere. As far as humans discovering the ruins, I suppose it's just a matter of time—and luck. Or maybe they're buried so deep it'll never happen. I really don't know."

"Wow—that would be a project worth pursuing. You sure you can't remember the locations?'

"I'm sure, and even if I did remember, I think prudence would require that I keep it to myself—at least until talking to some of my associates in the continuum. Now, my young friend, I've got to get out of this room or I'm going to go nuts. There's a pool hall across the street. What say we shoot some pool, have a few beers, and celebrate our quest."

"That sounds great, Max, but are you sure?" and Maley walked to the window to check it out himself. "Wait a sec, Max. That looks like the kind of place Truman's troops would call home. I don't think so..." but he was talking to an empty room as Max was in the hallway walking toward the stairs, having left the door open. "Damn...." was the best he could do, as he grabbed his coat and ran after his friend.

There were three or four men in the lobby of the hotel, mostly reading newspapers and keeping to themselves. No one, including the night manager, gave a rip who was coming down the stairs or where they were going. It was a pleasant evening, and Justin tried to talk Max into just going for a walk—not that he really looked forward to being on the street at night in a strange city and definitely on the wrong side of the tracks. It was just that being confined in a bar with what looked like a rough-and-tumble kind of clientele seemed like the last place they should be hanging out. Yet, Max appeared determined to shoot some pool.

The place was called "The Snug," with a totally incomprehensible derivation but looking like the kind of joint that would serve peanuts for snacks—the shells ending up on the floor—and pitchers of beer to wash away the salt. Then you needed more beer to replace the lost bodily fluids that the alcohol in the first pitcher washed down the ceramic urinal with the stinkiest, most recognizable smell of all: sorry, old-growth redwoods, but for aroma memory, the toilet in a beer joint has got you beat hands down.

The Snug was crowded but mostly in the bar area. Of the dozen or so pool tables, four were still available and, per Max's request, Maley rented the balls and rack and took up residence at the table of their choice. At least the tables were regulation size and not the "insert quarters" type that had been beaten to crap by drunk and pissed-off players. In fact, all the equipment looked to be in pretty good shape with the cues only slightly curved; plenty of chalk was on the tables, and white talcum cones were on the walls at convenient intervals. Maley began to change his mind about Max's idea—this might not be so bad after all.

Max had gotten them a couple of brewskis (using Maley's money, one more time), and offered to break for a game of eight-ball. In under sixty seconds, it was obvious that Maley was going to be doing a lot of sitting. When Max came around the table, with his back to Justin, Justin kind of whispered, "Hey, Max—you guys play pool in the continuum or somethin'?" He was ignored, as Max continued to sink the stripes until there was nothing left for him to sink but the eight ball, which turned out to be a full table-length bank shot— called and made.

As Maley racked up the balls again, Max looked around the room. *He's here, I can feel him. Where? Which one?* Even though he was supposed to break again, Max allowed his partner the honor, which gave Maley the opportunity to move the cue ball around some. He did fairly well until greater distances were involved and then he had to relinquish the table. Max reached for a chalk cube and felt the energy again—looking at him, but he couldn't make out the source: there was just too much stuff flying through the ether. He sank six

261

straight then choked on what should have been a slam dunk. Distracted, but it didn't matter. Maley sunk two more, missed, and then Max cleared the table.

"You rack 'em, Max. I gotta take a leak."

First, Max got two more beers, then began collecting the balls from the six pockets. Momentarily focusing on the business at hand, he never saw it coming—two cue sticks held tight by the skinny end with the fat ends smashing into the right rear quadrant of his skull, and apparently with full force. Max went down immediately and hard, and he didn't move; and an unconscious Max had no more power than a babe in arms. The attacker, who actually looked like a college student in his Dockers and CK Henley shirt, moved to stand at Max's feet. From underneath his windbreaker he pulled a 9mm Baretta from his backside waistband, took aim at the man on the floor, and just as casually as if he were stepping on a cockroach, put a round right through the old guy's heart.

The bar erupted with shocked and terrified patrons that began running for the nearest exit.

...Then another round...

Justin heard the first shot just as he'd started to pee, and stopping a full bladder at that stage is damn near impossible. He knew at once what he'd heard, not some bullshit "backfire" thing, and his gut told him who the target was. He tried to get his urine stream to stop, and it slowly was, but then he heard the second shot.

...Then the third...

Everyone was running away from the scene; no one seemed inclined to jump a man who had a dozen shots reserved for anyone so stupid. The exit doors were jammed with patrons trying to get outside—except for one man still standing at the bar. Detective First Grade, Gordon Nelson had been enjoying a friendly beer following another arduous day, and was watching the Orioles kick some Boston butt up at Camden Yards, when he heard the unmistakable thunk of a head being hit by a heavy object. His suspicions were confirmed when he looked up into the mirror behind the bar. He muttered an "Ah, shit" as he turned in preparation to break up a fight and maybe collar a couple of losers. His heart rate and level of urgency took a tenfold increase when he saw the Baretta clear the perp's jacket.

...Then the fourth...

The police academies may instruct their recruits to keep an empty chamber for safety's sake, but "Gordy's" mamma didn't raise no dummy; and on the streets of Wilmington, as in any big city, cops kept their weapons ready to fire right the hell now. And this was no time for niceties or Mirandas or any of that crap either, because the body on the floor had already taken four slugs and there was no sign the bad guy was going to stop. So, just as he'd been trained and had practiced a million times, Gordy pulled his own Beretta, and in one smooth sweeping motion raised it, cupped his right hand, cocked the weapon, aimed, fired and put one through the shooter's left ear. It had to be a head shot since the guy was sideways, but at less than twenty feet, it was a no-brainer, no pun intended.

The perp was instantly dead, not getting off his fifth for the night, and it was a shame that the beautiful green felt of the nearby table tops, along with the recently painted walls, would all have to be redone, and soon.

Justin came out of the restroom to find a gun swinging his way, so he automatically put his hands way up high. "Stop there, turn around, and face the wall. Don't move; I'll be with ya in a minute. Pete, you got my precinct number?"

"Yea, Gordy, I got it," said the bartender, coming up from behind the bar and shaking like a leaf.

"Call 'em now. Tell 'em it's me and I got a double homocide. Tell 'em we need two meat wagons and a full team here right the fuck now. You got it? Do it!" Detective Nelson then worked his way around one table and over to the "scene." It wasn't pretty—they never were—but neither was it new. There was no chance of either of these two pulling a fast one, so he began to relax. This one was going to be easy: no court room technicalities, a ton of witnesses, the murder weapon— just a bunch of paperwork and one more addition to his collection of nightmares. "Give me a double, Pete. You—over there by the restroom—yea, come here. Keep your hands where I can see them." He frisked Justin, checked his ID, and asked about his line of work and what he was doing here. Satisfied that Maley was okay, the cop quickly ignored him, leaving him to confirm his worst fears. He stepped away from the bar and circuitously made his way along the wall and to the form of his friend on the floor. It was all true. Max laid there with four obvious bullet holes in his chest and was clearly very dead. "Hey, magazine man, get the hell away from there, NOW!"

Justin took a last look, and wishing he could do more, but not wanting problems with the law, backed away as he was told. Since he had been in the restroom at the time, and didn't personally know any of the players (he lied), Detective Nelson allowed him to leave after providing a local address—as in across the street. Maley walked out the door to the sound of what seemed like a hundred sirens, went straight across the street, to his room, and locked the door—before losing it: Crying in uncontrollable sobs, gasping for air, stomach knotting up, he sat on the edge of the bed and wanted to scream but was afraid to. Reality had just hit him like a ten-pound sledgehammer. They had both known this could happen, that this was what the other side had been trying to do for four days. But Max was supposed to fend off all predators, and now Max was dead.

Now what was he going to do—Justin Maley, freelance journalist who had been looking for a story for months—all he lacked was a little subject matter. *Well, Justin, you dumb ass, you finally got your subject matter. Now what?* He'd come to like Max—a lot. It would have been bad enough tomorrow, but not like this. Oh, God!, and the sobs came on all the stronger. *And what about Truman Fucking Lawrence? Now what would happen? Would the continuum send someone else? What had been the back-up plan? What had Max said? Oh, Christ, he said there wasn't one.*

Justin got up, went to the bathroom and finished what he'd started earlier across the street, and he started crying again. *Could I have stopped it from happening?* Thankfully for the future of his mental health, the answer came immediately and clearly: No. He came back into the room, turned off the lights and looked out the window at the mayhem below. There were four patrol cars up and down the street, three others that looked to be unmarked, two ambulances, and a step van that said "Crime Scene Unit" on the side. He sat there on the windowsill, watching, spacing out, and then a gurney came through the entrance of The Snug and snaked its way to one of the ambulances. It carried a black body bag. *Is that you Max?* No, he would get no answer, not any more. An hour later, most of the action was done and gone, and a wasted, empty, emotionally drained Justin

got undressed and under the covers. He prayed—Ha! that's a joke—
for sleep, expecting none, but that night his prayer was answered.

———————

It was a great night to be a news anchor in Baltimore. Instead of
the usual Wednesday night drivel and human interest crap, Phil
Majors had a celebrity death in Duluth, Minnesota to talk about,
although that was mostly a national story with local color coming in
via on-site satellite trucks. The other event was local and they didn't
come any better, with a good, old-fashioned shoot-out nearby in
Wilmington. Even though it was in different state, it was close enough
to be considered "local."

Truman Lawrence and Adam Dempsey were both enjoying a quiet
evening together in the library, shoes off, feet on the table, each sipping their preferred late-night cordial. Adam deserved this moment
of intimate camaraderie, Truman had decided, for finally getting it
right—apparently.

He would have preferred that the story from Duluth not end up
on national TV, but that was inevitable. It's not everyday that a famous
and controversial "spill the beans" reporter ends up dying in the arms
(figuratively speaking) of a famous and also controversial vice-presidential candidate—particularly when the former was no doubt looking to expose secrets while the latter was no doubt trying to hide
them. No, there wasn't a chance in hell that that story would end up
on page twelve of the *Post* or *New York Times*. It didn't matter that
Lawrence was defacto cleared immediately of any wrong doing by the
lack of evidence to the contrary, the lack of trauma, and the eyewit-
ness accounts of two Secret Service agents. The bottom line was that
the reporter, sad as it was, had had a heart attack at a most inoppor-
tune time—for the interviewee, that is. On to the weather, please.

Nonetheless, the man relaxing on the sofa—the one with the
most to lose—was fortunate that the Duluth coroner did not have the
curiosity of a Quincy or a Jordan, a curiosity that would have
demanded, at least for his own benefit, an explanation for the strange
condition of the other organs and tissue of the deceased. It was
enough for him that the heart had obviously suffered severe damage

and was, therefore, ultimately the cause of death, no matter what other nasties might have been in wait around the corner. It certainly wasn't a homicide, so case closed—get on with electing the next vice-president, Duluth's favorite son.

As far as Wilmington, Adam had informed his boss on Truman's return from Minnesota that they had a lead on The Man from up in Delaware, and that Adam's best sleeper was heading there to investigate and take appropriate action. A police contact of Adam's confirmed that one of the two deceased was a Zack Marvin, which was indeed the false name of Adam's man. As he had put four shots into "an older man," it was assumed the dead guy had been identified as the proper target—let us hope.

In a final measure of relief, Truman Lawrence confirmed that the energy he had felt hanging around since the previous Sunday morning, and getting stronger as each day went by, was no longer being felt and therefore no longer the albatross around his neck. By unspoken agreement, Adam would live to see a few more days, and with the last sip of his B & B, the Senator headed for the bedroom and some blissful sleep. Two major obstacles had been eliminated in one day—quite an achievement unto itself—and now the future was looking real good—or bad, depending on one's viewpoint. He smiled at his own humor as he climbed the stairs.

Day Five

"A general review of priorities (a phrase which implies **consciousness***) is probably indicated, having now attained a level wherein we are willing to spend a like sum of money on 'teeth brighteners' as would feed a starving family of four for a week in any undeveloped country of the world."*

chapter seventeen

Goin' Home

Wilmington, Delaware

A knocking at a door did not fit the parameters of the dream, but even in dreams, it would seem, knocking at doors is an intrusion that cannot be ignored. So he left his place on the rocks above the stream, floated over the water to the far side, and reached for the glowing golden door knob, which pulsated with life. He opened the door—but there was nothing—just darkness, an abyss of emptiness, of nonexistence. The knocking continued, only louder. Where was it coming from? There were no other doors that he could see, still the intrusion persisted. It became a pounding, louder and louder, until....

Justin awoke with a start and sat up immediately, nowhere near being in his body and functional. There may also have been a knocking in his dream, but this knocking was quite real here in his hotel room—and then the reality of last night came screaming home. With an immense sadness and longing, Maley remembered that Max was dead—gone forever—mission not accomplished. Max, his newfound friend, had returned to—to the other side, to heaven, to the continuum, to whatever. Had the last four days been real, or had it all been part of the most elaborate dream of all time?

But the knocking at his door continued. To stop it, he fairly yelled, "Alright, alright, hold on a second." Maley looked at his watch, stalling for time, trying to get it together. *Who the hell could be bothering me at 4:35 in the morning? It's still dark out, for Christ's sake.*

He slid on his pants but nothing else, stumbled to the door, and demanded to know who was there. The only answer he got was more pounding. A growing anger trumped any waning fear, so he swung the door open ready to do his own pounding.

Standing before him, looking a little peaked, but there nonetheless, was one Max the Magician, still wearing the shirt laced with four fairly neat bullet holes—standing there, looking into his eyes, almost with a twinkle, and actually smiling.

For the first time in his life, Justin Maley fainted.

The fainting spell, that period of unconsciousness, didn't last too long. Justin's eyes opened, and this time he knew exactly where he was and what had transpired, although he had mysteriously ended up on his bed. He looked at his watch: 4:48 A.M.—ten minutes tops. Upon sitting up, a dizziness descended over his head, affecting both his moves and his thoughts. Max was laid out on the adjoining bed, sound asleep, sawing his logs. Justin shook his head in disbelief, and then he smiled, and then he chuckled—not so much at the fact that his friend had just come back from the dead (happens all the time, right?); but rather that no matter how dire the circumstances, the geezer could turn it all off in a second and catch up on his sorely needed *zzzzzzz*'s.

Still feeling tired and drained, and not wanting (or daring) to wake up Max, Justin laid back down. Pretty soon, a snoring contest was occurring in room 207 of The Balmoral Hotel of Wilmington, Delaware.

Justin awoke to the sound of a game show on the television. If memory served, it was "The Price Is Right," as evidenced by the bidding for anything from laundry detergent to sports cars. His suspicions were confirmed with the obnoxious invitation from the co-host: "Susan Taylor, come on down!" Suddenly, without any warning, the same words emanated from Max the Mouth: "Susan Taylor, come on down!" and spoken with almost perfect inflection. And then he started jiggling up and down on the edge of the bed.

"Jesus, Max, what's so damn funny?"

Max spun around, jumped up, closed his eyes, spread out his arms in invitation like the guy on TV, and said, "Justin Maley, come on down!" And he repeated the invitation, while Justin buried his head under a pillow. Unbelievable. Here's a guy who's talkin about changing the future course of civilization, and he's just gotten hooked on a stupid game show.

Maley came out from under the pillow, sprung out of bed, turned off the tube, all the while chewing on Max: "Max—forget the TV. What happened? You were dead—dead as a mackerel. I saw it—you. You took four slugs, *my* heart stopped, your heart stopped, the paramedics came, put you in a body bag and took off. Now fess-up. Are you immortal? Can you be killed? What?"

Max's head turned and looked out the window for a moment, even though the curtains were drawn—processing his answer. After taking a huge breath, and allowing a sigh just as big, he turned back to his partner. "The answer to your question comes in two parts: First, no, I think you already know that the soul you know as Max cannot be killed, any more than your soul can. Souls are permanent, as long as the Universe exists. But, I suspect you're talking about Max the body. So, secondly, this body is just as subject to injury and death as any other human body. The difference in this case is that the soul in this body, me, has the knowledge, confidence and experience to keep the body functioning. As long as my host body is in one piece and not burned to a crispy critter, I can repair injuries and hold off its fatal diseases, pretty much indefinitely, but at increasingly greater cost to my energy on a being level. Do you understand?"

The math wasn't too hard. "Yea, you can keep your body alive, but you as a being get weaker and weaker with the effort. Which means you're going up against Lawrence with a big disadvantage, right?"

271

"Yes," Max replied without hesitation, "but it won't matter. I'll win, he'll lose, planet Earth will remain in a semi-state of balance—end of story."

"You're not making sense, Max. If Lawrence has greater power than you, and he's young compared to your body, then how's he going to lose?"

Now Max got cryptic, "You'll see. You'll just have to wait. In the meantime, it'll help a lot that he thinks I'm dead, but I need to really watch my energy output or he'll be able to detect my presence again.

This was definitely not what Justin wanted to hear, but he'd played the game enough times with Max to know that no clarification would be forthcoming. Why is it that old farts get so hard-headed, he wondered, not considering that the body Max chose to come into could just as easily been that of a young man, or woman for that matter, and that the cantankerous answer would have been the same.

"Okay, so what happened after the paramedics took you to, to what—the morgue?" Justin wanted to know.

"They put me in one of those lockers, the cold ones, which was just fine. I needed privacy to do my repair work, and cool temperatures help, too. My body never did stop working. I just dialed things back far enough to fool everyone. I kind of put it into suspended animation, ya know? So, after a few hours, I got things patched up enough to get moving. I made the drawer thing open up, unzipped the bag, and found the nearest exit. No big deal..."

Right....no big deal! Lazarus makes a comeback....without any help from his Friend. Justin stared at, and through, Max, mind running in overdrive, wondering, with increasing overwhelm, how he could possibly document all the experiences and realizations of the past four, now five, days.

Max took the silent reverie as an indication that the Q & A session was over. He informed Justin of his need for more sleep before they headed to the stadium. Justin took a shower, dressed, and headed out for breakfast and some more think time.

Truman and Adam were savoring a special celebratory brunch courtesy of Simon, while going over plans for the evening's football game and party. For Adam, the chirping of his cell phone was an unpleasant interruption to the extended experience of rare intimacy with his boss, but chirping cell phones, like a dog that desperately needs to relieve itself, cannot be ignored.

"Dempsey!"

"Put Truman on."

It was the first time in his career with the Master that anyone had ever uttered those three words, or anything like them, and certainly without so much as a, "Hello" or a "Please." It was the wrong way to end the private reverie the devil's helper had been having with his devil.

Not wishing to disturb Lawrence any more than necessary while dealing with the intruder, Adam rose from the table and headed for the door as he challenged the caller. "Who the hell is this? And what the hell do you want. And who the FUCK do you think you're talking to?"

There was a soft chuckle at the other end of the line, then, in an equally soft and silky voice, "Listen to me, little man. I know *exactly* who you are, not to mention your boss; I know all about your 'little beasties,' Adam, and how you like to play with them—as well as yourself—in the darkness of your bedroom late at night. Shall I go on? Or perhaps you would like to pass the phone over to His Highness now. Hmm?"

Dempsey slowly pulled the phone away from his ear, moving it in front of his face, trying desperately to read beneath the "Unavailable" displayed on the tiny screen. His eyes rolled upward and locked on those of Senator Truman Lawrence who was staring at his associate in a most curious and intent manner.

"What is it, Adam?"

"I don't know," he cautiously replied, "but he wants you, and… and he knows things…."

Lawrence sat back in his chair and held out his hand, never taking his eyes off of Adam. He took the phone, "This is Truman Lawrence speaking…."

"Do not go to the game tonight," the handset uttered.

The instantaneous invectives that issued forth from the normally serene Senator from Minnesota made Adam Dempsey take several steps backward—seeking safety from the possible energy release he personally knew so well. But the Senator's energy was focused entirely toward the caller at the other end of the airwaves.

"You fucking moron... you imbecile... you can't do this. You know you can't do this. No one can know about you. What the hell are you doing? Why now, you asshole... we're so close."

Beyond all sense or justification, Lawrence went on for a good minute, totally losing himself in the emotion of perceived breach of security and threat to the consummation of his Grand Plan. When the spittle began forming at the corners of his mouth, he abruptly stopped his tirade, realizing with a sheepish look at the dumbstruck Adam that he was making a fool of himself and actually inviting any prying ears to take serious note of the call. Within a few seconds, Senator Lawrence returned from the visit to his alter ego and once again became the epitome of calm logic.

"There's no reason for me not to go to the game. Besides, it's all arranged and there will be nine important guests there with me. Why are you concerned?"

The caller, still unidentified—other than to Lawrence's intuition—explained, "I had a dream, that's all." But both men knew how important *their* dreams were. "There's danger for you at the stadium. In my dream, you were killed."

"Impossible," Lawrence replied. "Our friend has left us. Perhaps you watched the news last night. He was the unfortunate victim of a gunman in Delaware. His energy is no longer here."

The ensuing silence was the equivalent of a fifty word argument, then, "I stand by my dream."

"Your dream is insignificant. The danger is past and the game, along with my guests, is too important to the campaign to miss. Do not concern yourself... and never, ever call me again. Remember, you exist only if I fail." With that, Lawrence closed the cover of the phone and ended the call.

Somewhere around 12:30, after Justin returned from breakfast-lunch, Max was just waking up from his longish nap. He took a shower, put on different clothes (free of bullet holes and bloodstains) and declared himself ready at 1:00. Justin called a cab from the hotel room using his cell phone, then strolled to the front desk, ostensibly to get a newspaper, but in reality, clandestinely checking out the scene. Nothing seemed amiss—no lurking snoops, crows, warlocks, or just plain head thumpers, so maybe Max was right: Lawrence and company thought Max to be dead, and therefore no longer a threat to them or their plans. Apparently, they were in for a big surprise.

The Yellow Cab arrived, again with nothing weird or threatening from the driver, and they began the two-mile trip to the train station. Maley felt nervous and a little frightened, but Max looked downright calm—an almost sublime countenance all about him. Justin couldn't ignore the contradiction between appearance and purpose, so he asked: "Max, how can you sit there so peacefully when the fate of the world will soon rest in your hands?"

"Exhilarating, isn't it?" Max replied, with a smile and penetrating stare. "Justin, my friend, there's no small level of Karma that I will have cleaned up by the end of this journey—win, lose, or draw. This is as big a deal for me as it is for the residents of Earth, even if they don't know it. That's why I feel so good. Besides—I'm tired, and I'm ready to go home."

As frequently happened over the past five days, the humanness of Max touched Justin. There he was, sitting beside a—what—a man, a being—an entity that has the power to do almost anything? Once again, descriptive words failed him. For in truth, Justin still didn't know all that much about his companion. Five days together, with staggering revelations, and he still did not know the extent of Max's capabilities. He still couldn't really grasp the nature of the place Max called home. And it wasn't because he hadn't been listening and trying to understand. It was just too much—and not enough, at the same time.

They rode in silence for the remainder of the ride. Although the station was fairly busy, the time of day guaranteed short lines and Justin was able to get their tickets quickly. Max pulled a hat out of someplace that fairly well rendered his face invisible to any curious eyes. The concern, of course, was that one of Truman's troops, even though no longer looking for them, would accidentally recognize them and put out the alarm. However, they saw no one who looked the least bit threatening or interested, so they climbed aboard the #2159 train, found suitable seats, and pulled out of the station at 2:33 P.M. The train was the new express—the Acela—and was very quiet and comfortable in addition to being fast. Hopefully, this day would be free of derailments—now and later.

"Justin—we don't have too much more time together, and there's still some things to clean up. You okay with that?"

"Of course," *I mean, yea, bring it on, the more the better—what's a few more surprises when I can't figure out what to do with what I've got already.*

"You understand that today will be our last day together, right? Even if I should happen to luck out and be victorious, this body will not see another sunrise and my being will return to the continuum after the battle." He kept looking into Maley's eyes and nodded his head, prompting an affirmative "I understand" response from his friend.

But Justin was slow to respond—something seemed to have gotten caught in his throat. Finally, "Yea, Max, I understand, but that doesn't mean I have to like it. Okay? Ya know, I thought we'd become—kinda like buddies, or something, and it's not easy to leave real friends that you've been through thick and thin with; and having killers after you qualifies as thick and thin, ya know? So excuse me if I'm not too enthusiastic about the day's events."

Max stared at the side of Maley's face. He reached out and gently put his hand on Justin's shoulder, but Maley wasn't inclined to reciprocate. "Look at me, son."

Son? The new, softer form of address got Justin's attention, and he turned to look Max the Paternal in the eye.

In a sorrowful, regretful voice, Max said, "I have to go back, my friend, and I'm sure you know that and understand why. You also know that we'll be seeing each other again one day, although we'll look very, very different from what you see right now. Remember the squished penny? And we'll talk about old times and the journey we've been on together. And there will be lots of others there listening, too, Justin, because this is big-time Karma stakes we're playing—for both of us. The continuum is watching this round, with bated breath, and the bleachers are full. Corrective action this big seldom happens, and seldom with so much at stake. You've become a good friend, and I seriously doubt I could have accomplished my mission without you. But tomorrow, after I'm gone, it will be up to you to help your civilization understand what they've just witnessed. You're the record keeper,

Justin, the scribe for a monumental historical event that the future will want to study and comprehend..." then Max hesitated and kind of giggled, "...or maybe they won't. At any rate, the torch will become yours to bear. You were our back-up plan all along."

"When will you take another body," Maley asked. "I mean, will I see you again before I croak myself?"

"I don't think so—for a couple of reasons: if I did turn around and partner up another body right away and you did see me, it would be as an infant, or at least someone thirty-five years your junior. And even if that did happen, you wouldn't know me from a hole in the ground, nor I you. But mostly, I'm tired, Justin—just plain tuckered out. I'm not talking about the here and now, either, although that's real, too. Taking a body and working with it for eighty or ninety years is a lot of work for a being. That's okay when we're younger, but I'm an old fart being, Justin—been around a long time. I'm ready for that shady hammock in the continuum. When you're younger, full of piss and vinegar, it's a lot more fun to visit planets and do wild and crazy things."

"So what do you older beings do with yourselves—just waste away?"

"Hell no. We make lots of guest appearances in psychic classes, here on Earth and a few other planets. We come through what you humans call transmediums, and we get to hang out with bodies for a while, share some knowledge, tell fish stories, twist some arms—that sort of thing. Some of those classes get kind of sophisticated, and we can open up pretty good. Anyway, unless some other major emergency comes down the pike, that will probably be the limit of my visits to Earth. And even if some emergency does come along, they can send someone else. I've had it with putting out fires."

"So, when are you going to be 'passing beyond,' as you mysteriously put it?"

It was the one area of discussion that Max had steadfastly avoided, but the writer's brain and curiosity were obviously working just fine, and if their positions were reversed, Max was sure he'd be turning the Q & A toward that direction, too. "I don't have a clue, Justin, and there's no assurance I'll ever be leaving the continuum. Most don't."

"So, what's it like Max—that 'beyond' place?" Justin asked for the third or fourth time in as many days, always getting the same response, always perturbing Max and frustrating himself.

The old man shook his head, "You young pup—got a one track mind don't ya? Well, it hasn't worked before, and it ain't gonna work this time neither. Now forget it!"

There was another question on Justin's mind which Max might be more inclined to answer and which might end up in the same place, so he gave it a try. It was also a fundamental question in Justin's personal journal of Prime Secrets of Existence, of which he hungered for answers. "Okay, okay—maybe you can tell me this: what contains the Universe?"

"Say what?" the old man really wasn't sure he'd heard Maley right.

"What contains the Universe, Max?" and the immediate look of incomprehension from the elder spurred Justin to continue. "Max, everything is held or contained by something else. That Coke is contained by that glass; the glass is held by a table; the table by the train; the train and everything else on Earth is contained on the planet. The planet is contained in the Milky Way galaxy, and our galaxy is one of millions contained in the Universe. Everything, and I mean everything, Max, is contained by something. So, what contains the Universe?"

The sparkle in Max's eyes immediately told Justin that he was going to get shucked and jived: "The Beyond contains the Universe and everything else, Sonny-boy, and your end-runs won't work with this old geezer," and he began his good-natured cackle. "Nice try, though, and it is a worthy question. You'll just have to wait for the answer."

But now the illogic of the refusal began to piss off Justin. "Max, this is bullshit. You've entrusted many of the secrets of the continuum to me, and you even want me to write about them—some of them anyway. You've already made it clear that I need to use good judgement or some continuum nun is going to come down here—up here, whatever—and whack my knuckles with a ruler. So what's the diff? I'll leave this one out of the book, okay. This will be just between you and me, no sweat. Come on...."

"I can't...." and the old man was sinking lower in his seat, wanting the obnoxious inquisitor to go away. Not a chance...

"Why, Max? Why can't you share this little nugget wi..." and then the possibility hit him like the proverbial two-by-four across the head. He looked at Max the Messenger, long and hard, and then Max sheepishly looked up at him with those big blues, but not inviting conversation. But Justin was not to be put off, not this time, because he knew, and knowledge was power:

"You don't know, do you Max? None of you guys in the continuum knows what lies 'beyond,' just that there *is* something 'beyond' and sometimes beings go there, never to be seen or heard from again. The Jesus being went there, and for some idiotic reason, you seem to think that the Truman being may go there, but you don't even know where 'there' is."

Silence,

More silence, and then thought—a mind slowly putting it all together.

"You guys in the continuum, with all your knowledge and power are stuck in a kind of purgatory, aren't you? You can't do anything there but hang out, until you come to a planet and take a body, or until you're—invited?—to pass beyond. For all you guys know, all the Garden of Eden stuff in religions might be based on fact. There might be a supreme Being, or maybe not. There might be one God, or there might be a dozen all sitting around a table like in Greek Mythology. God might be a man, might be a woman, might even be a slug, for all you know.

"Oh, man—this is deep. Max, would you please tell me if I'm right or not? Please."

Max turned the other way, looking for salvation out the window somewhere; but, not finding it, he turned back to the man, the mind that had just put together the exact thing the others in the continuum were so worried about and why some had vociferously wanted him to have no contact with a human helper. "You're close enough."

Maley, sad deduction confirmed, sat back in his seat and turned to his own window, looking not for salvation, but for meaning. It was a great disappointment to him that upon reaching the continuum, the human version of heaven and hell, all secrets of the Universe would not be forthcoming. On the other hand, some mysteries are destined to remain that way, and the not knowing, along with the struggle to discover, is usually good as raison d'être. His struggle over this one would require some time to sort out, but in the meantime, Max looked like he'd crawled into a hole or something.

"Max—Yo, Max, ol' buddy—where'd you go?" but Max was sulking. *God, check it out: Here's an omniscient being, sulking like a defensive teenager.* He put his arm over Max's shoulder and got down close to his ear. "Max, it's okay. I understand why it has to remain a mystery—for all of us, you continuum guys included. There has to be a final mystery or we'd all just go home and call it a day."

And with those last few words, Max perked up at once, sat up straighter, and looked at his friend. "You do understand," and they both smiled. "You know, Justin, it's just as hard and aggravating for us as it is for you right now, and we've been dealing with it for eons. It really is a pisser!"

———————————

They pulled into New Carrollton station at close to 4:00—almost thirty minutes behind schedule due to some kind of emergency maintenance problem. But they still had plenty of time before the 8:30 evening kick-off, so they caught a cab for a nearby Marriott Hotel and got a room, as it was assumed that Justin would be staying the night.

The last problem they had, which couldn't be addressed until their arrival, was actually getting tickets for the game. Maley called the box office, but as he'd feared, and as with most NFL games, the stadium was sold out—not just for tonight's game, but for every game, thank you very much. The concierge desk in the lobby was used to this problem and offered to make a few calls to reliable sources on Justin's behalf—interpretation: be prepared to pay big time, much of it in buried service fees. Thirty minutes later, the concierge called their room with rare and wonderful news. Two tickets could be had for the meager price of two hundred dollars each. That was the legal face value of the ticket, of course (no scalping allowed), plus delivery fees, phone calls, etc. The concierge had figured his client correctly as Justin was in no position to complain, argue, bargain, or otherwise. He came to the desk, paid with what was almost all of his remaining cash and discovered the seats to actually be pretty good, rather than up high in the nose-bleed section.

The hotel offered a free shuttle bus service to FedEx Stadium, of which the two availed themselves, following a leisurely dinner in the hotel restaurant. They arrived in front of the stadium at 7:40, found the proper gate and vomitory and entered the stadium proper—their seats being near the top of Section 117 near one of the goal lines. Above them, they could see the private boxes and what they soon discovered to be the "club" section with lounge-like seating. Then, way above that was the nose-bleed section proper for those without connections, big money, and a helpful concierge. But none of that mattered to Max. They were not here to watch some silly football game after all. They got settled in, surveyed their surroundings and enjoyed the salty peanuts and soft drinks. At about ten minutes before the coin toss, it was time for business.

Max rose from his seat, but before he could say anything or take even one step, his destination was challenged by Justin. "Where are you going, Max?"

Mystery Man stopped, but didn't turn around—just turning his head a little for the eyeball connection with his partner. "To fulfill my destiny." However true, the answer just wasn't enough under the circumstances, and both knew it. They remained locked, eyeball to eyeball, blue penetrating brown, brown penetrating blue—or at least trying. The end was near. It was the appropriate time for "good-byes" if either man were the sentimental type, which of course, they both were. But for a warrior going off to do battle, there wasn't any room for sentimentality, or any other emotion, for that matter. At the moment, Max didn't have time or the luxury for such baggage—it was time to focus.

But Justin was different. He'd had thirty years to become unprepared for this moment of separation, for no matter how strong you are, when the instant comes for a good and close friend to be pulled from your heart and disappear forever, the void in your body is agonizing for a long time to come. One tends to delay the moment for as long as possible. And Justin now knew how special this man/nonman had become to him in just five short days. He wasn't ready to say goodbye, and his eyes said it all.

Max saw it, of course, and sat back down. "Justin, we can do this again if you need to, but this is it. It's time for me to go. Our time together is over—until we meet again on the other side."

"How, Max? If there's really a being for every single body on the planet, plus all the other planets, how the hell are you going to know when it's my time, much less be there?"

Max allowed a compassionate giggle while shaking his head. "Do you think I personally know, much less hang-out with, every being in the Universe? I'm good, ol' buddy, but I'm not that good. Just like you human bodies, we tend to congregate." And then his eyes lit up, as Justin had seen previously at times of pending cleverness. "Beings of a feather flock together," and Max cackled at his own pun.

Maley smiled, too, but just as quickly got serious as the possible ramifications of the words hit home. "Are you saying we already knew each other Max—on a being level?"

"Of course. Holy shit, Sonny-boy. There's 280 million bodies just in your country alone. I could have chosen any of them as my helper. I waited for you back there in the desert. I chose you—an old friend—but a friend with no other attachments and with the added benefit of being a writer: someone who could tell the story."

But the answer, as important as it was to Justin, only served to key-off an even more urgent question: "Max, how is it you were chosen, or volunteered, for this assignment? Why you, and not one of umpteen billion other beings?"

Max didn't answer. He stared at his companion, inviting him and wanting him to put it together, giving him the necessary time to see the picture.

And the fog suddenly lifted from Justin's eyes. "You have history with Lawrence, too, don't you? I mean, on a being level, or maybe even from some previous life. Right?"

Max smiled, nodded, "Take it another step, Justin. You're almost there" and Justin tried hard to see what Max was alluding to, but it was just too far out toward the edge. He shook his head in loss.

Still looking deeply into Justin's eyes, Max led him by the ethereal hand, "What do you think happened to the other half of Truman's being when he split it in two?" And now Max's smile turned into a great grin as Justin's eyes got huge, his mouth flopped open and he finally saw it.

"Oh my God, Max—that's you?" Max nodded. "You and Truman made up the same being: good, evil, not in balance, but soon to be once again. The continuum sent you, the obvious choice to bring your other half home." And now Maley shook his head in wonder, "Wow...."

"So, yes, we have some history together—been there, done that." Once again, Max looked down to the field. "It's time, my friend." Max looked into Justin's eyes for just a second longer, then stood and turned for the long line of concrete steps leading to a future that even he could not fully see.

And one last time, Justin yelled for Max to stop, and jumped up and toward the man about to leave his life forever. At the steps, Max turned, starting to get a little pissed-off at the source of these delays, but again, he softened, momentarily, at the pathetic look of sadness on the face of his partner. Still, it was time to end this sentimental journey and get on with the business at hand, so he brought in Max the Mouth, not caring that nearby fans were beginning to take interest in the "weird" conversation.

"Now listen up, Sonny-boy! What the hell did you think was gonna happen when we got here? HUH? Did ya think just our presence in this stadium would be enough….maybe scare the man into submission? And then maybe we'd just watch a good game while evil ran from the stadium with his tail between his legs?" Max shook his head back and forth in frustration and continued his tirade: "It takes a fair amount of work to remove evil from a planet, boy. The time has come for me to do my magic act, and to wake up this backward planet of yours at the same time."

"But you might die, Max. I can feel it….."

"Of course I'm gonna die," Max hissed and nearly yelled at the same time. "At least, this body is. Me, the soul, the important part, will go back to the continuum and 'live happily ever after,' while you and the rest of your kind get to muddle through your Karma until it's your turn to come home. I feel for ya, boy."

"What's going to happen, Max?"

Max was slow to answer, unsure of the future, "I'm gonna challenge Mr. Lawrence to do battle, Justin. I'm goin' down on that field there and call-out that evil son-of-a-bitch, and then we'll just see what we'll see. I promise ya this though. Win, lose, or draw, that boy's going to be done on this planet. When these 50,000 fans see the other side of that sparkling personality, he won't be able to get elected dog-catcher. It'll be a good show—better'n any football game, I'll betch'ya. The TV man's gonna love the ratings…" And as he laughed at his own humor, he turned to head down toward the field. A few steps away, he stopped, turned, and looked at Justin one last time, with the hint of a smile, nodding slowly, communicating a ton of thoughts in the movement:

recognition, thanks, camaraderie, secrets, friendship, even a kind of love. And then he went on his way—alone in the end.

The effort to keep the body shell alive and moving had been Herculean, and Max knew his powers had been lessened substantially as a result. He knew he'd get a mild infusion of strength when he was able to shed the organic visage, but it was still a little too soon for that. His plan was simple: draw the crowd's attention first—and taking his natural form might well freak the crowd so much as to cause a panic exit for the gates. No, he had to keep Max's body just a bit longer, draw in the crowd, slowly but surely allowing their curiosity to pin them to their seats. Then he'd go after Mr. Truman Lawrence, vice-presidential candidate of these here United States of America. Lawrence would have three choices: first, he could immediately leave the stadium, the "get out of Dodge" option, and thereby avoid the conflict; or second, he could ignore the challenge from the field, playing dumb and compassionate to the old codger's lunacy. But that wouldn't work because Max would zap him and terminate his command, on the spot, should he choose that option; and finally, he could come on down to the coliseum floor for some fun and games— 'fate of the world' kind of games. Max was pretty sure Lawrence would reject the first option, despite its being the smartest way to go—delaying the battle until a future date, perhaps at Lawrence's convenience and with no public witnesses. Max believed that the evil creature's ego would betray him into entering the killing field where the powers of eternity, creation, and destruction become focused as one. And the being that is capable of harnessing those forces, all together, and at one time, is indeed The Man—at least, for a moment.

No, the Evil One would not run—of that Max was quite sure. He approached the pipe barrier at the end of his long decent, noticing a perceptible increase in temperature at the bottom of the abyss. He climbed over the railing and dropped the short distance to the field below, and began walking, slowly but determinedly, toward the center of the field. The security teams noticed the uninvited guest even before his feet touched the ground, and the nearest began their move to intercept the potential terrorist or obnoxious fan or whatever he was. Little did they know…

The whole scene was visible to everyone in the stadium and became the center of attention, since both teams and the refs were still on the sidelines just prior to the coin toss. Their eyes, too, rotated toward the walking man. But then, something happened, something changed: idle, even humorous curiosity became the most intense kind of focus—the "don't blink your eyes" kind of focus because you might miss a key event.

As the first security cop approached Max and began reaching out in preparation for grabbing a collar or wrist or wad of hair, a blue crackly glow emanated in thin air about six feet behind Max. Even more amazing was the security officer's reaction: he quickly jerked his hand back to his body, and rubbed the burning appendage with his other, unaffected hand. And he stopped in his tracks in obvious total amazement and confusion, mixed in with no small amount of fear—mostly of the unknown.

Suddenly, there was a noticeable change in the background decibel level within the stadium: it instantly grew quieter—not hushed, not yet—but idle conversations ceased right after the thousands of, "Did you see that?"s.

Mystery Man kept walking, slowly, but the security people, having seen something strange, now became more concerned, so service weapons were drawn. Unseen to anyone on the field or in the stands, the allotted Secret Service and SWAT team sharp-shooters located on the roof, removed safetys and scope caps and got ready for business.

Another officer approached Max from the front, but his efforts were also rebuffed by what now appeared to everyone in the stadium as some sort of invisible barrier, like a Star Trek force field. And that made this a science fiction event—something along the lines of the impossible. The decibel level went down some more, curiosity ratcheted way up, and some palms began to get a little sweaty.

One pair of those palms belonged to Gil Thompson, the on-site producer for FBC. Located in the broadcast control trailer outside the stadium, along with his director, Thompson couldn't see the actual show developing before his eyes, so to speak—not like his announcers in their cushy box above the fifty-yard line. However, unlike anyone else on the planet, Gil was in charge of the signal going out to the world, or at least to the New York City network headquarters, and then on to an estimated 20 milllion national households plus the overseas and military stations. At the beginning of the old man's stroll onto the field, the few cameras that focused on the unusual action delivered their signal to the control booth where the feeds were recorded and then unceremoniously sent down the electronic floor drain. No signal of the grizzled man making a mockery of the security crews was being forwarded to New York: By informal agreement between the NFL and the broadcasters of their games, "wackos" did not receive the air time that they so zealously coveted. No one wanted to encourage the crazies of the world to become fifteen-minute stars, so although the fans and broadcast teams might get to enjoy a brief moment of excitement, no television viewers at home would be so bothered. That was about to change...

At first, Thompson believed that what he was seeing was some sort of fluke. But no longer—not after a second episode of the "strange but true." He requested that the director now order all appropriate cameras to focus on the guy moving toward field center. This action, by default, meant that the "crazy" was about to enter the consciousness of some 40 million viewers around the world. Simultaneously, the producer, who was in constant telephone communication with his counterparts in New York, advised the network of an immediate news event in progress at FedX stadium, and that he needed help. Although Gil's announcers might be the best in the business—for football events—they didn't know jack about anchoring a news event, and that was what seemed to be unfolding through the twelve different cameras at his command. If the old fart with the force field thing—well, whatever it was—was looking for attention, he had just succeeded beyond his wildest dreams.

Gil had his crew prep the recorded portions of Max's walk onto the field, including the attempt by two officers to stop him. The film was then transmitted to New York via a sideband hookup so the network pukes could see what he was talking about.

"What is that, Gil?" asked one of the associate producers in the network command center. "Some kind of stun gun or something?"

"Listen-up, guys. That's no stun gun—it's some kind of force field, and the boys in blue don't seem to be able to penetrate it, and the last time I checked, force fields were still science fiction. So this may be turning into something very, very big, and maybe you'd better get your ducks in a row up there—maybe call the news department, get some experts lined up, ya know? I'm sending you straight feed, no interruptions, no commercials, and my boys down here aren't the best for this kind of commentary. We need help from the news desk. You got it? Move!"

The old man was making life easy for Thompson: he seemed to be content now just standing still at field center. No quick or fancy camera work was necessary. Gil and crew could just switch around from one angle to another, looking for the best shot, while trying to keep the nonaction moving.

There were nine or ten officers around the stranger now, none of whom were too eager to be the next to approach the perpetrator, and perhaps feel the zap their brother officers had experienced. Those two officers were still on the field, still part of the pack, and seemed to be none the worse for their encounter. One of the other cops wisely jutted his baton in front of himself as he headed toward Max, and sure enough, the baton, along with the man holding it, came to an abrupt halt as the shield thing lit up like a trolley car's cantenary on a dark, wet night. But showing no ill-effects, the officer continued to probe with the night stick, looking for any holes or weak areas. The remaining cops duplicated his motions, but after a minute of fruitless effort, they all stood back, waiting for someone in a position of authority to come up with the solution and their instructions. In the meantime, the old guy inside the invisible shield seemed happy to just stand there, allowing everyone to do their best to get inside. The encircling officers began to look at one another, mostly confused looks, a little fear here and there, and they came together in twos and threes—talking over possibilities and whispering about impossibilities.

Despite the confusion and mystery, there was one thing that could be said for absolutely, positively true, and that was the fact that every single pair of eyes inside the stadium was focused on one spot, and one spot only. To that would soon be added everyone's ears.

Max was now satisfied that he had everyone's attention. He was now surrounded by maybe forty people, some of whom appeared to be military types. He was also confident that the TV people had had ample time to make any adjustments needed for their best possible advantage. In short, it was time to get on with the show....

Max did a three hundred sixty-degree turn at field center, both to let everyone know that something might be about to happen, and also to verify that Truman Lawrence was in the stadium: and he was, foolish man. He couldn't be seen by Max from this distance, but his energy stood out like a black smudge on a Rorschach card. There was no mistaking it, nor its general location within the stadium. Max ceased his turn on a line with the smudge of energy, and slowly, oh so slowly, lifted a tired right arm with a bony, arthritic, liver-spotted hand tipped with a knarly index finger, and pointed the whole pathetic thing toward luxury box number 226, more or less. All heads turned. All mouths closed. All ears opened, for something verbal had to be next. And it was.

Without microphone but clearly heard by everyone, and in a superb imitation of the late Rod Roddy, Max identified his purpose: "Truman Lawrence, come on down!"

Silence...complete and total...

New York asked for a sound check, and got it, because there was virtually nothing coming from the stadium. All eyes, all ears, all thoughts focused on the perceived end point of that most impolitely pointing finger. Although most fans in the stadium could not locate, much less scrutinize the Senator, the 40 million-plus outside the stadium had no such limitations: Camera number four, high above the fifty-yard line, was less than three-hundred feet away from luxury suite 226, and for a $250,000 primary game camera, that distance might just as well have been ten feet. A close-up of the suite came into focus on TV sets everywhere (including within the suite), and of the ten cushy seats provided, Lawrence was front row and centered. Though surrounded by friends and supporters, he was not laughing. He was not smiling. And he did not move.

The director had set up a split screen because the action was obviously centered on two places, and two places only. His work load was further reduced by the fact that this seemed to be a two-camera gig—no jumpin' around between twelve different units except for the occasional side angle shot just to keep things moving. With his finger on the trigger, he was ready to switch instantly between cameras four and nine, nine offering the best view of the guy on the field, as long as he was facing the victim of his interest. On a hunch, though, he had camera number seven at the Redskins' end zone maintain a wide angle shot that included both the old man on the field and the luxury box containing one challenged Senator.

The head of security, actually the senior Secret Service agent, had a bigger problem, now that his charge had just been identified as a potential target—of something. Lawrence had already refused to leave the stadium when advised to do so. When the old man had first walked onto the field, there was no indication of imminent danger to the Senator, or more germane to the Secret Service, the vice-presidential candidate. The old man appeared to be carrying nothing with him—certainly no bomb. But that initial assessment had radically altered the moment he displayed some means of avoiding apprehension by stadium security. Although he still appeared to pose no direct, physical threat, the fact that the security team on the field could seemingly do nothing to remove him was, at the very least, disconcerting. It was time to get his charge out of harm's way, but Lawrence still refused to move. And then came the verbal challenge, directed at Lawrence, and no mistaking an implied threat in the words and tone. Trained as he was, he immediately ordered the detail on the field to apprehend or stop the old man with any force necessary, including weapons discharge.

Phil Buchanon, senior agent on the field was reluctant to fire his weapon at the old man, not because of concern for the man's welfare—the geezer had long ago passed that threshold—no, his concern was the unpredictability of what the force field thing would do to a bullet if the bullet didn't penetrate. There were a lot of people who could get hurt by a ricochet. Buchanon called for, and got, a full-size pickup truck brought onto the stadium floor. Not wanting to risk anyone else's safety with his idea, the senior agent got behind the wheel, and from fifty feet away, gunned the truck and headed straight for the old man.

The last thing Buchanon saw before losing consciousness was his target turning his head, looking straight at him, and shaking his head. The truck hit the force field almost as though it were a concrete bridge abutment—almost, because some of the initial impact seemed to ripple the barrier and spread out. The force was still great enough that Buchanon struck the windshield. The cops and support personnel swarmed the truck to pull the steaming hulk away and recover the agent. After getting him into a waiting ambulance, the security people encircled Mystery Man once again, but now that one of theirs had been injured, they were ready to get aggressive. The last remaining Secret Service agent on the field, Jimmy Grant, instructed everyone to step back, as he would attempt the shot himself. The others did as they were told.

Gil Thompson, in the production van, was licking his chops with anticipation, as were all the execs in New York because this moment of wet-your-pants anxiety was being brought to the world by none other than FBC. Eat your hearts out, ABC, CBS, NBC, FOX, CNN, UPN. They also knew that word had to be spreading and that the audience was quickly increasing. If only they could break away for a commercial.

The agent approached the invisible shield, using a baton as gauge. Once the closest position was established, he raised his service weapon, pressed it against the shield, aimed at the left leg of the old man, and fired once.

The barrier rippled again, and amazingly, the slug hung in the barrier wall momentarily, intact, stuck, and then fell to the ground, totally spent of energy. No ricochets this time, as in the bus station back in St. Louis. Apparently Max could adjust the force field as he wanted. So agent Grant called all the other officers back to his position and instructed them to form a very tight firing pattern around his body, and fire into an equally tight target zone—the thinking being that all the energy in one spot might do the trick. It didn't occur to the agent that if it didn't work for a 4,000-pound truck, it probably wouldn't for eleven bullets. Nonetheless, they prepared, and on his "mark" they all fired as one, with exactly the same results as the solo effort.

Max had been watching this futile effort, giving them their opportunity to perform their duty because they would soon have to leave or risk grave danger. Max didn't want anyone injured other than the object of his attentions. But it was time to move ahead with the program.

"You boys done now?" Max asked the security people. It didn't seem to phase anyone, except maybe a few physicists here and there, that although bullets couldn't defeat the barrier, the spoken word passed through unimpeded. "It's time to back away—before you all get singed."

Then he turned back in the direction of box 226 and offered another invitation: "Last chance, Truman. Ya gonna come down here like a man, or am I gonna have ta come up there and gitch'ya?" Max the Mouth was in his element now—on a roll, and where he stops nobody knows...

Still, Lawrence did not budge.

So, Max raised his scrawny arm once again, pointing to Lawrence, only this time, more than words issued forth from Mystery Man's body: from the tip of his bony finger came a bolt of blue energy, very similar to a lighting bolt, but moving much slower—slow enough that the audience, all 50 million of them by now—could see the forward end of the bolt reach up to box 226 and the occupant of the front row, center seat. And the occupant finally moved. He raised his right hand, placing it between himself and the bolt of energy just a nano second before the bolt would have struck his body. The blocked bolt of energy splattered sideways in all directions until Max turned off the juice and the energy was expended.

As the former friends and supporters of Truman Lawrence veritably exploded from their adjoining seats, jamming for the one exit door (sorry, Truman, buddy, gotta go... let's do lunch...), there wasn't an eye socket in the stadium smaller than a silver dollar. The collective gasp of air through the stretched mouths had been audible. But, despite the rising fear, despite the unknown and the weird, everyone remained in his or her seats—except in Truman's box. On 30 million-plus TV sets, the open mics of the commentators were abused with one of those rare events where even professional talent forget the rules: "Oh, shit!..." was delivered in unison by two sportscasters in Washington and one news anchor in New York City. But the biggest response universally was the ever-appropriate, "Oh, my God...," in whatever native tongue the mouth belonged to. By now, the broadcast was going to international partners throughout the world, and although the details of what was happening were far from clear for anyone, what was clear was that a civilization-altering event might be happening at a stadium in the United States of America.

The football players, staff, and security types ran for the nearest perimeter wall, and in most cases climbed over—apparently believing, like little kids on a bed, as long as your feet aren't touching the floor, you're safe from the sharks and the other nasties that lurk in waiting.

And everyone was waiting for what would come next.

Now Lawrence stood—slowly, deliberately—lifting himself out of his seat, alone, isolated, and looking a little put out—more like livid, actually. The camera, from three hundred feet away, never left his face, and his face and eyes never left the image of Max the Spoiler, down on the field below, beckoning to him, challenging him to a little mano a mano. And like a cold slap across the face, Lawrence's consciousness finally brought all the pieces together and realized in one flash of hatred that his years of careful preparation, his close proximity to inevitable success, had just been destroyed—by the pathetic creature below. He realized that even if he beat the old man senseless, he had lost. His plans would never come to fruition now, and with that knowledge, the need to maintain the politician's polished image evaporated—a persona of any sort no longer mattered. His carefully crafted control began to fade. The Adonis façade began to melt as if he'd taken a dip in a vat of acid. Wrinkles appeared, as did sagging flesh, and the eyes began to issue a message to all who could see: the owner of these orbs is a hater of all things living. Finally, as the handsome, erect figure lost its tone, a sound—starting out like a moan—could be heard by those closest to the changling. The moan became louder and increased in pitch, and then it broke the bounds of normal bodies and emanated from the twisted mouth as a blast of air and rage, easily heard in every part of the stadium. Lawrence's arms, if the shape could still be said to be that of Truman Lawrence, raised above his head as the scream continued, not subject to the need for an interceding breath of air. Thousands of ears began to hurt; every single panel of glass in the stadium shattered—attacked either by violent frequencies or violent vibes, or both.

Suddenly, the shriek, for that's what it had become, stopped. Then, without delay, the body of former Senator Truman Lawrence, I-Minnesota, and vice-presidential candidate, levitated off the floor of luxury suite number 226, came over the concrete sill, and like a fastball from hell, hurled itself to the field below—hoping to bean the destroyer of his dreams.

The force field slowed the former politician's mass, but could not stop it. He oozed through the barrier and stood face to face with Max. Max waived his arm and the force field became much larger, almost to the limits of the field perimeter. Mustn't allow the fans to be injured...

Truman whispered something that only Max could hear, and then both men discarded any remaining semblance of human form and became translucent, fluorescing shapes at least twenty-feet tall, representing creatures not to be found in any earthly zoo. And the battle began, with each form crashing into the other, clawing, tearing, beating, and roaring. Somewhere in the melee, any recollection of which beast started off as which man became lost. There could, therefore, be no cheering for one over the other—if such a concept were remotely possible in the first place. Glowing, dripping flesh was being ripped apart here and there and being flung all over the stadium field, when abruptly, one of the forms released its grip, stood back and changed forms again: this time becoming some humanoid thing with an enormous sword-like weapon. The weapon was brought to bear on his opponent, who also began a shape-shift. But before the change was completed, with a brandishment of his own weapons, the first creature struck home with a seemingly devastating blow to what would have to be an arm—one of four, followed by a lunge to the torso. The sword struck home, penetrating completely, emerging from the back side. Unreal in appearance or not, the injured creature was obviously in a bad way. The attacker withdrew his sword for another attack, but this proved to be a mistake, for the injured one played possum, allowed the attacker's sword to come in for the decapitation, then dodged at the last second. The momentum of the swinging sword drew the attacker in close, right flank unguarded, and wide open for a sword thrust by the now severely weakened creature. The move was successful, the sword penetrating to the hilt. But the sword became stuck in place, gripped by electroplasmic sinew and muscle. The impaled creature, screaming with rage and pain, twisted away from the injured attacker, so now only one of the two had a sword. Apparently, in this magical world of unreality, a lost weapon was still a lost weapon, and the rules forbid the casual creation of another.

Both creatures, thusly wounded, faced off—one knowing that the end was likely near for himself. The armed attacker moved in for the kill, slowly, taking his time, enjoying the moment of victory, yet making sure to not be careless, lest the scenario become reversed.

But then, there was a change of strategy. For those glued to their monitors across the world, and for those hardly breathing observers in the stadium, a lesson was about to be learned. The mortally wounded creature began a shape change. The attacking creature, fearing a lost opportunity, rushed in as best his own injured body would allow. He drew his sword back for the coup de grâce as his opponent's final shape materialized: his appearance became that of a human being in a white robe, full beard and flowing brown hair. The human form went down on his knees, placed both hands over his heart, then bent well-forward, offering his neck to the creature, while at the last second pointing a finger at his executioner. Suddenly, the killing creature involuntarily began to change form as well, just as his sword reached its highest arc. He, too, became human, but with those vestiges that have long been associated by human beings almost everywhere with all things evil: small horns on head and neck, a pointed tail, blisters and boils oozing pestilence, and eyes that can belong to no one but the opposite counterpoint of the nearby image of kindness, hope, and humility—generously offering his head for the salvation and education of innocents the world over.

In his hatred and rage, the Evil One did not notice the forced change to his appearance, as the sword began its downward curve. Now that the good guy and the bad guy had been identified (or could it be a deception?), the crowd reared up in horror as the sickening conclusion became inevitable. Just as the fluorescing blue blade made contact with the presented neck, an enormous unified, "Nooo!" erupted within the stadium. The cut was clean, and the head rolled around in a half circle until coming to rest, eyes pointing straight up. The tinged force field instantly evaporated, and before the eyes of some 50 million people worldwide, the decapitated figure on the field began rippling and changing, much like a thing going through a transporter. When the process finished, Max was back as himself, whole, but lifeless on the ground. Then the victor morphed back into the slightly tarnished figure of "the former" Senator Truman Lawrence. Somewhere in the stadium, someone began booing. The sentiment was quickly picked up, and it spread, like "the wave," until the cacophony of anger, and pain, and sadness directed at the lone man standing became deafening. The man stood his ground, turning and looking, contemplating what might have been. The booing didn't bother him a bit. In fact, as group mind energy, it was absorbed and savored. But the noise abruptly ended as the crowd noticed movement from the other body—the dead body, lying prone on the field. Once again, a hush filled the stadium and the airwaves. Fifty million pairs of eyes watched as the slain creature/man arose, not with a struggle, not as a severely injured body, but as though he were weightless—a body filled with helium. He stood, turned, and faced his slayer from twenty feet away. A muffled gasp escaped 50,000 mouths in the stadium as both bodies began glowing within their abdomins, like a candle flame gently escaping the wax globe encompassing it—only this glow was blue. They stared at each other for perhaps ten seconds, then a flash of light emanated from the chest area of both bodies and a blue orb left each and hovered in the air; at the same moment, the former shell of both men collapsed to the field as would a dropped rag doll. After a few more seconds, the two blue orbs floated slowly toward each other, stopped maybe six inches before contact, hovered some more, and then continued their singular purpose—coming together in a final burst of light, joining as one. The softball sized sphere shone brightly for a few seconds, and then was gone—not up, not down—just gone.

Max had accomplished his mission.

"I once dreamed that there is a planet near the center of our galaxy that is so large, and populated with so many sentient beings that, by comparison, planet Earth would be considered nothing more than a village outpost on the cosmic road to somewhere else.

"The thought of this pleases me, for the residents of villages are historically well bonded, even if not all friends, as they share water from the same well, never dig their latrines upwind, or otherwise do anything to foul the source of their continued existence."

Eight Months Later

Moab, Utah

Justin enjoyed camping along a river perhaps more than anything else in his solitary life. Sometime after the Washington thing, he couldn't remember when, he'd promised himself that he'd return to the Colorado for another four-day trip through Cataract Canyon. So, he had made his reservation, paid the price, and had arrived at the spot south of Moab he knew was the jump-off for Western River Expedition's J-rigs. It didn't matter that he'd gotten there a day early. Staging area or not, it was quiet, he was alone, the mighty river was just a couple of leaps away, and the geology, as ever, was spectacularly powerful and beautiful. And for good measure, nature (or maybe it had been the continuum) had been kind enough to provide him a memorable meteor shower his very first night.

Being a smart and considerate camper, he had packed lightly for the trip, with the heaviest single piece of equipment being his double-spaced manuscript recounting the events of the five days last autumn leading up to the permanent resignation of Truman Lawrence from the human race. The work was almost complete, at long last, with just the final chapter needing some fine-tuning, and with a title that was still eluding him—even though he'd been casually thinking about it since near the beginning. Something would come to mind and feel perfect for a day or week, only to fall from grace with the passage of time. That was all right, though. The last time he'd had that problem, eight months earlier, he had been in search of inspiration—trying to force a title to become a story. No longer. With inspiration back in play, with the manuscript in place, the searching for a title had become a fun bit of business rather than a desperate act. It was an anology that applied to his whole life, of late. No longer the dried-up, sad, desperate journalist seeking answers to salvage his empty life, Justin was now a participant in the scenery around him instead of a distant viewer. He was a well with its pipe tapped into a universal reservoir of hope, creativity, curiosity, and understanding—and still seeking more answers with each breath taken. His was a state of mind as simply defined as being excited to rise each morning, ready to discover what new puzzle piece lay in wait for him during his day. Justin felt all this, and was *conscious* of all this, without forgetting that the shoe does drop from time to time. Shit does happen, but that's the nature of balance.

On a wider scale, things, referring to planet Earth, or rather the civilization that calls Earth home—had changed since the event in Washington, D.C. last fall. Thank God. Or thank whatever it is that lives "beyond": singular, plural, male, female, it. Whatever "it" is, the ultimate mystery of life was still safe and secure.

It had taken a month or so, but eventually every human being on the planet within viewing range of a television set finally saw what had happened that day in a coliseum full of people in the good old United States of America. They also realized that the location was solely a matter of convenience—that the event had worldwide implications well beyond the borders of the States. Therefore, the effects had been felt everywhere. Ready or not, here comes a new reality. There were many, naturally, who poo-pooed the whole thing, claiming that the network had crawled under the sheets with some special effects company to hoodwink the whole of humanity. Their arguments only served to show their preference for fantasyland, for there were 50,000 eye witnesses who knew better and were never hesitant to so inform anyone who cared to talk about the "evening that changed their lives forever."

The implied message that resulted from the brief "Battle of Titans," as the fight had come to be called, with an even shorter handle of "BT" when the conversation was fast and furious, was decidedly unclear—in the details, anyway. In generalities, however, the message was not lost on anyone: there was something out there, something not of the Earth, that had paid us a brief visit. The operative words, of course, were "not of the Earth," implying that someone, or something was in the cosmos with at least one eye on us, the inhabitants of the planet. And one could further deduce, as almost everyone did, that our beliefs structure could use a little tune-up, and perhaps we could all begin to live above the standard of behavior to which we had all become accustomed.

A familiar shriek grabbed Justin's attention, and he looked overhead wondering if his relatively new ornithological skills were right or wrong, but he saw nothing. Again, the shriek, but this time he didn't have to look around for the source. A large raptor landed on a rock outcropping across the river and downstream a bit. Justin studied it intensely, just as the bird of prey was focused on Justin. Then the bird jumped off its perch and actually flew towards him, landing on a rock protruding from the water, directly across the river from Maley. The head-on, beak-on, view from fifty feet was unmistakable: This was the falcon, or its twin, that had taught Justin a lesson in courage (or fear) all those months ago. The raptor drank from an eddy pool beside the rock, stared at Justin a few more seconds, then leaped into the air, returning to his cliffside perch. Justin stayed with the magnificent creature for at least a minute, smiling all the while, flashing back to those heady days when his life did a one-eighty.

He checked his watch, noted it was 8:15 (in the morning), then he stoked the fire a little, warming up his coffee in the process, and wondered what time the other river rats would arrive, along with the truck with one, disassembled rubber boat.

Leaning against a rock, working on the final chapter of his book, he heard the caw of a crow above him and its sound, too, instantly sent him back in time—as their call frequently did these days. He tilted his head back and saw the single bird high in the shore-line tree behind him. "Hello, Mr. Crow. Are you a friend or foe today—a spy or a navigator?" He watched the big black bird drop down a few branches and disappear into what looked to be a nest, but Justin had to turn away as his neck was beginning to cramp. He looked over at the falcon so close by and wondered why the crow wasn't scared or attacking the raptor, or vice versa. But all was calm.

Returning to the manuscript, he had just reentered the world of Washington, D.C. when the crow cawed again from behind him, but it was on the ground this time. As always, the ignoring of the noise was not allowed, so Justin set his work down and focused on the ugly thing to his rear. The crow was rummaging through the sand and dirt and river debris, apparently looking either for baby food or nesting materials. Out in the open like that, Justin became amazed that the falcon remained content on his perch. The crow's beak worked furiously—up and down, left and right—as if there were no time to waste. Justin smiled. Here he was spending some "quality" time with a bird that might be the same one that so tenaciously spied on him and Max last year. The bird found something, took it to its nest, and the squawking of babies indicated it was almost breakfast time. Justin thought, *so you crows can be okay critters, too. You need a place to live, to raise a family, just like the rest of us. You have to find food, a mate, and you like to hang out together.* Another crow approached the nest and landed on a nearby branch—apparently one of the parents. Suddenly, a message came to Justin's mind: *crows have as much right to be here as humans—and falcons.* And then, another thought: not all crows are bad, nor are they all good. He took the thought a final step: *like it or not, good or evil, clean or soiled—we all live in the same nest. We all belong here, to sink or swim—together.*

Justin returned to his book, wanting to get something productive accomplished before twenty people and a boat showed up. But that was not meant to be: In a moment of pristine quiet, red pen in hand and hovering over a passage, something fell from the sky on his right quadrant—and thunked into the sand. It wasn't enough to frighten, but enough to cause a jerk of his head. His eyes fell upon the object, and he froze—as did sound, as did time, as did his life. One of the crows descended to a rock about twenty feet distant and settled in—without a sound, without fear, just staring at the visitor. Half-buried in the river sand, little more than an arm's length away was something that had no *Earthly* business being there, and without doubt, it was meant for him and no other. It was a very flat, utterly squished, copper penny. Justin looked at it most carefully, not yet willing to touch it, as though it might be hot off the press and coming in at 500°F. He cocked his head a bit after seeing some kind of pattern on the visible face of the object. Recollecting that day back in Wilmington, he recalled Max pointing out a pattern, saying that beings in the continuum looked somewhat similar to that image. On the Colorado River, eight months later, Justin recognized the same pattern. A chill went through him as his hand began to shake a bit.

Without moving, his eyes rose above and beyond the penny to the rock with the resting crow. It, too, had not moved, nor had it made a sound, which was eerily strange for the species but definitely in keeping with the moment. A few hundred feet beyond the crow, the falcon was also still—just staring. They stared at each other for the longest time—maybe ten or twenty seconds, before the large, ugly crow jumped from his perch to the sand and confidently, still without fear, hopped to the copper penny. Maley knew little about birds, but he knew enough to know that none, except perhaps the pigeons in city parks, ever exhibit this kind of behavior—especially the elusive black crows. Yet here it was, stopping at the penny, five feet away. It grabbed the flat piece of copper in its beak and flung it hard into the body of the the man before it. Then the bird lifted off and returned to its nest.

Justin felt tears well up in his eyes, and he didn't bother with his usual logical deductions because there was no way he would be able to talk his way around this one. Nor did he particularly want to. The message was clear: Max had just dropped by to say hello. Perhaps he had gotten demoted and was in the body of the crow, and the thought was good for a smile.

"Hello, Max," Justin said out loud, then picked up the copper and began twirling it around with his fingers. Above him, the crows began their cawing again, and without another thought, the writer knew he finally had his title. He opened his manuscript to the cover page that was conspicuously missing the crucial element, and in big, bold letters, wrote "Crow's Nest."

Just then, a car pulled up nearby, parking behind his own well-used Mustang. An elderly couple got out, stretched and waved at him, and then began unloading their car. Overhead, the pair of crows flew off from the intrusion, and a second later, the raptor followed them. The new arrivals weren't first-timers either, packing very lightly, but also bringing along a cooler. They locked up the car, and brought their stuff over to the riverbank, staying a few yards away from Justin's space. They could see he was working, so they kept to themselves while getting their feet wet and generally frolicking in the spirit of their vacation. Justin watched them from the corner of his eye. They had to be in their 80s if not older, and both looked to be in good health, which one had to be to take the river trip.

They came back to their belongings, traded affectionate pecks, and began putting sunblock on each other. The writer had seen enough and lost control of his thoughts: "You two look mighty happy," he observed to the couple. It was kind of a silly comment, but comments like that are always received with a smile.

They both giggled and the man said, "Well, son, sixty years of marriage will do that to a couple—that and three kids, five grandchildren, and, two great grandchildren," at which point, they both smiled some more and looked at each other kind of adoringly. Then the man went on. "Hi there, my name's Dick, and this here good-lookin' gal is Doris. What's your name?"

Ol' Dick and Doris must have thought the poor man across from them had just seen a ghost, which is exactly what Dick said. "You okay son? You just got all pale, like ya just seen a ghost or somethin'."

It took Justin a few seconds to recover his composure, but when he did, he just couldn't help but laugh—God, it was going to be a great trip, what with two new friends and his trusty talisman. Then he explained his reaction, kind of, to the couple: "Dick, Doris—might you two have visited Monument Valley, back in—oh, say 1943?..." Their reaction confirmed his suspicions.

They both frowned, looked at each other, and then back to the stranger before them. What he was alluding to was the day Dick had proposed to Doris—right out there on that gorgeous promontory, in front of God and everyone—sixty years before. After a few seconds of trying to piece together the mystery, Dick asked, "Do we know you, son? Have we met?"

The simple question gave Justin pause as an involuntarily complex answer formed in his mind: *Of course you know me, and I you, and we both know those crows flying overhead and the falcon that's trying to eat them. We've known each other for eons. We've shared this planet, and others, many times. Perhaps you were my father one time, or my son, or my arch enemy, or perhaps my mate. Do we have Karma together? Is that why we're here together in this moment? Or maybe we're about to create some Karma. How far back do our connections go? How deep are the layers that make up our existence? And how do I share with you two what I've learned in the last eight months—without scaring you, without sounding like Nurse Ratched's final escaped basket case? Perhaps now was the time.*

Justin Maley smiled at his new friends. "Let me tell you a story…"